LOST GUARDIAN

By G.A. Wilson

CHAPTER 1

Wednesday December 12, 2012

Egyptian tribal music crackled from the old radio in the ferryman's cabin, the earthy drumbeat lending an atmospheric soundtrack to the ferry crossing. The long barge-like craft cut smoothly through the sparkling waters of the Nile. Only the day before Kate had eagerly anticipated making this journey on a more romantic vessel. None of her daydreams had featured the worn boards of the rustic car ferry or the fumes in the air, a combination of fuel and the questionable food offered by a vendor who had joined them for the crossing. She had imagined trailing her fingers languidly through the rippling water; instead, she found herself waving away a gang of persistent children determined to sell their wares. On any other day, she would have happily bartered with them for small souvenirs. But not today. Today her world was collapsing around her ears.

The poorly dressed but smiling children moved to a couple of tourists sitting nearby, leaving Kate alone to contemplate the calm river. Papyrus reeds crowded the river's edge, blowing gently in the pleasant breeze. Palm trees and the occasional acacia lined the banks. She could see a majestic cruise ship in the distance, making its leisurely way towards them, looking strangely out of place in this untamed environment.

'Did you know that according to the ancient Egyptian horoscope calendar, this is known as the Season of Emergence?'

Kate turned towards a stocky young man who was wearing Ray-Ban sunglasses and a baseball cap. His accent revealed him to be American, the stars and stripes on his grubby t-shirt further evidence of his proud heritage. A dirty backpack was slung over his shoulder, and he looked as though he hadn't shaved for days. As Kate took a deep breath and pasted on a smile, she realised he may not have showered for some time, either.

'Well, I'm very glad the waters of the Nile have receded,' she said drily. 'According to your calendar, what's the prediction for the day?'

Grinning, the man visibly puffed up under her politely interested gaze.

1

'Oh, today is very adverse.' He shook his head ominously. 'Isis and Nephthys weep for poor Osiris. You shouldn't listen to singing or chanting today.'

Raising an eyebrow, Kate cocked her head to listen to the intermittent music coming from the radio. With an ironic half-smile, she turned her attention back to the river. *So I should have stayed at home and shut myself away. The horoscope is absolutely right.*

'Long day?' the persistent American asked.

'Very long day,' she replied quietly. 'I've travelled down from Cairo.'

In truth, she had attempted to sleep for some of the long journey to Amarna, in the hope of escaping the turmoil in her brain. But she had been unable to get comfortable in the back seat of the dusty Land Rover and so had only managed to catnap. Driving through busy, noisy Cairo had been interesting – and hair-raising – but the long stretches of desert road that followed had seemed endless. She and her two companions had left the Ramses Hilton in Cairo not long after five in the morning and had stopped only once on the journey. Having left her watch safely in her suitcase, Kate had no idea of the current time. Judging by the position of the sun, it was late morning – and hot.

The backpacker had sidled closer. 'Are you on a sightseeing tour?' he asked hopefully.

'No, she's part of an archaeological team,' a gruff voice said from behind them. 'As am I.'

'Oh, really?' The young man tried to sound interested, but looked somewhat unnerved by Kate's grim-faced companion. 'What will you be doing out here?'

'Digging,' David Young muttered unhelpfully.

Kate sighed in exasperation. 'We're running a field school for students from Edinburgh,' she explained. 'We'll be helping out with the restoration work in the old city and excavating graves at the southern cemeteries. You could help the Amarna Trust's conservation plan by leaving a donation at the visitor centre, if you like…'

The mention of donations had its desired effect, and the man made a courteous but hasty departure to the other side of the craft. The hairs on the back of Kate's neck prickled as they always did when David stood behind her. How could she be angry with him and still want him to slip his arms around her and make her feel better?

'I'm sorry we didn't get to sail down the Nile as I planned,' he said softly.

'Given the circumstances, I expect it would have been really awkward.' Kate bit her lip to stop it from trembling.

Less than eight hours ago, she had tried to take their turbulent relationship to a more intimate level, but he had rejected her clumsy attempt to seduce him. He had provided no explanation for his reticence. She was left feeling scorned, wounded, and mortified by her presumptuousness.

Kate's gaze shifted to the man who stood behind David. Doctor Ethan Forbes leaned against the Land Rover, idly watching the antics of a young woman who was well aware of his attention. The girl's clothing was inappropriate for the region; she focused on giving David's best friend an eyeful of all the flesh she could expose without actually stripping.

Once again, Kate's memory flicked fretfully over the events of the past few months. A new job at the National Museum of Scotland had preceded the most upsetting and surreal year of her life. Her marriage to solicitor Mark Forrester, which had never been idyllic, ended when she discovered Mark's affair with one of her oldest friends.

Perhaps it had been loneliness, or the lack of intimacy in her marriage, which had brought forth disturbing dreams of a man she had never met, a handsome Victorian archaeologist named Edwin Ford. A close friend, Jess Mortimer, encouraged Kate to seek regression therapy. And so she discovered a past life in Victorian Edinburgh, where she had been the daughter of Professor James Grahame, the museum's director.

Kate endured three regression sessions, as the dreams continued to haunt her sleep. Research exposed a family connection to her past life: she was, in fact, the great-great-great granddaughter of James Grahame. She shared his daughter's name, and photographs showed an uncanny similarity between the two women.

In her Victorian lifetime, she had married Edwin and travelled with him to Amarna. Edwin held the prestigious position of expedition leader, in charge of a team who sought the tomb of Akhenaten. They spent some weeks at the site before holidaying in Cairo for the Christmas of 1891. When Katherine revealed she was pregnant, Edwin left her in the care of friends while he returned to Amarna. In his absence, Katherine suffered a miscarriage and became gravely ill. Her husband returned to Cairo in time to hold her as she died in his arms at the tender age of twenty-one.

While Kate struggled to come to terms with this tragic knowledge, Fate dealt her another crippling blow in the form of Edwin's ghost. For several weeks, he haunted her, while Kate began to fear she was nearing insanity. Nevertheless, the sad spirit provided a form of comfort as he imparted details of their life together. Before he disappeared for the last time, he implored Kate to travel to Egypt, implying she would find her soulmate in Amarna.

Unsurprisingly, Kate fell into a deeply melancholic state. The pain and grief from that other existence plagued her, mixing with the sorrow she felt over her life and her many failings. Her self-esteem plummeted until David took her in hand and helped her to recover. He had been a good friend – a stable, supportive presence in her life.

Professor David Young taught archaeology at Edinburgh University and was also the museum's Egyptologist. As a member of the Education and Events department, Kate had helped David with workshops and museum lectures. Even though he was already ably assisted by a graduate archaeologist named Steven Brodie, Kate quickly became invaluable to the often-taciturn professor.

To the surprise of their colleagues, David appointed Kate as his aide and provided basic field training so that she could accompany him to Egypt as the field school's student liaison.

David had doggedly tried to cultivate a relationship with Kate, but his efforts proved fruitless. When Kate finally confided the details of her past life, David assumed that she yearned for her Victorian soulmate. And then, a few days after Kate's thirtieth birthday, a row erupted which resulted in a three-month estrangement.

When at last they were reconciled, Kate realised that her feelings for David were no longer merely platonic. She had hoped that the trip to Egypt would help them make a fresh start.

David had arranged for Steven to work in Amarna with Ethan. The newly appointed Doctor Brodie escorted the students to Cairo while David and Kate travelled to Egypt on a later flight. While the students proceeded to Amarna, David and Kate enjoyed a luxurious two-night stay in adjoining rooms at the Hilton. The couple spent a day in bustling Cairo, and all had been wonderful – until the previous night.

And then, this morning, they had been met by Ethan. An employee of the Egypt Exploration Society and the field director of their expedition. David's friend since their university days. And the image of Kate's past life husband, Edwin Ford.

Although David had seen pictures of Edwin, he had not warned Kate of the Victorian's eerie resemblance to Ethan. So naturally, when she had come face to face with her past soulmate on the steps of the Hilton, Kate had been shocked.

Apparently, Ethan had already formed a low opinion of Kate for, since meeting her, he had been curt to the point of rudeness.

'You've hardly said a word all morning,' David murmured, interrupting her gloomy reverie, and Kate felt his sigh on the top of her head. No doubt, their thoughts were running along the same tracks.

Unable to look at him, she kept her eyes on the river, watching as the ferry manoeuvred for docking at el-Till. 'What would you have me say?' she inquired. 'I've just discovered that the man I trusted has been lying to me for six months…'

David placed a hand gently on her shoulder but dropped it again when she tensed at his touch. 'I'm sorry, Kate,' he said softly. 'I know you're hurt and angry, and justifiably so. I know we have to talk about this, but please hang on a little longer, okay?'

4

Hearing the pain and sincerity in his voice, she turned to face him. He looked almost haggard, but dark shadows only accentuated the green of his eyes. His dark blond hair, usually tidy, looked boyishly tousled. Kate nodded, too tired to vent her anger.

'You look exhausted,' David remarked, briefly touching her warm cheek.

'She's been lounging in the back of the car all morning,' Ethan taunted as he approached them. 'What's exhausting about that? Or were you two up all night?' He eyed Kate's blushing cheeks, not realising that she and David *had* been awake all night, but not for the reason he imagined. 'She'll have to get used to early mornings and long working days.'

He was treated to a scowl from each of them as they returned to the Land Rover. The other ferry passengers noisily climbed into the minibus parked at the front of the craft.

Once off the ferry, the minibus pulled up behind a tourist police jeep containing two armed, uniformed men who would be their escort around the site. Ethan drove alongside the minibus and stopped when he spotted the girl who had been tossing her hair at him on the ferry. Leaning out of the driver's window, he smiled disarmingly at the young woman, who hung chest-first out of her window and gave him a broad, bleached smile.

'You're a guest in a largely Muslim country,' he said evenly, his smile disappearing. 'Show some respect and dress accordingly.' With a mock salute, he gunned the engine and pulled onto the road ahead of the two vehicles.

David shook his head, appalled. 'That was unnecessary,' he snapped. 'And a really rotten thing to do!'

Ethan shrugged. 'The daft bimbo is dressed like a tart! She can't go about the place with her -' He glanced at Kate's horrified face in the rearview mirror. '- with it all hanging out. We're in the middle of the desert – what's the need for perfume, make-up and jewellery? What's next – stilettos? I hope you're paying attention, Miss Grahame!'

Kate did not respond, but her mind turned instantly to the silver, heart-shaped locket tucked among the clothes in her suitcase. She mentally caressed the engraved angel wings and wondered if she would ever wear David's birthday gift again. They had fallen out in July because she had refused to accept it; now she couldn't bear to be parted from it.

They sped past clusters of square, one-storey dwellings with small windows. Some of the brick walls were painted in cheerful colours, but many of the houses appeared rundown. Kate was reminded of the sprawling Lego towns constructed by her young nephew, Luca. Absently, she twisted the plastic mood ring that had been given to her by Luca's younger sister, Rebecca. The little girl had solemnly presented the colour-changing ring to her aunt, claiming it would keep her safe and help her find her handsome prince. Kate smiled sadly out of the window as houses and green fields made way for the barren desert.

In its heyday 4,000 years ago, the ancient city of Akhetaten stretched for twelve kilometres along the east bank of the Nile, and was about five kilometres wide. It had been the masterpiece of the eighteenth dynasty pharaoh Amenhotep IV, who had introduced the monotheistic religion known as Atenism. Rather than follow the pantheon of ancient Egyptian gods, the king revered one god: the Sun Disc, known as the Aten. In the fifth year of his reign, the king changed his name to Akhenaten and built a new capital city in the territory known as 'The Horizon of the Sun's Disc'. There he reigned with beautiful Queen Nefertiti until his death some thirteen years later.

Upon his demise, the people rejected the new religion and abandoned Akhetaten, returning to the gods and cities of pharaohs past. Workers dismantled stone temples and other buildings, transporting the blocks so that they could be used elsewhere. All evidence of the heretic pharaoh was removed; inscriptions bearing his name or image were systematically defaced. Historians still debated whether the king had been a freethinker ahead of his time or a tyrant.

The archaeological site was vast, occupying a semi-circle of desert with the river to the west and a crescent of limestone cliffs to the east. They travelled south on a road known locally as the Road of the Sultan. It had once been the Royal Road of Akhenaten, upon which he had driven his magnificent golden chariot.

Trying to get her bearings by remembering the pictures and books she had studied, Kate craned her neck to see out of the dirty windows. On her right, lush palm groves and patches of cultivation lined the wide bank of the Nile. To her left lay the scant remains of the ancient metropolis; the northern suburb gave way to the Central City and the Great Aten Temple. The barren, reddish-gold landscape undulated with mounds of sand, and the spoil heaps of many archaeological expeditions. Ruins of buildings were partially visible in the depressions, their decrepit walls made from the stone blocks known as talatat. As they passed the site of the Small Aten Temple, David pointed out the famous replica of a lotus-bundle column, towering over the excavation trenches and exposed foundation walls.

Prominent members of Akhenaten's court had built their tombs in the high northern cliffs, while others had chosen the lower cliffs to the south. Many of the tombs were unfinished, while others had been completed but left unused. Not all the tombs could be easily accessed; tourists had to be prepared to climb steep paths and punishing flights of steps. They also needed to hire drivers to take them from one part of the site to the next. The pharaoh's tomb was a few kilometres from the main city, along a road built in a dry valley known as the Royal Wadi. There were no treasures to see,

6

and very little artwork remained due to decay, looting and ancient vandalism.

A visitor centre had opened recently, which exhibited models of the city and some artefacts, as well as providing refreshments and shelter from the heat. The only way to fully appreciate the area, however, was to see it from the air, and so air-ballooning tours were under consideration by the tourist industry.

Nowadays Akhetaten was known as Tell el-Amarna, El-Amarna or simply Amarna. Many would be unimpressed by this unprepossessing site; it looked rather like the desolate surface of the moon. For Kate, mysterious Amarna held memories from her soul's past and perhaps also the key to her future.

After driving for about five kilometres down Akhenaten's old drag strip, Ethan turned left. Within a few minutes, they had reached the large, L-shaped dig house that would be their home for the next nine days.

With foundations that had been built by Akhenaten's workmen, the Amarna dig house had been used in Edwardian times, but for many years had lain abandoned and open to the elements. Almost forty years ago, the derelict single-storey ruin was rescued by the EES; the main house was restored, and given an impressive new façade featuring two arched doorways that led into a large dining room. The house resembled a Mexican hacienda in appearance, although the roof displayed a whimsical collection of pinnacles.

Over time, other buildings were added, and existing facilities upgraded. The main building possessed a modern kitchen, and a cosy living room complete with fireplace to bring comfort on cold winter nights. Attached to the house were small guest rooms with strange, conical roofs. The complex also offered laboratories, a photographic studio, office space, and secure storage facilities for artefacts.

In the centre of the facility, a welcoming courtyard paved with mosaic tiles offered respite from the harsh desert. The area nearest the dining room was partially roofed, and tables and chairs were set out for those who wished to dine al fresco. At the other end of the yard, a large acacia tree provided shade for the residents and the stray cats who frequently curled up at the base of the trunk.

Doors and window frames had been painted a cheerful cerulean blue to complement the dazzling white walls. The kitchen and some of the guest room doors faced onto the main yard while a smaller, lower courtyard led to the shower block. Stubborn plants attempted to thrive in pots that had been strategically placed near stone benches and plastic patio furniture, while pink bougainvillea crept over some of the buildings. A well-used stone barbecue told of the happy social gatherings of a small, harmonious community. This pleasing notion was slightly tainted, however, by the presence of soldiers.

Since the first Gulf War, residents of the dig house had been protected by a small garrison who staffed a guardhouse near the road. The house roof, which boasted a small tower, was marred by pillboxes for this armed security force.

Armed men aside, the house was a haven for archaeological teams, some of whom lived in the house for the duration of their visit, while others commuted from Mallawi, ten kilometres to the north.

A few hundred metres away from the east and west walls, cultivated areas offered verdant relief from the desert landscape. The village of El Hagg Qandil nestled nearby, providing a lifeline in what might otherwise have been an isolated location. Half a kilometre to the south lay the ruins of Kom el-Nana, the site of Nefertiti's sun temple. Excavations in this area had produced evidence of a garden and subsidiary buildings, including the remains of a bakery and a brewery.

Various vehicles were parked at the side of the dig house: a jeep, a scrambler motorbike, a pickup truck, and another Land Rover. Ethan parked next to the jeep and began muttering irritably when he saw four people gathering at the front door. Clearly, his passengers were to be greeted by a formal Egyptian welcoming party. A middle-aged woman and two men were being herded into an orderly line by a wizened old lady swathed in traditional robes of dark purple.

'Damn!' Ethan muttered in irritation. 'Just what I need!'

David's voice revealed his pleasure. 'She's still here? I thought she'd be long gone!'

'I'm beginning to think she's immortal. She gets weirder every year. She's been hanging about since I got here, giving me strange looks, and muttering. She says she's waiting for "the little cat".' Ethan shook his head in exasperation.

Kate peered out of the window at the old woman, who met her curious gaze with coal-black eyes that seemed to pierce her battered soul. Climbing stiffly out of the car, Kate started to feel very nervous as she realised that her conduct would now be under scrutiny. As she followed Ethan and David to meet these new companions, a small boy ran out of another doorway and took his place at the front of the line. Hanging back a little, Kate watched David greet these people like old friends, while Ethan stood at his elbow looking impatient. Her attention was diverted by the little boy, who snatched her right hand and shook it vigorously.

'Hi, honey!' he called, attempting an American accent. 'I am Hassan! Pleased ta meetcha!'

Laughing for the first time that day, Kate shook the small hand. The boy was about nine years old, with a shock of black hair that fell over his mischievous brown eyes. He was wearing faded jeans and a red Coca Cola t-shirt. Hassan received a gentle cuff on the back of the head from the man standing next to him, and a soft reprimand in Arabic. This tall, clean-shaven Egyptian looked about the same age as David, and a strong family resemblance indicated that he was Hassan's father.

Expecting to be greeted as an inferior species, as she had been by men in Cairo, Kate was surprised when this man gave a short bow over her proffered hand and then spoke to her almost reverently.

'My name is Ahmed, Miss Grahame. I am most honoured to meet you.'

Disconcerted by the man's frank stare, Kate returned his courteous greeting, aware that Ethan was watching her thoughtfully. Moving up the line, she now faced another tall man. He was older than Ahmed, with a greying beard and kind eyes. He wore a long white galabeya tunic and white cap. With a broad smile that revealed yellowing teeth, he shook Kate's hand firmly.

'I am Ali Suefy,' he announced. 'I am the caretaker here, and Ahmed is my son.' He gestured to the matronly woman standing next to him. 'This is my wife Samira. She speaks a very little English -'

Ali stopped talking as Samira interrupted in a rush of soft Arabic, her cheerful smile trained on Kate. Ali nodded, and then turned back to Kate. 'She is very happy you are here, and wishes to be of service to you whenever you require.'

Kate took up Samira's hands and smiled at her. 'Please tell Samira I am grateful for her kindness,' she said, not looking at Ali. 'But I am here to assist wherever necessary; please let her know that *I* would be happy to serve *her* whenever she needs my help.'

Ali seemed taken by surprise, but he translated, and Kate received a warm embrace and a kiss from Mrs Suefy. The woman then passed a comment to David in Arabic, and he smiled proudly in return; Ethan merely pursed his lips.

David stepped forward to greet the old woman, who took his hands and spoke to him softly in Arabic. To Ethan, she was brusque and dismissive, eliciting a sardonic smile from the Egyptologist, who left to unload the luggage from the Land Rover. As Kate stepped timidly forward, she noticed a younger woman come out of the house and stride eagerly towards them. Small and slim, the Egyptian girl wore trousers and an open-necked shirt, her long black hair flowing loosely across her shoulders.

'Assalamu alaikum,' Kate stuttered as the frail old woman took both her hands in a tight grip. She hoped she had delivered the formal greeting correctly, and glanced up at David for approval. Nodding, he smiled at her encouragingly.

'Wa alaikum assalam, qitah.' The woman looked inordinately pleased to meet Kate, and gave her a broad smile. 'Ana ismee Anai.' She pointed to

9

her bony chest, and then placed a palm over Kate's heart. 'We are family.'

The gesture was a little puzzling; Kate assumed it was a local custom and offered up a warm smile, before trying out another Arabic phrase. 'Ana ismee Kate.'

Kate grinned as Anai cackled and clapped her hands together, but her smile faded as she noticed that the young Egyptian woman was holding David's hands and looking fondly into his eyes. Worse, he was reciprocating in kind. The pair exchanged a few quiet words – in French.

'You're improving, Tasmina,' David told the exotic beauty. He received a shy smile from lusciously full lips.

Seemingly satisfied with his praise, which Kate knew was not easy to acquire, the girl turned to Kate and offered her right hand in a more Western greeting. 'My name is Mina. I help my Aunt Samira in the house. Anai is my grandmother. I am very pleased to meet you at last.'

'See, Mina!' Anai cried, reverting to heavily accented English. 'The guardians have returned. All together again!'

'Not this again!' Ethan spat as he rejoined the group. 'Mina, I wish you'd keep your grandmother at home – I'm sick of listening to this nonsense about guardians and lost stuff!'

Anai glowered at him and pointed a bony finger in his direction. 'You would rather hide from the truth than learn and move on to a more righteous existence! It has always been so with you!' She lowered her voice to a grumpy mutter. '*Ahbal!*'

'Very nice,' Ethan retorted sarcastically. 'I'm fed up being called an idiot, too!' He scowled at David as he heard his friend snigger.

Anai smiled sweetly at Kate and David. 'You two will come to my house for food. I will tell you when the time is right.' She quickly turned to Ethan. '*You* are not invited!'

Ethan snorted. 'Mind what you eat,' he advised David. 'The last time I ate at her house, I'm sure she laced my food with something. I've been having weird dreams ever since! Now, can we get on?' He walked off towards the front door of the house.

'We accept your kind offer, Anai,' David said respectfully, in English for Kate's sake. Anai nodded, her sharp chin lifted imperiously. She reached out to pat Kate's cheek, before shuffling off around the side of the building, her family in tow. Kate watched them thoughtfully, her mind already filling with questions.

'Anai's family have worked with European archaeologists for generations,' David told her, pre-empting her inevitable queries. 'Her father was English, but the locals treat her as an oracle. She dabbles in mystical things and yes, some of the things she says don't make sense. She must be in her eighties now. I don't know what she meant about the guardians returning. I do know that "qitah" is Arabic for "cat". The word "ahbal" loosely means idiot -'

'I'd worked that out,' Kate interrupted. 'Though it's tamer than some of the words *I'd* use to describe him…' Ethan had left their luggage by the car; Kate retrieved her small suitcase and laptop bag. 'And Mina?' she asked carefully, hefting the laptop bag over her shoulder.

'Her father was French. Both her parents are dead; her grandmother raised her and made sure she had an education. She enjoys looking after us -'

Kate's eyes narrowed. 'Oh, really?'

David gave her an admonishing look; she had no right to be jealous. 'She's a *girl* – no more than twenty. We're friends. I taught her French.' Taking Kate's case from her, he moved towards the door, silencing any further discussion about his relationship with the vivacious young Egyptian. As if on cue, Mina reappeared and tried to take David's laptop bag. Playfully turning away so she couldn't reach it, he strode into the house.

Dolefully, Kate trailed behind, listening to the pair converse in three different languages, forgetting to look over her new home, her eyes on David's back. Mina asked David if he had brought her a present; David replied in the affirmative. She chatted girlishly, frequently touching his arm and looking up at him adoringly with her striking, golden brown eyes. She used the French pronunciation of David's name, which rolled seductively off her tongue like a caress. Kate stifled the urge to make the 'vomit face' behind Mina's back.

The interior of the house was pleasantly cool, and quiet save for the muffled sound of a radio playing in a distant corner of the building. They walked along a narrow whitewashed corridor punctuated by wooden doors on both sides. Ethan was waiting impatiently at one of the doors; once they had caught up, he opened it and stepped inside a small room. It was sparsely furnished with a bed, a desk, a couple of chairs, and a small wardrobe. Another door led to a tiny shower room. Kate stared awkwardly at the double bed, aware that Ethan was watching her with vindictive amusement. Mina looked almost horrified.

'We need *two* rooms, Ethan.' David fired his friend a venomous glance, while Kate blushed furiously and stared at the tiles on the floor. 'I thought I had made this clear.'

Ethan raised a dark eyebrow. 'Did you?'

'Yes,' David replied through gritted teeth.

Ethan shrugged nonchalantly. 'I thought you'd appreciate the field director's room…' His brooding gaze swivelled back to Kate and settled on her face. 'Besides, I don't think we've any spare rooms. She'd have to bunk up with somebody else…'

'There are seventeen bedrooms in this place!' David protested.

'Yes, but we're not alone – there's an American team here and they're not all staying in Mallawi. Yusuf and another inspector will be joining us later today. I've kept our people on this side of the building, but they're already sharing rooms, and -'

Kate squirmed, fidgeting with the strap of her bag. 'It's fine,' she stuttered, avoiding Ethan's scrutiny. 'I don't mind sharing a room...'

'You'll do no such thing!' David sounded appalled. '*I* can share with one of the other men.' He turned to Ethan. 'Which of the guys has room?'

Ethan sighed irritably, rolling his eyes at David's gallantry.

'No, David,' Kate interrupted. 'I'm happy to share a room with one of the female students. It'll help me get to know them, which will help me do my job better.' She allowed some of her indignation to bubble to the surface. 'Besides, I wouldn't want to interfere with Doctor Forbes' housekeeping arrangements...'

Ethan frowned at her with obvious distaste. 'I'm *not* the housekeeper,' he told her, enunciating each word. This time, Kate did not look meekly at the floor. She returned his gaze with a fiery look but was unable to formulate a suitable rejoinder.

Mina spoke up in Arabic, her tone and expression terse. With a theatrical sigh, Ethan picked up Kate's suitcase and headed for the corridor.

'Follow me,' he commanded Kate. 'It seems there's a spare room after all, but it's at the other end of the house. So hurry up – it would be nice if we could get *some* work done today.' He glanced back towards David, who still stood staring at the bed in his room. 'I'll be back in a minute. I need to talk to you.'

Feeling irked because Mina had taken a seat on David's bed and resumed their animated conversation, Kate glared at Ethan's back as he walked quickly along the corridor. He looked like Edwin, even sounded a little like Edwin. But she could not sense her Victorian husband's essence in this brash, sarcastic, modern-day version who had treated her with contempt since the moment they had met in Cairo.

They left the main building and crossed the courtyard to the long block that housed the secure storage rooms and several workrooms. The sound of engines and voices signalled the return of the workforce for lunch. As Ethan strode past the acacia, a black cat ran out from behind the tree, hissed at him then ran off in the direction of the kitchen.

He led Kate through a wooden door almost hidden from the courtyard by the tree's foliage. A few steps along another hallway and he pushed open another door. Kate was surprised when he stood back to let her enter the room first.

It reminded Kate of a cell; the small window had bars across it, painted in the same shade of blue as the window frames. Shafts of sunlight shone through, highlighting the dust motes that filled the air. There was a single bed, covered by a mosquito net. A small, narrow wardrobe stood in one corner, next to a cracked hand sink. A lamp and a desktop refrigerator sat on a wooden desk, along with a pile of books that had presumably been left by the previous occupant. Two paintings of the landscape graced the white walls.

'Probably not what you're used to...' Ethan commented sarcastically. 'Mina uses this room sometimes,' He flashed her a nasty smirk. 'She probably won't need it for a while. The lock on the door is broken, but I'll ask Ali to fix it.'

Alarmed by the prospect of sleeping alone in an unlocked room, Kate began to protest, but the words died on her lips as she glanced up at him. There was no empathy in his piercing brown eyes, only cold implacability. Kate's stomach lurched queasily.

'You made quite an impression with the locals,' he remarked.

'I hope it was a good one...' Kate stuttered, realising he was undoubtedly referring to her defiant response to Ali's comment about his wife being of service. She tried to meet Ethan's gaze, but failed.

'Am I going to have trouble with you?' he asked, and his eyes narrowed ominously.

Kate made sure her expression revealed nothing of her anguish. 'I'm here to work for David.'

Ethan's gaze shifted as he heard footsteps approaching from behind them. Kate turned, and her heart sank even further as Amy Reardon appeared in the doorway. She offered Kate a tight, clearly faked smile.

Amy idolised David and saw Kate as a rival for his affections. As a result, Kate had failed to build a rapport with the third-year archaeology student.

'Are you back for lunch already, Miss Reardon?' Ethan asked briskly.

Amy gave him a glorious smile, and Kate wondered if the girl had switched allegiance. 'We've been slogging away all morning, Doctor Forbes!' she gushed. 'I left something in the workroom along the hall, which is why -'

'I'm glad to hear you've been working,' Ethan interrupted, and dropped Kate's case on the floor. 'Especially since Professor Young has arrived and will be casting his critical eye over your work very shortly. Show the professor's *assistant* where everything is.' He glanced coldly at Kate. 'Grahame, when you've unpacked you can grab some lunch. I'll be taking Professor Young around the site in about an hour. I expect he'll want you to come along.'

Once he had gone, Amy took the opportunity to appraise Kate's room. Kate took comfort in the fact that Amy would be unable to tell her fellow students that David's assistant had been given luxurious accommodation while the rest of them were doubling up in single rooms.

'You're next door to the Bone Room...' Amy commented.

Suspecting the remark had been made to unsettle her, Kate decided not to give Amy any satisfaction.

'How are you settling in?' Kate asked, walking to the bed and laying her case upon the striped blanket. She turned towards the student, forcing an amiable expression onto her face.

'Fine,' came the somewhat truculent reply.

'I understand this is your first trip to Egypt?'

'Yes.'

Kate felt as though she were pulling teeth, but continued doggedly. 'What have you been doing since you got here?'

Amy shrugged, plainly unimpressed with Kate's attempt to befriend her. No doubt she was another person who believed that a mere museum employee like Kate had no place on an archaeological field trip, and certainly should not own a position of authority.

'We toured the site and looked at some recently-excavated artefacts.' Amy gave Kate a pointed look. 'We've been waiting for the professor, so we can actually do some fieldwork.'

Undaunted by Amy's sarcasm, Kate's gaze did not waver from the student's freckled face. 'Well, he's here now.'

Turning her back on the young woman, she proceeded to open her suitcase. Amy stood awkwardly in the centre of the room, emanating ill feeling. Kate tried once again to foster goodwill. 'Would you like to join me for lunch?'

Amy looked surprised by the offer. She pushed a long strand of blonde hair back from her face. 'I have to write up my notes on this morning's work,' she muttered. The guarded expression slipped a fraction. 'But thanks for asking…'

Kate smiled, pleased that she had made a little progress. 'Another time then. Listen, if you have work to do then go – you don't have to show me round; I'm sure I'll get my bearings...'

Amy nodded and swiftly left. Kate slumped onto the bed, feeling the mattress sink depressingly under her slight weight. She lowered her face into her hands and sighed, gathering the inner strength she would need to face the inevitable trials to come. She tried to steer her attention towards her role as student liaison.

The professor was a fine teacher, but he had no patience for the petty dramas of his students. Kate's job was to deal with such minutiae so David could concentrate on teaching. Her feelings, confused though they might be, were of secondary importance.

Back in Edinburgh, she had assured her friend Jess that she would forget her inane romantic obsession with a soulmate long dead, that she would leave her love life in the hands of Fate. Fate who had regularly screwed her over in her thirty years in this lifetime.

But before she pushed her personal issues to one side, she had to confront

David.

The suppressed frustration of the two men made the room seem even smaller. David, his face like thunder, slumped down on the bed, which creaked dangerously. Picking up a small statue of Bastet from the desk, Ethan pulled out the chair and sat down. He fidgeted with the black figurine as he regarded his truculent friend.

'Hey, I gave up my bedroom for you!' Ethan teased. 'Show some gratitude!' He looked around the room. 'I think I cleared all my stuff out...'

'Except for your pet,' David commented, nodding at Bastet. 'I'm surprised you still have that thing after all these years...'

'She's my lucky mascot,' Ethan replied, tickling the statue under its proud chin. 'She never fails me!'

'Why do I feel like the conversation is about to take a salacious turn?' David sighed.

'You need to pack in the banter with Mina,' Ethan said, his face grim. The girl had excused herself as soon as Ethan had returned to David's room, as though eager to escape the field director. 'She's not a child anymore; she'll get the wrong idea, and then you'll be in trouble. Her uncle and I are in the middle of finding her a husband -'

David's laughter was laced with irony. '*You're* helping to find her a husband? That's rich! What are you now, the local sheikh?'

'Belt up! Ali asked for my help, so I'm helping. Actually, Anai gave me first refusal. She said that a marriage to Mina would be my soul's redemption...' He paused, staring into space for a moment, then caught David's quizzical stare. 'The old crone wasn't best pleased when I declined her offer. In fact, I think she put a curse on me and my entire lineage...'

'Please tell me you haven't been amusing yourself with Mina...' David began, sighing heavily.

'No!' Ethan protested. 'You know I never mess about with the local women -'

'Just every *other* woman -'

'Don't start! Everybody knows you brought your "assistant" to keep you warm at night – so keep Mina at arm's length and don't screw things up! Mind you, I have to wonder why Anai didn't offer the girl to *you*...' Ethan paused, his mind drifting back to the enthusiastic welcome Kate had received on her arrival. 'Why did it sound like Anai was expecting Kate?'

David shrugged irritably. 'Maybe she read it in the tea leaves. Where are the students?'

Ethan knew it was important to act in a conciliatory manner; he would be testing the limits of their friendship over the next few days. 'I gave them the afternoon off so they could perfect their notes for their very particular professor.' He tried a winning smile, which David ignored.

'And have they done any work at all, or have you left them to their own devices while you wandered about the cliffs looking for a lost tomb?'

'Don't get all high-and-mighty with me!' Ethan cried defensively. 'You were supposed to arrive with them two days ago! Steve and I have been covering for you so you could woo your assistant!' He paused and scrutinised his friend through narrowed eyes. 'Judging from the strained atmosphere in the car this morning, I gather things didn't work out as you planned? Either that, or she was terrible in -'

'Stop it!' David snapped. 'For once in your life, can you think about something other than sex? Nothing happened. Whatever I wanted...well, it's over.'

Ethan looked incredulous. 'What – just like that? When you've spent months pining for her? Mind you, it would be the wisest course of action. I always thought she was leading you on. Women like her -'

'We're *not* discussing Kate!'

'I won't allow her to hamper this expedition!'

'*Now* who's acting high-and-mighty?'

Unwilling to quarrel with his friend, Ethan calmed down. 'D'you want to talk about it?' He grimaced at the floor.

David caught the expression of reluctance. 'I told you, no. There's nothing between Kate and me. And nothing will interfere with my work here. Now, what have the students been doing?'

Ethan grunted, mollified for the present. 'We've followed your itinerary for the field school. By the time we arrived on Monday there was only time for a lecture on recent finds and our expectations for the season. Yesterday, we toured the city and saw the boundary stelae. This morning, they went to look at their allocated dig site in the southern cemetery. Obviously, Steve's done most of the work, since I had that meeting in Cairo yesterday with the man from the MSA...'

As though he had wished to thwart his friend's romantic plans, Ethan had summoned David to the Cairo museum the previous morning to relay his suspicion that the northern cliffs of Amarna hid an undiscovered tomb. By law, they needed permission from the Ministry of State for Antiquities before any archaeological work could begin.

'And you were told that a proper search for a tomb was out of the question. There would be no funding, no equipment, and no extra staff.'

'Actually, our inspector's willing to look over the area and report back to Cairo.' For a moment, Ethan looked smug. His tiny triumph was short-lived.

'And what's he going to look at, Ethan? What makes you so sure there's something there?'

'Intuition...?'

David rolled his eyes. 'Do you have any *concrete evidence*?'

'I've looked over the area numerous times,' Ethan replied defensively. 'I've taken photos and I've examined old maps and geological surveys. I want us to go out to the site together, so I can show you the lay of the land. There's a weak seam in the cliff face, which would have been the perfect place to dig a shaft. There are signs of an old path, and the rock formation generally just doesn't look…right.'

'What about your work here?'

Ethan shrugged in frustration. 'It's *desk* work. Paper pushing. Managing things for the EES and sending endless reports. Accounts. Paying the workers. Making the shopping lists…' He stood up, giving the impression of a caged animal. 'I need to get *out there*! Please, Dave, help me with this admin work so I can spend time at the cliffs. I promise I'll help you with the students. I know there's something out there!' For a moment, his eyes glazed over, as though he could imagine himself discovering a tomb that had lain hidden for millennia.

David looked pensive, caught between loyalty to his friend and his moral obligation to uphold the law. Ethan had endured a difficult year. He had suffered a severe fall while mountain climbing in the Scottish Highlands at the end of last winter. A head injury had forced an induced coma, and Ethan had lain in the Edinburgh Royal Infirmary for over a month. Since then, he had been restless and dissatisfied with life. Excavating without permission would be a career-ending move, perhaps for both of them. Nevertheless, David was inclined to indulge him. Compassion overruled the jealousy that gnawed at him as he looked into a face that resembled that of his dead nemesis. It wasn't Ethan's fault that he looked like Edwin Ford. David wondered how many times a day he would have to remind himself of that fact.

Ethan observed David's hesitancy. 'I promise I'll be discreet…' He placed the statue back on the desk.

David gave a disbelieving snort. 'When have you *ever* been discreet?' His friend was renowned for bedding any female who took his fancy, regardless of marital status.

As if on cue, there was a knock on the door and it opened to reveal a stunning redhead dressed in the popular uniform of the archaeologist: boots, cargo pants, cotton shirt.

David's eyes fixed on Ethan's; they exchanged a look that warned Ethan of a stern reprimand to come.

'Professor Young!' The woman approached David with open arms and gave him a fierce hug. David's response was perfunctory, his smile tight.

'Doctor Deveraux. What a surprise.' He glared at Ethan over the woman's shoulder. 'Are you here with the American team?'

The woman's tinkling laughter filled the room. 'Oh, yes,' she drawled in a Texan accent. Stepping back, she gave Ethan a conspiratorial wink. 'And we're enjoying your hospitality immensely!'

David stood. 'I'm sure. You can tell me all about it later. Right now I have to catch up with my team and find something to eat.' He paused as an idea occurred to him. 'Ethan, if we're going out to the city this afternoon, I want to make one specific stop…'

'Well, tell me on the way,' Ethan replied. 'You go on to the dining room. I'll catch up in a couple of minutes.'

Shaking his head in exasperation, David left his room and went to look for Kate.

He found her trying to hang up the beautiful dress she had worn to dinner at the Hilton the night before. Kate had looked radiant in the long, simply cut dress of midnight blue chiffon. Her dazzling smile had been full of hope, her face flushed with excitement and anticipation…

'It'll be safer in your suitcase,' David advised her gently, watching her stroke the sleeve. When she glanced at him, there was a tear at the corner of her eye. She made a sound of agreement and returned the garment to her suitcase, stowing the case under the bed.

David made a quick survey of the room and tutted in consternation. 'This is no bigger than a mouse hole. And it's miles away from everybody else -'

Moving to the desk, he perused the stack of books, finding a romantic novel, a history of Amarna, a self-help book and a book on ancient Egyptian magic.

'Well, at least it will be peaceful.' Kate felt suddenly brazen. 'And I might not have needed my own room, if you'd -'

David shook his head, hearing the sound of Ethan's voice and approaching footsteps. 'Don't. Not now.' He saw her brown eyes pleading for an explanation. 'Soon, Kate. I promise.'

Ethan stuck his head round the door. 'I thought I'd find you here. Right – quick bite to eat, and then we're going out.'

CHAPTER 2

The dining room was homely and welcoming, with windows overlooking the courtyard. Cupboards lined the walls, and Ethan rummaged to find a suitable snack for himself. Kate remained in the doorway, wishing she could absent herself and so deny Ethan's existence for a little longer. Her eyes wandered to the flies hovering over the bowl of fruit that lay in the centre of the marble table that dominated the room.

Mina appeared from the adjoining kitchen, carrying a plate of sandwiches and some bottles of water. She smiled at Kate and beckoned her to the table. 'Come. You must eat if you are to walk in the desert.'

Ethan sat down and helped himself to a sandwich. Pulling out a chair for Kate, David waited for her to sit, and then took a seat next to her. Ethan and Mina both looked surprised by the polite gesture but said nothing. With a satisfied nod, Mina left the room.

The sandwiches were tasty and, discovering she was hungry after all, Kate devoured hers with gusto. Ethan held David's attention with details of a recently excavated anthropoid coffin, unaware of the disquiet caused by his handsome features. Kate caught the occasional tic in David's firm jaw and fervently wished she had never confided in him about her past life. Then she alone would be filled with trepidation.

The three looked up as a young man entered, and Kate grinned widely at Steven Brodie, pleased beyond measure to see him. Steven had helped with Kate's training, supplied her with his own study notes, and patiently answered her endless questions. Having recently attained his PhD, Steven had accepted his first appointment with enthusiasm and hoped it would lead to a fulfilling and lucrative full-time job.

'Steven!' Kate cried, rising from her chair in order to hug her friend. Steven's grim expression made her stop dead in her tracks. She received only a muttered greeting, and then Steven helped himself to a bottle of water and sat down next to Ethan. Bemused by his sullenness, Kate resumed her seat.

'The students are updating their notes,' he told Ethan. 'After lunch, Ahmed will drive us down to the city; we're going to help repair the walls around the Great Temple. I've told them all to reassemble here at dinner time – so they can greet Professor Young and his "assistant".' The barb was unmistakable.

'How are you, Steven?' David asked tersely.

'Fine,' the young archaeologist muttered. 'But I'll be glad to be relieved of my babysitting duties – or to be able to share them, at least.' He gave David a meaningful look, which the professor chose to ignore.

Kate looked from one to the other warily, bewildered by Steven's uncharacteristic belligerence.

'If the students have been difficult, I apologise.' David offered mildly.

'Yeah, well, I *do* have my own work to do.'

Trying to placate him, Kate smiled at him. 'If we have time this week, perhaps you could show me some of the tombs -'

'I'm not a tour guide,' Steven snapped. 'And I don't have time to nursemaid *you*, either -' He faltered as he saw Kate recoil from his venom.

David's eyes narrowed dangerously. 'Steven! Apologise to Kate. *Now.*'

'It's not necessary, David,' Kate said hastily. 'Steven's right. He has a lot of work to do…'

'And I'd be grateful if you could call me *Doctor Brodie* in front of the students.' Steven rose and moved towards the door.

It was a step too far; David started to rise from his chair, until Ethan pulled him back down again.

'*Doctor* Brodie, we're all on the same team, here. Miss Grahame is Professor Young's assistant. Regardless of her qualifications – or lack thereof – you'll treat her with respect. Is that clear?'

Steven's eyes were icy, but he nodded reluctantly and continued on his way. Before he reached the hallway, he stopped and returned to the table. Leaning down, he lowered his voice, his expression contemptuous. 'You should know that there's gossip…'

David's jaw tightened. 'Oh?'

'People are wondering why you two came out alone, after the rest of us. They wonder why Kate is here at all.'

David snorted. 'I don't care about idle gossip -'

'It's not *you* I'm concerned about!' Steven snapped. 'Your lack of professionalism casts a shadow on the whole expedition.' He strode quickly from the room.

David watched him go, his expression troubled. He sighed heavily, as Kate realised what was amiss.

'We were supposed to come out here with the students, weren't we?' Kate asked quietly. He had insisted on arranging their travel plans, and she had acquiesced without question.

'Don't worry about him,' Ethan said dismissively, squeezing David's shoulder. 'Some of the students have had problems adjusting to the change in diet. One of the boys – Jonathan, I think – puked all over Steven the other day. He's still narked about it!' He stood up, restless to proceed with his plans for the day. 'But he's right – you two are the main source of gossip right now.' He fixed them with a curious stare. 'I don't know what's going on with the pair of you, but you have to put the work first. If you're a couple, be discreet. If you're not, then you have to find a way past your issues; I don't want any soap opera dramas on my watch -'

David looked up, indignant and angry at Ethan's patronising attitude and Steven's inexcusable rudeness. 'Are *you* really going to lecture *me* about *that*?'

Ethan raised an arrogant eyebrow. 'Dunno. Let's see how it goes.'

They began at the west-facing North Palace, which stood 1500 metres north of El-Till. It had been built for Nefertiti but was later passed to her eldest daughter, Meryetaten. The remains of mud-brick walls delineated the rooms and courtyards of this rectangular compound that had once overlooked the Nile. As with the rest of Akhetaten, conservation was ongoing. The city could never be restored to its former glory, but the boundaries of the main buildings and other prominent features would be clarified to provide an indication of how the city had looked. Smaller, less significant areas would be buried by sand, an effective and cheap method of preservation.

Locally made bricks had been used to cap the eroding walls of the palace, and repair their weathered sides. Stone blocks marked the boundaries of rooms and courtyards, so that visitors could at least see the floor plan and dimensions of the place. Pillar bases and old thresholds had been reconstructed. Even so, envisaging a grand palace took a great deal of imagination.

Rows of chambers overlooked the garden court, which had been surrounded by pillars. The garden had contained a pool in its centre, which had cooled the palace by means of evaporation. During the excavations of the 1920's, magnificent friezes had been discovered depicting vibrant scenes of a papyrus marsh, with lifelike birds cavorting among the reeds. A reconstruction of one of the paintings had been fixed to a wall in a chamber known as the Green Room; the beauty of the piece was unexpected, the colours dazzling.

There were also the remains of animal houses, workshops, a throne room, a bathroom and a toilet.

Speaking quickly, and with a hint of impatience, Ethan explained that conservation work on the palace was complete. The local workforce had moved on to the Central City, where they would soon begin to clean and restore the front of the Great Aten Temple.

'Which is where we're going next,' Ethan announced loudly.

Looking down at her feet, Kate was lost in thought; she was standing where Queen Nefertiti had stood. She was in the home of her favourite Egyptian, and Kate was starstruck.

'Kate…' David called softly, and Kate looked up at him with a goofy smile.

'I'm in Nefertiti's house…' she said.

Gazing at her tenderly, David chuckled. 'I know, but we have to go; there's more to see.' He walked with Ethan to the Land Rover.

After taking some photographs, Kate followed, walking backwards nearly all the way to the car.

The Great Aten Temple was a short drive south on the Royal Road. The expanding community of El-Till was gradually encroaching on the temple and parts of the city; the walls of the Muslim cemetery were already butting against the edges of the temple. When it came to the preservation of a national monument, the local people exhibited an apathetic attitude. Under pressure from the MSA, the local council had recently cleared a rubbish dump that had covered part of the site. There was, therefore, an urgent need to accurately mark out the temple and create firm boundaries between temple and village.

In its day, the temple complex had been surrounded by a brick wall, creating an enclosure whose area measured 240,000 square metres. Entrants to the temple would have passed through massive ceremonial gates on their way to make an offering to the mighty Aten. Only two buildings inhabited the space, the largest of which was the Long Temple. As its name suggests, this was a long rectangular building comprising of six courtyards, each separated by a grand doorway. Most of the courtyards were filled with small tables for offerings; the foundations of these stone tables were still visible.

Towards the rear of the enclosure, the roofless Sanctuary had been built. It, too, had been filled with offerings tables. In front of this building, a square enclosure had been used to slaughter cattle. Evidence of more offerings tables had been discovered in the open space around the Great Temple; excavators estimated there had been almost 2,000 of these tables in the complex.

Conservation of the Great Aten Temple was underway, starting with the exposure of walls and foundations. Ancient paving could be seen under a thin layer of sand, along with the bases of pillars. Local builders were already repairing walls, and members of an Australian field school were working in the area of the Long Temple. They reminded Kate of industrious ants.

As David and Ethan talked with the Arab foreman at the temple, Kate wandered around the area, trying to imagine the impressive roofless structure in its heyday. The workers glanced at her and flashed the occasional smile, but they did not engage her in conversation.

A group of tourists arrived, having journeyed to the temple in a trailer hitched to a tractor. Their Egyptian guide herded them together and proceeded to lead them about the site.

Closing her eyes, and ignoring the noise around her, Kate absorbed the sounds and scents which surrounded her, feeling the energy of the ancient site and enjoying the healing warmth of the sun on her face. *I'm lucky to be here,* she told herself. *David has taken a risk in bringing me; I have to make the best of this and not let him down.* She heard him call her name, and obediently returned to his side.

They walked down the road for about half a kilometre, the heat reflecting off the tarmac onto their faces. David took a hand-drawn map from his shirt pocket and pointed out the indentations in the sand that marked the remains of a bakery, noblemen's houses, the Records Office and the King's House. On the other side of the road, nearer the Nile, Akhenaten had built the Great Palace, which had boasted its own bridge linking the palace to the King's House. The bridge's foundations still stood, the remnants of what surely must have been a feat of engineering.

While David pointed out the most interesting areas of the city, Ethan walked several metres in front, hands in pockets, a proverbial black cloud above his head. He contributed nothing to David's informal lecture, but his dour presence created an uncomfortable atmosphere.

It was quiet around the Small Aten Temple, but a handful of men laboured near one of the buttresses at the southern end of the enclosure.

This temple was almost precisely aligned with the mouth of the Royal Wadi and was assumed to be Akhenaten's mortuary temple. New limestone blocks marked the outline of the compound; new paving had been laid and walls had been repaired where necessary. Pieces of the original pillars remained, but the most eye-catching piece was the reconstruction of a sandstone papyrus-bud column. At around ten metres high, the column was striking, and contained some of the preserved fragments from the original piece.

Craning her neck to look up the length of the pillar, Kate was suddenly overcome with embarrassment. Here she was, in the company of men, and staring intently at the distinctly phallic-shaped landmark. Quickly turning away, she moved to examine a partial pillar, which sat on a limestone plinth nearby. Then, realising that Ethan and David were walking out of the temple towards the remains of the central city, she took some more photographs and hurried after them.

The heat was intense in the open desert, and a stiff breeze blew sand into Kate's face and mouth. Tired and thirsty, she continued determinedly, suspecting that Ethan was expecting her to flag.

Having all but ignored her for the entire afternoon, he had commandeered David's attention once again. The pompous field director carried on a ceaseless monologue about different excavations and plans for the site, while David listened intently and interrupted with occasional questions. Kate stopped listening to Ethan as she heard a horse whinny from somewhere behind her. She turned to see a black horse galloping towards them from the general direction of El Hagg Qandil, a young man in hot pursuit. A mocking jeer went up from the Egyptian workmen at the Small Temple, who were preparing to down tools for the day.

'David!' Kate hissed urgently, tugging his sleeve as the horse approached them without slowing down. Its dark eyes were wide; the animal was terrified.

David moved quickly in front of Kate, taking a firm stance in the sand with his arms raised above his head. Although he was directly in the path of the fleeing horse, he stood calmly and began to call soothingly to the animal. Miraculously, the horse faltered. Without thinking, Kate moved to stand beside David as the horse slowed to a trot.

'Kate, get out of its way!' David commanded in the same quiet voice. The horse, saddled and bridled, pranced sideways and snorted.

'He's only frightened,' Kate replied, slowly reaching into the pocket of her trousers. Pulling out a packet of mints, she placed a sweet on the palm of her hand and held it out to the trembling horse. As she walked slowly towards the animal, it snickered, and shook its thick black mane. Craning its neck, it sniffed Kate's hand, took a hesitant step forward, and then gently took the mint from her palm. Kate seized the opportunity to capture the reins, and stroked the horse's nose as she murmured softly to it.

The youth ran towards them, shouting even though he was out of breath. Ethan came forward to talk to him, but Kate's attention was on the horse. Noticing flecks of blood in the spittle around its mouth, Kate moved to examine the bridle and bit. Enraged, she discovered that the bridle was too tight, causing the bit to pull cruelly at the horse's mouth. She moved to the horse's neck, stroking its silky coat as she went. Old scars told of excessive whipping. The saddle was of reasonable quality and sat upon a colourful blanket, but Kate could barely get one finger under the girth.

Lifting the saddle flap, she loosened the girth. Her actions resulted in an angry tirade in Arabic from the young man, who rushed over to her, gesticulating wildly without getting too close. Rolling his eyes, Ethan attempted to intercede.

David stood back, and waited for Kate to vent her anger on the two arrogant men. He knew she would hold her own and didn't need him to defend her – not when there was a horse involved. Back in Edinburgh, he had reintroduced her to her old passion for horse riding. He had watched her mollycoddle his two rescue horses as though they were the most precious creatures in the world. At times, he had almost felt jealous of Ginger and Zack.

'Let him have his horse back,' Ethan told Kate peevishly. 'You're making a scene!'

Kate's eyes flashed, and David saw her jaw clench. 'He's mistreating this horse!' she fumed. 'The girth is far too tight, and so is the bridle. Look at the bit!' She pointed to the blood around the horse's mouth and proceeded to loosen the bridle and reposition the bit. 'He shouldn't use a bit again until the horse's mouth has healed. And the poor animal has been whipped! It's barbaric!'

The youth raised his voice even further, sounding close to hysteria at Kate's interference. Ethan tried to placate him, but when he turned back to Kate once more, she could see the anger in his eyes. His expression was devoid of compassion as he addressed her curtly. 'He claims the horse can't be controlled in any other way. It's a high-spirited brute -'

'He's an Arab stallion,' Kate corrected, rubbing the horse's nose. 'Tell the stupid prat he'll get more out of the animal with kindness than cruelty.' She glared at the horse's owner. 'Ahbal!'

Ethan relayed a censored version of Kate's message to the Egyptian, apologising on her behalf for the insult she had fired at him. The pair exchanged a few sentences then both laughed, like men sharing a dirty joke. Ethan turned back to Kate with a sneer. 'He says horses and women should be treated in the same manner.'

David stepped towards the two chauvinists, incensed by the insult. Before he reached Kate's side, however, she had lifted her foot to the stirrup and hoisted herself up into the saddle, ignoring the indignant yells of the horse's owner. Behind them, the curious workers drew closer and watched the scene unfold.

'Get down from there, you idiot!' Ethan growled.

Kate scowled at him, hiding her nervousness at being so high up and on the back of a temperamental horse. 'I'll get down when I've proved my point to this ignorant chauvinist pig!'

Gathering the reins, she looked quickly away from David's concerned gaze before he had time to admonish her. With only a light touch of her heels, the horse set off at a gentle walk. Kate spoke quietly to her mount as they rode a little way from the group. He was still jittery, his ears twitching at the sound of his master's harsh voice. Kate stroked his ebony shoulder with gentle hands.

After a few metres, both horse and rider overcame their nerves, and Kate wished they could just ride in peace for the rest of the afternoon. Determined to make her case, she urged the horse into a graceful trot and laughed joyfully as her new friend whinnied and flamboyantly tossed his head.

Turning in a wide arc, they headed back to the three men. The owner had fallen silent at last, cowed by his horse's display of perfect behaviour and sickened at being humiliated in front of his countrymen by a woman. Ethan's face showed his displeasure as Kate halted the horse before him. David took hold of the horse's reins and gave Kate a reproving glance, but she thought she saw his lips twitch.

Dismounting gracefully, she ran up the stirrups then stroked the horse's neck. In response, the stallion turned his head towards her and butted her backside. She giggled as he nuzzled her trouser pocket in search of more mints. Kate obliged by giving the horse another treat, before turning defiantly towards Ethan and the Egyptian.

'As you can see, he's perfectly obedient when his tack is positioned correctly and he's treated with respect. Tell your friend he needs to see to the horse's mouth. I would be happy to supervise him.' Her eyes glinted wickedly.

Ethan glowered at Kate, momentarily speechless. He quickly recovered and translated an abridged version of Kate's suggestions. After another short discussion, during which the Egyptian gestured at Kate dismissively, the youth led his horse back towards El Hagg Qandil.

Ethan turned on Kate. 'What the hell did you think you were doing?' he shouted. 'We need to keep the villagers on side, you daft woman, not alienate them! They won't want to help us if we allow our women to interfere and belittle them!'

'It sounds more like you're worried about your own reputation!' Kate snapped. 'Are you concerned about your masculinity being questioned if they think you can't control "your women"? And in case you hadn't realised, Western women are not considered the property of men!'

Had he possessed any of Edwin's nature, Kate knew that at this stage in the argument, Ethan would say something flippant to lighten the mood. He would use the magical talent he had possessed to defuse her anger. Instead, his voice dripped barely concealed contempt.

'Keep behaving this way, and you'll be on the next flight home. I don't need another burden on this expedition. And in case you hadn't realised, you've been brought here against my wishes – you'd be well advised to remember that. Just get on with your work and keep your head down!'

'Ethan,' David's voice was threateningly quiet. 'Kate's a member of *my* staff. She's my responsibility, not yours.'

'Then get her under control!' Ethan spat. 'Now come on – I have a lot of work to do back at the house.' He stalked back towards the road like a man in need of escape.

'You promised we could make one more stop,' David reminded him.

'That was before your assistant blew it -'

'Ethan, you want my help this week – so we're making one more stop!'

Muttering under his breath, Ethan continued on his way. David turned towards Kate, who fought to blink angry tears from her eyes. Nevertheless, she looked up at him rebelliously and waited for him to continue where his friend had left off.

'I will never admonish you for stepping out from behind your mask,' he told her kindly. 'Nor will I yell at you for coming to the aid of a suffering animal. But we must all be mindful of our behaviour here. In this matter, Ethan's correct – we need to be diplomatic with the locals. And as a woman, you have to behave with...' David hesitated, because he knew she would inevitably lose her temper at the next word. '...decorum.' He pointedly took a step back, out of her reach. Instead of inflaming her anger, the deliberately comical move made her giggle weakly.

'I'm sorry,' she said sincerely. 'I don't want to make things difficult for you, but when men treat me that way, it just makes me so...' She shook her head and bit her lip. *It reminds me of being a Victorian woman, desperate for the freedom enjoyed by Victorian men.* 'Ethan's not...'

'He's not what you expected.'

Kate shook her head helplessly and looked down at the sand.

'Let's go, you two!' Ethan's shouted at them cantankerously. 'Have romantic interludes on your own time!'

Kate looked past David to where Ethan stood a short distance away. *He's obnoxious,* she thought. *He's nothing like Edwin.*

Placing his hand lightly on the small of her back, David shepherded her back the way they had come. In response, she leaned her head against his upper arm. She felt exhausted, and they still had an unpleasant discussion ahead.

'I can't believe you gave that horse a Polo mint,' David told her with a smile. Kate merely shrugged, too tired to offer a defence.

Grateful for a seat in an air-conditioned vehicle, Kate drank nearly all of her water as David drove them further down the road, past the temples and buildings of the main city. He eventually pulled off the tarmac and parked the Land Rover at the side of the road. The men climbed out, Ethan's face stony. Nonplussed, and suppressing a weary groan, Kate jumped onto the flinty ground and followed them as they headed further into the desert.

There were numerous soil heaps, and indentations in the ground marked areas where dwellings had once stood in the city suburbs. Partial walls peeked out from ground level while some stood taller, delineating the rooms of houses long abandoned. Broken pieces of pottery crunched under their feet, and Kate was alarmed to see one or two bones, hopefully just the remains of a desert animal's meal.

By the time David paused to consult his map, they had walked for nearly half a kilometre, and Kate was wilting. She stopped to wipe the sweat from her eyes with her sleeve, only to have Ethan's critical gaze fall on her once more.

'Didn't you bring a hat?' he snapped. 'Or water?' He had been slugging from a two-litre bottle for most of the walk.

'I have a little water,' she replied. 'My hat's in my bag.' She patted the satchel across her shoulder.

'Not much use in your bag, is it?' he commented.

'Never mind,' David soothed. 'We're here.' Smiling sympathetically at Kate, he gestured to the remains of a group of houses. He led the way to one particular house, where some of the walls reached up to Kate's chest, marking several rooms. Stepping inside one of the rooms, David beckoned for Kate to follow. She looked around the space, her imagination attempting to fill in the missing pieces.

'D'you know where you are?' David asked.

She glanced up at him, puzzled. 'In a big house?' From outside the house, Ethan snorted.

'This is Thutmose's workshop,' David explained.

Her eyes widened. 'The sculptor of the Nefertiti bust?' David nodded, grinning.

With the toe of her boot, Kate brushed at the surface of the ground. 'She was found *here*?' she asked breathlessly.

'Right where you're standing – on December 6th, 1912.'

'Allegedly,' Ethan added. 'There are those who believe the whole thing was faked – a sensational discovery conveniently made on the very day that foreign royalty visited Borchardt at Amarna.'

'Sour grapes,' David retorted, and turned his back on Ethan, who sighed and began walking slowly back towards the car.

Kneeling down on the ground, Kate sifted a handful of sand through her fingers, awestruck. A stone caught her eye, and she picked it up; dark red with darker striations, it twinkled slightly when it caught the sunlight.

'Red quartzite,' David asserted. 'It was used for making busts and statues – and this *was* a sculptor's studio. I can show you a 3D model of what we think the workshop looked like…'

'Can I take this piece home?' Kate asked.

'For Luca?' David guessed, and Kate nodded. 'He emailed me a few days ago and asked me to bring him back a dinosaur bone. I didn't tell him we'd be looking for *human* bones, but I suspect one of those would bring him almost as much pleasure…' He chuckled, but Kate was perturbed by her nephew's actions.

'You're right; he's fascinated by any kind of bone – it must be because his dad's a doctor. But I'm sorry if Luca disturbed you. I'll talk to him about that when I get home -'

Crouching down beside her, David gave her a warm smile. 'He didn't disturb me. I'm happy he got in touch, and he can keep emailing me for as long as he likes. I'm a teacher – I like to teach.'

Forgetting she was supposed to be upset with him, Kate impulsively kissed his cheek. 'Thank you for bringing me here – it's amazing.'

Standing, and pulling her up beside him, David glanced towards Ethan's retreating figure. 'Well, take some pictures, because we need to go home; it'll soon be Mister Happy's feeding time.'

The dig house was teeming with hungry people on their return, all lured to the kitchen by the delicious smell of food. Mina and Samira had prepared a rich stew, accompanied by vegetables, couscous and bread. Some of the diners sat at the table while others took their plates to the veranda and enjoyed an al fresco dinner in the rosy evening light, despite the threat of mosquitoes.

Ethan introduced David and Kate to the two inspectors who had recently arrived from Cairo. Yusuf Shoukry had worked with David and Ethan for several seasons; he had given Kate a short tour of the Cairo museum when David had been summoned to a meeting with Ethan. Yusuf was shrewd in a typically Egyptian way, but fair-minded and not above bending the strict rules of his office in the pursuit of knowledge and the discovery of artefacts. Moumdah el-Aaswany, on the other hand, was a stickler for protocol and wore a dour, disapproving expression. Both men were quite dismissive of Kate and focused their attention on David and Ethan.

The loud and jovial American team was from the University of California in Los Angeles. The three female and two male students all seemed to exude a kind of Hollywood glamour, as did their lecturer, Doctor Marianne Deveraux. The team's photographer, however, ogled Kate as though she were a banquet to be savoured; Kate was very glad to discover that Brandon Taylor returned to a hotel in Mallawi every evening with some of his colleagues.

The Americans, who had been lingering around the table with after-dinner coffee, got up and left the dining room. As soon as they had gone, the room filled up again with David's ravenous students. The British group greeted their teacher with cautious civility; David was their professor and had no wish to be their best friend. He addressed them with his usual reserve then sat down next to Ethan, who had naturally taken a seat at the head of the table. Steven shuffled in morosely and sat down on Ethan's other side, his eyes fixed on the plate of stew Samira set before him. Fluttering around him like a mother hen, Mina set David's cutlery and napkin before him, before bringing a heaped plate of food and a cold bottle of beer.

Kate had received awkward but nonetheless welcoming hugs from Jonathan Ritchie, Dominic O'Hare, Russell Palmer and Celine Pierzak before they scrambled to sit at the table. Julian Noble and Amy greeted her politely, with an air of mild disapproval. Still, the students seemed to be in good spirits as they tucked into their food, only mildly intimidated by David's presence. Sitting at the opposite end of the table from Ethan, Kate picked at her food and used the time to observe the students discreetly. She had been their liaison in the weeks leading up to the expedition, answering their queries, sweating beside them during David's punishing gym sessions and generally helping them to prepare for their trip. Regrettably, time had not allowed her the opportunity to interact with them on a more personal level.

Once the food had been devoured, and the plates had been cleared away, the students placed their notebooks on the table so that David could peruse their field notes. They all looked slightly anxious; David had very exacting standards, and they had all been on the receiving end of his acid tongue on at least one occasion.

'*I'll* read the notes tonight,' Steven offered. Throughout dinner, he had contributed little to the conversation. Now he looked at David with contrition. 'I've been working with them, after all. You can take over tomorrow.' His apparent remorse did not extend to Kate, however, whom he had pointedly ignored since entering the room.

'Fair enough,' David replied, getting stiffly to his feet and looking around the table at the eager young faces of his team. 'Kate will put tomorrow's work schedule on the notice board in the hall outside. We'll be leaving for the excavation site at 7.30 sharp. Have a good night's sleep.' He nodded to Ethan and Steven and headed for his room, gesturing for Kate to join him. The moment they had both dreaded had finally arrived.

Closing the bedroom door behind them, David ran a hand through his hair and mentally steeled himself for what was to come. She had waited hours to confront him, had been forced to bottle up emotions that would now be unleashed on him. He was surprised, then, when Kate merely stared at the floor, anxiously wringing her hands. The defeated stance was worse than a display of her fiery temper.

'You've known about Edwin for six months,' she murmured. 'Why didn't you say anything about his resemblance to Ethan? Why didn't you warn me?' Her hands curled into tight fists, a sign that she was fighting to control her emotions. 'I thought we were -' Kate's voice faltered. 'And all this time, you *knew*…'

David passed his hand across his eyes as he tried to deliver a suitable confession. 'I'm sorry,' he began, and decided only the truth would suffice. 'I have no plausible excuse, other than my selfishness.' He moved a step closer, his expression earnest and sad. 'When I saw the photo of Edwin Ford from the museum archives, I didn't know what to do. We thought it would be better for you to find out when you got here -'

Kate looked up sharply. '*We?*' she repeated. 'Who else knew?'

David groaned softly at his poor choice of words. 'Jess summoned me to a meeting in October. She gave me a rollicking for treating you badly after we fell out over that stupid locket. I showed her the wedding photograph I'd found of you and – and *him*. I expressed my suspicion that you were waiting for whomever Edwin might be this time round. But that was the first time she and I had ever discussed it -'

'I can't believe Jess knew about Ethan all along…' Kate looked bewildered and hurt.

'Don't blame Jess,' David said quickly. 'It's not her fault. She wanted to fix things, for you to be happy. I begged her not to say anything about Ethan.' He reached out for her clenched fist and held it. 'I wanted you to myself, Kate, for just a little longer…'

When she looked up at him, Kate's eyes glistened with unshed tears. 'You didn't want me last night…'

David raised his other hand to her cheek. 'I did,' he told her firmly. 'More than you can imagine. But knowing what was about to happen, I couldn't stay with you. It would have been wrong.' He pried her fingers open and held her hand in his. 'If we had spent the night together, it would have made this even more difficult to bear. For both of us.'

'You made me feel so rejected…'she accused.

'And how would you feel now, if I had acted differently?' David became indignant; she wasn't the only one who was suffering. 'How can you act so…so *injured*, when you've repeatedly rebuffed me for the best part of a year? I tried to be patient and understanding because I thought my only competition was your cheating ex-husband. But I'm just a normal guy, Kate, and I've *never* understood this unshakable belief that you would find Edwin Ford again and live happily ever after. What made you so sure?'

'He told me himself…' she whispered. She hung her head, fearful of his response.

David stared at her warily, unsure if he had misheard. 'He…what?'

She looked up, and he saw a spark of anger in her eyes. 'So Jess didn't blab *everything* to you then?'

David sighed wearily. 'Jess didn't tell me *anything*. She's been completely loyal to you throughout this whole blasted nightmare. And now, there's a ghost…'

He regarded her warily, not sure if he would be able to cope with another fantastical revelation. 'Kate, please, I'm begging you – tell me the whole blasted story so that I know where I stand. I think I deserve to know the truth.'

She took a deep breath. 'Around the time I broke up with Mark, Edwin…appeared to me. First in the Egyptian gallery of the museum, then at home.' She glanced up to gauge his reaction; David kept his face carefully blank. 'I saw him several times. Jess saw him move an artefact in the museum, so I know he wasn't a figment of my imagination.'

David's mouth felt dry, and he dearly wished for some whisky; he swallowed hard before talking again. 'And did he communicate with you?'

'He told me that my inability to be a good Victorian wife caused problems in -'

'Stop it!' David snapped automatically. She had incessantly picked at her supposed flaws for too long. Worse, she had reverted to a mode of speech that always filled him with fear – talking as if *she* was Katherine Ford.

'He told me about my – *Katherine's* – death, and a little of what happened to him afterwards. He said he'd come back to make sure I took the right path. I'd made bad decisions in the past, which had somehow prevented me from meeting my soulmate.' She looked up at him then, her wide eyes pleading for understanding. 'He said I would find…answers…in Egypt…'

As she spoke, she stepped closer and laid her cheek on his chest. David refrained from slipping his arms around her, even though he longed to comfort her. Receiving no response from him, Kate stepped back again, looking utterly disconsolate.

'It seems he said a lot,' David began, his dislike of the long-dead Edwin Ford rising to the surface. 'Without actually saying very much.'

'He could be annoyingly vague,' Kate agreed.

'And it sounds like he helped to chip away at your already crumbling self-esteem!'

Kate sighed. 'Don't, David. I needed him…'

'You had *me*.' David glared at her accusingly.

'We hardly knew each other.'

There was a long silence, while David strove to find a solution to yet another problem.

'He's no longer "with" you?' he asked, dreading the answer.

Kate winced at the sharp tone of his voice. 'He said he couldn't stay. The day after he left me, Ethan woke up from his coma.'

David's mind reeled as he tried to find a connection between these events. 'You think he's in Ethan? Just because they look similar?' Exasperation made him raise his voice. 'If Edwin was anything like Ethan,

I can't imagine why you would have married him!'

'Ethan doesn't recognise me,' she murmured, shaking her head. 'He doesn't even seem to *like* me. And I can't sense Edwin in him...' She stared into space for a moment, and then looked back at David. 'Ethan's insufferable. He's not like Edwin at all.' Kate wrapped her arms tightly around herself, an indication of her insecurity. It was a gesture David had not seen her make for some time. 'The worst thing is, I had decided to move on with my life and stop letting the past rule the present. Or the future...'

She looked so lost, so fragile, that David put his arms around her and pulled her gently to him. Nestling against his chest, Kate shivered.

'Well,' David began, struggling to find a practical solution. 'Once again, your past life has reared up to slap us in the face. You have no choice but to try and bond with the man you believe to be your soulmate.' She started to protest, but he kept talking. 'If you're meant to connect with Ethan in some way, then it will happen.' He cupped her chin in his hand and made her look at him. 'But Kate, you have to know that he sees women as a short-term diversion. I've never known him to nurture a meaningful relationship with a woman, but I *have* seen him toss many to the kerb. Luckily, he seems to stick to those who share his values. This isn't bitterness or jealousy, Kate – it's a warning. Do you understand?'

Kate nodded. 'I thought he was your best friend?'

'He is, but that doesn't mean I approve of his actions all the time. I think he behaves the way he does because he battles with a restlessness he can't control. He's always been unsettled, and since he woke from the coma he's been much worse.' He held her face between his hands. 'I won't stand in your way, but you should also know that in this particular crusade, you stand alone. Please don't ask for my help with this.'

'I'm so sorry, David...' she murmured, swallowing a sob.

David kissed the top of her head. 'Don't, angel...' he whispered into her hair. *Please allow me to protect myself. Please help me to gather the strength I need to face the trials ahead and still do my job.* He began to relax his hold on her, but in response she held him fiercely.

'Kate,' David said gently. 'Ethan won't give you the time of day if he thinks we have feelings for one another.' He smiled sadly. 'He does have *some* scruples! We can't give people the impression that we're anything but co-workers. So we shouldn't do *this*.'

In spite of his words, he couldn't bring himself to release her completely. Reluctantly, he pulled her arms from around his waist and brought her hands to his lips, kissing the cold knuckles.

'Are you going to freeze me out again?' Kate asked miserably. 'Turn your back on me and treat me like dirt?'

David bowed his head in contrition, still ashamed of his ill-treatment of her during their three-month rift. His anger at her rejection had caused him to draw out his vengeance and abuse his role as her supervisor. He had taken grim pleasure in the allocation of onerous tasks and an evil delight in picking her work apart with endless criticism. He had denied her even the most basic courtesy – all because he loved her beyond reason.

'No, Kate. I will *never* behave that way again. But I have to treat you as my assistant...' He looked at her regretfully, fully aware that he was a hard taskmaster. Steven and Kate were the only ones who had endured in a role which could be both demanding and thankless; all David's other aides had either resigned or been dismissed.

Kate made one last, desperate attempt to retain some claim on his affections. 'What if I say that I don't want it to be like this?'

David's jaw tightened. 'A part of me wouldn't believe you, just as a part of you would always wonder what might have happened if you had met Ethan without me in tow.'

'No, I wouldn't -'

'Kate, if we were lovers, would you want to share me with another woman?' She looked shocked, then indignant, and fervidly shook her head. 'I feel the same way; I'm not sharing you with a ghost. As I told you in Cairo, I won't be second best.'

Kate stepped back. 'I understand,' she said, sounding calmer than he felt. Moving past him, she headed for the door and opened it. 'Goodnight, Professor.' Her voice echoed in the hallway. As did her footsteps, as she made her way to her lonely room, so very far away from him.

In a little house on the edge of El Hagg Qandil, Mina knelt in front of the fire beside her grandmother. The old woman murmured words in an ancient language and tossed a selection of herbs and spices into the fire, causing orange flames to leap up the chimney. A strange odour pervaded the darkened room which made Mina's eyes water. On the stone mantelpiece above, a row of figurines looked down on them, the old gods and goddesses of Egypt. A beautifully painted statue of Isis took pride of place in the centre of the arrangement, her mighty wings outstretched behind slender raised arms.

'Grandmother,' Mina began in a pleading tone. 'Must we do this?'

'Yes, Tasmina,' Anai replied firmly.

'Why must you tamper with them? Why can't you leave David – for me?'

Anai's tone was sharp and full of conviction. 'You will have the one you deserve, the one who will help you reach your destiny. But we must enlighten the three, and avenge those who were lost. Then perhaps there will be peace and prosperity in our family. Come, child – it is the time of the full moon, and we have much work to do.'

Bowing their heads, the two women began to pray to the ancient gods of death and rebirth.

CHAPTER 3

Exhausted from the day's travails, Kate had been unable to find respite or warmth under the blankets on her narrow bed. She had fought with the mosquito net, which seemed intent on suffocating her. The house had whispered around her; she imagined she could hear footsteps outside her door. In the desert, wild dogs had howled continuously, and the distressing sounds of dying prey seemed to go on forever, the hapless animal's painful shrieks agonising to hear. In the end, she began reading the book on magic by the insufficient light of the bedside lamp until she finally fell asleep.

Rising at 6am, Kate quietly opened the door at the end of the corridor and crept outside into the shadowy, silent courtyard. The cold air caused her to inhale sharply, and she shivered as she hastened to the communal shower block. Luckily, she encountered none of the other occupants of the house and was able to shower and dress in relative peace before rousing the students. Her first duty of the day complete, she made her way to the dining room, where Mina and Samira had laid out a buffet breakfast. Kate winced at the bright lights, and the loud voices of the American team, as she made her way towards the spread of bread, fruit and cereal. She stared numbly at the food, trying to decide whether she was hungry, and was about to turn away when David came to stand beside her. A glance around the room told her that they were being observed by several pairs of inquisitive eyes.

'Have some breakfast, Kate,' David urged.

'I'm not hungry…' she murmured and stole a glance at his face. He looked as though he hadn't slept, and he hadn't bothered to shave.

'I'm not moving until I've seen you eat something,' David hissed in Kate's ear. 'You hardly ate yesterday. I'll cook you something myself if I have to – in front of all these people, who are surreptitiously watching our every move.' He nodded in the direction of their nosey housemates.

She wondered if they were going to return to their usual pattern of behaviour. Countless times over the last nine months, they had agreed to act as platonic workmates, and then David would ignore the ground rules and continue to flirt and chip away at her defences. He seemed unable to help himself and she – albeit reluctantly – enjoyed his attentions. Inevitably, one would offend the other; they would argue and proceed to sulk for a few hours or days while the tension simmered around their environment and long-suffering colleagues. Once they realised that they missed one another's company, whoever was at fault would apologise for their transgression, and the whole maddening cycle would repeat itself. And yet, it was better than being pushed away altogether. It was better than facing his remoteness or his cruelty.

Kate's eyes glinted defiantly at David's comments, but she obediently picked up a plate and perused the buffet wish fresh eyes, trying to ignore the flies hovering above the exposed food. She selected some fruit that she could peel, and a bottle of water, before following David into the spacious kitchen.

An impressive cooking range dominated this room, flanked by marble worktops. Wooden cabinets lined the walls. Another door, half-open, led out into the courtyard. Samira and Ali sat at a small table, enjoying breakfast together. David bid them good morning, and helped himself to some plates from one of the cupboards. Glad that Mina was not within fawning distance, Kate watched him toast some bread in the ancient toaster. She smiled at his frown of concentration as he monitored the bread's progress, fishing it out when he deemed it ready. Spreading the toast with golden honey, he placed it on Kate's plate along with a few plump strawberries.

'Bossy!' she muttered tetchily, as they walked back into the dining room.

'You're no good to me if you're weak with hunger. Now eat, or I'll feed you a strawberry. And you'll be mortified.' He held a strawberry in front of her lips, his eyes challenging a retort that she was set to deliver until Ethan approached them.

'I'm going to El-Till to pick up supplies this morning,' he announced to David. 'I need an extra pair of hands. Can you spare your assistant for a couple of hours?'

Both Kate and David interpreted the request as a deliberate gibe at Kate's lack of archaeological qualifications. Her expression impassive, Kate looked at David and waited to see if he would remember his promise not to become an impediment. To her disappointment, he shrugged and nodded his assent.

'Good,' Ethan said briskly, helping himself to a cup of tar-like coffee. 'Grahame, the supply depot will call me when the provisions have arrived. Make yourself useful while you're waiting – help Samira with the dishes or something.' Nodding his thanks to David, he sat down at the table next to

Marianne.

'I'll stay if you want me to,' Kate offered. 'I'm on *your* team, not his.'

'You need to spend some time with him alone.' He sounded almost indifferent.

Kate's eyes dropped to her plate. 'I'm not sure I want to.'

'You won't know peace until you've given this your best shot...'

Ahmed drove David and the students to their dig site in an old military truck. Kate remained behind and, as Ethan had spitefully suggested, helped Samira and Mina to clear up in the dining room and kitchen. The Egyptian women were cheerful and kind, but seemed to look at Kate with something akin to pity.

Almost two hours had passed by the time Ethan reappeared and ordered Kate to join him in an old Ford pickup truck. They made the short journey to El-Till in stony silence. Kate leaned against the passenger door of the truck, the seatbelt cutting into her neck as she stared out of the window. She barely registered the clear blue sky or the stark beauty of the landscape. She didn't want to be alone with Ethan Forbes. Out of the corner of her eye, she saw him glance in her direction, shake his head, and then return his attention to the empty road. He could undoubtedly sense her displeasure, and he would have noticed that she had placed herself as far away from him as possible. Kate blushed, embarrassed; he had probably added 'immature' to his list of her faults.

'You look very familiar,' he said suddenly, and for a moment, Kate held her breath. 'Have our paths crossed before?' She replied in the negative. 'You've always lived in Edinburgh?' She gave a short nod of affirmation. 'You've set yourself some narrow boundaries. No desire to see the world?'

'I wanted to see Egypt. And here I am.'

With a resigned sigh, Ethan parked in front of the supply depot near the ferry port. 'You're almost as taciturn as David,' he commented drily. 'Perhaps you two are well-matched, after all.' Before she could reply, he jumped out of the truck and shouted a greeting to a man who was already stacking boxes outside the small building.

Pulling a folded sheet of paper out of his back pocket, he handed it to Kate as she disembarked.

'This is our shopping list. Check that we have everything, and get it loaded onto the back of the truck. I have to go inside and check on some equipment I sent for.' He strode off but then stopped and looked back. 'Make sure we've got David's chocolate supply, will you? He's grumpy enough as it is!' Ethan grinned, just like Edwin Ford.

Common ground made Kate smile nervously back at him. 'Peanut M&M's?' she asked, chuckling at David's passion for these particular sweets. Ethan nodded and stepped inside the depot.

For a moment, Kate took the opportunity to study him through the open doorway, seeing him clearly for the first time. The resemblance to Edwin was startling, but the two men were not identical. Like Edwin, Ethan was tall and athletic. His hair was almost black, like Edwin's, and he had the same dark brown eyes. But Ethan's gaze was cold, arrogant and calculating. His climbing accident had left a three-inch scar on his forehead, near the hairline, and his face was beginning to look a little careworn.

It struck her then that the details of her past life – which had once been as vivid as her reality – had faded into distant memory. In recent weeks, her mind had been happily occupied with work and study – and David. Now those recollections of Katherine Ford's life were resurfacing once more, bringing the pain and anguish Kate had worked hard to overcome.

Suppressing her fears, she focused on her assignment, checking that the supplies in the boxes tallied with those on the list. As well as foodstuffs and cleaning products, there were several large bags of sweets for David and a well-concealed case of beer. Satisfied that they had everything on the list, Kate began to load the provisions onto the back of the truck, gritting her teeth against the weight of huge tanks of water for the water coolers. With unlikely chivalry, Ethan came out in time to help load the heavier items.

Their next errand was to purchase some equipment for a repair to the dig house roof, and Ethan bought a new lock for Kate's bedroom door. Although he was friendly and talkative with the local tradesmen, Kate did not even merit a benevolent glance. She was thankful when Ethan announced that their shopping trip was over. However, instead of taking the Royal Road, Ethan took a different route on a smaller road that turned into a dirt track and began to ascend towards the north cliffs.

After a somewhat alarming drive along a ridge only a little wider than the truck, Ethan parked at a safe distance from the edge of the escarpment. Kate's eyes widened at the beautiful scene far below. The wide expanse of the Nile meandered into the distance, a number of small fishing boats dotted along its calm surface. On either side, the broad stripe of cultivated land seemed to end abruptly when it reached the desert, rather like a green carpet laid across the barren sand. Amarna was already being trampled on by tourists; from her vantage point, Kate could see cars and minibuses traversing the site.

'It's beautiful,' Kate murmured, captivated.

Ethan slouched back in his seat, regarding her with the lazy, derisive gaze he reserved just for her. He seemed unimpressed with the view, and Kate supposed he had brought many women to this spot, perhaps as part of his much-vaunted seduction technique. Why, then, had he brought *her*?

'In Akhenaten's time, the uncontrolled floods would have ensured a wider expanse of fertile ground,' Ethan told Kate, in a tone that suggested he was bored. 'The Aswan dam put paid to that.'

Kate turned towards him, but found herself still unable to meet his gaze. His presence was unnerving, predatory and disdainful all at once. It was as if their energy fields clashed, making her feel almost nauseous.

'David has kept you very close to his chest,' he declared, smirking at the double entendre.

Kate turned back to the view. 'I'm sure David has told you that we're just colleagues,' she replied, sounding defensive. 'And friends.' His penetrating gaze caused an involuntary shudder. Even though it was sunny, she felt cold.

'He has – several times. But I've known him for a long time, and I've never seen anyone get under his skin the way you have. So tell me, are you leading him a merry dance? What's your agenda, Miss Grahame?'

Finally, Kate's fiery eyes met his. 'Our relationship – *whatever* it may be – is none of your damn business!'

He seemed to enjoy this new facet of her character, for his eyes glinted, and he continued to goad Kate. 'Well, the pair of you fairly ooze unrequited passion, so I gather you're not sleeping together...'

Kate's eyes widened at the inappropriate remark, but she could find no words to voice her repugnance.

'Who rejected whom?' Ethan prodded.

Her look of outrage changed to one of guilt, and Ethan sat back, a look of satisfaction on his face. Kate stared at him mutely, unable to believe his audacity. As memories returned, of the last year, of the night at the Hilton, her expression became one of torment.

Perhaps he owned a tiny modicum of compassion, for Ethan's voice softened a fraction. 'Are you the reason he broke up with Diane?'

Around the time Kate's marriage had dissolved, David had ended his own seemingly unfulfilling relationship.

Kate slowly shook her head. 'I didn't know him very well when he was dating Diane. I don't know why they split up.'

'But he started going out with you soon afterwards?'

'We started "going out" as friends who had both suffered break-ups...' Kate decided to stop allowing herself to be browbeaten by this supercilious fishwife. 'He was very worried about you when you were in a coma, you know. He looked after your parents, too. Were you aware of that?'

Ethan had the decency to look contrite. 'He's a good man.' An ironic smile appeared on his lips. 'A real knight in shining armour, with a taste for lost causes.' He gave her a meaningful look. 'I've often thought about buying him a white horse...' Ethan chuckled and gazed wistfully towards the blue horizon. 'He's too noble for his own good...'

Kate nodded sadly. 'Yes, he is.'

They sat in silence for a while, each lost in their thoughts of David.

Finally, Kate turned to Ethan. 'Doctor Forbes, do you remember anything about being in a coma?'

Ethan kept his eyes on the skyline, recalling the disjointed dreams of his comatose state. He keenly remembered waking to an overwhelming sense of loss, a gnawing emptiness that still haunted him. Nothing seemed to fill the cavern in his soul, and his vivid dreams had turned his nights into an alternative, more disturbing reality.

'Not really.' He shrugged dismissively. 'I think I may have dreamed. I woke up confused and disorientated...'

'Are you better now?'

'Miss Grahame, you can rest assured that I am of sound mind and able to perform my duties more than adequately.'

'I didn't mean -'

'Did you bring your camera?' Ethan waved a hand towards the river. 'Good place to take some photos, don't you think?'

Flustered, Kate retrieved her camera from her bag and climbed out of the truck. Ethan watched her train the camera on the landscape, his eyes automatically roaming her figure and marking her assets out of ten. He wondered if she was genuinely shy, or merely playing the coquette. As a rule, he preferred confident, worldly women. He felt a momentary spark of irritation; Kate Grahame was going to be difficult to fathom.

Climbing out of the truck, he stretched and turned his face up to the sun, aware that Kate was unconsciously stepping towards the edge of the track. He moved swiftly as she took another step forward, grabbing her around the waist and pulling her back to safety. Squealing in surprise, she spun round to face him, one small hand lifted as if to slap his face. Instead, she disengaged herself, pushing his hands away from her body.

'You're too near the edge,' he scolded, and looked into her face for several long moments. The breeze blew a strand of curling hair into her eyes, and she lifted her hand to tuck the tendril behind her ear.

Ethan's eyes followed the gesture, his gaze pensive. 'Are you sure we've never...met?'

The question seemed loaded with innuendo, and Kate frowned in response. 'If we have, then it obviously wasn't very memorable. For *either* of us.' Striding back to the truck, she climbed into the dusty seat.

The drive back was made in contemplative silence.

Under David's supervision, the Edinburgh students spent the morning preparing their dig site in the cemetery below the southern tombs, at the mouth of a wadi strewn with pieces of bone and broken pottery. Previous GPS surveys of the area indicated many graves, ostensibly belonging to Amarna's working-class citizens. Excavation of such graves provided invaluable information about these people's lives, mortality rates, illnesses, physical abnormalities, nutrition and religious beliefs.

As their professor observed and supervised, the students marked off two plots with poles and string, each area measuring two metres by four metres. They then progressed to removing the top ten centimetres of sand and gravel. This was a painstaking process, as every shovelful had to be sifted through large circular sieves. Nothing of note had been found that morning, but the students remained undaunted and returned to the house in an optimistic mood. Aware that they still needed to grow accustomed to working in the heat, David rewarded them with a long lunch break.

As he slowed down to turn into the grounds of the dig house, Ethan spotted a motorbike speeding along the road towards them. Frowning when he recognised the rider, he glanced over at Kate in order to assess her reaction. Her expression was one of disbelief as she watched David manoeuvre the trail bike in order to turn in behind them. His lithe passenger clung to him, arms wrapped tightly around his waist, black hair flying behind her from under her helmet. As David parked the bike beside the pickup truck, Mina pulled off the helmet, her tinkling laughter filling the air.

'Did you get everything?' David called as Ethan climbed out of the truck. Mina came to stand beside David, linking her arm possessively through his.

Walking around the far side of the truck, Kate opened the tailgate and began unloading the supplies. Mina ran to help, and the pair began to carry the boxes to the kitchen.

'What the hell are you playing at?' Ethan demanded.

David's euphoric grin slipped from his face, to be replaced with a puzzled expression.

'Mina needed to take something to her cousin's house,' David replied defensively. 'I gave her a lift. What took *you* so long? You should've been back ages ago.' His gaze wandered in the direction of the kitchen.

Shaking his head, Ethan began to unload a tank of water. 'If *this* is how you tried to get Kate into bed, it's no wonder you failed! But if you're still trying to win the girl, you're doing a lousy job. Unless you're trying to win a *different* girl…'

Once the boxes of provisions had been carried into the house, Kate joined the students in the courtyard. Washing hung on a line at one end of the yard, the modern clothing somewhat incongruous in a place where 18th Dynasty building work was still visible. The black cat sat under the acacia, people watching with feline disdain.

Anai sat on a plastic chair under a large parasol, holding court at a circular patio table, her knobbly fingers busy with some sewing. The students – three Scots, one Englishman, one Irishman, a Polish girl and four Americans – clustered around her, listening to folk tales as they tucked into oversized sandwiches.

Marianne gestured for Kate to sit next to her on a stone bench while Ethan perched restlessly on the other side of the American archaeologist. Mina fussed around David, pulling a chair into the shade for him, and then disappearing into the kitchen. She returned minutes later with a plate of food for the professor, and then sat cross-legged at his feet. Ethan stared at David in disbelief, and then squinted at Kate. She, too, had witnessed Mina's excessive attentiveness and now looked completely dispirited as she turned her attention back to Anai. The old Egyptian woman had evidently been regaling the students with ghost stories, for one of the girls had just asked if the dig house was haunted.

Anai snorted. 'Many have died here. Many souls wander the desert. Some of them are among us at this very moment...' She looked up towards the stone bench, her shrewd gaze passing from Ethan to Kate, then flicking across to David.

'So the house *is* haunted?' Amy asked. 'Or d'you mean they've been reincarnated?'

Anai nodded vaguely, her attention on the shirt she was darning. 'There are spirits, shadows, and souls which suffer pain...'

'Here we go again...' Ethan muttered under his breath, earning himself a poke in the ribs from Marianne.

'Do you know who they are?' Amy pressed, frowning at Dominic as he burst into disbelieving laughter.

Anai put down her sewing in a somewhat theatrical gesture. The young people around her seemed to lean forward as a group, listening with baited breath for the next revelation.

'They return again and again...' Anai sighed, shaking her head.

'Why?' Marianne asked. 'Aren't they at peace?'

'The gods ordered them to protect this land,' Anai told her, her voice growing stronger. 'But the guardians made many mistakes and failed in their duty. They have wronged the people of Amarna – and each other...'

'So they've come back to put things right?'

In answer to Marianne's question, Anai nodded and slowly stood up, signalling the end of the discussion. Mina sprang up from her place at David's feet and ran to help her grandmother.

'Thank God!' Ethan breathed. 'She's finally going home!'

Leaning on Mina's arm, Anai steered her granddaughter towards the stone bench. Her dark eyes settled on Ethan. 'You must atone,' she told him quietly, handing him a small object from a pocket in her robes. 'And then you will be forgiven.' She turned to Kate, reaching out to pat her cheek.

43

'You also, qitah.' Anai pressed something into Kate's hand, and then presented David with a third small object before shuffling towards the kitchen door, murmuring in Arabic.

Throughout Anai's cryptic tale, David had watched Ethan and Kate. She had appeared spellbound, but uncertain. Ethan had been typically restive, his face showing scepticism. There was no indication that they had used the supply run to begin forging a tentative friendship.

Lips pursed, Ethan rubbed thoughtfully at the small metal disc in his palm, his fingertips tracing the engraved surface. He looked across at David. 'She's given me a talisman of Anubis.'

David chuckled; Anai often referred to Ethan as a jackal, and now she had presented him with an engraving of the jackal-headed funerary deity.

Frowning at David, Ethan shifted his gaze to Kate. 'What did she give *you*?'

'An engraving of Bastet,' Kate replied pensively.

They both looked expectantly at David. He knew the coincidence would unsettle Kate. She had inherited a figurine of the cat goddess from her late aunt, which she suspected might once have belonged to Edwin.

'Sekhmet,' he announced.

The group sat in silence as they mulled over the old woman's words. Finally, David stood up; like his companions, he felt mildly disturbed by what he had witnessed, but he needed to remain grounded.

'Right – back to work. Amy, please make sure you have the right tools this afternoon.'

'Yeah,' Dominic taunted. 'You can't do much without a trowel!'

David watched them amble back inside the house, Dominic's Irish brogue rising above the other voices. When he turned back, Kate was on her feet and awaiting his orders. 'Kate, come with me to the equipment room – you can get some tools and join us.' He smiled as he saw her eyes light up.

'Hang on a minute,' Ethan called. 'I don't want her in the field. She's not qualified.'

'She's had proper training,' David attested. 'And she handles artefacts all the time at the museum -'

'I don't care -'

'You're being irrational.' David's condescending remark stopped Ethan in his tracks. Kate and Marianne stared at David, surprised that he would talk to his friend so bluntly in front of them.

'Doctor Forbes,' Kate began, in a mollifying tone. 'Part of my job is to write a daily blog for the museum website, so that people are made aware of the work going on out here, and its significance. I also have to send regular reports to Deputy Director Gray. I can't do any of that if I -'

Ethan eyed her suspiciously. 'You have to send reports to Gray?' Kate nodded, flushing under his intense, angry stare. 'So you're here to spy on us? Looking for another way to cut our funding?'

'No, of course not! I -'

'One of the reasons Kate's here is because she has a family connection to this place,' David interrupted.

'Ah, so you bought your place with a large donation?' Ethan asked with a sneer.

'I did not!' Kate cried, indignantly.

'Her great-great-great grandfather was James Grahame, one of the museum's directors.' David wanted to grind his teeth in frustration. 'His daughter married an archaeologist who worked on an Amarna expedition. Gray's a power-hungry control freak, but Kate is not in his pocket. We can trust her to deliver reports that will be sympathetic to our work.'

Ethan paused, assimilating this new information, before turning to Kate once more. 'I want to read these reports before you send them. Every single one of them.'

'Ethan, don't be ridiculous!' David was incredulous.

'I mean it!' Ethan barked. He glowered at Kate, whose face had paled under his verbal assault. 'Now, if you want something to do, Mina needs help to put away the supplies. On your way, Grahame.'

Kate hurried away with her head bowed in shame. Marianne stood and moved to follow her at a slower pace. She shook her head as she passed Ethan. 'Idiot!'

Infuriated by his friend's high-handedness, David glared at Ethan. 'She's right – you're an idiot. Kate's not a kitchen hand -'

'I won't have unqualified personnel at the dig site.'

'She *will* be present at field school excavations, Ethan. End of story. Get off her back!'

Ethan strolled towards the acacia tree, jolting the cat from its slumber. The animal yowled crossly and fled. Two long wooden staffs leaned against the gnarled trunk, each just over a metre in length. He tossed one to David. 'Fight for her then, Galahad. If *you* win, she can go out on the dig. But if *I* win, she stays in the house.'

'Don't be a prat! We're supposed to be in charge here, not behaving like testosterone-fuelled louts!'

Ethan walked out of the courtyard to the bare ground behind the house, expertly twirling the staff as if it weighed nothing. 'Well, if anyone comes along, we can say we're giving a demonstration on ancient Egyptian stick fighting. What's the matter, Dave? Afraid I'll beat you?'

Testosterone prevailed; David followed, testing the weight of the staff, finding the centre of balance as Ethan circled him.

'This is stupid,' David grumbled. 'And I'm out of practice.'

'You look like you need to get rid of some tension,' Ethan chuckled. 'You should've made use of that double bed, mate!'

45

Swinging the staff in a wide circle over his head, he brought it down sharply near David's shoulder. An experienced swordsman, David easily intercepted the move and knocked the staff away. His answering lunge was also knocked off course, making him stumble slightly.

'I'm surprised you didn't take the double room yourself...'

David executed another swing, aiming for a body blow; Ethan jumped back out of the way, but the end of David's staff grazed his bare arm.

You know me; I'm resourceful.' His staff connected with David's hip before it was batted away. 'Don't always need a bed. A darkened corner's just as good. Or the floor -' Ethan moved swiftly backwards as David launched another assault. 'A chair, a desk -'

What had begun as a light-hearted bout slowly became more heated as David remembered his training. They had learned the art of stick fighting as students on their first expedition. Every time they returned to Egypt thereafter, they practised with the locals, honing their skills. Since Ethan now lived in Egypt for much of the year, his technical expertise far outweighed David's. As the captain of the university fencing team, however, David was more nimble than his opponent.

'You're disgusting!' David spat, forgetting that he was in combat with a friend. Repressed anger rose from his gut; he looked for an opportunity to catch Ethan off-guard. 'You wouldn't be so vile if you were mature enough to embark on a proper relationship...' Another attack from each man, both staffs deflected. Neither noticed that the students were watching from the side of the house. Ethan and David circled again, sweat beginning to stain their t-shirts in the sweltering heat.

'Variety's the spice of life,' Ethan sneered. 'Why would I want to limit myself to only one woman? Is that really what you want? A lifetime with your little mouse?' The staffs clashed together, each man pushing against the other's stick to gain ground. Ethan's eyes narrowed as he stared through crossed staffs at David. 'She looks like she could do with being bent over a desk...'

The Arabic name for Tahtib is *Fann el Nazaha Wal Tahtib*, which roughly translates as 'The art of Uprightness and Honesty through the use of the stick'. David forgot all about such values as he swung his right fist into Ethan's jaw, sending his friend sprawling backwards into the dirt. Dazed, Ethan rubbed his cheek but rose swiftly to his feet as he saw David approach him with a murderous gleam in his eye. Before he could attack again, Ethan retaliated with a right hook of his own. David swayed on his feet but stayed upright. He made a grab for his opponent who, at that moment in time, had ceased to be his friend and now represented the man who stood in the way of his happiness.

Steven emerged from the house in order to gather the students for the afternoon's work, but found them standing staring out beyond the boundary wall. Above him, the two guards on the roof were laughing and catcalling. Following their line of vision, he spotted David and Ethan exchanging punches. One tripped the other, and the pair tumbled to the ground, where they continued the struggle. Cursing, Steven ran over to the men, dodging a couple of random blows and a flailing foot. At last, he managed to separate them and hauled them to their feet.

'What the hell are you doing?' he cried in disbelief.

'Training,' Ethan muttered, wiping at a cut on his lip. 'Holy shit, David! I was only joking!'

Wincing, David glared at him. 'In the future, keep your foul views to yourself.'

Mina had sent Kate to the small infirmary to put away a box of medical supplies. The white, windowless room contained well-stocked cabinets, a sink and an old hospital bed. The local doctor lived in El Hagg Qandil, but the nearest hospital was almost an hour away in Minya.

As Kate stowed rolls of bandages in one of the cupboards, Steven stomped in. 'You've got first aid training, right?'

'Yes. Why? Who's hurt?' Kate looked worried.

Steven fixed her with an arctic stare. 'David and Ethan have been stick fighting. Looks like it got out of hand; they need patching up.'

'What were they fighting about?'

'Ethan said something David didn't like.'

'That doesn't sound like David...'

Blue eyes grew even frostier. 'Yeah, well, what subject never fails to get him hot and bothered?' He glowered at her accusingly, and left.

When Ethan and David limped into the infirmary, they were treated to a glacial scowl from Kate. Tight-lipped, she pulled two chairs into the centre of the room, under the light. She tried to ignore the two perfect naked torsos in her line of vision; the men had removed their t-shirts and had used them to wipe sweat and dirt from their faces. Her eyes fell on the tattoo that adorned Ethan's left shoulder blade: beautiful Arabic script curled across his olive skin, exotic and mysterious. Hastily, she looked away and remembered she was supposed to be angry. Heaving an exasperated sigh, she forcibly opened a drawer and pulled out a first aid kit, banging it down on the trolley beside the bed.

Feeling strangely vulnerable in the face of her disapproval, the men pulled on their shirts. David looked down at the floor, shamefaced.

Amused by the ferocity in the eyes of this small, quiet woman, Ethan watched her open the first aid kit and peruse the contents while she chewed her lip. His eyes followed her as she strode to the freezer in the corner of the room and returned with two ice packs. Deftly, she wrapped one in a cloth and applied it to David's bruised cheekbone. He winced but looked up at her gratefully and held the pack against his cheek.

'How come he gets treated first?' Ethan grumbled. 'I'm the senior archaeologist here. And besides, he started it!'

'I'm *his* assistant. I'm not *yours*!' Kate snapped, before wrapping the other ice pack and slapping it indelicately against Ethan's jaw. He hissed as icy cold met searing heat, and his black gaze snapped up to meet her equally dark look. 'And what kind of example are you setting, anyway?' She glanced at David. 'Acting like children, the pair of you! What's it all about? Did you just fancy flashing your six-packs at all the women in your vicinity?' Both men looked at their dusty boots, and shuffled their feet like teenagers hauled in front of the head teacher. 'Well?' Kate demanded, tapping her foot on the tiled floor.

'We were just letting off some steam,' Ethan muttered.

'We got carried away,' David finished. 'It's nothing…'

'Titillating the female contingent was an unforeseen bonus,' Ethan added, giving her a sidelong glance. 'Though I didn't see *you* there…'

Kate's expression became venomous. 'I prefer men who behave like responsible adults.' She moved over to David. 'Not toddlers pretending to be grown-ups!'

'I'm the same age as David,' he protested, sounding less self-assured.

'*He's* not going grey,' Kate retorted, temporarily silencing the egotistical archaeologist. Gently, she took David's chin in her hand and lifted his face to the light. He had cut his lower lip; dowsing a cotton bud with antiseptic, she dabbed at the injury while David gazed adoringly into her face.

'Did you hurt anything else?' she asked tenderly, removing the ice pack and smoothing some arnica cream over David's reddened cheekbone. She ignored Ethan's snort of derision.

'I bumped my head,' David murmured, and Ethan heard him sigh with pleasure when Kate began to run searching fingers through his hair and over his scalp. Inadvertently, she leaned over so that her chest was close to David's face. David couldn't help but smile at the view before him.

Watching his friend, Ethan stifled a chuckle. 'Peaches or tangerines?' he muttered in David's direction. Thankfully, Kate appeared to be engrossed in her examination, and so David remained engrossed in his study of her cleavage.

'You realise I'll have to write this up in the accident log…' Kate muttered tetchily.

'Minor injury caused during recreational activity,' Ethan piped up. 'Covers a multitude of sins…'

Kate completed her examination, apparently finding no wound or bump on David's head. Unfortunately, she then discovered where David had fixed his attention. Stepping back, she folded her arms and blocked his view. 'So when you come out here, you forget your manners altogether?' she questioned tartly.

Ethan started to laugh and David, too, could not repress a rueful smile. 'I'm sorry,' David muttered, gazing at her like a very appealing puppy. Sure enough, her gaze softened. But then she turned to Ethan.

'And you?' she inquired coldly. 'Did you hurt your head, too?'

Ethan gave her his most charming smile, but it had little effect. 'Oh, definitely,' he said enthusiastically. He heard David snigger. The animosity between them was forgotten; in accordance with tradition, they had offered each other an apology and a handshake. Ethan's ogling hopes were dashed, however, when Kate moved behind him and examined his scalp without the tenderness she had shown David.

'There's nothing wrong with you,' she told him. 'At least nothing I can fix.'

Ethan pointed to the graze on his left forearm, and then held up his right forefinger. 'My arm's bleeding and I have a splinter.'

'Oh, for God's sake!' Kate muttered and proceeded to clean the small scratch on his arm, spitefully slapping a large Band-Aid over the superficial wound. Then, taking his hand, she peered at his 'injured' forefinger. A tiny sliver of wood could be seen just under the skin, and Kate conceded it would probably be troublesome. She moved off to rummage in a cupboard and returned moments later with tweezers and a sewing needle. Pulling up another chair, she prepared to apply the needle to the tiny hole caused by the splinter's entry.

'I hope you've sterilised that needle...' Ethan grumbled, noticing that she'd buttoned up her shirt. Kate's eyes flashed wickedly, and she stabbed Ethan's finger with the needle. He yelped, and she responded with an insincere apology.

'Your bedside manner is appalling!' Ethan complained, gritting his teeth.

The needle touched the edge of the splinter and Kate used the point to pull the skin back a little. 'Well, at least it's only my bedside manner,' she replied, not looking at him. She recalled how she had felt as Victorian Katherine, the first time she had sat next to Edwin Ford. She had felt hot, almost breathless by his proximity and her heart had raced. Ethan Forbes evoked no such reaction. She felt nervous, certainly, but sensed no mutual attraction or connection of souls. Involuntarily, she glanced up at David, who watched them curiously.

'Pay attention to my finger,' Ethan ordered, and Kate dipped her head to her work once more.

David watched her swiftly remove the offending splinter with tweezers, clean the miniscule wound, and cover it with a plaster. She kept her eyes resolutely on her work and betrayed no signs of nervousness. Still, it was hard to control the irrational stab of jealousy that made him wonder if her apparent hostility was solely for his benefit. His suspicion diminished when she glanced his way, and he saw her deflated expression. Ethan's contemptuous verbal attacks, however, seemed relentless.

'I have just the job for you, Grahame,' he called to Kate as she tidied up and updated the accident log. 'It will make good use of your apparently excellent office skills.'

Kate turned to face him, her hand sweeping back her hair in a gesture of tired frustration. 'Please stop calling me by my surname.'

After a moment's consideration, Ethan grinned. 'Well, how about if I call you Friday? Since you're Dave's Girl Friday?' Kate shrugged in defeat, and Ethan continued to twist the small, blunt knife into her heart. 'We're starting to digitise the old records, but it's time-consuming and we have more important things to do. Mina's been helping when she can. You can start this afternoon – with the records from 1891.'

'1891?' Kate repeated hoarsely, turning pale.

'Ethan,' David interjected. '*I* need Kate's help -'

'You can spare her for a few hours.' He turned to Kate. 'What's the problem with 1891?' He paused, as though awaiting elucidation. 'Don't tell me your ancestor was on *that* expedition? It was an Italian operation...'

'No, it wasn't,' Kate replied defensively. 'The Italians took the credit for its success, and no doubt made a profit out of it. It was a British expedition first...' She looked to David for support.

'Yeah, but we don't talk about that.' Ethan sounded scornful. 'The British expedition leader couldn't hack it and he ran home in disgrace. Hardly our finest moment...'

'*That's not true!*' Tears sprang to her eyes, provoked by Ethan's contempt.

'Oh, wait – don't tell me *he* was your ancestor? The idiot who brought his wife on a field trip? No wonder he failed!'

'Ethan!' David barked, desperate to avert an impending calamity. 'The leader's wife was Kate's great-great aunt. She died in Cairo. Her husband returned to Edinburgh with *his wife's body.*'

Moderating his tone, Ethan pointed at Kate. 'Why's she so upset about someone who died over a hundred years ago?'

'She's proud of her heritage – as she should be. Kate's done a lot of research into her ancestry, so she's bound to take it personally when you insult her family. And what happened to her aunt was a tragedy; have some respect. There was no failure – not in archaeological terms, at least.'

David looked compassionately at Kate, his eyes willing her to be strong. 'If you would like to help with the digitisation, you can. You'll be ensuring there's a permanent record of their work, and so you'll be making a valuable contribution. If, however, you'd rather not do this, I have plenty to keep you busy.' He fired a bleak look at Ethan. 'In the field and the office.' When his gaze returned to his assistant, he could see her eyes pleading with him for guidance; David looked down at the floor.

'Alright,' Kate conceded quietly, turning a cold gaze on Ethan. 'But my work for David takes priority.'

'Yes,' Ethan agreed, and Kate knew another barb was coming her way. 'You have to earn your keep. Come on, I'll get you started.'

He walked towards the door, and Kate felt a moment of wicked pleasure as she saw him check his hair furtively in the mirror on the way. As she passed David, he reached out and lightly brushed her fingers with his own.

A short distance along the corridor, Ethan opened the door to one of the offices. Blue metal shelving units stood along one wall, filled with labelled plastic containers and metal boxes. A long wooden table with a desktop computer and printer lined another. Two desks had been pushed together against one of the shorter walls, each with its own computer. Kate took a seat at one of the desks, while Ethan pulled a small metal box down from one of the higher shelves.

'Details of this expedition are sketchy,' he explained, still managing to address her with disdain. 'We don't have much in the way of records; perhaps it wasn't their strong point.' He switched on the computer and accessed the digitisation programme. 'I need all the info in the box to be added to the database. Everything needs to be scanned and accurately transcribed. Any questions?'

Glancing into the open box, Kate saw that it was full of yellowing papers and file cards. She looked from the box to the screen, to Ethan. She had swapped one office for another. 'No. I've used this software at the museum; I'll be fine.'

'Well, crack on with this until you're needed elsewhere. As you say, you're Dave's assistant – don't let this get in the way of your *"assisting"*. If you get stuck, Mina can help. Unless she's busy running after David or doing his laundry or something…' He headed for the door, as though anxious to escape her presence.

Astounded, Kate blurted, 'She does his laundry?'

Turning in the doorway, Ethan gave her another hateful smirk. 'When David's here, Mina endeavours to do *anything* to make him happy.' The bombshell successfully dropped, he left.

CHAPTER 4

Left alone in the room, Kate stared blankly at the computer screen, her mind filled with troubling images of Mina and David. She had many questions about their so-called friendship, but she knew she had no right to demand answers from David. The contents of the metal box called to her, however, and she pushed away her feelings of jealousy in favour of immersing herself in the past. *Her* past.

A quick look through the box indicated that there were several lists of provisions and equipment, some accounts, several letters, and a collection of cards detailing artefacts recovered from the site. Although it was tempting to begin searching for correspondence relating to Katherine or Edwin Ford, Kate knew she had to embark on this task methodically, or risk Ethan's wrath. She divided the paperwork into categories, beginning the digitisation process with lists of provisions. Each piece of paper was scanned then carefully transcribed. Most of them had been written by the same hand in a fluid, typically Victorian style. The author had noted his initials at the bottom of each page: RY. Naturally, as the afternoon progressed, Kate began to contemplate what kind of person RY had been. She assumed the author had been male, as her fragmented memories recalled that Katherine Ford had been the only Western woman on the expedition. Her active imagination created a soft, deep voice that spoke to her from the dry pages. She smiled to herself as she heard him whispering words such as 'camels', 'donkeys' and 'flour' as though he were murmuring seductively in her ear.

The work soon became absorbing, and time passed quickly. When her mouth started to feel like sandpaper, Kate took a short break and made her way to the kitchen for some water. She was gratified to see Mina alone in the kitchen preparing dinner and not fawning over David. Her guilty satisfaction waned when Mina proudly announced she was making David's favourite soup. Muttering a response that was socially acceptable, but not heartfelt, Kate returned to her new office and 1891. Still rankled by Mina's unswerving devotion to David, Kate found herself grumbling to the mysterious 'RY'. He remained unhelpfully silent.

As the afternoon progressed, Kate was pulled deeper into that other life, her soul crying softly for its lost counterpart. Memories she had sensibly packed into the recesses of her mind crept back into her awareness and began to gnaw at the psychic defences she had worked hard to erect. She remembered Edwin washing her long hair over a basin, his fingers massaging her scalp and neck. He had introduced her to coffee and had always brought her a mug before leaving at dawn. The wind had howled in the night back then, just as it had last night, and he had held her in his arms to soothe her. She could almost remember the smell of his skin, and the way his hands had felt on her body…

A loud bang from somewhere in the house jolted Kate out of her daydream, and she hastily resumed her work. Feeling ill at ease, she quickly transcribed the list for bricks, tools, blankets and foodstuffs. Her efforts were rewarded by the signature at the bottom of the ragged page: RY finally revealed himself as Captain Richard Yorke.

'Hey, Kate! Why are you holed up in here?'

Turning towards the door, Kate saw Dominic peering in from the corridor, Russell and Jonathan behind him. The three students were dusty, red-faced, and grinning. Bounding into the room, they pulled chairs up to Kate's desk, curious as to why she had chosen to spend the afternoon in an office.

After providing a brief explanation, which held no denigration of the expedition leaders, Kate asked about their day in the field. The boys were excited; they were in the process of uncovering a grave that may miraculously have been spared from looting. David had covered it with the intention of resuming excavation in the morning.

In addition to the grave, they had also discovered a soil heap nearby and planned to begin investigating it the following day. Although this activity was rather like sorting through a pile of rubbish, it often yielded exciting discoveries. In the distant past, archaeologists discarded many small artefacts as worthless; today they were considered invaluable.

Ethan had not been present for the day's work in the field; he and Steven had driven to the north cliffs with survey equipment. The Americans had been in the 'Bone Room', the lab next to Kate's room that stored numerous boxes of bones awaiting examination. Marianne had spent the afternoon showing her students the wealth of information that could be gleaned from the study of Egyptian skeletons. The American photographer, meanwhile, had spent the day taking pictures at the Great Aten Temple.

Their thorough report delivered, the boys left to clean up for dinner; as usual, they were famished. Kate packed up the metal box then began to type her report for Deputy Director Gray, following this with a short but interesting entry for her blog. She had almost finished when Jonathan reappeared and quietly sat down beside her. The curly-haired Edinburgh student was the youngest in the group and was having difficulty acclimatising to this new way of life. Lacking the confidence of the other three boys, Jonathan often appeared withdrawn and was frankly terrified of David's disapproval. A shrewd observer of human nature, Kate had quickly discerned the young man's fears and established a rapport with him. She soon discovered an insightful intellect and a dry wit underneath the reserve.

'Can I ask you a favour?' Jonathan asked warily.

Kate gave him an encouraging smile. 'Of course! What do you need?'

He slid his notebook across the table towards her. 'Would you mind looking over my field notes before I give them to Professor Young? As well as expecting our reports to be technically accurate, he demands perfect English. I heard that you've helped him write lecture notes and that you create a lot of the handouts for museum workshops, so I wondered...' He flushed and chewed his lip. 'This is my first year with Professor Young, and I want to create a good impression...'

Pushing the keyboard to one side, Kate smiled sympathetically and opened the boy's notebook. She was not surprised to find that he had provided a succinct account of the day's work. Tentatively, she suggested a couple of minor alterations but ended by praising Jonathan and offering her assistance in the future.

'Some of the others might want you to check their notes, too...' Jonathan informed her.

'That's fine, but you should have more confidence in your abilities. Professor Young really isn't that bad, you know...' Her voice tailed off, as she completed the blog entry, saved her work and shut down the computer. A group of Americans passed the room, chatting animatedly as they headed for the dining room.

'Everybody's going to dinner,' Jonathan told her.

'Yes,' Kate's tone was dry. 'I believe Professor Young's favourite soup is on the menu.'

Jonathan looked concerned. 'D'you know what's in it?'

'Hopefully nothing funky.' She grimaced, making Jonathan grin. 'Probably just veggies; I assume we're on a budget.'

'Wish it was pizza,' the student sighed. 'Or chips.'

The pair walked to the dining room together, listing all the food they would never take for granted again. The other students had taken their bowls of soup to a table in the outdoor dining area. Kate hovered uncertainly in the kitchen with her bowl. David, Ethan, Steven and Marianne were already seated at the dining room table and involved in a lively discussion about the pathology of bones found in Amarna. The thought of joining them made Kate feel slightly sick; she certainly had nothing to contribute to their debate, and was afraid of seeming stupid in front of her new colleagues.

Seeing her quandary, Jonathan invited Kate to join him outdoors, and so the seven crowded round the table, the students eagerly discussing their day while Kate listened avidly. When the conversation wandered to the fight between Ethan and David, Kate steered it away onto safer ground.

Soup was followed by another stew, which they picked at suspiciously before devouring. When Mina brought a tray of pastries to the table, the group was much more enthusiastic about their new diet. The sun began its descent, turning the sky breathtaking shades of pink, violet and orange. The temperature cooled, a warning of the cold temperatures to come. Samira served Egyptian coffee, but Kate discovered that she intensely disliked the bitter, syrupy drink.

Their leisurely meal at an end, the students considered their options for the evening. Some had notes to perfect, while others wanted to watch a movie on a laptop. A game of poker with the American students was arranged in comical whispers, but silence befell the group as David approached their table. Kate noticed a relaxed, satisfied expression on his face that she hadn't seen before, as though he were content in these surroundings. Even his gait seemed more laidback; a different David was emerging in this less officious environment. The students, however, became immediately alert.

'Good work today, everyone,' David smiled. 'I look forward to reading your field notes, but right now I want you to fetch some camping gear from the equipment stores. We're sleeping out. I've picked a nice spot near the grave we found today.'

The boys were enthusiastic, but Amy's face fell. 'In the desert?' she squeaked. 'What about scorpions? And snakes? Is it safe?' She looked up at David with huge, fearful eyes.

'One of the guards will stay with us and another will patrol the surrounding area, so we should be safe from bands of homicidal maniacs. As for scorpions and snakes…' He rubbed his chin, and with a straight face, said, 'Make sure your clothing is secure where it needs to be and don't take off your boots. If you do, check them in the morning. Oh, and you'd better check the sleeping bags before you climb into them. Take some rope to place in the sand around your tent – snakes won't climb over rope. And don't pitch up near rocks or greenery. We'll be leaving in an hour.'

Unsure of the truth behind their professor's advice, the group ambled inside. David watched them go, and then sat down next to Kate. His eyes roamed greedily over her lovely face, but he kept his expression neutral.

'Did you enjoy your soup?' Kate asked, and he thought he detected a note of sarcasm in her tone.

David shrugged. 'It was delicious.'

'Mina made it especially for you…'

A warning bell rang faintly in David's head. 'She's a kind girl. She also wants to keep her job, I suppose…'

'Is that why she does your laundry?'

David executed a move he knew would knock her off her current path: he stared deep into her eyes. 'How's the digitisation? Did you find anything interesting?'

Kate blinked, and swallowed. 'Lots of lists. There's more to be done, if I have the time. I've typed up a few paragraphs for the museum blog and drafted the report for Gray. I'll send it when our fascist leader gives his approval…'

David noted her resentment but did not defend his friend's actions. 'You should be having dinner with *me*, not the students.' Kate cocked her head, eyes questioning. 'They have to see you as one of the team leaders, not one of *them*.'

Kate began to draw patterns on the table surface with one finger. 'I was getting to know them.' She glanced up at him, eyes fiery. 'And I didn't feel like another verbal battering from your so-called friend!'

'I'm sure that once you've got your bearings, you'll give as good as you get,' he smiled. 'You've never been afraid to give *me* a piece of your mind!' David reached across and gently tucked a stray lock of hair behind her ear. A year ago, Kate had possessed a thick mane of long, curling tresses. A few weeks after joining the museum staff, her glorious dark brown locks had been shortened to shoulder-length. For the trip to Egypt, Kate had opted for an even shorter cut that reached just below her chin. But however she styled her hair, one adorable curl always fell over her face.

'So tell me,' David continued. 'Based on the time you've spent with them in Edinburgh and here, what are your observations of our students?' He knew she would be unable to give him an accurate assessment, as she had not spent time with them in the field. David was simply grasping an opportunity to spend some time with her. If they discussed work issues, there was less chance of a quarrel.

'Well, Celine seems quietly competent, but I'm not sure she'll opt to specialise in Egyptology. Amy, as we know, is a work in progress. I can't determine if she's struggling yet, but I'm slowly weakening her defences –'

'As you do with everyone…' David remarked quietly.

'Jonathan is shy, but very sweet. I think he's having a little trouble finding his place in the group, but he'll get there. His stomach seems to have settled down, but I'll keep an eye on him…' For a brief moment she looked wistful, and David wondered if her thoughts had turned to Luca and Rebecca.

'I see he's fired up your maternal instincts,' David teased. 'How's he getting on with the work?'

Kate's glance was mildly reproachful. 'He's very bright and conscientious, the sort of quiet, thoughtful guy who notices the little things missed by those who are brash and overconfident.' She paused meaningfully; David merely smiled and waited for the rest of her report.

'Dominic and Russell are strong characters, but they know what they're doing, and they're pretty ambitious. All of the students are keen to please you, but these two – they want to *be* you. I'd watch your back in a few years if I were you.' Uncharacteristically, David poked his tongue out at Kate's facetious remark.

'Our lone Englishman is vying for position as the alpha male. Julian doesn't interact with me much, but he's quite arrogant around the others. Having said that, I haven't noticed any animosity, although the other students think it's funny that Julian dresses like Indiana Jones – right down to the hat.' She giggled, her eyes twinkling. 'On the whole, they seem to be coping, though I'm not sure about this camping idea...'

'Archaeologists don't always have the luxury of a dig house, Kate -'

'Or a personal maid, I imagine...'

David refused to take the bait. 'Camping out is part of their education.'

Seeing that Kate's eyes were fixed on the kitchen door, David turned his head to follow her gaze. Mina hovered in the kitchen doorway, watching them intently.

'I'd better get some camping gear together -' Kate sounded tired as she stood up, bringing the 'meeting' to a close.

Ever the gentleman, David also rose to his feet. 'You're not coming,' he told her decisively.

'Why not? I can pitch a tent.' Her brother had given her lessons before the expedition as she hated camping and had not ventured into a tent since childhood.

'I want you to stay here.'

'That's not a good explanation...'

'They're two-man tents,' David explained. 'We have four boys and two girls – and only four tents.' He hoped the weak excuse would satisfy her, and that she wouldn't check the equipment store.

Kate pondered this explanation, unsure how to further her argument. She wanted to suggest that they could share a tent. To be honest, she *wanted* to share a tent with him, but not with eavesdropping students around.

'No,' David said firmly, leaving Kate wondering if she had inadvertently voiced her idea. 'That wouldn't be wise. Besides, you need to stay here – without me in the way.'

Now she understood. David was leaving her alone – with Ethan. Or did he already have someone to share his tent? Kate couldn't hide her disappointment, so she simply nodded and returned to the office.

Wishing to sit alone and mope, she was irritated to find Marianne in the room with her assistant, Thea. They appeared to be comparing images of bones on a laptop with photographs of Amarna bones recently exhumed.

The discussion on pathology continued. Kate's mood darkened even further when she saw Ethan and Steven standing at the long table comparing pictures, maps and surveys.

The women smiled warmly at Kate as she took her seat; the men barely glanced in her direction. Unable to concentrate on the digitisation task, Kate used the opportunity to check her emails and edit the reports waiting to be sent to Edinburgh. She wondered if she should ask Ethan to approve her work, but the idea chipped at her pride. As though he could read her mind, Ethan turned to her.

'Have you done your report for Gray yet?' he asked brusquely.

Kate flushed as everyone stared at her inquiringly, and nodded. She sat back as he pulled up a chair and proceeded to review her work. Feeling mildly queasy, Kate looked meekly down at her hands. Apparently satisfied with the contents of the report, he moved his attention to the blog entry. Kate cringed, certain that the other three people in the room were waiting for Ethan's inevitable censure. Outside, the students were moving around the corridors, preparing for their camping trip. The office, which had been pleasantly cool all afternoon, suddenly felt oppressively stuffy.

'You've really dumbed this down, haven't you?' Ethan observed, his lips curled in a mocking snarl.

'It's for the museum website,' she stuttered quietly. 'It's meant to be a light-hearted account of my experiences here and it's supposed to appeal to all age groups.'

He nodded thoughtfully. 'You work with kids, right?'

She glanced at him warily, suddenly ashamed of the job she loved. Part of her felt angry that she seemed unable to defend herself against his constant needling; her past connection to him made her weak. Again, she could do nothing but nod her head.

Ethan rose to his feet. 'It shows,' he muttered cruelly. 'Send your "reports".' Glancing towards Marianne, he was treated to an admonishing look from the redhead.

Returning the chair to its place, Ethan turned to Steven. 'I'm going down to the campsite with David,' he announced to his assistant. 'I'll take the map and pictures and discuss them with him, see if we can come up with a plan.'

Ethan gathered up the paperwork on the table and left, his mind already on something else. He completely ignored Mina, as she passed him in the doorway and stood awkwardly just inside the room.

Steven fixed Kate with a cold stare. 'Shouldn't you be getting your camping gear together?'

Blushing again, Kate looked up at the young man who had once been a good friend and now seemed to detest her. 'I'm not going,' she murmured, mortified by Marianne's look of surprise.

'What a shock!' Steven scoffed. 'Afraid you'll break a nail?'

Stunned by his rudeness, Kate stood up, at last finding an ounce of courage. 'Professor Young wants me to stay here -'

'I hear you had lunch with my mother last week. Is that right?'

Bewildered by the sudden change of subject, Kate could only stammer, 'Yes, she -'

'Back off, Kate. You've got a family of your own – stop trying to worm your way into mine!'

His hurtful remark brought tears to her eyes; she fought them, refusing to let him see how upset she was. 'Steven, why are you so angry with me? What have I done?'

Steven shoved his hands into his pockets, balling them into fists. He wasn't angry with her, not really. But she was an easy target for his frustration.

'David has paid out a fortune to bring you here,' he told her, deliberately revealing information David had concealed from Kate. 'And still you're leading him around by the nose and coming between him and Ethan. I'm stuck between the pair of them, and I'm still being bossed around! I want to do archaeological work, but because you're so – so *incapable* – I'm having to babysit the students! Why couldn't you have stayed in Edinburgh and given your place to someone who would've been of use! *David doesn't need you!'*

He stormed out of the office, unable to meet Kate's stricken face, hating himself for his cruelty towards a woman who had always shown him unreserved kindness.

Mina chewed her lip thoughtfully; surely, this discord could not be part of her grandmother's plan? *Men are very stupid,* she thought. *We have to clean up after them all the time. They are worse than donkeys!* Taking a deep breath, she made her announcement.

'My aunt and grandmother wish to spend some time with you,' she told Kate, who had slumped back in her chair. 'Come with me now, Kate. We will go to my grandmother's house, and you can spend the evening with us. The men can take care of themselves. Come, we will have a good time!' She held out her hand to Kate and smiled at Marianne and Thea. 'You two are also invited.'

'A girls' night out is just what we need!' Marianne grinned. Quiet, bespectacled Thea eagerly agreed.

'I can't leave until I'm finished here.' Kate sounded defeated. 'And not without permission from Professor Young…'

'Hah!' Mina's derision was like a small explosion. 'Meet me by my car in ten minutes. We will creep away like desert foxes!'

Intimidated by the ominous silence of the vast desert, and the burial grounds

59

in their vicinity, the students huddled around their small fire and spoke in lowered voices. Even though they could see the twinkling lights of houses less than a kilometre away, they felt isolated and vulnerable. Their armed security guard paced the perimeter of the campsite, and then sat down nearby with his back against a rock.

A short distance away, David and Ethan brooded over their fire near David's tent, sharing an illicit flask of whisky. Ethan showed David the photographs and surveys of the area he wanted to search. Half-heartedly, David suggested examining the area from the top of the cliffs and offered no protest when Ethan decided to plan a secret outing. The evening's work concluded, they sat in silence, watching the flames and lost in their own dark thoughts.

'I've been offered a job at the University of York...' David blurted unhappily.

Ethan poked the fire with a stick. 'Oh?' He waited for David to reveal more details, but as usual, his friend remained reticent. 'That would surely be a good career move, right?' David shrugged. 'Are you going to take it?' Another shrug, but Ethan guessed the reason for David's lack of enthusiasm. 'You're hesitant because of Kate...'

'Ethan, don't start on me again...' David sighed. 'And don't start on her, either. You don't know anything about us...'

A pack of dogs howled in the distance, startling the already jittery students. Dominic anxiously built up the fire as the group huddled even closer together. Ethan watched them, trying to recall if he had been as nervous on his first night out in the desert.

'It's time you were getting some sleep,' David called to them, and they immediately prepared to retire for the night.

'Your girl seems much caught up in her ancestry,' Ethan remarked. 'How did she find out about it?'

'It's not my story to tell,' David replied. 'She's done a lot of research...'

'Well, I'm surprised she was able to find out anything. That expedition has hardly been acknowledged; the British team didn't find much before they were disbanded. Her aunt died out here?'

'She died in Cairo.'

'D'you know how she died?'

'You should ask Kate about this...'

'I'd rather ask *you*.'

Despite the fact that they could not be overheard, David lowered his voice. 'The woman got pregnant on the boat over to Egypt but didn't tell her husband until they were in Cairo for the Christmas holidays. He left her there and went back to Amarna, planning to take her home to Edinburgh once his replacement arrived. She fell, miscarried, and then contracted an infection that killed her.'

'He shouldn't have brought her to Egypt in the first place…'

'Apparently their relationship was very…intense. By all accounts it was a love-at-first-sight, whirlwind affair.'

Ethan laughed quietly. 'You sound jealous!' he teased, but David's countenance remained grim. 'What happened to the archaeologist?'

'His career took a nosedive and he died a few years later. They're both buried in Edinburgh, not far from Kate's house, which hasn't helped her get over this obsession…'

'Has it messed with her head?' Ethan experienced an odd sensation, as if a long-forgotten memory was trying to reinstate itself. He rubbed at the scar on his forehead.

'She learned about this while she was going through her divorce, and her emotions were all over the place. She's sad about what happened to her great-great aunt – the *other* Katherine Grahame. One of the reasons she came out here was to try and connect…'

'But you brought her here for an entirely different reason…' This time there was no mockery in Ethan's tone. David was tired and confused, and he needed to confide in someone.

'She's asked me to leave her alone so many times. But I can't seem to help myself.'

'I still feel she's got you dangling. If she doesn't want you, she should let you get on with your life.'

'She finds it hard to trust people, Ethan. I get that. Her husband hurt her. *I've* hurt her. And yet, I know she cares for me. I know she needs time to heal, but I can't wait for her any longer. I have to move on…'

'Are you really ready to settle down?' Ethan sounded incredulous. 'It's too soon, surely?'

'Ethan, I'm thirty-five! Yes, I want to settle down and have a family. Don't you?'

Bitterly, Ethan stabbed at the sand with his stick. 'Who would have me? I think we both know I'd be a rubbish husband and father…'

'So are you going to spend your life wandering around Egypt?' Now it was Ethan's turn to shrug. 'Your folks aren't getting any younger, and they miss you. You have a brother, a sister, nieces and nephews -'

The sound of tyres screeching to a halt stopped their conversation. Steven had parked the pickup truck on the sand a few metres away and was running towards them.

'I can't find Kate,' he called to them, sounding agitated. 'I've looked everywhere!'

Ethan sighed impatiently. 'What's the panic? She can't have vanished off the face of the earth.'

Steven glanced warily at David. 'We had words. But once I'd thought about it, I realised I might have been too hard on her, and I went to find her so I could apologise -'

David was already on his feet when Amy materialised at Steven's side. She smiled winsomely at the young archaeologist. 'Kate, Thea and Doctor Deveraux have gone to Anai's house with Mina. I heard them discussing it as we were preparing to leave.'

'See?' Ethan piped up. 'Princess Kate has not been abducted!' He smirked at Steven's sheepish expression.

'Thank you, Amy,' David said pointedly, and gave the girl a look that plainly told her to make herself scarce. Amy beamed up at Steven, her new idol, before returning to the relative safety of her tent.

Ethan watched David pull on his jacket. 'You're not running off to her rescue, are you?' he scoffed. 'Mina will bring her back.'

David ignored him, so Ethan reluctantly roused himself from his slouching position and pulled on his sweater. 'You've been drinking, and you know you get tipsy after two nips of whisky – *I'll* drive. Steve, stay here with this lot until we get back.'

Music floated towards them from Anai's house, a warm glow radiating from the small windows and the half-open door. As Ethan and David approached the house, there was the sound of applause and cheering, followed by girlish laughter. Doubtful whether they would be welcomed into a house full of women, the two men crept furtively to one of the windows and peered inside.

Three women stood in the centre of the softly lit room, dressed in the flimsy, tinkling garb of Egyptian belly dancers. Coloured silk scarves covered their heads and cascaded over their bodies, and their faces were partially veiled. A small group of women sat cross-legged in a corner, observing the dancers who moved in time to an earthy Baladi rhythm emanating from an old CD player. Marianne and Thea sat in their midst, looking out of place in their modern clothing. Anai sat on an armchair, an elderly queen reclining on her throne. Even from outside, the men sensed the heady, seductive atmosphere, and knew they were intruding on an exclusively female gathering. Ethan gave a low whistle of appreciation at the sinuous movement of hands, arms and curvaceous hips.

'We shouldn't be spying on them,' David whispered, and respectfully turned his back.

'Don't be daft!' Ethan muttered. 'We can't see their faces, in any case.' He stared, squinting at one of the women. 'Wait a minute – David, you might want to look at this...'

'At what?' David queried, turning back to the window.

Ethan pointed at one of the dancing women, whose stomach muscles undulated provocatively, causing the coins on her hip scarf to shimmer and tinkle. 'One of these girls is not like the others…'

David stared at the central figure, who turned in a graceful circle as she danced, her hands moving delicately in the air in front of her abdomen, thus highlighting the movement of her hips. Even as the tempo of the music increased, David realised that the smooth skin on display was paler than that of the other dancers. As the woman began to shimmy, he heard her giggle and realised he was watching Kate. Despite his assertion that they should be respectful, his eyes became glued to her supple form.

The women in the room clapped and cheered in encouragement as Kate lost herself to the rhythm, raising her arms above her head and closing her eyes. The dance filled her with a joy that was evident in her abandonment.

'She's magnificent…' David breathed, feeling a little tipsy. 'She's been attending dance classes for a few months, but I never imagined she would be *this* good…'

'Holy cow!' Ethan exclaimed in disbelief. 'David, how have you managed *not* to sleep with this woman?' He glanced across at his friend and Ethan saw the love plainly written on David's face, an expression that quickly turned to indignation.

'With immense difficulty!' David whined. 'And stop leering at her like that!'

'You do know it's impolite to spy on people?' Mina called from the doorway.

The men turned towards her, feeling only slightly remorseful at their intrusion. Mina had been one of the dancers but had modestly donned a blue linen robe over her costume. She gestured for them to enter, and watched the men carefully as they trooped sheepishly into the room. Music and dancing ceased immediately as the women surveyed the male invaders.

Bowing his head, Ethan addressed Anai respectfully in Arabic, apologising for their intrusion and explaining that they had come to take their womenfolk home. He then turned to Kate, who glared at him accusingly as she removed her veil.

'Go and get changed,' Ethan ordered harshly, casting a distasteful eye over her costume. Nervously, he fingered the talisman in his trouser pocket.

David, on the other hand, stared at her appreciatively; he had never seen her wearing red. A full skirt embroidered with gold thread sat becomingly on her rounded hips. A matching hip scarf embellished with rows of gold coins shivered with a life of its own. Gold coins also edged the cropped top whose scooped neck displayed Kate's very alluring cleavage. Her dark hair was tousled, the sweet curl falling over her eye and caressing one flushed cheek. His open scrutiny caused Kate to wrap the wide scarf around her body.

'I'll only be a minute…' she stuttered.

'No, you must keep the costume, qitah,' Anai called to her,

metaphorically poking the fire. 'A gift for your fine dancing!' Grinning, she said something to Samira, the third dancer. The two women laughed, and Samira nodded to Kate encouragingly.

'Yes,' David agreed, his voice low so only Kate could hear him. 'Please keep, qitah…' He gave her a goofy grin. Kate blushed as red as her costume and fled to the bedroom to change her clothes.

When she finally emerged in a thick sweater, leggings and boots, Ethan had taken Marianne and Thea to the pickup truck. David stood in the room with Mina and Anai, and his face lit up with a loving smile when he saw Kate, her newly acquired costume folded carefully in her arms.

'Ah, good, good,' Anai murmured.

'Shukran, Anai,' Kate smiled. 'Thank you.'

'A'afwan,' the old woman replied, patting Kate's cheek. 'You have pleased the gods with your dancing, little one. You will bring us good fortune.' She looked up at David. 'Tomorrow night you will both eat here.' It was not a request.

David merely nodded, bid the Egyptian women goodnight, and led Kate outside.

Once the Westerners had gone, the atmosphere changed in the house. Samira and another woman returned to their homes, but three remained and awaited Anai's attention. To one young woman, Anai presented a canvas pouch filled with a concoction of herbs. As payment, the woman gave Mina a small cake and then left. The second woman handed over a number of small coins and received a pot of salve. The third paid for a bottled potion with a delicate bracelet.

When only Anai and her granddaughter remained, Mina gathered the materials they would need for that night's work. The full moon brought a powerful energy, enhanced by the guardian's summoning dance; Anai would harness that power and use it to manipulate past, present and future.

Outside, and unaware of the activities taking place in the house behind him, Ethan was pacing the length of the truck. 'What kind of exhibition do you call *that*?' he demanded. 'Is it the norm for you to prance about half-naked in front of strangers? I've told you before – we have to toe the line here!'

'I was *dancing*!' Kate protested.

'Very nicely, too…' David interjected with a slightly drunk giggle.

'With *women*!' Kate continued, glaring at Ethan. 'Nobody invited you to peer through windows like a pervert!' She heard David snigger behind his hand. 'I, on the other hand, was *invited* to Anai's house and *asked* to dance! It's none of your business what I do in my own time!' Her wildly gesticulating hands made her stumble slightly.

Ethan's eyes narrowed. 'Have you been drinking the local hooch?'

'I certainly have not! I don't need alcohol to relax and enjoy myself.' She looked from Ethan to David. 'Unlike *some* people!'

'Come on, Kate, get in the truck,' said David, leading her by the hand to the passenger door. 'It's cold.'

'Get in the back!' Ethan almost shouted. 'Marianne and Thea are sitting in the front.'

'There's room for Kate if they squash up -' David pointed out.

'No, no – it's fine!' Kate said, matching Ethan's volume. 'I don't want to sit with him anyway! *Stronzo!*' Even in Italian, Kate couldn't bring herself to call him anything nastier than an idiot, although she had learned some fairly explicit insults from her Italian sister-in-law.

'*Gerek akh set er teftef-ek!*' Ethan retorted. 'Now get in the truck!' Climbing into the driver's seat, he slammed the door.

'David,' Kate began as he pushed her up into the truck. 'What language was that? What did he say?'

David climbed up behind her, and they settled into the back of the pickup, using some folded canvas as makeshift cushions. 'It's ancient Egyptian. He said your silence is better than your blethering.'

Ethan's knuckles whitened as he gripped the steering wheel and tried to regain his composure. Tactfully, Thea put on her headphones so she could listen to music instead of a disgruntled archaeologist.

'Why are you so mad at her?' Marianne chided. 'We were just having some fun! She needed to let her hair down...'

'There was no need for her to go to extremes!'

Marianne laughed. 'You sound positively medieval! A bit hypocritical, don't you think?'

Ethan started the engine and pulled onto the road. 'She drives me insane!'

'Why? Is she getting in the way of your bromance with David?'

Ethan glared at her indignantly. 'No! I don't know what it is about her that annoys me so much. And *that* drives me insane!' He resisted the urge to speed; David was sitting unsecured in the back. 'She's rude, disrespectful, and disobedient!'

Marianne snorted in disbelief and amusement. 'Well, I think she's sweet.'

Noticing that Kate had begun to shiver, David reached for an old blanket and, as he raised one arm to place it around her shoulders, she seized the opportunity to snuggle up next to him. Sighing, he wrapped the blanket – and his arm – around her and rested his chin on the top of her head. The exotic smell of incense clung to her hair and tickled his nose as she wriggled to get her head comfortable against his chest.

'David…' she murmured.

'Hmm…' He stifled a yawn, relaxing in the warmth of her body.

'I *have* been drinking a little,'

'S'alright,' he whispered into her hair. 'I have, too…' But the warm glow acquired from a dose of single malt was slowly dissipating in the crisp night air. He felt Kate's arm tighten around his waist as Ethan drove over a bump in the road.

'I had a really nice time…'

'I noticed.'

'Anai asked for a lock of my hair as a remembrance. Wasn't that sweet?'

Basking in the luxury of holding her, David ignored the faint voice in his head that warned him of a possible threat. 'Well, your hair *is* beautiful.'

'This is the best place in the world…' she murmured sleepily.

David looked up at a black sky filled with twinkling stars. The huge full moon cast an eerie, bluish light over the shadowy landscape.

'Yes,' he replied absently. 'Egypt's pretty amazing…'

'Wasn't talking about Egypt,' came the muffled response from the blanket cocoon. 'I meant *here*.' She placed a palm on his chest then replaced it with her cheek. At the same time, she pressed her body against him suggestively and gave an exaggerated, breathy sigh.

'Stop it,' David muttered, shifting slightly away from her.

'Please don't go camping, David…' Her finger traced a line down his chest as she closed the gap between their bodies. 'Stay at the house. I don't like being there alone – it's creepy.'

Unsettled by this unexpected behaviour, David cleared his throat. 'You won't be alone, and I've already pitched my tent…' He wondered if the last remark could be considered innuendo. *Oh, I should stop drinking whisky!*

'Then let me come with you.' She fixed huge brown eyes on him, and pouted.

'Kate, you know that we can't…' But his will wavered.

Ethan stopped at the side of the road near the campsite, and David reluctantly extricated himself from Kate and the blanket. She gazed at him forlornly.

'Get some sleep,' he told her. 'I'll see you in the morning.' He turned and jogged towards the cluster of tents, suddenly feeling very, very cold.

The fire in the hearth blazed, the flames spitting a rush of singeing sparks over the grate. Standing in the centre of the room, Anai held her arms aloft and recited an incantation in a strong voice, her eyes frighteningly wide. The innocuous sideboard was now a candlelit altar on which three small wax figures lay. Using a technique passed down through the centuries, Anai had used soft wax to fashion two male figures and one female. Bizarrely, the female figure had dark brown hair.

Mina glanced at the open book beside her on the rug, her eyes flicking over symbols and words she didn't understand. Wringing her hands, she waited for Anai to end her demands.

'Please don't hurt them,' she begged. 'They don't deserve to suffer.'

Ignoring her, Anai continued the ritual, a bony finger touching each of the wax figures in turn. 'Wake!' she commanded them, as the flames burned even brighter. 'I command you to wake!'

'Ti amo,' Ethan whispered, nuzzling her ear, inhaling the scent of violets from the thick auburn tresses spread across the pillow. He pulled at the ribbon that fastened the nightgown at her ample bosom, opening the flimsy silk garment. His lips moved to the lace edge of the low neckline, teasing, waking her desire. Writhing against him, she released a soft moan into the secret space created by the curtains of the four-poster bed. The nightdress gaped open, allowing him to trail soft kisses down her body, his tongue flicking her navel as she clutched his hair. 'Sei cosi bella, amore mio...' Gently, he slid the nightdress off her shoulders, down her arms and body, pushing the fabric down her thighs as she shifted her legs to free herself from the garment. He kissed the soft flesh of her inner thigh as his hands explored her hips. She was delicious, and innocent still. His to teach in the ways of love. His alone.

'Please...' she whimpered, her small hand clutching his muscled shoulder and attempting to pull him upwards. He obeyed, sliding sensuously against her as his lips traced a return path. His eyes gazed into hers, the candlelight in the room beyond the curtains suffusing their nest with a soft glow. Her new wedding ring glinted as she reached up to stroke his cheek.

'I love you,' she whispered.

He gazed at her with an adoring smile. 'And I love *you*, my beautiful wife...'

The impact of his backside hitting the tiled floor woke Ethan. Sitting up, he realised he had fallen out of bed. Then his dream returned with startling clarity, bringing with it every sensation, every scent, the memory of those beautiful eyes and an innocent, eager young body. Kate. But not Kate. As he climbed back into bed, he was filled with apprehension and guilt. He had dreamed of Kate Grahame before...

An unexpected sound woke David, and he reached for the torch he kept within reach. Switching it on, he was startled to encounter a form kneeling just inside the tent, wrapped in the blanket from the truck. As he moved the beam upwards, the light fell on Kate's face.

'What are you doing here?' he whispered hoarsely. 'The students -'

'I don't care about the students,' she replied, her voice unusually husky. The blanket dropped from her shoulders, and David gaped. She was wearing the red hip scarf – and nothing else. The coins shivered lightly as she crawled towards him, arching her back like a cat. The moonlight filtering through the canvas tent gave her skin the luminosity of some unearthly creature. Straddling him, she began to unfasten his shirt. He watched her lick her lips and appraise him through heavy-lidded eyes, looking every inch the wanton seductress.

'Kate, this is wrong...' he told her in a strangled voice.

'Don't you get tired of being so noble and self-controlled? Don't you want me?' Leaning down, she flicked her tongue over his ear, took his hands and placed them on her hips. He breathed in the smell of her favourite perfume, a scent that never failed to bamboozle his senses.

'You belong to *him*,' David murmured.

She took his face between her hands, and looked into his eyes. 'I'm *yours*, David,' she whispered. 'Only yours...'

David's eyes snapped open. The breeze had strengthened, loosening the tethers of the tent flap. Moonlight filtered through the gap, showing David that he was alone in a sleeping bag, and not on a bed amid a pile of silk cushions making love to a very receptive Kate. It hadn't been the first intimate dream he'd had about her, but it had certainly been the most vivid. David reached for his bottle of water and breathed deeply to calm his pounding heart. Just once, he wished he could get to the end of the dream before waking up...

The sound of a door opening invaded Kate's consciousness, waking her. The hairs rose on the back of her neck as she slowly sat up and pushed the mosquito net out of the way.

Ethan stood just inside the room, silent and immobile like a dark shadow.

'Doctor Forbes?' Kate's throat felt constricted. He did not respond, but she sensed he was looking straight at her. 'Ethan?' Forcing her feet to the floor, she stood up. Something was wrong, something other than the fact he had come into her bedroom in the middle of the night.

'Kate...' His voice sounded strange, distant.

Gasping, and then pressing her lips together to suppress the sound, Kate padded towards him. In the faint light from the corridor, she saw that his eyes were blank and staring; with surprise, she realised he was sleepwalking. Tentatively, she touched his cold cheek, and was startled when he held her palm to his face.

'I'm sorry, my love,' he murmured. 'So sorry...'

'I-it's alright,' Kate whispered, and felt her heart skip a beat. 'It wasn't your fault.' A dry sob rose in her throat. 'Edwin?' A whimper escaped from her lips as he seemed to look straight at her. Or through her, to another. He turned his face to kiss her palm, and then shuffled silently out of the room.

For a few moments, Kate was unable to move. Hot tears trickled down her cheeks as her heart beat painfully in her chest. By the time she managed to command her feet to walk to the hallway, he had gone.

For the rest of the night, Kate dozed restlessly with the light on. As the world spun in its endless cycle, a shaft of moonlight filtered through the window, bathing the desk and the Bastet amulet in its silvery light. The talisman shimmered, a faint glow appearing to emanate from the crude engraving of the cat goddess.

CHAPTER 5

Friday December 14, 2012

As usual, the dining room was a hive of early morning activity. Members of both teams sat at the table and stood around the room in small groups, eating and talking with enthusiasm. Yesterday had been a productive day, and everyone anticipated similar satisfaction in the hours ahead. The people she knew greeted Kate cheerfully as she entered the room, unaware of her disturbed night or the haunted look in her eyes.

Before braving the day, she had firmly reminded herself that Ethan would recollect nothing of his nocturnal visit to her room. He was ignorant of the relationship between Edwin and Katherine Ford, and she was not about to enlighten him. Her eyes sought out David. He sat with Ethan at the far corner of the table, both of them seemingly fascinated by their bowls of cereal. As though they felt her gaze upon them, the men looked up – and blushed when they caught sight of her. Puzzled at this reaction, Kate watched them return their attention to their food, and then made her way to the kitchen to make some toast. From their seats, David and Ethan watched the object of their most recent fantasies disappear through the kitchen door.

'Why the hell are you blushing?' Ethan hissed crossly, taking a gulp of coffee.

David frowned. 'More to the point, why the hell are *you*?'

In the kitchen, Mina was already preparing vegetables for lunch while talking to Ahmed in hushed, urgent tones. Their conversation ended abruptly, and the pair adroitly switched to English small talk as soon as Kate entered the room. Mina's amiable cousin was a tour guide, and he offered to take Kate to visit the best-preserved tombs sometime during her stay. Mina handed her a bowl of fresh strawberries, but Kate noticed the absence of the girl's usual good cheer. Realising she was probably intruding, Kate wandered back to the dining room, taking a deep, fortifying breath as she approached the two difficult men in her life.

'Whose assistant would you like me to be today?' she inquired, standing over them. Picking a plump strawberry from her plate, she took a bite of the luscious fruit, aware of David's full attention. Ethan avoided looking at her altogether.

'The village workers are due to be paid tomorrow,' David explained. 'I've left the accounts book on the desk in my room. I'd be grateful if you could make a list of the payments due.'

Kate refrained from pointing out that this was the field director's responsibility. 'Anything else?'

'When you've finished you can join us on the dig,' Ethan offered gruffly. 'Take photos, make notes, but stay out of our way.'

'Oh, so you're actually going to be an archaeologist today then?' Kate retorted tartly. 'No wandering off to the cliffs on a wild goose chase and leaving David to do all the work?'

'Are you going to be doing any illicit dancing for the locals today?' he snapped back.

David rolled his eyes and stood up, his chair scraping the tiles.

Kate pretended to consider Ethan's suggestion. 'I don't know. It was such good fun the last time – I'll see how the day goes...'

'Are you finished, Kate?' David interrupted hastily. 'We can go and get that accounts book...'

A bored-looking grey donkey watched the sweaty humans as they sieved the gravel and sand from a large soil heap. Observing from her perch on a flat-topped rock, Kate smiled whimsically and wondered if the sweet-faced animal thought they were all idiots. Two Egyptian children carried small buckets of sifted grit to the large panniers attached to the donkey's back; this worthless dirt would be deposited a short distance away. Perhaps in a hundred years, archaeologists would excavate this new pile in the hope of finding fragments of history.

Today's soil heap had already yielded some pieces of tile and an old sardine can. Steven, Amy and Jonathan worked silently and methodically, placing their discoveries in a large, shallow basket and making notes and sketches of each piece in their notebooks. The donkey's owner was using a shovel to loosen the soil on the far side of the mound. Since it was a Muslim holy day, he and his children were the only Egyptians on site.

Not far away, the other students continued to work on the plots they had marked out. Their job for the day was to dig out and sift through another ten centimetres of soil, but their attention frequently strayed to the work progressing a few metres away.

Standing with folded arms and an air of self-importance, Yusuf paced the perimeter of a larger area marked off with poles and string. Kneeling within the cordoned-off zone, David and Ethan worked on the newly discovered grave. A canvas screen had been erected to protect them from the hot mid-morning sun. As Kate stood to take photographs of her companions at work, David glanced up and offered a quick, shy smile. A few moments later, he called out to his students to gather round the grave. The youngsters immediately dropped their tools and hurried to find the best vantage point outside the barrier of string, notebooks and cameras poised. An air of hushed anticipation settled on the group.

Finding a space next to Steven, behind where David knelt, Kate endeavoured to keep the distaste from her face. They had cleared just over half a metre of soil from the grave; enough dirt had been removed to expose a skeleton. Bumps in the ground promised relics for collection. With a small trowel and brush, David carefully revealed the edges of the skull while Ethan focused his attention on a large knobbly shape further down near the ribs. The students remained respectfully sombre in the presence of their first exhumed corpse.

'Kate, pass me a container,' David ordered, and Kate immediately complied. David lifted an irregularly-shaped piece of bone from the grave and placed it in the container.

'Is that from the skull, Professor?' Dominic asked, pen hovering over his notebook.

'I can't say for sure until we get her into the lab,' he replied, not looking up from his work.

'Her?' Russell repeated. 'It's a woman then?'

'I believe so, judging from the jaw and...' David glanced quickly up at Kate. 'Hips.'

They all jumped as Ethan swore and pushed back from the grave, a look of horror in his eyes.

'It's a child,' he muttered, pointing to the small skull nestled close to the ribs of its mother. 'A baby.' He looked up then, at Kate. Their eyes met and locked. Ethan struggled to grasp a memory that seemed just out of reach, a traumatic event, a disabling grief. As he stared at Kate, he felt she knew the source of his distress.

David had followed Ethan's gaze, and seen that Kate was as troubled as her soulmate. 'I can handle this,' he told Ethan quietly. 'You've been out here for hours. Go and rest.' He sat back on his haunches and turned to Kate. 'You too. Go back to the dig house and prepare your report. We'll get the pictures you need.'

Gratefully, Kate nodded, and Ethan stood to let Steven take his place. David watched Ethan and Kate walk back to the dig house together; Ethan's head was bent to the ground, and Kate's arms were wrapped defensively around her body. He felt a wave of sympathy for the pair, but returned diligently to his work.

Ethan followed Kate to the office and sat down opposite her. He watched her take a notebook, pen and camera from her satchel and place them beside the computer. To the outside observer, she was the picture of efficiency, but Ethan noticed that her fingers shook, she frequently bit her lip and, as usual, she avoided looking directly at him. He couldn't decide whether he enjoyed unsettling her; perhaps he should seek the solitude of his own office instead...

'Can I get you anything?' Kate asked tentatively, interrupting Ethan's internal debate.

Ethan looked up, surprised by her concern. 'It's a headache,' he told her, irritated at himself for showing weakness. 'Nothing more.'

'I'll go and get you something,' Kate decided. She left the room and returned ten minutes later with some headache pills, water and biscuits.

'I expect you find this very amusing...' he accused as she handed him the tablets.

'Why would I?'

'An archaeologist upset by a skeleton? Pretty pathetic!'

Sitting down, Kate gave him a small, sympathetic smile. 'It just shows that you're not a completely unfeeling dork *all* the time.'

The remark elicited a self-deprecating grin. Kate hid behind the computer screen as Ethan devoured half a packet of biscuits without offering her one. He continued with his contemplations, his eyes roving over her head and shoulders while she typed.

'Your hair wasn't always that short, was it?' he asked suddenly.

'What makes you think that?' she asked warily.

'You seem uncomfortable with it.' He frowned, not sure how he could justify the observation.

'I had it cut short for coming out here; I thought it would be easier to keep it tidy that way.'

'It's not working.' He waited for the angry flash from her brown eyes and smirked when he received her cutting stare.

'You're obviously feeling better,' she said curtly. 'Perhaps you should go and do something constructive.'

Ethan sighed, and then rose to sit at another computer. 'I think I'll email home first,' he murmured thoughtfully. 'Since we appear to have Wi-Fi.'

Kate glanced at him with a raised eyebrow. 'Really?' she asked, sounding surprised. 'You mean you have an actual human family?'

Taken aback by her impudence, Ethan laughed abruptly. 'I have a very nice family!' *They deserve a better son than me.*

Ethan came from a large, boisterous clan. The youngest of three, he had proved the most difficult to set on a straight and honest path. His parents had tried to set firm boundaries in an attempt to harness his wild, restless ways. But Ethan had broken through every one of them, hurting and

73

exasperating his loving parents. As a result, Ethan hardly ever returned to his home on the outskirts of Carlisle; he had no desire to cause them more pain and trouble.

'My father is very interested in my work,' Ethan continued, reminiscing about that calm, dependable man. People said he looked like his father, having inherited the dark good looks that had their origin in some distant, Mediterranean ancestor. 'And I have a great-uncle who likes regular updates; he had aspirations of becoming an archaeologist in his youth, but common sense prevailed. And like you, I have Victorian ancestors with connections to this noble profession. But *unlike* you, I don't care about the details…'

Turning to the computer in front of him, Ethan effectively cut off further discussion. For a while, he just stared at the screen, the text in front of him a blur.

They were still in the office an hour later when David joined them. By this time, Ethan was sitting at one side of the long room behind a tower of file boxes. Kate, meanwhile, sat at the other end with her back to both Ethan and the door, typing furiously on the computer. David walked quietly to Ethan's desk.

'I've covered the skeletons with tarpaulin,' he informed his friend. 'Yusuf wants to supervise their removal…'

Kate turned at the sound of David's voice but continued typing. Ethan stole a furtive glance at her before looking up at David. 'Will we be examining them here?'

David frowned at Ethan's trepidation. 'I'm not sure. Hopefully, we can have some supervised access before they're removed. The child will likely be taken to Cairo, to more delicate hands than ours. Why are you acting so squeamish? We've dealt with this stuff before.'

Ethan raked his hand through his hair. 'I don't know. This one's different, somehow…'

'Perhaps you're getting broody…' David suggested, eyes twinkling.

'Not likely,' Ethan replied, and then grimaced. 'I assume then, that the MSA will want to take full credit for the find?' He was suddenly full of righteous indignation. 'Oh, for those heady days when we were able to divide the spoils!'

'Those days ended a long time ago,' David pointed out. 'The MSA wants the same as we do – for everything to be handled with respect, then preserved and made available for study…'

'Oh, Dave, you and your nobility! It would be nice if, now and again, we could make some money and receive some recognition for the work we do! You know as well as I do that some artefacts make it to the black market or to private collectors – it's a lucrative business. Don't you ever wish that some of those riches would come *your* way?'

'No, not like that. I'm paid well enough, and I enjoy what I do. I'm teaching the next generation of archaeologists – if I do a good job of that, then that's legacy enough for me.'

Speechless in the face of his friend's integrity, Ethan covered his eyes for a moment, sighed, and then rose wearily. He stopped in the doorway and turned to Kate.

'See?' he cried in exasperation, pointing to a bemused David. 'D'you see what sort of man he is?'

'Yes,' Kate replied calmly, looking from one to the other with a small smile. She had overheard their conversation, and her heart had swelled with pride at David's honest, humble declaration. 'The very best sort of man.'

Shaking his head, Ethan threw up his hands in defeat and left the room in search of coffee.

David moved to stand behind Kate, his hands resting on the back of her chair as she resumed typing. 'Thank you for that,' he said, pleasure in his voice. 'Though I'm not sure I deserve it…'

'Well,' she replied softly. 'You're a better sort of man than he is. Though, at the moment, I can't work him out at all…'

Ethan's words had saddened her; to the best of her knowledge, Edwin had shared David's point of view and had not sought wealth and fame through his work.

'Are you alright?' he asked carefully, referring to their grisly discovery.

Kate nodded, still typing. 'Of course,' she assured him, an image of the recently opened grave flashing into her head. She tensed her body to quell a shudder. 'I'm just putting your discovery in my blog…'

'I can understand why you might be disturbed by what we found -'

She looked up at him with her trademark stubborn expression. '*I* did not lose a child, David.' She nodded towards the door. 'Neither did *he*.'

He looked over her shoulder at the small pile of ageing cards at the side of the keyboard. 'How's it going?'

Kate stroked the cards fondly. 'I've started on the cataloguing cards. There are some lovely sketches of the artefacts that were found – mostly pieces of pottery, one or two amulets, and lots of amulet moulds…'

'Nothing of note, then?'

She gave him a mischievous smile. 'I think I'm developing a crush on Captain Richard Yorke, whoever he was. Even when he's writing lists and cataloguing bits of broken tile, he manages to inject a kind of passion…' She started to giggle at David's disbelieving – and rather envious – look. 'He has lovely handwriting.' Rifling through the cards, she held up one up for David's perusal. 'I imagine he was very dashing. It's a pity there are no photographs…'

His eyes scanned the words on the card. 'I was worried that, once you'd immersed yourself in this, you'd become despondent. I'm grateful to Captain Yorke for providing a welcome distraction.' He handed the card back. 'Keep me informed of your progress. Will you come out to watch us lift the skeletons?'

Kate made a face. 'I'm not sure – you know how I feel about disturbing the dead. Of course, if you need me, I'm there.'

David straightened. 'I'll leave it up to you, then. Don't forget tonight…'

She perked up. 'Our date? How could I forget?' Kate gave him a disarming smile.

'We're eating with a cantankerous old woman who seems to have a mysterious agenda of her own,' David mumbled. 'Hardly the date I would prefer.' He moved to escape; she had succeeded in making him flustered.

'Shouldn't we take something?' she called after him, hiding a satisfied smirk, surprised to see him blushing when he looked back at her.

'What do you suggest?' he asked gruffly. 'A bottle of wine and a bouquet of flowers?'

'No need for sarcasm!' Kate tapped her lips with her fingertip; David's eyes locked on the gesture. 'I could make something…'

'Origami?' he quipped.

'The Hieratic text reads as follows: "You are more dazzling to my eyes than all the stars of heaven, the sun and the moon. You are my heart and my life. I enslave myself to you for all eternity, my Queen". The author of this may have etched his name into the tablet, as some characters have been erased. The cartouche of Nefertiti appears on the top left-hand corner. Found in square U36 by Katherine Ford, who claims this piece is a tragic letter to Queen Nefertiti by an impoverished, lovelorn scribe. (Perhaps Mrs Ford was that very queen in a past life. If so, many such letters would have been composed.)'

The words in brackets had been scored out but were still decipherable under the censorious line of fading blue ink. The card was tucked inside a folded sheet of paper, upon which a detailed sketch of the tablet had been skilfully drawn. The stone love letter was now on display in the Cairo museum. Dated December 1891, the drawing was signed with a flourish: Captain Richard Yorke. Wistfully, Kate read the card again then carefully scanned the image and added the details to the database.

A short while later, she found some cards which had been written by Katherine. In small, neat handwriting, her ancestor had proficiently recorded the relevant data for some shards of pottery and several pieces of painted tile. As she entered the cataloguing information into the computer, she could almost hear Katherine's voice in her ear, reading out the words as

Kate typed up a more permanent record of the ill-fated expedition.

One particular annotation caught Kate's eye. It provided information on a hair comb cut from a singular piece of light brown wood, with thirty-two pointed teeth between two thicker end pieces. The accompanying sketch looked similar to a modern-day hair lice comb. Katherine had ended her description with a personal remark: 'Although I believe this to be a lady's hair comb, and the teeth ends are stained with what may have once been scented oil, Captain Yorke insists it is a grooming tool for donkeys.'

Kate emitted a snort of laughter when she read an additional comment from Captain Yorke, scribbled beneath Katherine's tidy script: 'If the teeth are indeed stained with a substance, it is more likely to be ancient horse liniment. Unlike Mrs Ford, who claims she can detect something akin to exotic perfume on the comb, I can only smell old, rotting wood.'

'Oh, Richard,' Kate sighed longingly. 'I wish I remembered *you*...'

She felt sure that the pair had been friends. It warmed Kate's heart to think that Katherine might have found someone to chase away the loneliness she must have felt. She imagined the pair working together in the cataloguing tent, whiling away the hours with gentle banter. There would have been no unchivalrous behaviour from Captain Yorke, of that Kate was certain. She had constructed an image of him in her mind: a tall, handsome, gallant soldier. A steadfast guardian of Amarna, and perhaps also of Katherine. For Kate had noticed the distinct absence of Edwin Ford in the expedition paperwork.

At length, Kate packed away the expedition records and made her way to the kitchen, a rather frivolous idea forming in her mind. Pleased to find the area deserted, she rummaged in the cupboards for ingredients then stealthily began preparing cookie dough. It seemed somewhat surreal to be making biscuits in a house in the middle of the Egyptian desert while her companions were digging up skeletons, but Kate was determined not to go to Anai's house empty-handed. If she were completely honest, she was also a little jealous of Mina's ability to produce culinary delights that David then raved about.

By the time she had placed three trays of chocolate chip cookies in the oven, she could hear voices outside and within the house. The ancient Egyptian woman and her child had been brought to a new, temporary place of rest. Kate remained in the peaceful isolation of the kitchen and silently apologised to any disturbed spirits who may now seek to haunt them.

Taking a seat against the kitchen wall, Ethan leaned his head against the sun-warmed stone and contemplated the scene before him. David's students relaxed around their usual table in the courtyard, avidly discussing the skeletons. Jonathan was reviewing the photographs he had taken; he tried to involve Celine in the editing process, evidently keen to engage the Polish girl in conversation. Amy watched Steven as he sat alone in the shade, engrossed in his report on the day's findings.

Exhilarated by the day's success, David had allowed himself to be cornered by Hassan, who spent much of his free time around the dig house. The boy had brought out a selection of old cars in a small box, and now played with them on the ground. Aware that David usually had sweets in his pockets, Hassan called to the professor and begged him to race the cars with him. The students stared in disbelief as their usually austere leader lowered himself to the tiled floor and selected his vehicle.

Ethan smiled wistfully as he watched his friend playing with the little boy, chatting in a mixture of Arabic and English. Yes, David was ready to settle down; Ethan could see that now, and he reluctantly understood his friend's yearning for a family of his own.

David's parents had always been career-driven; despite their advancing years, both still enjoyed successful and often glamorous careers in the Foreign Service. Once she had given birth to David, Estelle Young had returned to work almost immediately. She had made it clear that, since she had dutifully provided a son and heir, there would be no more children to obstruct her ambitions. David had been left in the care of nannies until he was old enough to be sent to boarding school.

His only experience of a truly loving environment had been during the school holidays, when he was sent to stay with his father's parents. David's grandparents had adored their grandson and showered him with affection while teaching him the values and good manners he carried on into adulthood.

On his grandfather's death two years ago, David had inherited their pretty cottage in the Cambridgeshire countryside. Although he currently rented out the property, Ethan knew that David dreamed of raising his children in this little corner of paradise. He wondered whether David had ever discussed his life plan with Kate. Could she be persuaded to leave her precious Edinburgh, and the ties that bound her to that city?

As he tried to see into the future, Ethan could only see thick, impenetrable fog. It was always the same, as if nothing lay before him. Sighing in resignation, he attempted to tune in to the present moment instead.

The early evening light cast a soft glow on the courtyard and its occupants; the air was pleasantly warm and almost soporific. A light breeze caressed the sprawling acacia, gently rustling the leaves. The black cat lay curled in its favourite spot, half-dozing, its ears twitching at sounds it deemed too loud for comfort.

Stretching his long legs before him and slouching in his chair, Ethan closed his eyes and tilted his face to catch the breeze. Someone stepped out of the kitchen and paused, drawing in an audible breath. With his eyes still closed, Ethan inhaled deeply, not quite believing the scent that wafted up his nostrils.

Opening his eyes in order to confirm his suspicion, Ethan's gaze fell on Kate. She stood not far from him, holding a plate of biscuits. He scrutinised her profile as she surveyed the courtyard, noticing a smile appear on her face as she spotted David racing cars with Hassan. Her expression softened as David's boyish laughter rang out, but Kate's demeanour changed when Mina rushed past her and headed towards David, holding a bottle of beer. The girl led David towards the stone bench and sat next to him, her lovely face animated. Hassan climbed up on David's knee, having cajoled some sweets from the professor. He tried to steal some beer, but David playfully batted the boy's hand away. Ethan had to concede that the three looked like the perfect family unit. When he looked back at Kate, he witnessed the disappointment and sadness on her features and the sudden wilting in her posture.

The American team had returned from the Great Aten Temple and were now commandeering the showers. Their photographer lounged in the kitchen doorway, holding a mug of coffee. Brandon Taylor was in his forties, with dirty blond hair that was too long and unkempt. Uncaring of his thickening waistline and craggy complexion, he believed he was irresistible to women. Ethan watched as Taylor ogled Kate's rear and legs, undoubtedly speculating on the rumours circulating about the English professor and his mysterious assistant.

'I hear you're quite the dancer,' the American drawled to Kate's backside.

Startled, Kate turned quickly, noticing Ethan and the photographer at the same time. She blushed and smiled awkwardly.

'Perhaps you could give us all a dance sometime...' Brandon suggested, his eyes settling on her bosom.

'I don't think so,' Kate murmured coolly.

Taylor moved to stand beside her, too close. She could smell onions on his breath and sidestepped, her fingers clutching the plate of cooling biscuits.

'Well,' he whispered in her ear. 'If you ever get bored with Professor Stiff-Upper-Lip over there, you can always come and dance for me.'

Kate stared at the man, offended by his proposal and the accompanying leer. Anger overwhelmed her; with a twisting step, she pretended to stumble slightly towards him, knocking the mug of coffee all over his shirt. 'Oh, I'm so sorry!' she cried, sounding entirely insincere. 'I'm so clumsy! I hope that wasn't your last clean shirt?'

The photographer's face contorted with pain from the scalding liquid. 'You stupid -' Realising that some of the people in the yard had witnessed the incident, he stumbled back into the house.

The flames left Kate's eyes as her gaze fell on Ethan, and she waited for further castigation. Instead, she was surprised to receive a slight nod of approval and a lopsided smile.

'Did you get bored digitising records?' he inquired, eyeing the plate she held.

Inexplicably, Kate flushed. 'I wanted to take something to Anai's, and this was all I could think of, but I made way too many…' She looked down at the ground, watching his boots as he walked towards her. He helped himself to a cookie and chewed slowly as he watched David watching them.

'Nice idea, Friday,' Ethan muttered. 'And they don't taste too bad, either.' Catching her eye, he flashed her a wry grin. 'But Scottish shortbread might have been a more fitting gift…'

Having first smelled and then spotted Kate's offering, the students called her over to their table, offering a welcome escape. Sitting down, she placed the dish in the centre of the table and watched them fight good-naturedly over the biscuits. Thankfully, she had already put some aside for Anai, for very soon there were only three left.

'Can I take one to Doctor Brodie?' Amy asked, picking up the plate. When Kate shrugged, the young student sashayed across to Steven, but the truculent archaeologist shook his head and went back to his work. Amy returned, crestfallen. Hassan snatched the remaining cookies from Amy and ran back to David and Mina with his stolen treats. Turning her back on the trio, Kate perfunctorily performed her role as student liaison until it was time to get ready for dinner with Anai.

When Kate emerged from the house, Ethan and David were leaning against the Land Rover laughing softly at a shared joke. She had showered and changed into blue trousers and a blue printed blouse. The night air felt fresh on her face, but Kate still felt as though sand clung to her. The full moon hung low in the clear night sky, as though it were too heavy to climb any higher. Clutching the container of home baking, Kate suddenly felt full of trepidation.

The men straightened as Kate walked towards them. David saw her glance nervously at Ethan, but she avoided looking at her supervisor altogether, as though she feared he would read something in her expression she preferred to keep hidden.

'You look nice,' David commented, thrown off-guard by her reserve. She was wearing the same outfit she had worn on their single happy day in Cairo. His words evoked a smile that quickly faded.

'I hope you've got your lucky charms…' Ethan teased, pulling the talisman of Anubis from his pocket and staring at the engraved image with a puzzled frown.

'Is that what they are?' Kate asked. 'Why did she give them to us? And what do they mean?'

'Well,' Ethan began slowly. 'She gave you Bastet, which makes sense, I suppose...'

'Bastet's a goddess of protection and hope -'

'Also a bit of a schizophrenic,' Ethan interrupted, and gave David a playful wink. 'She was the daughter of the sun god, Ra, and could be both docile and aggressive. In her hostile and belligerent mode, she was portrayed as a goddess of fire and sunlight. When she was feeling peaceable, she displayed the gentle temperament of a domestic feline and was associated with the moon. You're right; she is a protector of the home. But she's also the goddess of fertility...' He gave Kate a very direct look, making her blush. 'Of course, Anai also calls you "cat" and your name is Katherine. Or Kat, I suppose...'

'I hate being called Kat,' Kate muttered; her ex-husband had called her Kitty Kat, which she had detested.

'Yes,' Ethan replied. 'It doesn't suit your "sweet girl from the posh side of Edinburgh" persona...' Before she could retaliate, he turned to David with a mischievous smile. 'Now, Sekhmet...'

'Goddess of war and retribution,' David supplied. 'She represents the destructive force of the sun.'

'Hmm,' Ethan mused, shaking his head. 'Yes, there are some nasty stories about old Sekhmet...' Grinning, he gave David a furtive look. 'Wasn't she renowned for her fierce temper?'

Catching on, David smiled. 'Indeed she was.' He feigned a moment's contemplation. 'Perhaps Anai got the amulets mixed up...' Both men looked meaningfully at Kate.

For a moment, Kate basked in their teasing. Pursing her lips, she gave them an admonishing look. 'Sekhmet is also a goddess of healing and surgery,' she continued. 'And she is a protector of truth and justice. "She is the one who loves Ma'at and detests evil", or something like that...' Her eyes softened as she caught David's look of affectionate pride.

For the first time, Ethan gave Kate a genuine smile. 'I see she's not the only protective one. Since you've obviously done *some* homework, can you tell me why the old witch gave me Anubis?'

'Well, you were the god of mummification...' Kate said warily.

'What, me personally?' Ethan quipped as his fingers fidgeted with the amulet.

'Guardian and protector of the dead,' Kate continued. 'Lord of the sacred land and...' She glanced at David uncertainly. '...and the patron of lost souls...'

Crying out in surprise, Ethan dropped the amulet abruptly and sucked his forefinger. 'The blasted thing bit me!' he snapped, then laughed at their alarmed expressions.

Retrieving the amulet, David shoved it in Ethan's shirt pocket and moved to stand beside Kate.

'Have a nice evening,' Ethan told them and started to walk away. He stopped midstride and turned back. 'Friday, Anai has a box of stuff from the 1891 expedition. I don't know what's in it, but she won't let me have it. You might have better luck...'

All business, Kate nodded. 'I'll see what I can do, Doctor Forbes.'

'And mind what you drink,' he warned them. 'I mean it.' He kicked a stone all the way back to the house.

As she turned towards the passenger door, Kate felt David's eyes on her; she felt he analysed every interaction between her and Ethan, looking for the rekindling of a flame long extinguished.

'Wrong side,' David told her, taking the container from her grip and handing her the car keys. Eyes wide, she stared at him, stunned and fearful. 'You have a licence, right?' he asked.

'Yes, but -' *I'm too scared to drive.*

'Well, it's my job as your boss to provide opportunities for your development. Get in.'

Fighting the childish urge to cry, Kate climbed into the driver's seat. As she adjusted the seat, she felt sick. It had taken three attempts to pass her driving test. Each time she got behind the wheel of a car she became a nervous wreck. She had never needed to drive in Edinburgh and, using this as her excuse, had never built up confidence as a driver. Apparently, David had perceived her fear.

'It's only a little way up the road,' David said. 'But if you can't do it, it's okay.'

Torn between pride and cowardice, she glanced at him, and then squared her shoulders. Remembering all the appropriate pre-drive checks, she finally turned the key in the ignition as David smiled into the darkness. With his gentle encouragement, Kate amazed herself by managing to drive the short distance to Anai's house. But, by the time she parked and switched off the engine again, she was trembling. Before she could berate him for coercing her, David gathered her into a gentle embrace across the gearstick.

'Well done,' he murmured into her hair. 'As usual, you exceed your own expectations.'

'I feel sick,' she muttered into his jacket.

He chuckled. 'Not a good thing to say when we're going to eat!'

By local standards, Anai's house was furnished to an almost luxurious standard. The plastered walls were the colour of pale terracotta, and colourful rugs covered the stone floors. Although many families had to share one bedroom, Anai and Mina each had their own small room. A separate bathroom containing an old sitz bath was considered by their neighbours to be the height of decadence.

Greeting them at the front door, Mina invited them to remove their footwear and gave them soft slippers to wear. She then led them into the room Kate had danced in the night before, which was dominated by a large fireplace. A wooden table had been moved to the centre of the room and laid with a bright cloth. Further warmth radiated from the oil lamps and candles, which softly lit the room and created dancing shadows in the corners. The mistress of the house rose from her armchair to welcome her guests. She wore a fine cotton galabeya in a rich shade of purple, and a long string of multi-coloured beads.

As soon as Anai's shrewd black eyes settled on him, David knew the old woman had her own plans for the evening.

Kate made her offering of home-baked cookies, which their hostess accepted with genuine pleasure. Anai graciously invited them to sit at the table, and offered a beverage that she assured them was a locally produced, non-alcoholic wine enhanced with honey, herbs and spices. Kate hesitated, mindful of Ethan's warning, but then followed David's example and sipped at the strange-tasting drink.

Their meal was simple and typically Egyptian: a little meat with vegetables and couscous served in earthenware bowls and accompanied by bread. The flickering light in Anai's single public room made it difficult to discern exactly what was in her plate, but Kate ate heartily while an image of mushroom pizza floated tantalisingly in the back of her mind. Gentle Sufi music drifted into the room from the house next door.

At first, conversation was polite and, for Kate's benefit, mostly in English. Mina quietly and efficiently served them and cleared away their empty plates, her behaviour much more restrained in her grandmother's presence.

Anai watched her guests carefully throughout the meal. As the evening progressed, and her guests imbibed more of the nameless wine, the old woman began to ask probing questions about their backgrounds, their lifestyle in Edinburgh, and their relationship. Kate grew increasingly tongue-tied as the heat in the room affected her concentration; David, however, did his best to divert Anai's attention by discussing the expedition and asking questions of his own.

After dinner, David helpfully moved the table back against the wall so that they could sit in front of the fire. Anai lowered herself into the single armchair, while Mina took up a position on the floor at her grandmother's feet. Pulling a chair closer to the fire for Kate, David also sat on the floor, resting his back against Kate's legs. A look of disappointment crossed

Mina's face as she saw Kate furtively brush her fingers across the back of David's neck.

'So, qitah,' Anai breathed. 'When did you begin to dream of your soul's last journey?'

An uncomfortable silence reigned for several moments while Kate struggled with uncertainty. David felt his heart sink into his boots.

'I don't know what you mean…' Kate muttered weakly.

'Come, now.' Anai smiled enigmatically. 'We know who you are, and why you have returned. Your lover's soul resides in the lost jackal, but guilt prevents him from finding peace.'

'Anai, Kate does not wish to be ruled by events that may or may not have happened in the past,' David spoke up. 'Please don't drag her back there.' Feeling Kate's hand on his shoulder, David reached up to hold it and felt her tremble.

'I came here to be with David,' Kate blurted, squeezing his hand. She felt a moment's surprise that she should so readily accept Anai's awareness of her past life. But then, she had been forced to accept so many implausible truths in the last year. 'And to see the place where my ancestors worked. It has nothing to do with the past – or Ethan.' She hoped she sounded convincing.

At a gesture from Anai, Mina reached under the armchair for a battered tin box.

'I have been keeping this for you, qitah,' she said gravely, as Mina handed the small box to Kate. 'It has been with my family for safe-keeping. For a very long time.'

With trembling fingers, Kate lifted the lid. For a moment, she held her breath. The box contained some paperwork and sepia photographs of an archaeological expedition.

'Oh, God!' Kate whispered. 'These are…this is -' She picked up a picture of a fresh-faced young man, smiling up from the depths of a ditch. '*Jackson!*' She had remembered him briefly in regression therapy, a junior archaeologist who had worked with Katherine on the day she had found the tablet.

Handing the photograph to David, Kate rifled for more. There were some pictures of Amarna, scenes of the men at work, a table of small artefacts, and the camp doctor. Finally, her fingers closed on a formal grouping. Two rows of people, the front row sitting stiffly on folding chairs. Smiling Egyptian workers stood in a small group at one side of the British team. A solitary woman sat in the centre of the front row, long auburn hair hanging in a curling rope over one shoulder. Defiant in her trousers, boots and masculine shirt, Katherine Ford beamed at her niece.

Behind Katherine, a hand possessively resting on her shoulder, stood a grim-faced Edwin Ford. Even from the ageing paper, his dark eyes stared out at Kate accusingly. Swallowing the tears that nearly always accompanied memories of her soulmate, Kate's eyes slid to the man next to Edwin. Staring out at her with a slightly amused expression stood a tall soldier wearing the uniform of a cavalryman. He had light-coloured hair and a handsome, intelligent face. A face she knew well. David's face.

Wordlessly, Kate passed the photograph to David and left him to stare at the evidence in front of him. Pulling a small rectangular magnifier from the pocket of his trousers, he examined the picture. Taking a deep breath, he fought to still his trembling fingers, his foggy brain struggling with recognition. He *remembered* posing for this photograph. He *remembered* a deep resentment for a living, breathing Edwin Ford.

Kate had taken a torn piece of paper from the tin. The letter was badly creased, as though it had been crumpled into a ball and then smoothed out. It was dated January 1892:

Dearest Harriet,

Although I have received no new orders, I will be returning to my regiment in the morning. Disaster has befallen this expedition, and our team is disbanding, to be replaced with an Italian group. We have found many interesting artefacts during our time here, but the pharaoh's tomb has eluded us.

Worse, we have been crippled by a tragic event. Our leader's wife, Katherine, died from an illness a few days ago. Her passing was unexpected and needless. Her husband had left her in Cairo, in the care of people who were only mere acquaintances, while he returned to Akhetaten. I only hope she did not die alone and every day I wish I had stayed with her in Edwin's stead.

In the short time we spent together, Katherine and I enjoyed a wondrous friendship. She was the daughter of my tutor, the esteemed James Grahame. You will remember that I was supposed to return to Edinburgh in 1890 with artefacts for an exhibition. Military orders called me away, and Edwin travelled to Edinburgh in my place. And there he won beautiful Katherine. Not a day passes that I don't curse the Hussars for taking me along a different path.

My dear sister, I believe I loved Katherine, and the grief I feel at her loss threatens to engulf me. My only comfort is that her husband has taken her back to her family in Scotland and not buried her in Egypt. I hope he suffers a lifetime of guilt for his neglect of her, for she lost their child along with her life.

I am unsure where my next posting may be and, at this time, I care not. Please give my regards to the other members of our family and assure them of my safety. I cannot say when I will be able to write to you again.

Your brother, Richard

His grief almost permeated the thin sheet of paper.

'Poor Richard...' Kate whispered, a lump rising in her throat.

'Do you mean Richard Yorke?' David sounded confused, his eyes flicking from the snapshot he held to the paper in her hands. She handed him the letter, saying nothing, refusing to interfere with his dawning comprehension.

Another photo in the box caught her eye, and she pulled it out. In this picture, Katherine had been caught off guard and stood on a ridge contemplating the vista before her. It must have been a windy day, for one hand held her hair back from her face. Her expression was undeniably sad.

Regression had shown Kate that Edwin and his wife had not enjoyed an idyllic marriage. Both had been stubborn, passionate and hot-tempered, and Katherine had hated the restrictions placed upon her as a Victorian wife. This candid photograph seemed to provide evidence of Katherine's dissatisfaction.

David gently took the picture from Kate's fingers and gazed upon the young woman with Kate's face and melancholy expression. For a brief moment, he felt as though he had loved this woman as much as he adored the flesh-and-blood version of her sitting behind him.

'I can help you remember more, qitah,' Anai said gently, watching David's face as he struggled to find a logical explanation he could believe with absolute certainty.

'How?' Kate asked.

'Kate, don't,' David begged. 'Please, don't do this again...' And yet, *he* wanted to know more.

'It is not your choice!' Anai snapped. 'Once she understands the past, she will go towards the future with an open heart and do what is right.' Her eyes narrowed shrewdly. 'That is what you wish, is it not?'

'How will you help me remember, Anai?' Kate pressed.

'There were herbs in your wine,' Mina confessed. 'They serve to relax you. Another potion will help to open your mind. We will help you into a state of deep relaxation and set you on your journey...'

'It is a full moon and a new day,' Anai commented. 'An auspicious time for such an endeavour, for it is a kind of magic...'

'Wait,' David interjected. 'Are you talking about witchcraft? I won't allow Kate to -'

'It sounds more like a primitive method of hypnotherapy,' Kate said. 'Alright. I'll do it.'

'Then I'm doing it, too,' David spoke up.

As Kate began to protest, and David countered her argument, Mina rose, walked over to the sideboard and opened a cupboard door. Removing a dark-coloured silken cloth, she draped it across the surface of the cabinet. David's eyes strayed to the carved wheel hanging on the wall, which he recognised as a Wheel of the Year. Since ancient times, magicians and witches had used the wheel to symbolise the four agricultural and pastoral festivals, and the four solar festivals.

David wanted to escape, to protect Kate from these women who apparently imagined themselves witches. But perhaps due to the liquid he had naively consumed, or because he now had his own questions, he felt unable to stir himself to action. Instead, he took Kate's hand and held it tightly.

With great reverence, Mina withdrew a small bowl of soil and laid it on the cloth. Next came a ceremonial dagger, or athame. Its hilt was carved in the shape of the goddess Isis, the crosspiece a pair of wings with a scarab at the centre.

A bronze disc engraved with a pentacle was placed beside the sacred blade, followed by a candle to represent the element of fire. Finally, Mina brought a bowl of water from the kitchen, turned down the lamps and opened the small windows to allow the bright moonlight to shine into the hot room. She filled two thimble-sized glasses with a dark-coloured syrup and handed them somewhat ceremoniously to David and Kate. Anai, meanwhile, had taken a position in front of the fire. Closing her eyes, she rocked gently as she began to chant in a low, guttural voice.

'You don't have to do this, David,' Kate pleaded quietly. 'I would feel better knowing that you were conscious and in full control of your faculties…'

'Now I need answers too, angel,' he replied, sounding more confident than he felt. He refrained from reminding her that he, too, had been drugged. 'Perhaps we'll find them together.'

'You may not travel the same road,' Anai piped up. 'Throughout the ages, your paths have crossed but never merged.'

'Doesn't mean it'll be like that this time,' David retorted. 'I believe we can change our destiny.' He turned back to Kate, lowering his voice. 'I would love to know how she knows all this stuff. Harbinger of doom…' He tapped the rim of his glass against Kate's and downed the foul-tasting syrup.

Mina had placed a blanket and some cushions on the floor near the fire; she invited David and Kate to lie down. As they complied and made themselves comfortable, Anai used the dagger to draw a circle around them.

Above them, statues of Isis, Anubis, Sekhmet and Bastet stared down from the mantelpiece. There were smaller likeness of other gods, and Kate strained to identify them, but her vision was beginning to blur. She tilted her head against David's upper arm, a rush of guilt washing over her. He was willing to submit to this ritual in the hope of connecting with her in the past. There seemed to be no end to the trials he would face for her. She did not deserve such a loyal champion.

Seeming suddenly sprightlier, Anai dropped easily to a kneeling position at their heads. She anointed the centre of their foreheads with oil as Mina wafted incense about the darkened room.

David inhaled deeply, the cloying scent filling his nostrils, his awareness becoming foggy. Mina began speaking to them in a low, soothing tone, gently urging them to a place of relaxation so that they could begin their journey to the past. She was telling them to concentrate on the place they wanted to visit, the face they most wanted to see.

As David closed his eyes, he felt Kate take his hand. From some distant place, he could hear the sound of a gentle wind tapping against canvas…

CHAPTER 6

The papers on the rickety desk fluttered in the warm breeze, and he absently secured the rumpled pile with a small rock. Aware that someone approached the open flaps of his tent, he looked up, momentarily dazzled by bright sunlight. Then he rose quickly to his feet.

'Mrs Ford.' His tone of voice conveyed respect as he stood to attention. The pose was second nature to him, honed from his years at Sandhurst and then on campaign.

'Captain Yorke,' the young woman addressed him nervously, in a soft voice made sweeter by its Scottish lilt. She looked up at him as he stood rigidly at the side of his desk. 'I'm sorry to disturb you. I was looking for my husband...'

Richard Yorke's gaze rested on her face only as long as was considered proper. He avoided looking down at her lithe young body clad in a man's shirt and trousers, but he felt his ears start to burn nonetheless. It was no secret that Edwin and Katherine Ford enjoyed a fairly unconventional, but fiercely passionate relationship. Only the previous evening, Richard had happened to walk past their quarters and had inadvertently overheard what had obviously been an intimate and intensely pleasurable encounter.

'I'm sorry, Mrs Ford,' Richard stuttered, forcing the memory from his mind. 'He has not returned from the northern cliffs.' He saw her look of disappointment. 'Might I be of assistance?'

With a slight shake of her head, Katherine gave him a weak half-smile. 'No thank you, Captain Yorke. I only wished to discuss a small housekeeping matter. It is of little importance...'

At that moment, a young man ran up, holding a teapot in a linen cloth. 'Your tea, Captain Yorke!' he announced, setting it on the desk before running off to his next errand.

Katherine eyed the pot, and then her curious gaze roamed the contents of the tent. His quarters were those of a soldier: typically sparse, orderly and impersonal. A folding bed sat on an almost threadbare rug; a desk and chair; a functional but featureless washstand; a battered trunk with a pile of books on top. The other senior members of the team had moved into hastily constructed mud-brick houses, but he had remained in his tent on the outskirts of the camp.

Richard studied her discreetly. She was beautiful but so very young. He wondered what had possessed Ford to bring his new wife to such an inhospitable place. She was the only woman in their group; no doubt she was lonely, especially since Ford spent much of his time away from the campsite on his quest to find the pharaoh's tomb. Over the last three weeks, Richard had admired the determination with which Katherine had attacked her living conditions. She had worked hard to provide a comfortable living space for herself and Ford, ably carrying out domestic duties without complaint. She had crashed fearlessly through the barriers of language, culture, gender and, at times, propriety. She had involved herself with the cataloguing of artefacts and had even joined them on the dig. Katherine Ford was an admirable force of nature. And yet, despite her efforts to appear resilient, he had caught glimpses of vulnerability and discontent.

'Would you care for some ginger tea?' he offered, pouring some into a battered tin mug. 'Army-issue beaker, I'm afraid...' He gave her a rueful smile.

She looked surprised by his attempt at humour, as though she had not expected such a comment from so stern a countenance. Returning his smile, she looked longingly at the mug but remained standing just beyond the threshold of the tent. Realisation dawned, and Richard pulled his chair around to the open entrance of his bachelor quarters. He gestured for her to sit where she was in plain sight of other people, and handed her a mug of tea.

'I've never tasted ginger tea...' she mused, sniffing the hot drink. Katherine sipped and made a small sound of appreciation.

'It soothes the digestion,' Richard replied tactfully, in reference to their sometimes-unidentifiable meals, which made army rations seem like luxury.

She sat quietly, demurely drinking her tea while Richard paced like a restless lion. He felt awkward in her company, aware that she was unchaperoned and the wife of the expedition leader. The sounds he had heard the night before echoed in his ear, taunting him.

At last, he moved the books from atop the trunk and sat on the edge of the box. 'How are you faring?' he asked carefully.

She gave him a small smile. 'Fine, I think.' Her expression changed, and she looked at him with wide-eyed concern. 'Does it look as though I am struggling?'

Richard's eyes sparkled. 'It looks as though you are your father's daughter!' He was delighted to receive the gift of a dazzling smile.

'You know my father?'

'Your father was my professor at university, Mrs Ford.' Richard smiled wistfully at distant memories of carefree youth, before the darkness of battle had descended like an impenetrable cloud. 'He was kind enough to provide extra tuition in his free time, in your house in Heriot Row. Your mother plied me with tea and scones on many occasions.' He paused as her face transformed with an expression of utter longing. 'You and I have already met, though you were only a child...' Katherine's face fell. 'What vexes you?'

Her eyes were downcast. 'Was I really awful?' she asked in a small voice. 'My parents say I was a very precocious child...'

Richard chuckled, an unfamiliar sound. 'There is no harm in being curious about the world.'

'No, not if you are of the male gender...'

'Mrs Ford, your father was immensely proud of the fact that you were a spirited, intelligent child. He often marvelled at the thought of you growing into a woman who knew her mind.'

Katherine gazed dolefully into her mug. 'I'm afraid these traits have often landed me in trouble, Captain Yorke.'

Richard shrugged. 'We are none of us saints. And you are not the only one who has shrunk under Professor Grahame's withering scowl. He was less than pleased with *me* when I applied to military school once I had finished university. He foresaw a glittering career in archaeology, which I turned my back on in favour of duty to my country.' He frowned then, remembering the disappointment on James Grahame's face when he discovered his favourite pupil had chosen a dangerous, uncertain course.

Rising, Richard lifted the lid of the trunk and began to rummage among the contents. He placed his dark blue cavalry tunic reverently on the neatly made bed. A long, shining sword followed suit, and then Richard found what he was looking for. Taking the mug from her without touching her fingers, he placed a slim volume in her hand and returned to perch on the edge of the trunk.

She read the spine and gasped. 'Archaeology: Methods and Practices – by James Grahame!' She looked up at him. 'My Father wrote this?'

'A long time ago, I believe. Look at the flyleaf – he wrote me a message.'

Katherine opened the book and saw her father's flamboyant script: *To Richard - Follow your dreams. Best Regards, James Grahame.* She touched the words with her fingers, and Richard thought he saw a glistening tear at the corner of one eye.

'You miss him,' Richard declared softly. It occurred to him that, in the time she had been sitting with him, he had all but forgotten that they were in a bustling, noisy camp. Requisitions and accounts had vanished from his mind. The bloody scenes of battle that haunted him had dissipated like steam from a kettle.

'I miss all of them,' Katherine murmured. 'We've never been so far apart…'

'Perhaps there will be a letter waiting for you in Cairo. You must be looking forward to returning to civilisation for a few days. Such as it is…'

Katherine nodded thoughtfully, one small hand absently caressing the cover of the book she held. 'Will you be joining us?'

'Yes. I'm in charge of transportation. We need to gather some supplies, and I need to collect my correspondence.' He looked morosely at the uniform on his bed. 'I am presently on leave, and awaiting new orders. For the last few years, it has been my good fortune to be able to spend some of the winter as an archaeologist. As a matter of fact, I was on the expedition that resulted in your husband's journey to Edinburgh.' He saw Katherine's lovely eyes widen in surprise. 'I was supposed to make the trip myself, but new orders arrived, and Edwin took my place.'

Richard sighed, somewhat regretfully. 'So you see, if Her Majesty's Cavalry had not intervened, we may have met again.' He stroked his hand through his dark blond hair. 'It certainly would have been more pleasant than the Sudan Campaign…'

He rose and once again lifted the lid of the trunk in order to return his uniform to its resting place. Picking up his sword, he balanced the shining scabbard between his palms, his expression distant.

'Three swords broke at the Battle of Gemaizah in 1888,' Katherine said softly as she rose from her chair and moved closer to him.

Richard wasn't surprised that she was aware of the fact; she was, after all, James Grahame's daughter. Armoury was another of the museum director's passions.

'I know,' Richard replied, one hand moving to grasp the simply fashioned hilt. 'I was there…' He could still smell blood, gunpowder, burning flesh.

'I'm sorry,' Katherine's voice was full of pity, and Richard believed her compassion was for him. He turned towards her, taken aback by her reaction. Most women either fawned over him as though he were a gallant knight in shining armour or looked down their noses at him because they considered him a savage killer.

'Some say that there are those in the cavalry who refuse to carry the latest firearms because they consider it beneath them to dismount in order to fight.' Katherine looked up at him warily, and Richard saw she had no wish to be antagonistic.

'There is no place for foolish pride on the battlefield,' he replied grimly. 'I can assure you that my fellow Hussars and I carry whatever is necessary to survive.'

She pointed hesitantly at the sword in Richard's hands. 'May I?'

Wordlessly, Richard handed the sheathed sword to the petite young woman and was pleasantly surprised when she showed no girlish concern at the weight. Carefully but confidently, Katherine unsheathed the weapon and laid the scabbard on the desk. With two hands holding the hilt and the point towards the floor, she reverently studied the length of the polished blade. Richard watched her appraisal with growing amusement; Katherine looked very like her mother, but at this moment, she reminded him of James.

'The blade length is thirty-four inches,' she recited, as though remembering her father's teachings.

'And a half,' Richard added with a smile, finding her pursed lips endearing. Shyly, she returned his smile, and then resumed her perusal of the weapon that was more than half her height.

'Including the hilt, the sword measures forty-one inches.' Katherine gave him a mischievous glance. 'And a half.'

'Put that down, Mrs Ford,' a voice commanded from behind them. 'You're fearsome enough without weaponry!'

Richard and Katherine turned to see Edwin standing at the entrance to the tent, looking rakishly dishevelled. Handing the sword back to its owner, Katherine rushed to her husband, her face suffused with open adoration. He caught her in his arms and kissed her nose, then turned his attention to Richard, who had replaced the sword in its scabbard and returned it to the trunk.

'How are you progressing with the accounts, Captain Yorke?' Edwin tucked his wife against his side, his hand curled around her hip possessively.

Richard didn't miss the unmistakably proprietary gesture or the slightly superior tone in Edwin's voice. He also noticed the expedition leader's furrowed brow and the troubled look in his eyes.

'Everything is in order, Mister Ford,' Richard replied, stifling the desire to stress the word 'mister'. 'Mrs Ford was looking for you...'

Katherine picked up the book from Richard's desk and held it up to her husband. 'Look, Edwin! Captain Yorke has a book written by Father!'

Richard clasped his hands behind his back, once more the detached officer. 'You may borrow it, Mrs Ford, and return it once you have read it.'

Edwin turned, hiding his face from Richard's view and whispered something close to his wife's ear. Whatever he said caused Katherine to blush to the roots of her hair and lower her gaze to the ground, a secretive smile on her lips. Richard's sharp eyes followed the unconscious movement of her hand as it slipped protectively over her abdomen.

'Thank you for the delicious tea,' she said to Richard, her calm demeanour all a-fluster in the presence of her charismatic mate.

'If it would please you, I could send some to your quarters.'

Katherine smiled at him disarmingly. 'I would be very grateful, Captain Yorke. I am growing weary of Egyptian coffee.'

Richard couldn't help himself. 'The last time we met, you called me Richard,' he said softly and was gratified to see Edwin frown and cast a speculative glance towards his wife.

Her flushed cheeks reddened further, and she smiled nervously. 'Yes, but I was…' She tilted her head, mentally calculating.

'Ten,' Richard supplied with a smile. Out of the corner of his eye, he saw Edwin exhale with relief.

'We should return to our quarters,' Edwin decided, taking his wife's hand. He turned to Richard. 'Thank you for your hospitality towards my wife.'

Richard bowed gallantly to Katherine and watched her weave her way through the camp until he could no longer see her. He made a mental note to have a pot of ginger tea sent to her each morning, for his keen observation of Katherine Ford had told him something that her husband had not yet realised…

Feeling David's fingers grow cold, Kate held them tighter, shifting closer to him as she closed her eyes. The pungent incense enveloped her until she felt as though she floated on a scented cloud. Anai's quiet monotone was soothing, leading her to a warm, comfortable place where she felt safe. Behind her eyelids, the darkness grew steadily brighter, and shapes began to form. She could hear music, faintly at first but growing louder. Drowsily, Kate began to hum along to a waltz…

'I'm sorry, sweetheart. I know you wanted us to spend this evening together, but I must keep them sweet – I need their permission to extend the perimeter of the dig site.'

Kate averted her eyes from her husband's handsome face. 'I understand, Edwin.'

His dark eyes sought hers once more. 'Your face tells me different, love.'

They waltzed in silence, Kate battling to hide her misery. It was New Year's Eve; she was in a beautiful ballroom in Cairo, wearing a magnificent gown of midnight blue, and dancing in the arms of the most handsome man in the room. She should feel happy. Instead, her husband had tactlessly announced that he would be using the event as a means to promote his work. Prominent men from the Department of Antiquities were attending the celebrations, and Edwin needed to curry favour with them in order to maintain their support for his expedition.

Involuntarily, Kate's eyes sought out Richard Yorke. He danced with a pretty, fair-haired young woman who was obviously smitten with the dashing cavalryman. Dressed in the dark blue dress uniform of the 20th Hussars, Richard cut a striking figure. As though he sensed her eyes upon him, his gaze moved up from the top of his partner's head and fell on Kate.

He gave her a small smile, before Edwin's body blocked her view.

'I *did* tell you I would have to work, Kate...' Edwin sounded slightly peeved by his wife's perceived sulkiness.

Kate looked up at him, her eyes absorbing every feature of the man she loved. 'I know.' She didn't want to fight, not when their time together was so tightly scheduled, as it had been since they had returned from an idyllic honeymoon sixteen months before.

'And there are many people here whom you know. You can sit and gossip with the ladies. I'm sure you won't be short of a dance partner, either.' He smiled wryly, leading her to one side of the room as the dance ended. Conveniently, they now stood beside a group of seated matrons. Amelia Hamilton, a recent acquaintance, gave Kate a welcoming smile and gestured for her to join them.

'Look,' Edwin squeezed her hand. 'Here's your champion. Good evening, Captain Yorke!'

Edwin was so obviously desperate to make his escape that Kate almost felt like weeping. She held onto his hand, struggling to maintain an amiable countenance. He was making polite conversation with Richard, preparing to entrust his wife to someone else's care when all she wanted was to be with him. At last, Edwin turned back to her and tenderly touched her cheek. At last, she saw the love in his eyes as he moved her out of the way of couples dancing a vigorous polka.

'You *know* I can't dance with another man all night,' she told him quietly, almost pleading. 'And if you're leaving, I'll be here on my own. People might talk...'

His voice was soft and cajoling; Kate knew the tone well. 'I'll be in the smoking room next door. You never had a chaperone the whole time we were courting – although there were a few occasions when you definitely needed one – so I refuse to believe you feel one is necessary now.' He kissed her lips, and Kate heard some of the women gasp in surprise at the impropriety. 'Save me the waltzes, my love.' And he left her, quickly disappearing in the throng of people.

Feeling bereft, Kate walked slowly to the tall, partially open windows of the ballroom and looked out into the night. Flame torches lined the terrace, and illuminated the landscaped garden beyond. People sat outside in the cool evening air, enjoying drinks and cheerful discourse. Kate suppressed an indignant sob and forced back tears. Her hand went to the gold heart-shaped locket at her throat, where a lock of Edwin's hair nestled entwined with a curl of her own.

'It would be my honour to escort you until his return,' Richard said quietly from just behind her. 'I'm confident he will not be able to stay away from you for long.' Kate turned her head to smile wanly at the compliment. 'Besides, I expect you've already filled your dance card.'

Kate pursed her lips, youthful rebelliousness returning. 'I did not accept a dance card; I am not a mere bauble to be passed from one man to the next for their entertainment!'

Richard's eyes sparkled with mirth. 'Why am I not surprised by such a response from you? Very well then – I will have to approve all your partners in the absence of your husband!'

'You will do no such thing!' she huffed, turning back to the window and glaring at her reflection. She resisted the urge to fold her arms across her chest and pout. 'You do not need to stay with me,' she continued, hearing self-pity in her voice. 'There are many beautiful girls in the room desirous of your attention; you should go and enjoy yourself while you can. I have no wish to spoil your evening.'

'And I have no wish to go and pretend to be something I am not. So please let me stay and take on the duty of protector to the darling of our expedition.'

In spite of herself, Kate smiled at his impertinence. 'Stop teasing me!' she chided, watching a young couple dancing on the terrace. They had eyes only for each other, oblivious to the noise and bustle around them. Feeling a stab of envy, Kate swallowed the lump in her throat. Her emotions felt scattered, and she wished she could find a quiet place to sit alone and wallow in her disappointment.

Richard watched her reflection in the window. 'Have you forgiven me for your unsatisfactory journey to Cairo?'

Kate scowled at him. 'My teeth are still rattling from travelling in that awful baggage wagon!'

Richard grinned. 'It was the nearest thing to a carriage I could find. Had Edwin been in charge of the transport arrangements, I am sure he would have chosen the same.'

'I am a competent horsewoman – I could have managed perfectly well on horseback. A *camel* would have been more comfortable than that cart!'

Richard lowered his voice, his expression grave. 'I would not allow you to take such a risk.'

Kate became guarded. 'Why not?'

Even in murky reflection, his green eyes were intense. 'Katherine, you *know* why not.'

Kate flushed as her hands crept over the satin bodice of her gown. 'Captain Yorke, you're making inappropriate presumptions -'

'I have two sisters, both of whom have children. I have lived in barracks where my men's wives have given birth; I know the signs well enough. I will not be contrite for ensuring your safety. No doubt your husband shares my views.'

The orchestra began to play music for a Gay Gordons dance, and jubilant whooping pierced the air as dancers flocked to the floor. The camp surgeon approached, nodding a greeting to Richard as he asked Kate to dance. Without seeking Richard's approval, she took the doctor's arm. The music reminded her of parties in Edinburgh, where she had danced this very dance with her beloved father.

'Aye, we're a long way from home,' the portly doctor sighed, twirling Kate under his raised arm. He was a kindly Scotsman in his fifties, with a bushy grey beard. 'Scotland seems very far away tonight, eh lass?' Kate merely nodded, homesickness adding to her sorrow. 'I've just heard your man agreeing to meet with officials from the Department of Antiquities tomorrow. It sounds like he's won them over with that silver tongue of his.'

Kate's step faltered. 'But tomorrow is New Year's Day!'

'Ford's a driven man, as you well know. And he's sure he's close to finding the tomb; he says he just needs more time, which naturally means more funding.' He gave Kate a shrewd glance. 'Since he'll be out, I'll call on you in the morning and give you a proper examination. Then we'll know for sure, one way or the other. And you can talk to your husband, at last.' Kate coloured, and opened her mouth to protest. 'I'll brook no opposition from you, lassie. You've hung onto your suspicions long enough.'

The Gay Gordons ended, a two-step began, and Kate was whisked off by one of the junior archaeologists. Amelia Hamilton's husband then swept her off for a polka. The building excitement in the room, the cordiality, the lively music, helped raised her spirits a little, and she began to enjoy herself. Richard refrained from dancing, choosing instead to stand on the sidelines where he could keep an eye on her. During a mazurka with another cavalry officer, she peeked around the man's arm and poked out her tongue at Richard. Her guardian pretended to look offended and frowned back.

At last, the orchestra conductor announced the last waltz of 1891. The guests sought out their spouses or singled out a particular partner. Kate stood near the door to the smoking room and waited for Edwin to appear. Violins started to play a beautifully romantic waltz, the lights dimmed and the room seemed to hush. But there was no sign of her husband. A tear trickled slowly down Kate's cheek, just as she felt a warm hand lift hers.

'Come, Katherine,' Richard said softly, bringing her gloved hand to his lips. 'Edwin will find you…' He led her onto the floor, and they joined the dance.

He was much taller than she; her eyes focused on the gold frogging on his tunic, and the Egypt medal pinned to his chest. Through blurry eyes, she saw that the bars denoted valour at Toski and Gemaizah. The medal suspended from the blue-and-white striped ribbon depicted the head of a veiled Queen Victoria on one side, with a sphinx atop a pedestal on the other. Kate knew from the time she had spent in his company that, although he was proud to serve queen and country, he took no satisfaction in the actions forced upon him during that service. Not for the first time, Kate felt grateful to have made such a friend as he. Not for the first time, she wondered what might have happened if they had met earlier, before Edwin had burst into her life. Her husband's sardonic observation had been astute: Richard Yorke had become Kate's champion, quietly providing for her comfort, requiring no acknowledgement or reward for his kindness.

As the days at camp had become more difficult to bear, and Edwin had all but vanished from her presence, she had sought Richard's company, enjoying his stillness as well as his wit and keen intelligence. She knew she would miss him if new orders required him to leave. And she would worry for his safety.

'You look radiant,' he told her.

She gave him a playful smile. 'You've hardly danced all evening. It's a shame, when you look so dashing!' Her eyes glinted mischievously; she found she enjoyed teasing the stern captain. It seemed to take him by surprise every time.

'I was waiting to dance with the most beautiful woman in the room,' he retorted. 'But she has been passed from man to man all evening – rather like a bauble.' He smiled as Kate giggled, his fingers pressing gently against the bodice of her gown where they rested at her back. 'I'm relieved you wisely decided not to throttle your ribs in too tight a corset.' He looked nonchalantly over Kate's head as the couple next to them glanced in their direction, their eyebrows raised in astonishment. 'But then, you seemed to discard that restrictive garment almost as soon as you arrived in the desert…'

Kate blushed, askance. '*Richard!*' she hissed indignantly.

'I'm surprised that your husband hasn't noticed the rather obvious clue which has been staring him in the face all these weeks.' Richard's tone was suddenly sharp.

'Edwin knows that I have always despised being trussed up like a Christmas goose. In fact – *oh!*' She looked quickly away, embarrassed by her lack of decorum. Once again, her eyes searched the room for Edwin, but still there was no sign. Suddenly she felt distraught by his thoughtlessness; it would soon be midnight, and he had forgotten her. Her hand gripped Richard's arm as her peripheral vision began to blur, and she began to feel weak.

'Richard…' she murmured, swaying unsteadily in his arms.

Adroitly, he steered her towards the terrace and helped her to sit on a stone bench near the wide French doors.

'Breathe deeply,' he told her as he stood before her, trying not to draw attention. 'Shall I get you something to drink?' Kate shook her head, her fingers clutching the edge of the seat as she tried to control her heaving stomach. Automatically, her hand moved to her belly as if to soothe the life within.

'Then let me fetch Edwin -'

'No!' Kate was vehement. 'I'll be fine in a moment...'

Heedless of the rules of their society, Richard crouched before her and looked into her fearful eyes. 'Katherine, why have you still not told him about the child?'

Kate bowed her head in shame. 'I'm afraid he'll be angry with me...'

'Why?' Richard asked in surprise. 'Does he not want children?'

'Yes, of course...' Kate replied, too quickly. 'But the timing...he so desperately wants this expedition to be a success.' She looked down at the paved terrace. 'He made it clear before we came to Egypt that now would not be a convenient time...' Kate cringed, knowing she should not be discussing such a personal matter with him.

'Then why did he bring you?'

'I begged him – I could not bear to stay in Edinburgh. And most definitely not without Edwin.'

'Why did you want to leave Edinburgh?'

'Oh, Richard, I felt so confined! And now I feel ashamed, for I should have stayed there instead of becoming his burden!'

'Katherine,' Richard said in a soothing tone. 'You are not a burden. Edwin is very lucky to have you for his wife. But you *must* tell him -'

'I'm afraid he will send me home!' She clenched her fists together on her lap.

Richard placed a hand over hers, flouting the rules of propriety even further. 'No – he will *take* you home.'

'He will not leave Akhetaten, Richard. He will remain here to finish his work, and he will send me home. And he will be right to do so...'

Richard's face became grim. 'Yes, it's true he is ambitious -'

'Not ambitious!' Kate rose to her husband's defence. 'He has always said he has no need for riches or fame. He strives only to bring knowledge to the world...' She faltered as she saw Richard's doubtful expression, and just stared at him helplessly.

'You must tell him,' Richard urged. 'I am sure he will be overjoyed with the news and his primary concern will be for your welfare, not for some old tomb which has lain undisturbed for thousands of years. He will want to look after *you*. Both of you.'

Kate felt a flutter of hope in her belly. 'Do you think so?'

Richard's smile was reassuring, though his eyes looked sad. 'Dearest Katherine, how could he not? How could he not want to be with you, to witness every moment of this miracle you have brought into being? Do not deny him this, I beg you! He will want to feel every kick, witness every tiny development. He will want to be present when you bring this child into the world, be the first to hold him in his arms, be the first to kiss him and profess his undying love to you both.'

His passionately spoken words made Kate want to weep. Her lip trembled. 'Are you certain? How do you know?'

Richard leaned down to kiss her hands as the revellers began counting down the seconds to midnight. 'Because it's what *I* would do…'

People began to flock to the terrace in anticipation of fireworks and the chiming of Christian church bells. Taking Kate's hand, Richard helped her to her feet, just as Edwin appeared and wrapped his arms around his wife from behind.

'Here you are!' he exclaimed, kissing her bare shoulder.

Kate's eyes held Richard's and imparted her heartfelt gratitude. Richard responded with a barely perceptible nod then he respectfully turned away from her to look out at the colourful fireworks. A group of people began to sing 'Auld Lang Syne'.

'Forgive me, Kate,' Edwin murmured, and she believed he sounded sincere.

'You missed the last waltz of 1891,' she said reproachfully.

'Then I will have the first waltz of 1892,' he smiled. 'And the first waltz of every year hereafter. And every waltz in between until we no longer have legs to dance.' Ignoring the people around them, he turned her to face him and erased all disharmony by claiming her lips for a New Year kiss…

Mina's voice was gentle but firm. 'Kate, it is time to return. You must leave that life behind…'

'No…' Kate moaned. 'I don't want to leave yet! Please let me stay…'

David sat up groggily, his heart twisting with jealousy. *She's with Edwin*, he thought bitterly. *She wants to stay with him. Any minute now, she's going to call his name…*

'I want…Richard…' Kate murmured, and David's torment ceased.

After several more minutes of soothing words, Mina finally managed to bring Kate out of a trance state. But when at last she opened her eyes, Kate sat up and began to cry. Pulling her knees up to her chest, she gently rocked back and forth.

'Did she go to the moment of her death?' David looked at Mina and Anai accusingly. 'You should have steered her away from it!' Forcing his tingling body into a kneeling position, David pulled Kate into his arms, one hand stroking her back while she sobbed quietly, her eyes tightly closed.

'That is not why she weeps,' Anai told him.

'She's crying for *him*?' David asked. 'Again?'

The old woman shook her head and lifted Kate's chin. 'Look at me, qitah.' Reluctantly, Kate looked into Anai's wizened face. 'Do not grieve for what was lost, for it will be returned to you. You will not have long to wait.'

Sickened, David let go of Kate and stood up. Pacing the small room, he finally came to a halt at the window and stared out into the night.

Mina took David's place at Kate's side, her dark eyes full of concern.

'I was pregnant,' Kate whispered hoarsely 'I felt his child inside me…'

'Your connection to that life is indeed strong…' Mina observed. 'Most people can only glimpse images from their past lives.'

Anai, meanwhile, had moved to the sideboard and retrieved a bottle filled with dark brown liquid. Carefully pouring out two small glasses, she stood over her guests while they drank, assuring them that the mysterious beverage would help clear their heads and stem their anxiety.

'Did you see his child?' she asked Kate.

Looking up at Anai, Kate noticed the fearsome intensity in the old woman's eyes. For a moment, Kate was almost afraid of her.

'N-no. I did not…' How could she, when that child had been denied life? She sniffed, her lip trembled, but she refused to cry. The grief was not hers; her tears would not bring peace to her ancestors.

'Think, qitah!' Anai persisted. '*Remember*. You must have seen -'

'Anai, stop it!' David cried, and earned himself an admonishing scowl from the elderly witch.

'She has more to learn,' Anai continued, pointing at Kate. 'And she must forgive. She cannot move forward until she can forgive herself and those who hurt her. In both lifetimes.'

'We understand – her happiness is dependent on her ability to forgive,' David interjected, seeing Kate struggling to grasp the connotations of Anai's words. 'I think that's enough for one night. Thank you both for all you've done, but I think we should go home.' He looked at Kate sorrowfully, wishing that they could go back to Scotland and forget all about past lives and lost loves.

Anai glared at him, suddenly imperious. 'You do not decide for her!' she cried angrily and pointed at Kate. 'She is in need of understanding, as are you. There are lessons to learn from the past -'

Defensive anger rising within him, David took Kate's elbow and helped her to her feet. 'She needs to learn how to live in the present. The past is suffocating her, and clouding her judgement. She can't see what's in front of her because she's too busy moping about what's gone before!'

Taking Kate's hand, he led the bewildered woman to the front door, picking up the box of mementoes as he went. Remembering his manners, he took a deep breath and turned to Anai and Mina. The look of concern on their faces made him regret his outburst. 'I'm sorry – I don't mean to cause offence. We need time to process this – in private. Perhaps we could discuss this another time, when we've had time to think…'

After delivering the apposite farewell in Arabic, he bundled Kate into the Land Rover. She offered no protest or reprimand, just stared silently into the darkness as her head began to clear.

Halfway to the dig house, David parked on the side of the road and turned off the engine. Sighing heavily, he turned and opened his arms to Kate.

'I don't need to be coddled!' she huffed, clearly appalled by his rude behaviour at Anai's house.

'I *do*,' he replied, and pulled her into his arms. She remained belligerently rigid at first, and then relaxed against him.

'You shouldn't have done it!' she scolded. 'Did you see something awful? You don't have to tell me...'

David tried to put his experience into sensible phrases, still fearful that he might have been hallucinating. 'I was Captain Richard Yorke, cavalry officer of the 20th Hussars, but also an archaeologist. I knew Katherine Grahame as a child, and then we met again on the Amarna dig. It seems a friendship grew in the constant absence of her husband...' David smiled wistfully as he vividly recalled the diminutive Katherine Ford holding up a cavalry sword as if it weighed nothing at all. 'I – *he* was quite enamoured of the tiny brunette with the iron will and fiery temper. Not so taken with her arrogant, thoughtless husband...' He brushed his cheek against her hair. 'Kate, I don't know how to talk about this...'

'I know. I suppose we have to discover the lessons Anai claims we must learn...'

'Am I allowed to ask why you were so distressed?' He steeled himself for the answer.

Remembering Richard's mischievous smile and sparkling eyes, Kate smiled against David's chest. 'They were at a Hogmanay party. Edwin left to schmooze officials in order to extend the site boundaries, leaving me in Richard's care. He was so kind. I – she – felt faint because of the pregnancy and he realised that Edwin didn't know about the baby. He convinced her to tell Edwin.' She sighed. 'He said the nicest things...'

'Such as?'

'He told Katherine that Edwin would want to take her home to Edinburgh and look after her. That he would want to be with her throughout the pregnancy, to share -'

'To share every single moment. He would want to witness the birth, and be the first to hold his child. He would promise you both his undying love and protection until the breath left his body...'

Kate stared at David's shadowed face. 'How did you...?'

David's voice held a note of sadness. 'It's what *I* would do. It's what I *will* do, when the time comes.'

'That's what Richard said...' She pressed her lips against David's sweater, a secret kiss over his heart. Her feelings of longing at that moment were overwhelming – for David.

'Is that why you were upset?' David asked carefully. 'Because you remembered being pregnant?' Kate nodded slowly. 'I'm sorry, angel…' His arms tightened around her. 'Anai said you would regain what was lost. Perhaps that's what she was talking about…'

Kate was suddenly glad of the darkness. 'I don't think we should be discussing that particular topic.'

David smiled at her embarrassment. 'Then tell me more about this ball. Was Captain Yorke a good dancer?'

'Wonderful. Better even than Edwin Ford!'

'Very shrewd reply, Miss Grahame.'

Kate shifted to lift her face to his. 'He called her Katherine. Not Kate, or Katie. She liked it. And she thought he looked very handsome in his uniform. In fact, I think she may have had some…feelings for him.' *Or are they my feelings, transferred?*

'She had a crush on another man?' David feigned incredulity.

'I suppose she was lonely.' Kate sighed. 'Edwin was more ambitious than I thought. I've always held him up to be noble, a crusader who didn't need wealth or fame. I don't think that was the case. I think Katherine was becoming aware of Edwin's real priorities, and that's why she was scared to tell him about the baby. She feared he didn't love her enough…'

Kate paused as a feeling of apprehension crept up her spine. Throughout this latest regression, her love for Edwin had not seemed as all-consuming as it had been before. But there was a growing, hidden affection for Richard Yorke. 'You don't think that Katherine and Richard ever…?'

David's reply sounded definite. 'No. She was a good and loyal wife, even though her blind adoration for Ford was misguided. And Yorke was an honourable fool. I do, however, wonder what would have happened if Yorke had gone to Edinburgh instead of Ford…'

'Everything might have been different…' Kate sighed wistfully.

David pulled away suddenly, and his expression became stony in the faint light from the dashboard. 'This changes nothing,' he said firmly to the windscreen. 'I'm not going to run off and research what may have been my past life, so don't even suggest it. I don't care who I might have been; I care about who I am now and who I will be in the future! This knowledge will not govern the rest of my life – and it certainly won't hold me back! Besides, who's to say we weren't hallucinating? She drugged us, and the letters and photographs could have acted as some sort of autosuggestion. How do we know we didn't just see what we wanted to see?'

Kate sighed, tired of their wrangling with this subject. 'I get it. You're saying that all this time I've just been weak-minded and on drugs. How pathetic I am…' Absently, she folded her hands across her barren belly, remembering the strong feelings of protectiveness and anticipation. She jumped as David slammed his hand down on the steering wheel.

'That's not what I meant and you know it! Stop being so nauseatingly self-pitying!' Even in the darkness, David saw her eyes flash angrily.

The regression had rattled David. He was angry that, even in that other lifetime, he hadn't been allowed to be with the woman he loved.

He turned to face her, his eyes pleading for some form of comfort. 'Kate, up until I met you, my life had a sense of order. It might not have been the happiest existence, but I knew what was real and what was not. Now I've been forced to consider concepts that have no scientific foundation, and accept them as the truth. In so doing, I feel as though I'm losing my grasp of reality -'

'You make me feel like this is all my fault!' she cried defensively.

David snapped. 'It *is* your fault, damn it!' He heard her gasp at his frankness, but he was unable to rein in his temper. 'Christ, Kate, you've put me through hell these last nine months! And all because you've been wallowing in your misplaced grief over a *ghost*! Sometimes, I think you actually *enjoy* the drama of it!

'You've moaned and wailed about feeling trapped as Edwin's wife; you've complained about experiencing similar constraints in this life. But you don't seem to realise that you also set *your own* limitations!' His jaw clenched as he delivered a cruel barb. 'Perhaps you like it that way. Perhaps it's safer than pushing your boundaries and realising true freedom. Katherine bravely tried to escape her chains at every opportunity – a quality worthy of admiration. But you seem content to lie beneath yours and utter hollow protests when the going gets too tough.'

Her hurt look tore at his heart, but David was unable to silence his anguish. 'God, how I wish you'd never volunteered to help me with that lecture last February! Why couldn't you just have gone home to your husband and left me to admire you from a safe distance?'

'What are you talking about? You were in a relationship last February – and I was *married*!'

'A blind and deaf alien from a distant galaxy would have been able to see you were miserable with Mark! Our whole office knew it! And I wasn't happy, either. The day I discovered you were divorcing Mark I went home and broke up with Diane -'

'Don't say that! Your break-up isn't my fault -'

'You were the catalyst! And then – what happens? I spend months chasing you, only for you to block me continually. And yet, despite being repeatedly kicked by you, despite knowing about your ridiculous plan to find a resurrected Edwin Ford, I keep coming back for more! I'm such a damned fool!' Enraged, he glared at her. 'Have you ever once stopped to consider *my* feelings?'

Kate recoiled from his anger and the failings he had exposed in her character. Still, his temper had inflamed her own, and like a wounded animal, she offered an ill-considered defence. 'Well, tomorrow I'll do everyone a favour and go home! I'll resign from my job at the museum, and you won't have to see me again!'

'Yes, do that! Run away from me again! But this time, let's hope I have the good sense not to follow you like a masochistic lapdog!'

'I'm sure you'll be fine! After all, there are plenty of women desperate for your attention! I'm sure Mina will eagerly provide consolation! Or perhaps one of your esteemed American colleagues! Or even -'

Kate was silenced by David's lips pressing hard against hers, his hands pushing her back against the seat. She made a muffled sound of protest and tried to push against his chest, but he would not be deterred. He held her upper arms and kissed her with a fierce passion, months of frustration rising to the surface. He wanted to hurt her as she had hurt him; he wanted this cycle of unrequited love to end. He had tried to walk away from her, but their time apart had been dark and empty. A life without her would be meaningless. David's fingers tightened, holding her motionless as his lips devoured hers. Sadistically, as soon as he felt Kate respond to his kiss, he let her go and sat back.

'I'm sorry,' he muttered hoarsely. 'I shouldn't have done that. It won't happen again.'

Kate's fingers touched her stinging lips as she watched him wipe his mouth with the back of his hand, as if he wanted to erase their kiss. His insensitivity cut her to the quick, but she turned to stare blankly out of the window, grinding her teeth together, determined not to cry. David started the engine and drove recklessly through the night to the dig house.

Seeing Ethan leaning against the wall near the front door made Kate want to scream. As soon as David halted the vehicle, tyres screeching loudly in the silence of the desert, Kate jumped out and stalked into the house.

Ethan tactfully refrained from asking questions. Instead, he walked over to the car, where David sat in the driver's seat looking defeated.

'Steve took the students out to the campsite as you asked,' he informed David. 'If you've got what you need, I'll drive you to your tent and bring Steve back.' He scrutinised his friend's face. 'Or I could stay with you if you like.'

Shaking his head, David slid over to the passenger seat and gratefully let Ethan take the wheel. They drove in silence; once at the quiet campsite, David relieved a disgruntled Steven and sought the solitude of his tent.

When she crept into bed that night, Kate's mind was still reeling from David's ferocious outburst. His harsh words stung like a thousand tiny cuts. Shame sickened her, as she faced the stark truth behind his criticisms; she was guilty of all the charges he had made. He had acted as though he hated her, as though she made him utterly miserable. And yet, despite his cruelty, she had felt a moment's elation when he had kissed her, and wholly dismayed when he had broken contact. Miserably, she tried desperately to find a way to resolve this bleak state of affairs, one that would perhaps secure David's forgiveness.

At last, she dozed off, but a deep, peaceful sleep eluded her once more; Kate tossed and turned, strange dreams causing her to moan and call out. Finally, she woke, startled by the sound of a baby crying. Sitting up, she strained her ears and thought she heard the sound again. Pulling on boots and a sweater, she crept into the corridor.

Seemingly of their own accord, her feet started to move towards the Bone Room, where the newly excavated skeletons had been taken for examination before their journey to Cairo. Stopping outside the door, Kate listened but the only sound she could hear was the wind whistling outside. Without thinking, she opened the door and stepped inside, her fingers searching the wall for a light switch.

From the other side of the room, a lamp flicked on, causing Kate to jump and cry out in fright. From his chair in a corner, Ethan stared at her, his expression unreadable.

'You frightened the life out of me!' Kate exclaimed. 'Why are you sitting here in the dark?' It occurred to her that he might be sleepwalking again; she waited for a coherent response.

'I'm keeping watch,' he muttered, sounding wholly unconvincing.

'Do you often do that when you exhume bodies?'

'Actually, this is the first time.' For a moment, he looked perturbed. 'There's always the risk of burglary…'

'Is that why we have armed guards protecting the house?'

Ethan looked unhappily at the floor. 'Egypt's not the place it used to be.' He shook his head sadly and sighed. 'There's a storm coming…'

Kate chewed her lip, eyeing him warily. 'I'll leave you to it, then…'

He lifted his head, alert once more. 'Why are *you* here?'

'I – I thought I heard something…' In fact, now that she was here, she wanted to sit with the skeletons for a while as a mark of respect, even though to do so would fill her with an irrational fear. The bodies lay on a large table in the centre of the room, already resting in closed makeshift sarcophagi. The infant's coffin was painfully small.

'If you can't sleep, stay for a while. Perhaps we can bore each other into a dozy stupor.' Ethan gestured to a second chair, and she obediently sat down. 'You and David have had a fight?'

She merely shrugged, hugging herself; the room was uncomfortably cold, and Kate felt self-conscious in her blue pyjama bottoms embellished with cavorting sheep.

'Nothing to do with him playing happy families this afternoon, I suppose?'

'He's entitled to enjoy himself,' she muttered lamely. 'He works hard enough…'

Ethan chuckled. 'You're loyal even when you're mad at him!' He gazed at her intently. 'Friday, what you saw – you shouldn't read anything into it. David likes kids; he's always said he wants to be a father one day. I think he's almost ready. Sad, really…'

Sighing wearily, Kate stared at the small, pathetic coffin. Her brain was too full of morbid thoughts, and too tired to think rationally. She longed for the comfort of her own house and her own bed. And her mother…

'Don't *you* want kids?' Ethan asked, yawning.

She glanced at him briefly, choosing her words carefully. 'My ex-husband didn't want children…'

'And you?'

'I…I had hoped…' *Whatever I say will be met with derision. I can't talk to him.* 'I have a niece and nephew. What about you?'

He looked surprised at the question. 'Me?' His lips twisted in a sardonic smile. 'Oh, you want to know if I have a horde of offspring scattered across the globe…' Kate shrugged again, refusing to appear embarrassed or apologetic. 'As far as I'm aware, I'm not a father. And as for the future…' He frowned, and his eyes grew distant. 'There's too much work to be done here…'

'How many years have you worked in Amarna?'

Ethan tilted his head, calculating. 'Dave and I first came out as students. I've worked here almost constantly for about ten years, although this is the first time I've been field director. Dave has other interests as well as Egyptology, so he's travelled all over the place. And of course, he likes to teach…' He made a disapproving face.

'Do you like what you do?' she asked, and he got the feeling she was referring to more than his career. 'I mean, working in Amarna all the time?'

'Working here is like a calling I can't ignore, but…' *Something is missing.* Uncomfortable because she was leading him towards introspection, Ethan stood up. 'Well, I'm sufficiently bored. We'd better get some sleep; we have to be up at first light, which is only a few hours away.' He held open the door for her. 'Goodnight, Friday.'

It wasn't the last time Kate saw him that night. An hour or so before dawn, intuition invaded her sleep to warn her of a presence in her room. Jolting awake, she found him standing by her bed, his eyes staring blankly down at her. Choking off a cry of alarm, she sat up, intending to help him back to his room, which was one of the guest rooms that opened into the courtyard.

In the grey light, she could see the look of despondency on his face. Slowly, as if the movement pained him, he reached out to touch her face through the mosquito net. Desperate for some form of comfort, she held his hand between her own and kissed it gently. Ethan turned and walked out of the room, leaving Kate to weep quietly in her lonely bed.

CHAPTER 7

Saturday December 15, 2012

From her lonely position at the top of the tower, Kate looked over the eccentric crenellations at the forbidding landscape. Sounds below broke the pre-dawn silence, and she watched disconsolately as David and Mina rode towards the cliffs on two fine Arab horses, creating a cloud of sand in their wake. She hugged herself, shivering in air not yet warmed by the sun, feeling physically and emotionally weak.

'Does it bother you?' a deep voice asked from behind her.

Kate didn't turn to greet Ethan as he came to stand beside her, a mug of steaming coffee in his hand. Mulling over his nightly visits to her room, Kate considered it unwise to mention it to him. There was enough tension in the air without adding more fuel to the fire.

She shrugged. 'Why should it bother me?'

Ethan eyed the small woman beside him, whose slim body was swamped by a huge hooded sweatshirt. She had pulled the hood up over her face, and he couldn't see her eyes. Not that he was able to figure her out by looking into her eyes; Kate Grahame was still a mystery to him. Before meeting her, he had assumed Kate to be a manipulative femme fatale who was using her feminine wiles to keep David under her spell. So far, he had seen none of these traits in this quiet, shy young woman.

There had been many women in Ethan's life, but none of them had held his attention long enough for him to attempt to empathise with them. Perhaps it was for David's sake that he wanted to get to know Kate a little better.

'You're a strange pair,' he commented, swallowing a mouthful of coffee.

Turning away from the two receding figures in the distance, she sighed. 'I've already told you, we're not a pair.'

Ethan caught a glimpse of her face, and saw a tortured expression flit across her countenance. Once again, he was struck by a feeling of familiarity. He was unable to understand why he needed her to think well of him; this inexplicable influence she had on him was disconcerting. All his adult life he had divided women into two camps: those he wanted to bed, and those he didn't. Kate was in a group of her own.

He watched her walk slowly towards the stairs, and an idea entered his head that drove him to talk without thinking. 'I'm going to Akhenaten's tomb to check on the rate of deterioration,' he called after her. 'You can come along if you like.' He frowned, surprised at himself.

Kate stopped and half-turned towards him, her gaze focusing somewhere around his feet. 'I can't,' she muttered and continued her escape, taking another step towards the stairs.

It pained him to see her shrink from his gaze, obviously desperate to be away from him. No woman had ever displayed such blatant antipathy towards him. Even her body language emanated hostility.

Ethan contemplated her discomfort as he finished his coffee. 'I see my reputation precedes me,' he observed. 'You've nothing to worry about; David's my best friend – you'll be quite safe. Bring a notebook, in case I need you to take dictation.' He saw her raise an elegant dark eyebrow and offered her a self-deprecating smile. 'I can't make notes to save myself.'

'I should stay with the students,' Kate stammered. 'David's taking us to a tomb to practise epigraphy, and he wants to get an early start…'

Ethan nodded towards the cliffs. 'David's busy. And Marianne has offered to get your students organised for their trip, although I suspect you've already briefed them…' He had observed Kate's work methods, and knew she took her trumped-up role seriously.

'Yes,' she murmured glumly. 'I've already done my "liaising" bit…'

The tone of her voice suggested that Kate was beginning to realise that the role of 'student liaison' was not a recognised position at all, but one David had invented for his own benefit. Nevertheless, Ethan admired the rapport she had built with the students while still maintaining her authority.

'And I hear you've also been persuaded to write some of the students' field notes…'

'They asked me to check their field notes before they submit them to David. If I can save them from an ear-bashing over a misplaced semicolon, then I'm happy to help them out.'

'Alright then, but don't be a pushover. Now, go and get ready – I want to get out of here.'

Nodding meekly in acquiescence, she returned to her room to prepare a bag.

The Royal Wadi was roughly five kilometres northeast of the dig house, an indentation in the cliffs between the north and south tombs. They sped along the road in the jeep, the reddening cliffs rising on either side as they drove towards the sunrise. Eventually, they turned left into a narrower valley and travelled on for a short distance before Ethan slowed and parked at the side of the road. The silence around them was intimidating as they approached Akhenaten's tomb. It had been built facing east, presumably so the king could begin his afterlife by walking back into the world in the direction of the rising sun.

The custodian awaited them, a tall Egyptian in a dark blue galabeya and matching cap, who toted a rifle over one shoulder. Nodding to Ethan in greeting, he opened the locked entrance gates as Kate drew out her camera and took a couple of pictures.

The caretaker remained guarding the entrance as Ethan led the way down a long flight of steps, lit inadequately by lights fixed almost at ceiling height. As they progressed deeper, Ethan switched on a torch whose beam disappeared after a few metres.

Due to the poor quality of the stone in the region, the walls of Amarna tombs had been plastered first and then decorated. Over the centuries the plaster had decayed, and the scenes that had been expertly carved into the walls were badly damaged. And so these tombs were almost bereft of the stunning artwork that graced those found in other parts of Egypt.

Ethan stopped occasionally to scrutinise some of the faded illustrations that had survived at the top of the walls. Amarna was famous for its art, a softer and more natural style than the rigid, precise painting used by previous generations. Akhenaten's artists had lovingly decorated tiles, walls and paving with images of birds in flight, bulrushes and flowers swaying in the breeze, and scenes of daily life in beautiful colours.

As they walked carefully and silently into the flank of the hill, the staircase ended on a brief landing. A steep ramp followed, which seemed to lead into a dark nothingness. Ethan remarked that some of the light bulbs had blown since his last visit and would need to be replaced. Kate paused on the landing and took a deep breath of stale air, her fingers touching the cold limestone of the nearest wall. As she followed Ethan down the ramp, she became increasingly disorientated, and her head began to spin slightly. As though he sensed her unease, Ethan stopped and turned around.

'Are you claustrophobic?' he asked sharply.

Shaking her head, Kate swallowed hard, unable to explain why she felt so strange – as if a part of her was no longer in her body. Bringing her attention back to her immediate surroundings, she realised they had stopped before a dark opening in the wall on their right. Kate knew that the passageway beyond this doorway led to an unfinished suite of rooms assumed to be an additional royal tomb.

'Nefertiti's burial suite,' she announced, with absolute certainty. She tried to steady her breathing as she felt the walls and ceiling closing in on her.

'Like so many of the tombs here, the chambers were never finished,' Ethan supplied. 'It's generally accepted that Queen Tiye – Akhenaten's mother – would have been buried here, too. But yes, I've always thought those rooms were Nefertiti's...' His voice trailed off, and he started walking again.

The ramp ended at another landing, and they stepped into a room measuring about five metres square with a ceiling of about three metres high. Kate followed the beam of Ethan's torch as it travelled over the walls, highlighting scenes of a tragic, premature death. The reliefs showed Akhenaten and Nefertiti grieving over the body of a girl who lay on a bed, the sun disc presiding over their mourning. Although the figures were now barely visible, and the royal features had been defaced, their grief pervaded the air. Meketaten had been the second daughter of Akhenaten and Nefertiti, and she had died in her early teens. The scenes in the chamber also depicted a wet nurse tending a baby, suggesting that the princess had died in childbirth.

Two short passageways in the far wall led to a small, unfinished room reputed to be a storage room. This room led on to a small funerary chamber with a much lower ceiling; Ethan bowed his head a little as he stood inside the room and examined more scenes of mourning. Aware that he had brought Kate here on the pretext of giving her a job to do, he dictated some notes on the ongoing deterioration of the room and the woeful state of illumination. He had visited this tomb many times over the years, seeing it only through the eyes of an archaeologist. But today he had felt compelled to bring Kate, and now they seemed to share a sense of foreboding. The atmosphere was thick with the stench of failure, both ancient and current. Suddenly, Ethan wanted to leave and return to the dig house, where everyone believed him to be a shallow wretch and treated him accordingly.

Another steep flight of steps brought them to the well chamber, the purpose of which had been to protect the pharaoh's funerary chamber from floods. A brick wall had originally sealed the burial room beyond the well. When the tomb was discovered in 1892, the wall was destroyed. The limestone bricks were used to fill the well so that funerary goods could be removed from the burial hall. The well chamber had once borne inscriptions and reliefs of the king and queen making offerings to the Aten with their six daughters. Now only meagre traces remained.

The final, short flight of steps led into the desecrated burial chamber of Akhenaten himself. It was a large room with a high ceiling, and a platform along the left side, edged with two square pillars. A plinth in the centre of the floor marked the place where the king's sarcophagus had been laid to rest. Apart from some badly eroded inscriptions near the ceiling, all artwork had been destroyed shortly after the king's death in 1336BC. Perhaps in order to provide something of a happy ending to the story of the heretic pharaoh, some historians hypothesised that the king's body had been removed by his son, Tutankhamun, and taken to a safer location in the Valley of the Kings.

Since the tomb had been looted in antiquity, there had been little left of value for modern archaeologists to find. The red granite outer sarcophagus had been put on display outside the museum in Cairo, and up until recently had been used as a receptacle for litter and cigarette ends by careless passers-by. The inner coffin had been smashed in hatred by the pharaoh's own people; remnants had been found scattered on the floor of the chamber when the tomb had been discovered. However, the ancient thieves and vandals had left behind over two hundred shabti figures, and fragments from an alabaster canopic chest, all of which were now on public display.

'There used to be scenes of women mourning the king's death on the wall,' Ethan told her, his voice echoing as he stood in the middle of the chamber. 'But now all that's left is up there.' Tilting his head back, he pointed at the fragile gypsum plaster at the top of the wall, which bore the titles of Akhenaten and Nefertiti.

'Destroying the faces of Nefertiti and Akhenaten was a vicious act of hatred,' Ethan mused, reaching out to touch the wall. He glanced at Kate then looked back at the vandalised scene on the wall in front of him. 'The ancient Egyptians believed that the soul worked through the face, the eyes, the nose, the ears and mouth. The vandals sought to destroy the souls of the pharaoh and his wife, so they hacked off the images of their faces.'

Not sure how to respond, or if he even cared about her opinion, Kate stood quietly and waited for him to continue.

'History's dissolving into the desert as we speak,' he muttered gloomily, and glanced once more at his silent companion. 'You probably wish your ancestor had found it...'

Kate stood beside one of the pillars, feeling humbled by her surroundings but aware of a throbbing pain emanating from the back of her head. 'Edwin did his best,' she murmured and looked away as he stared at her, his eyebrows knitting together in consternation.

'Is that *your* ambition?' she asked softly. 'To find an undiscovered tomb full of riches?'

He snorted derisively. 'Are we not all the same?' He spread his arms wide, encompassing his profession. 'We may tell the world that we want to educate and find the truth, but all we really want is fame and glory.'

A feeling of nausea rose within Kate, and she sat down on the platform. The atmosphere was becoming oppressive. 'I don't believe you...' She took a bottle of water from her bag and sipped, grimacing when she discovered the water was tepid. 'David's not like that - '

'Money – and lots of loose women...' he continued, but he sounded less confident as he gazed down at Kate, who wrapped her arms around her raised knees and lowered her head. 'Are you feeling alright?'

'I'm fine. Just feeling a bit sick…'

'I assume it's not morning sickness?' His tone was mildly sarcastic.

'Most definitely not.' Kate felt her cheeks flush. 'I missed breakfast, and it's stuffy in here.'

Ethan swept the torch beam around the chamber once more. 'Well, I'm done. We can go.' He turned to see her take a small sample bottle from her bag, and fill it with earth from the floor. 'What are you doing?' he asked, surprised.

'Taking it home,' she replied.

'Are you going to put it on your ancestor's grave?' Ethan asked, giving her a curious look. 'I suppose that's…nice…if a little odd.'

Breathing deeply to combat her queasiness, Kate stood unsteadily and leaned against the pillar. Ethan came to her side, and she waited for him to roll his eyes in disgust. 'I suppose I just reinforce your belief that women shouldn't come on expeditions…' she said weakly.

Taking her elbow, he began to lead her towards the well chamber. 'I have no objections to women on expeditions,' he told her, for once speaking gently. 'I've worked with some very clever women. But I would never bring along someone I cared about; it would be too much of a distraction.' He hesitated. 'Not that I'm ever likely to be in that position…'

They continued in silence, up the stairs, up the steep ramp and the last flight of steps. Kate felt an enormous weight on her chest, and swallowed the bile that rose in her throat. When they finally stepped out into the dazzling sunlight, she took in a massive gulp of fresh air. Ethan commanded her to sit on the custodian's folding chair in the shade of the modern concrete structure that marked the tomb's entrance. Retrieving a packet of biscuits from the jeep, he paced the dirt track as Kate ate an impromptu breakfast. She suppressed the urge to apologise for her weakness, but felt pathetic nonetheless.

'Did you drink something at Anai's last night?' he asked her sharply. 'Something she said was a local brew?'

When Kate nodded unhappily, Ethan cursed at the ground. 'She spiked your drink. Did David take it, too?'

'Yes!' Kate began to panic. 'Has she made us ill on purpose?' She stared at Ethan. 'Doctor Forbes, is Anai a witch?'

Ethan lowered himself to the ground, sitting cross-legged at her feet as though it were the most natural position in the world. Kate watched him uncertainly, hoping he could provide answers without judgement.

'You have to understand that witchcraft has been practised in Egypt for thousands of years,' he began. 'There is no dividing line between white and black magic. The Egyptians used magic for personal gain and the benefit of others; they used magic to make the crops grow. By reciting specific incantations in a particular tone of voice, they believed they could encourage the gods to do their bidding. The Book of the Dead is full of spells and incantations, and ancient Egyptian doctors used magic to treat the sick. It was just an accepted way of life and, in many parts of the country, it still is. There's a book about Egyptian magic in your room; you should read it…'

Ethan paused; how had he known there was such a book in Kate's room? A quick glance in her direction showed that she was pondering the same question. Taking a deep breath, Ethan resumed his monologue in the hope he would distract her.

'Anai makes up spells and potions in exchange for money, or food, or some other small gift. Women go to her to have their fortunes told, or to help them conceive, or to have her cast a love spell on some unsuspecting guy. I've seen her prowling around the ferry port or the visitor centre, using her "skills" to extort money from gullible tourists. You've heard her talk about "returning souls", right? Well, you wouldn't believe the number of reincarnated scribes and water-bearers we've had through here! In fact, the pharaoh himself has been back for a look at his kingdom, disguised as a Dutch television producer. The Suefy family ate well for a month, after *his* visit!'

'Can't you do anything to stop her?'

'I have to keep the locals sweet,' he told her, not realising that Kate had recently heard those exact words from her soulmate while under hypnosis. 'These people are poor, and they have families to feed. Anai's not doing any harm, so I tend to turn a blind eye. But should she injure those under my supervision, or the people I care about – well, then she's crossed the line, and I *will* do something about it.'

He gazed at her intently, feeling his defences weaken a little; there were few people in Ethan's life who knew the man beneath the façade, but David's would-be lover was chipping away at Ethan's armour.

'I'll talk to her,' he decided. 'And perhaps threaten to invite Christian missionaries to stay at the dig house for a season. She would consider that a blasphemous violation of her territory.'

Kate observed a smile edged with sadness, as if he were burdened with regret. His kindness, though long awaited, was a double-edged sword. Even so, she tentatively returned his smile, handing him the packet of biscuits.

'She said the wine was mixed with spices and herbs,' Kate revealed, watching him devour a biscuit. 'Do you think it was harmful? Did she give you the same thing?'

Ethan shrugged. 'Have you had trouble sleeping?' he asked. 'Are you having strange dreams, or hearing strange sounds in the night? Are you having trouble concentrating?'

'All of those things…' Kate glanced down at her feet and waited for him to pronounce her insane.

'Then yes, she gave me the same thing. I think it must have been some kind of homeopathic hallucinogen made from plants. I should go and check her vegetable plot for magic mushrooms…'

Noting his troubled expression, Kate knew she had to tread carefully. 'Why did she give it to *you*?'

'I have no idea why she would drug us; she certainly wouldn't rob us while we were out of it – no satisfaction in *that*. I was invited to dinner, and she gave me her home brew. She's a nosey old crone, so she always asks lots of questions. She went on about me needing to face a crime I had committed in a past incarnation. Next thing I knew, it was morning, and I had spent the night on the floor in front of the fire. That in itself didn't bother me – it's not the first time I've passed out through drink and woken up in a strange place.

'Anai wanted to know about any dreams I'd experienced, but…but I couldn't remember the details. It took a few days for the effects to wear off, but I'm mostly fine now. Obviously, she must have given you two a weaker dose because David was able to drive you home. Do you remember what happened?'

Here was her opportunity to tell him everything. She opted for the safer, more cowardly option. 'Like you, she wanted to regress us to a past life. There was chanting, and incense, and we drifted off to sleep for a little while. I don't remember much, just that she sent us home with that same order to forgive so that we can move on. What do you think that means? And aren't you the least bit concerned?'

Ethan made a sound of contempt. 'We all seek forgiveness for *something*, and we all need to forgive *somebody*. There's nothing portentous in her words, just ambiguity. In my case – well, she doesn't like me, and she can't manipulate me, so naturally I'm destined to be eternally miserable because of my wickedness. Although she also claims that if I change my ways, I can be "saved" – somehow.' He gave her a lopsided smile. 'Take her with a pinch of salt, Kate. But be wary around her, for she's a wily, scheming old bat.'

There was a short silence, while Kate struggled to decide what she should do or say next.

'Do you believe in past lives?' she blurted.

He stared at her intently. 'What I believe is that this life I'm living is hard enough. I've made too many mistakes in *this* lifetime; I don't need to know I've been just as stupid in another one.'

By way of avoiding further difficult questions, Ethan checked his watch, got to his feet and stretched. He had a short conversation with the custodian, who had locked up the tomb and was waiting for them to leave before making his departure. Kate's nausea had passed, but a headache throbbed at her temples and the back of her skull. She rubbed at the back of her neck, seeking some relief from the pain, wondering if any good would come from this conversation with her past soulmate. At the very least, she hoped they could call a truce to their rancour. Then she would only have to deal with David's enmity.

'Well, back to the joys of an archaeologist's life...' Ethan said, in a tone of voice that was anything but joyful. He remained standing in the same spot, contemplating a few puffy white clouds in the morning sky.

'Are you happy, Doctor Forbes?' Kate asked at last. 'With your way of life? You sound as though you have misgivings...'

Shifting his gaze from the heavens, he looked perturbed by the question. 'If you're going to start asking personal questions again, you should probably call me Ethan.' He pursed his lips. 'I like being an Egyptologist. But, in all honesty, I'm not enjoying being field director...'

Kate understood. 'You can't stand the desk work or the bureaucracy; you'd rather be in the field, making discoveries, travelling the world.' She couldn't resist a gentle dig. 'Meeting new "people"...'

Ethan's bark of laughter was self-mocking. 'Either you're preternaturally intuitive or David's been talking about me! Archaeology is my life, and I imagine it always will be. I'm not the type to settle down and have a family.'

'Not ever? How can you be so sure?'

'There are so many beautiful, willing women in the world. Monogamy is not for me. I'm not David.' A coldness crept into his tone, and his expression bore a hint of cruelty. 'And you're hardly the best advertisement for married life...'

Ethan faltered as he saw her stricken look and realised he had gone too far. Repentantly, he leaned towards her and reached out to touch her arm. 'I'm sorry, sweetheart. I didn't mean -'

Kate gaped at him, shocked to hear the endearment. She rose to her feet, anxious to return to the house and its throng of people.

'I'm sorry,' Ethan muttered, sounding bewildered. 'I didn't mean to say that. I don't know why -'

'Forget it,' she interrupted. 'We should be getting back to the house...'

'Yes,' he agreed, worried about the repercussions should she tell David about his faux pas. 'We definitely should.'

The sense of unease that had plagued them all morning worsened as Ethan drove the final few metres along the road to the dig house. David was waiting outside the building, pacing irritably beside a canvas-covered truck as the students loaded their rucksacks into the back.

'He's angry,' Kate blurted. 'I should've stayed -'

'He can't go to the tomb without an inspector,' Ethan told her, in an attempt to allay her fear. 'And Moumdah is in the car behind us.'

Ethan slowed and turned into the unmarked driveway, aware that David now stood glaring thunderously at them. He deliberately parked the jeep at the far end of the row of vehicles, partly to annoy his friend, partly to buy them another minute while he considered warning Kate of David's job offer. As a rule, Ethan avoided involving himself in any kind of relationship, let alone someone else's; it would be best not to become more embroiled in his friend's problematic love life. On the other hand, wasn't it his duty to help?

Before he could entangle himself any further, he heard an angry rap on Kate's window followed by the opening of her door.

'You're still here then?' David asked acidly.

Half-expecting Kate to run away in tears, Ethan was surprised when she turned to him calmly and spoke with quiet dignity. 'Thank you for the tour, Doctor Forbes. I'll have those notes typed up by the end of the day and leave them on your desk.' She wasn't quite quick enough to hide the slight trembling of her lower lip as she exited the vehicle, avoiding David's burning gaze.

'We'll be leaving in ten minutes,' David told her, obviously disconcerted. Kate didn't reply as she headed towards the house.

'The inspector will no doubt wish to avail himself of our hospitality,' Ethan called after her as he climbed out of the jeep. 'Get some breakfast.' She kept walking, so Ethan raised his voice. 'That's not a suggestion, Friday! You're no use if you're faint from hunger! And take something for that headache!' He turned to face his friend's ire, sighing wearily.

'You can't just commandeer my staff,' David blustered. Then Ethan's words finally sank in. 'Is she ill?'

'I think she took a dizzy spell in Akhenaten's tomb. She told me she'd missed breakfast.'

David looked thoughtfully towards the house. 'She stops eating when she's upset...'

'Really? Well, I wonder what could be making her upset...' Ethan's voice dripped sarcasm. 'She saw you riding off into the desert with Mina – what conclusions do you think she might have drawn? I took her with me to distract her. Why are you acting like such an idiot? And what the hell happened at Anai's house? I've heard all about her making you swig from a poisoned chalice – another reason's Kate's not feeling well. But, apart from your botched hypnotherapy, something obviously went wrong between you and Kate last night. She's miserable, by the way.'

Feeling suddenly angry with David, Ethan began to walk towards the inspector's car. 'You know what? I don't want to know about your issues. But if you want to monopolise her attention, stop sneaking off with other women!'

Weary from two nights of camping in the unfriendly desert, the students wilted under the added stress caused by their professor's foul mood. David barked at them to cease their endless dawdling and get into the truck. Cowed, the trainee archaeologists helped each other into the back of the vehicle and took their seats on the hard benches screwed into the floor. Even though it was still early, the sun beat down on them mercilessly; everything they touched felt hot, even the breeze felt like a hot breath on their skin. By comparison, the photographic equipment required for the trip was safely stored in the cooler, air-conditioned cabin.

Moumdah and one of the guards took refuge in the inspector's car. Keen to get the trip over with, David waited impatiently for Kate, and was about to go back into the house to retrieve her when she rushed out of the front door looking dishevelled. His lips pressed tightly together, he held open the passenger door for her but she rejected the gesture and walked past him to join the group in the back of the truck. Fuming, David climbed into the driver's seat and banged the door. As they travelled to Meryre's tomb in the north cliffs, tension hovered over the group like a black, ominous cloud.

Meryre's burial place was one of the largest tombs in Amarna but like all the others, it was in a pitiful state. After the fall of Akhenaten's empire, the tomb had been altered to accommodate the Coptics who had resided there for a time. One of the most beautiful tombs in Amarna due to its size and craftsmanship, the monument had mysteriously been left unfinished; the builders had never constructed a funeral shaft.

The group parked the vehicles and carried their equipment up a long flight of steps to the entrance, where a painted sign announced Meryre as 'The High Priest of the Aten, the Fan-Bearer on the King's Right Hand and the Chancellor of the King'. The builders had cut into the cliff face, creating a courtyard in front of the door. The overhanging stone acted as an awning over the doorway, which was fitted with an iron gate.

A custodian waited in a tiny square of shade as the sun-flushed group approached. David exchanged pleasantries with the elderly caretaker, and handed over the obligatory baksheesh. The students waited impatiently to enter the tomb and escape the heat of the sun. As the guard took up his post in the shade with the custodian, David began the day's lesson.

Just inside the entrance to the tomb, he pointed out a relief of the tomb's owner. Meryre stood with arms outstretched in adoration, reciting the prayer to the Aten that was carved around him. The ceiling was divided into three rectangles of typical Egyptian friezes, muted blue patterns on a faded yellow background.

They stepped into a square antechamber, softly lit to protect the artwork, where more inscriptions could be seen. One wall was decorated with a huge bouquet of flowers arranged in tiers, the blue and red colouring still faintly visible. Naturally, the sun disc was also in evidence. The next room – the first hypostyle hall – made the students gasp in one collective intake of breath.

Inexplicably, David moved through the pillared room to the second hypostyle hall. Although similar to the first in design, this semi-dark chamber was undecorated and unfinished. The pillars, though impressive, were irregular. The floor, too, was uneven, and the shrine beyond had not been completely excavated and lay in darkness.

Clearly distracted, David gave only a brief explanation of these two chambers before moving back into the first hall, where a small wooden table and chair had been set up near a power outlet. As he gratefully removed the heavy equipment bag from across his aching shoulders, he let the awestruck students gaze around the room. It was lit from floor level, the better to display the artwork covering the walls and the two pillars that graced the right side of the chamber.

Quietly, Kate unpacked the heavy digital camera and folding tripod. She kept her eyes diligently on her work, but David's gaze was often drawn to her, and he frequently found himself stuttering, or losing his chain of thought altogether as he tried to recall the information he wished to impart.

'Let's look at the entrance to this room,' he decided suddenly, beckoning the group to the short passage leading from the antechamber to the hall.

Some of the students exchanged puzzled glances; their professor usually followed a strict, organised lesson plan and rarely digressed.

'You'll notice on the west wall that Meryre is facing the entrance in an attitude of prayer -'

'I think you mean the *east* wall, professor,' Julian interrupted, sounding mildly patronising. 'The *west* wall depicts the priest's *wife.*'

One of the boys cleared his throat in embarrassment; David's sour expression warned them of his aggravation. Taking a deep breath that signified his impatience, he resumed his lecture.

'On the *east* wall, we can see Meryre reciting the prayer known as the Small Hymn to the Aten – as opposed to the Great Hymn of the Aten. Does anyone know what the Small Hymn is about?'

Julian fairly puffed himself up. 'It's about the solar cycle and its consequences on creation,' he said, looking at each member of the group in turn as though *he* were the teacher. 'Then there's a bit about the unique relationship between Akhenaten and the Aten.'

David nodded, but his bleak mood demanded a dig at the arrogant student. He pointed at the wall in question. 'Can you translate any of it?' In the soft, green-hued lighting, he saw Julian's face fall. 'No? Something to work on, then…'

He heard Kate's irritable sigh as he turned to the opposite wall to continue the tutorial. 'As you pointed out, Mister Noble, on the *west* wall we can see Meryre's wife, the lady Tenra, described as "the great favourite of the Lady of the Two Lands" -'

Julian did not like being humiliated. Testosterone insisted upon revenge. 'I think her name was Tinro -'

A nerve in David's jaw twitched; the other five students seemed to take a step backwards. 'Thank you, Mister Noble,' he said coldly. 'Since you feel qualified to educate the group, please take over the lesson.'

The party watched in disbelief as David strode from the hall and headed out of the tomb.

Striving to remain calm and efficient, Kate gathered her wits and stood up. 'Right,' she began, harnessing the attention of the wide-eyed students. 'What you're going to do today is practise your drawing skills.'

Studying the walls of the imposing chamber, she attempted to find the illustrations David had planned to use. It saddened her to see how brutally the people of Amarna had hammered out evidence of their pharaoh and his wife; the damage was everywhere she looked. One wall depicted the investiture of the high priest; Akhenaten and Nefertiti had been savagely removed from the sunken relief.

A large part of the west wall and some of the north wall showed a breathtaking representation of the royal family going to the temple of Aten, surrounded by adoring subjects. The royal couple drove chariots pulled by magnificent horses wearing plumed headdresses. Again, the king and queen had been deprived of their features. Nevertheless, the whole scene gave the impression of movement and splendour, the horses still showing a faint red tinge. The people had been carved with realistic features, including the famous paunch and, in some cases, wrinkles.

Furnishing the students with squared paper and pencils, Kate commanded them to sketch the journey to the temple, taking a section of the wall each. Throughout history, archaeologists and epigraphists had recorded friezes and inscriptions in this manner, the drawings updated on each expedition. On this occasion, photographs would be taken of the mural and, on their return to the house, David would demonstrate the latest epigraphy software. This new computer programme used digital images to provide 3D representations of inscriptions, wall art and artefacts.

Leaving the students to work under the scrutiny of the inspector, Kate went to find David. The professor was standing some way down the flight of steps, gazing out across the shimmering desert. From this viewpoint, all of Amarna could be seen: the Nile, the villages, the lush areas of cultivation that gave way to the desert and the remains of Akhetaten. In the distance, the southern cliffs curved in the direction of the dig house.

David's stared in the direction of the North Palace, once a grand palace built for a beautiful queen. In one of his dreams from the previous night, he had been in a palace with his own beautiful queen, entwined with her in a soft bed, her silky auburn hair fanning across the silken pillows…

'Are you listening to me?'

Kate's angry voice disrupted his reverie, and he turned, briefly startled as his eyes fell on her *shorter* hair. David had taken the box from Anai's house to his tent the night before, and had spent a long time looking at the photograph of Katherine Ford gazing out over Amarna. In his dreams, the two women had become interchangeable and on one occasion, he had found himself in a cavalryman's uniform. He wondered if the dream had been the result of Anai's herbal concoction. Or had he truly stirred memories of a past life? Either way, David felt disturbed, disorientated and angry.

'*Professor Young!*'

Finally, David crawled reluctantly into the present but found his eyes wandering to Kate's lips. His brain brought him the vivid memory of a fiercely passionate kiss taken in anger. With startling clarity, he remembered how her lips had felt and tasted. He wanted to repeat the experience, over and over again.

'Your behaviour back there was completely unprofessional!' she berated him. 'Get back inside and do your job properly!'

He found himself incapable of an apology, or indeed any suitable response. Each day he felt less in control of himself, resenting his obligations, his environment, and his companions. Kate had placed him in an intolerable situation, and yet he couldn't bear to let her go. Not when there might still be hope…

'I thought you wanted to leave…' he muttered reprovingly, cringing inwardly at his immaturity.

Kate hesitated, looking nervously over his shoulder as though she couldn't bear to look at him. 'I have responsibilities here,' she replied. 'To the students. And to the museum.'

Tilting his head, David waited for her to add that she had a responsibility to Ethan, to Edwin, to *him*. But Kate would not give him the satisfaction.

Finally, their eyes met, sparking an undeniable need. David's eyes narrowed as Kate licked her lips. A noise below alerted them to a group of tourists alighting from a minibus a hundred feet below on the plain. Slowly, David began to ascend the steps towards Kate, his eyes never leaving her face.

As she crossed her arms across her chest, David spotted bruises on both her upper arms. Taking hold of one elbow, he lifted her arm to examine the purple marks that resembled thumbprints.

He stared from the marks to her face, horrified and immediately contrite. 'Did I do that?' he whispered.

Rather than sounding injured or fearful, Kate's lowered voice sounded peeved. 'Yes you did!'

'Christ, I'm sorry! I won't -'

Pulling her arm out of his grasp, Kate waved away his apology with one hand. 'Oh, you already told me – you won't do it again. You made it quite clear you didn't like kissing me.' She pointed to his hand as he absently wiped his dry lips. 'See, you're still wiping yourself clean!' Huffily, she turned her back on him and pretended to admire the scenery.

'I probably didn't come up to Edwin Ford's standards, anyway,' David groused.

She spun back to face him. '*Child!*' she spat reproachfully, her eyes fixing on those luscious, skilful lips. Thinking about his kiss made her weak at the knees, and that made her even angrier. 'Apart from you, I've only been kissed by one man in my life – and it wasn't Edwin Ford!' She glared at him. When she stamped one foot in a fit of temper, David laughed, mocking her.

'Oh, please, go on and make fun of me, too!' Kate cried, enraged. Pouting, she pushed past him with her chin in the air. From their vantage point, the security guard and custodian chortled at this amusing scene.

'You should be glad we have an audience,' David muttered darkly, making her halt and turn to glare at him. This new revelation added to the unbearable tension between them. Her inept ex-husband had been the only man to claim her; she was almost an innocent. His eyes glittered and darkened with a sudden, untimely desire to kiss those pouting lips again this very second.

'You're all talk!' Kate huffed and sashayed back into the tomb.

Momentarily frozen as he watched her swaying hips, David bounded after her and caught up as she entered the silent antechamber. Catching her by the wrist, he pulled her to a halt and manoeuvred her against the wall.

'Our infuriating circumstances prevent me from taking more definite action,' he informed her, his voice barely more than a whisper as his eyes burned into hers. Reaching behind her, he held both her wrists tightly. 'Believe me, if I'd taken you up on your offer in Cairo, you'd have forgotten all about all those other "responsibilities" by now.'

Kate's face was a mask of furious defiance. 'Oh, you're so full of yourself!' she hissed. 'Did Diane like this type of behaviour?' She wriggled, futilely trying to break free from his vice-like grip.

'Are you asking about my physical relationship with Diane?'

'Of course not, you arrogant thug!'

He leaned down to whisper in her ear. 'It was energetic. Acrobatic.' He took a deep breath. 'And completely choreographed. There was no spontaneity. And no intimacy. In fact, I don't even recall what she felt like…'

David let go of her wrists, his hands encircling her waist. 'Now tell me, *Katherine*, did your husband ever manage to ignite that fire you keep so carefully suppressed?'

Kate shoved him away roughly, eyes aflame with rage and repulsion. 'You're disgusting! You get more like Ethan every day!'

'And you're lying when you insist that Mark was the first man to kiss you.' He smiled mysteriously as if he knew she was nursing a secret.

As the first tourists reached the courtyard, Kate stumbled back to the students.

CHAPTER 8

Upon their return to the dig house, David herded the group into the room Kate had been using to digitise the old records. With an indifference that perplexed his students, the professor uploaded the photographs taken at Meryre's tomb and demonstrated the new epigraphy software. The cold, objective images were then compared to the students' sketches. Once the lesson was over, David sent the class for an early lunch but ordered his assistant to remain in the room.

'Where did you go with him?' David asked abruptly, as he watched Kate tidy the room.

'He asked me to accompany him to Akhenaten's tomb – to take notes…' She looked away, probably realising how implausible this explanation sounded.

David snorted in disbelief. '*Notes?*'

'Yes. On the rate of deterioration. And places where the lighting needs repaired.' Kate became defensive. 'I can show you my notebook if that will make you happy!'

'Nothing about this makes me happy! He goes up there to escape his responsibilities here – why did he feel the need to take *you*?'

'I don't know! And anyway, I'm not answerable to you!' Kate's stifled inner teenager was emerging, another side effect of this horrendous situation.

'Actually,' David said evenly. 'You *are*. Did you tell him everything – now that the two of you are so friendly? Or were you too busy to talk?'

In two strides she was standing before him, clasping his face between her hands. 'Stop this,' she begged him. 'This isn't you; please stop it. I told him nothing, *nothing*. But I discovered that Anai practises witchcraft, and she may have given us some kind of herbal hallucinogen last night. She did the same thing to Ethan, but he claims he doesn't remember anything. Whatever she professes to know about our alleged past lives together, she hasn't enlightened Ethan.'

'So you now believe that what we saw was just a drug-induced hallucination?'

Kate knew he wanted her to say yes, but her experience had been too real, the images and emotions too intense. She shook her head. 'No.'

She saw a look of defeat in his eyes, and he tried to pull away from her, but she held on. 'But what happened…afterwards, and how we've behaved today – that's probably down to the drink she gave us. Ethan and I have suffered the same side effects -' Now she saw resentment, and changed tack. 'Please, David, I'm scared. I don't know how much Anai knows, or how she found out, but I'm worried about what she's doing to us. Ethan seems to be completely blasé…'

Tired of being needed, of always having to be strong, David wrenched his face from Kate's hands. 'What do you have to worry about, Kate?' he asked roughly, as he walked towards the door. 'You're with your beloved soulmate, now. And it seems you're working some magic of your own – on Ethan. So go and tell *him* about your fears.'

'But I don't want him, David…' Kate said quietly. But David was no longer there to hear her.

The Edinburgh faction resumed digging in the southern cemetery that afternoon, accompanied by Yusuf and the field director. It was important that excavations continue in the open grave, in order to remove any burial goods before opportunists stole whatever artefacts lay concealed in the sand.

Although Yusuf insisted that only qualified archaeologists be allowed to work in the grave, David permitted his third-year students – namely Dominic, Russell and Julian – the opportunity to excavate the edges of the grave for short periods. Around them, Steven and the remaining students worked on the other marked-off plots and the soil heap.

Camera and notepad at the ready, Kate sat nearby and waited, her mind pondering several issues while she perfunctorily crafted her next report for the museum. She was saddened by David's outburst and sorry to be the cause of his pain and confusion. Morosely, she fixated on the many negative aspects of this trip. Challenging relationships, animosity, uncomfortable accommodation, wearying temperatures, and strange food all conspired to weaken her resilience. And then there was the supernatural element to contend with…

As though subdued by the environment, everyone worked quietly. The discovery of small objects elicited only a muted response, rather than a cry of triumph. After two hours of careful excavation, the tray beside the grave held some pieces of textile that suggested the bodies had been wrapped in traditional matting. There were also pieces of pottery and some small, irregularly-shaped objects caked in dirt. Small brushes were used to clean away some of the soil, revealing amulets that would have been buried with the bodies for their protection. Julian announced that he had found a piece of jewellery; the small item glinted golden through its casing of dirt. Dominic scrambled over the sand to see Julian's discovery, but David gruffly instructed the Irishman to take care when moving around. Peevishly, the professor ordered the two students to the soil heap.

In a world of his own, Ethan seemed completely absorbed in his work. Surreptitiously, Kate watched him; he had lost the furrowed brow, the sardonic smirk, the guarded look. Apart from the occasional muttered observation, he and David worked silently and in perfect harmony.

After a while, David sat back a little and grinned boyishly at Ethan. Words were exchanged in low voices, presumably so as not to alert Yusuf, who had moved to one of the other trenches. Then the pair picked up small trowels and bent their heads over a small patch of ground in the corner of the grave. Kate observed them with interest, bemused by their behaviour. They worked swiftly, exchanging the trowels for smaller tools. All of a sudden, David stopped working, and Ethan looked up at him with a puzzled frown. There was more whispering, during which Ethan seemed to offer some protest. Then, to Kate's astonishment, the pair seemed to cover up whatever they had been on the verge of unearthing.

Climbing carefully out of the trench, David stretched. 'Doctor Brodie!' he called, and Steven looked up from his work. 'Take over, would you? I've got cramp in my hand.'

Handing his shovel to one of the Egyptian workers, Steven strode over to the grave and took David's place. Shaking his head in exasperation, Ethan applied his trowel to a different part of the trench. David sat down on the sand and made a show of massaging his hand, his expression indecipherable. Ten minutes passed, then Steven's face lit up, and he drew Ethan's attention to the area where he had been working.

'Friday!' Ethan shouted. 'Bring your wee camera over here!'

Steven had uncovered a small, rectangular box and now strove to prise it from the desert's clutches. With infinite care and Ethan's help, Steven freed the wooden chest and lifted it carefully onto the tray. By this time, the others had gathered around the grave; David stood behind Ethan as Kate knelt to take photographs of the intriguing artefact.

'Back off until I've had a look,' Steven almost snarled at Kate. 'And when you're writing your next report, don't forget to say it was *me* who found this.'

Tired of his animosity, Kate complied without argument and moved next to Ethan and David. She was half-tempted to reveal that the box had been found by *David*. It was clear to Kate that David had wanted Steven to make the discovery, probably in an attempt to make the boorish young archaeologist a little less unbearable.

'What's your assessment, Doctor Forbes?' David asked, brusquely.

As Steven carefully brushed the sand and grit from the surface of the box, faded symbols and images began to appear. A painting of Isis adorned the lid, her multi-coloured wings stretching majestically over the surface, her beautiful black eyes expressing benevolence. There was lettering on each side of the box, along with a winged scarab, and the symbols for the sun and moon.

'It could be a box for jewellery or toiletry items,' Steven suggested, sounding a little flustered. He slowly lifted the box, testing the weight. 'There might still be items inside; we should take it back to the lab and have a look…'

'I concur,' David agreed. He glanced at his students, and then pointed at the symbols on the box. 'You'll get a proper look at this later, but there's a clue as to the occupation of the owner.'

The students craned their necks for a better view; Ethan leaned closer, his lips moving silently as he read the faded hieratic text.

'She was a magician,' Ethan told them. 'Our girl was a witch.'

Marianne used her extensive negotiating skills on the two inspectors, and finally received permission to inspect the skeletons before their removal to Cairo. She invited the Scottish field school to join her students in the Bone Room.

The crowded laboratory was made even more cramped by the rows of chairs which had been set out. The bodies still lay on the large stainless steel table, waiting to reveal their secrets. The overhead lights shone brightly on the gruesome scene. Yusuf stood at the head of the table to ensure no ill conduct; no one would be allowed to touch the remains during this examination. Ethan stood next to him, eyes fixed on the pathetic remains of the baby.

Calling for the students to settle down, Marianne donned a white lab coat and latex gloves and walked slowly around the table. The constrictions placed upon her by the inspector were frustrating, and this was conveyed in her sharp tone of voice as she delivered her opening remarks.

Just as Marianne began her assessment, the door opened once again, and Ali entered, leading his mother. Flushing slightly, the caretaker apologised for the intrusion and asked if he and Anai could observe the proceedings.

'Highly irregular!' Yusuf protested, in English so that the Western party could witness his authority.

'She is one of us!' Anai snapped, and made her way to the front row of chairs. After some shuffling about, she and her son were given seats in the front row, and the inspection of the skeletons could finally begin.

According to the Texan archaeologist, the woman had been in her late teens or early twenties. Bone development suggested the woman had enjoyed good nutrition, and had been in good health. The shape of the skull confirmed she had been of Egyptian origin. Unusually for an ancient Egyptian, her teeth had been almost perfect. The dimensions of the pelvis indicated that she had given birth, and so was probably the mother of the child. The child itself had likely died not long after its birth, but the deterioration of the fragile bones made further speculation impossible.

Both had been wrapped in a winding sheet; fragments of cloth could be seen adhering to the bones. The matting that had been found at the site indicated that this material had been used as a final covering.

Strands of dark hair were still attached to the woman's skull, and the skeleton still had its fingernails and several toenails. There was also evidence of soft tissue; Marianne postulated that it might be possible to collect a DNA sample. Someone commented that the woman and child may have ancestors living in the vicinity, and several heads turned towards Anai and Ali.

With a rather defiant look at Yusuf, the redhead pulled the portable magnifier into position, adjusting the flexible metal arm so that she could examine the skull in closer detail. The magnifier was connected to a desktop computer situated in the corner of the room, which in turn projected the magnified image of the skull onto a large screen on the back wall.

As Marianne launched into detailed speculation about possible causes of death, Kate found it increasingly difficult to concentrate on the unfamiliar terminology. It didn't help that David had taken a seat next to her, or that his athletic body pressed next to hers in the confined space. In addition, he kept shifting his leg, and in so doing rubbed his thigh against her own. Marianne's words began to mean very little; she could have been speaking a foreign language for all Kate understood. In contrast, David appeared completely absorbed in the American's deliberations.

Having revealed all she could without touching the remains, Marianne gave Ethan a helpless little shrug. Even though she had corroborated the lecture with data from other excavations, the cursory examination had taken barely forty-five minutes.

Moving to the computer, Ethan quickly accessed photographs of the anthropoid coffin recently discovered in the southern cemetery, which had held the mummy of an old man. He went on to discuss the results of the CAT scans of the mummy, which showed protective amulets between the wrappings, an elaborate collared necklace and other pieces of jewellery. David began to rub at a smudge of dirt on his trousers, just above his knee; Kate's attention began to wander once more.

Yusuf considered himself less austere than many of his colleagues, and so allowed photographs to be taken of the skeletons before their coffins were sealed. He had prepared a list of the organisations present in the room; these would be official photographs, not tourist shots to be paraded on social media or sold via the internet. Naturally, he began with the representative of the EES. Ethan took the permitted three photos with his expensive Nokia camera, then stood back to allow Marianne and Taylor to take pictures. David was called to the table next, and Kate admired his look of concentration as he took photographs with a modest, well-used camera. She hardly heard Yusuf's voice calling for the next photographer.

'National Museum of Scotland!'

Startled, Kate looked at him dumbly. Rising to her feet, she realised she hadn't brought a camera or even her phone. As she made her way to the table, her cheeks flushed with embarrassment.

Surprisingly, it was Ethan who came to her rescue. 'Take mine,' he muttered, pushing his camera into her hands. 'It's all set. Just point and shoot – for the NMS.' He hid a mischievous smile as, out of the corner of his eye, he spotted David scowling at him.

Stepping out of the way, Ethan watched as Kate walked around the table, deciding on the photographs she wanted to send back to Edinburgh – without looking the adult skeleton in the eye socket. He grudgingly conceded that she selected better angles than he had done, thus displaying her creativity and loyalty to her place of employment.

Satisfied with her work, Kate returned the camera to Ethan and thanked him with a shy smile. Finding himself incapable of a verbal response, he merely offered her a grim-faced nod.

Anxious to seal the coffins in preparation for their removal, Yusuf nodded meaningfully to Ethan. Stepping to the front of the table, the director formally thanked Doctor Deveraux for her informative presentation. Marianne shrugged; her professional curiosity had not been satisfied, and she was disappointed that she would only discover the skeletons' secrets by way of another archaeologist's publication.

Before leaving, Anai approached the skeletons. The room fell silent as she muttered prayers over the dead, flouting protocol by lightly touching each corpse's forehead. Disregarding Yusuf's whispered words of indignation, Anai walked regally out of the lab, her son following meekly in her wake. Stunned, the students looked to their teachers for an explanation.

'I think we've all earned some time off,' Ethan announced impulsively. 'Professor Young and I will be honing our skills at Egyptian stick fighting, under the supervision of Mister Suefy. You're welcome to come and watch, and receive some basic training.'

His words seemed to lift the morale of the group as they left the room amid the scraping of chairs. David, however, was not so enthusiastic.

'They should be working,' he grumbled to Ethan, keeping his back to the students who hadn't left yet. 'I have to stick to the schedule. As everyone keeps telling me, I've messed around enough already on this trip.'

'They look shattered,' Ethan muttered in reply. 'They need some time to chill out. And so do you. Besides that, Yusuf wants to move the skeletons this afternoon; the transport arrived an hour ago. Some discretion might be wise.' He sneaked a look at Kate, who sat scribbling notes for her next report. 'I get the feeling not everyone approves of their removal...'

As he turned to look at Kate, David's eyes filled with longing. Ethan's correct assumption seemed to prove his deep connection with Kate, and this made David feel even more desolate. He was surprised, then, to hear Ethan laugh softly.

'What's so funny?' David asked irritably.

'You,' Ethan snorted. 'I know why you're camping out every night. It has nothing to do with toughening up the students. You don't trust yourself to be in the same building as her, do you? Mister Self-Control is actually scared of *losing* control -'

'Oh, bugger off!' David snapped, causing Kate to glance up inquisitively.

Yusuf's men entered the room and held a quiet discussion with the inspector about how best to transport the mother and child. Yusuf took them to look at the box David and Steven had found earlier, and they stood in a tight huddle, murmuring speculatively.

'Ethan,' David began, watching the Egyptians with suspicion. 'I'd like to take a closer look at that box. Preferably without being crowded by noisy juveniles and interrupted by stupid questions...'

'And you say you enjoy teaching!' Ethan chided.

'The box will be going to Cairo with the bones,' Yusuf informed them.

'Can't we keep it a bit longer?' David asked. 'It's a rare find – we're surely entitled to document it for our records...'

'Come on, Yusuf,' Ethan wheedled. 'The rule is that you examine all the finds at the end of the season. We've been following the same procedure for more than a century! You're taking the skeletons – leave us the box.'

Yusuf shook his head. 'No,' he said firmly. 'It needs conservation work, and so it will be taken to *our* experts.'

Having overheard the conversation, Kate stood up and moved to David's side. 'Professor Young *is* an expert!' she declared. 'He found the box – you should let him examine it. It's only fair -'

'*Miss Grahame!*' Ethan barked. 'Why don't you go and do *your* job and let the *men* do *theirs?* I'm sure the women need help in the kitchen...' Looking past her, he smiled at Yusuf, who nodded approvingly. Obviously embarrassed, David shifted uncomfortably from foot to foot.

Kate was appalled. 'I beg your pardon?' she hissed, favouring Ethan with a livid scowl.

'Actually, Kate,' David interrupted. 'I wanted to discuss tomorrow's schedule.' He gestured towards the door, and then turned to Yusuf. 'By the way, congratulations on the birth of your child. Your wife delivered safely?'

The inspector waved dismissively. 'Another girl,' he grunted, seemingly disgusted. 'If she does not provide a son soon, I may take another wife.'

As the Egyptian men – and Ethan – commiserated with the disgruntled inspector, David led a fuming Kate down the corridor to her room. By the time he shut the bedroom door, Kate had calmed down and now understood she had committed a grave faux pas.

'I'm sorry,' she said, turning towards David. 'I realise I spoke of turn and made you look bad in front of those chauvinist pigs. I didn't mean to emasculate you in public.'

He raised an eyebrow at her dubiously-phrased final comment. 'It doesn't matter,' he muttered. 'I've grown very thick skin in recent months. No comments from you about it matching my very thick head, please.'

She almost smiled, but anger still festered. 'But even though I made a mistake, Ethan had no right to talk to me like that! And what about that git Yusuf? His wife's just given birth, and he's *here*? He should be happy that his wife and child are healthy, not moaning because he doesn't have a son to raise in the way of the sexist pig!'

Chewing the inside of his cheek, David looked nonplussed. On another occasion, Kate might have laughed at his comical expression, but she was too cranky. 'And I'm not sorry about anything I said back there because I only spoke the truth. You *were* trained in Edinburgh, after all.'

'Are you done?' David asked. 'Or are you going to spit nails and stamp your foot?'

She settled for folding her arms and tapping one foot, eyes full of indignation.

Taking a deep breath, David attempted to appease her. 'Yes, you made a small error of judgement but you meant well – and thanks, by the way, for defending my honour, even if you *did* make me look like a wimp.

'No, Ethan shouldn't have spoken to you the way he did. Perhaps he's trying to empathise with Yusuf so that he can use it to his advantage. Or maybe he's lived out here too long. Neither is a good excuse for his rudeness, but I *did* warn you about him.'

David paused, feeling utterly worn out. 'Yes, Yusuf is a complete git, and I'm really annoyed with him because I really wanted to see what was in that box. I can't think why he would want to remove it so quickly – unless he's worried it might contain items pertaining to witchcraft. Such things might not be deemed suitable for public display, in case they have an adverse influence…'

'What – in case they give women ideas about strength and self-sufficiency, you mean?' Kate exclaimed. With an unladylike snort, she muttered a string of Italian swearwords and accompanied them with illustrative hand gestures.

'Indeed…' David agreed. 'Finally, he should most certainly be with his wife and daughter. You are aware, however, that this culture prefers sons to daughters.' He gazed at her intently. 'I don't share that view. I would love a daughter or two, as well as a son to raise in the way of the gentleman…'

She stared at him, unsure how to respond; he had effectively assuaged her anger, damn him. Noises in the hall signified that the skeletons were being carried out of the building; Kate grimaced in disapproval.

'What did you want to discuss with me?' she asked grouchily.

'Nothing,' David replied. 'I just wanted us to get out of that room without either of us losing face. Now I have to go and play with sticks…' His hand on the door handle, he looked back at her. 'You know that it was Steven who found that box, not me.'

'Liar!' Kate snapped, the word encompassing more than just the day's archaeological discovery.

David gazed at her steadily. 'Make sure that you attribute the find to Doctor Brodie. I'll see you at dinner.' Opening the door, he stepped into the corridor and left her to rant at the walls.

Anai relaxed in a lounger with the black cat at her feet, watching the young people gather around David and Ethan as they prepared to demonstrate stick fighting. Quarterstaffs in hand, the two men listened intently to instructions from Ali. The caretaker wanted to ensure there would be no illegal moves during *this* fight.

Some of the other students sat on the benches and chairs, reading or chatting amiably and enjoying the gentler temperatures of early evening. For the moment, the atmosphere was peaceful and convivial.

Anai sighed and closed her eyes, smiling as she sensed Kate settling down on a cushion at her feet. Stretching out a bony hand, Anai stroked her fingers through Kate's hair, feeling the troubled young woman tense slightly at her touch. There was no need to talk, for Kate was close to realising her purpose in Amarna. She would benefit from companionable silence.

The mock battle between David and Ethan began. Before long, laughter could be heard as the two archaeologists engaged in light-hearted badgering. Ali's goading of the combatants added to the students' amusement. Kate smiled but remained where she was.

'Ethan wears a mask,' Kate murmured to herself. Eyes still closed, Anai nodded in agreement. 'He puts on a front which acts as a barrier; no one gets close, so no one knows who he really is.' She felt a fog clearing in her head. 'He does it to protect himself because he doesn't want to get hurt.' She turned to Anai. 'He doesn't remember me, but he remembers the pain. Is that possible, Anai?'

A gentle smile graced once-full lips. 'Yes, little one…'

'Part of him feels responsible for what happened back then, but he doesn't realise it…'

'He punishes himself without knowing why. That is why he needs absolution. But for some sins, there can be no mercy …'

'But if I forgive him, will he know? Will it help him?'

'You must try and reach his soul, qitah. You can only do that when all is quiet…'

Resting her back against Anai's chair, Kate felt an inkling of hope; perhaps closure was possible, after all.

Footsteps signalled the end of their peace, as Marianne and Mina joined them, carrying delicate glasses of Egyptian tea.

Handing a glass to her grandmother, Mina sat on the ground next to her, her gaze immediately seeking David.

'Mina's been telling me that she wants to study medicine,' Marianne informed Kate as she gave her some tea and sat beside her. 'Isn't that interesting?' She nudged Kate lightly; Kate gave her a puzzled glance over the rim of the glass.

'She wishes to study in England,' Anai admitted, her attention seemingly on the activity in front of her. 'But we do not have the money; she would require a sponsor…'

Firing Kate a meaningful look, Marianne mouthed the words 'meal ticket', and then smiled across at Mina. 'Maybe you can find yourself a nice British husband, Mina,' she teased. 'He could whisk you off to England and put you through medical school.'

Mina blushed and looked away.

Satisfied that she had alerted Kate to the women's possible motives, Marianne sipped at her drink and observed the duel in progress. The two stick-brandishing warriors were now being lightly reprimanded by Ali. After a moment, battle resumed but it was clear that David and Ethan were clowning around in order to irk their referee.

'Damn, they look good enough to eat…' Marianne breathed.

Kate smiled, but remained silent. Although the American was friendly, Kate didn't know her well enough to agree with the assertion. Or to add that in her opinion, David was possibly the sexiest man on the planet, even when he was behaving badly.

Ahmed had joined the group on the sand, accompanied by Hassan and one of the boy's young friends. David threw the Egyptian his quarterstaff and invited him to best Ethan. Anai's grandson stripped off his jacket and made a show of twirling his staff, intending to display his prowess in the hope of impressing the female spectators. As David walked away from the area of battle, he was immediately mobbed by the two boys. Mina jumped up in order to take refreshments to the sweating professor. Hearing Kate muttering darkly under her breath, Marianne gave the younger woman a knowing look.

'Hassan has grown so much, Anai,' Marianne commented. 'He's going to be handsome like his father.'

'Hassan needs a mother,' Anai replied grimly. 'Ahmed seeks a new wife.' The set of her jaw suggested that there might be an unpleasant tale surrounding Hassan's mother, but it would remain a closely guarded secret.

Kate's eyes widened; the shrewd American was gradually revealing Anai's agenda, as though she were peeling back an ancient burial shroud and revealing a jewel-clad mummy. Her mind raced; in her naivety, she had not considered that the Suefy family – or at least, Anai – would see the Westerners as a source of income or advancement. This knowledge threw a whole new light on the situation and made Kate feel even more unsettled.

Seeing her worried look, Marianne drew Kate into a distracting conversation about their respective families. To Kate's surprise, Marianne was married to an anthropologist and had two teenage sons. Eventually, though, the Texan steered the conversation towards Kate's relationship with David, and Kate immediately clammed up. It was becoming too noisy, and she felt the onset of another headache, creeping up from the tension in her neck. The smell of food drifting from the kitchen made her feel slightly queasy. Beside her, Anai was snoring gently, despite the chaos a short distance away. Julian took a seat in the corner of the courtyard, and attempted to read a book. After five minutes, however, he seemed unable to tolerate the disturbance around him and returned to his room.

'So,' Marianne was saying. 'Will you follow David if he takes the job in York?'

Looking at her dumbly, Kate tried to make sense of what she had just heard. 'Pardon?'

Marianne looked uncomfortable. 'I'm sorry, I assumed you knew…'

Kate's eyes were fearful. 'Knew what?'

'Oh, hell, I've put my foot in it!' Marianne groaned. 'David's been offered a job at York University. I only know because I happened to be in the wrong place at the right time…'

As Ali's wife called out a summons to dinner, Kate stood. 'Please excuse me, Marianne. I have a rotten headache…'

'Sit with me at dinner, Kate. We can talk about -'

'Thanks, but I'm not hungry. I could do with an early night – and time to think. I'll see you tomorrow.'

Leaning against the bedroom door, Kate fervently wished there was a lock and thought fleetingly of barricading it with the single chair in the room. Her eyes fell on the battered metal box that had been placed on the bed. Pushing away from the door, she sat down and opened the box which had spent years gathering dust in Anai's little house, yearning to lose herself once more in that other life. It only took her a moment to realise that David had removed Richard's letter and the photographs of the Fords and Richard Yorke. She wondered if he had done this out of spite, but the voice of reason told her that David would not want anyone else to see the pictures. He was protecting them from unwanted attention.

Sadly, he had removed a source of comfort. The rest of the box contained uninspiring photographs of the dig in process, the landscape, and the Egyptian workers. There were tattered pieces of paper scored with faded pencil marks and the wrapper from a bar of ladies' soap. At last, Kate set the box on the floor and curled up on the bed, her mind in turmoil. Her room was so far away from the others that she could barely hear them, and so she fell into an exhausted doze.

At the other end of the house, the residents enjoyed an Egyptian buffet and relaxed in the balmy evening air. David and Ethan removed themselves slightly from the group to discuss plans to explore the cliff face for signs of a tomb entrance. Ethan announced that Yusuf would be willing to join their unsanctioned expedition as long as he was given control should they find a tomb. Ahmed had sourced some climbing equipment for them, and so the trip was planned for three days' time, when Moumdah would be in Minya. No one noticed Kate's absence, but the students' high spirits sagged again when David announced another night under canvas.

When Kate woke at dusk, the room was darker and colder. Rising, she pulled the coverlet over her shoulders and shuffled to the window. The beautiful evening sky was flame-coloured, shot with shades of pink and violet. The desert was blood red as the sun slipped below the horizon. A short distance away, near a bent palm tree, Ethan stood facing the sunset. Kate gazed at his elegantly chiselled profile, her emotions tangled. Her eyes stung, as in her mind's eye, she saw Edwin, not Ethan. He stood completely still, surveying the landscape as though he were on guard, darkness creeping over the ground behind him. Dressed in his trademark black, he would soon melt into the night.

'Go to him,' a voice whispered in the air around her. Or was it in her head? More than once since her arrival, Kate had heard whispers in the wind, seen fleeting shadows out of the corner of her eye. She had told herself that it was a product of her imagination, brought to life by Anai's fables, as well as the witch's expertise in herbalism.

'No,' she replied, although a part of her cried out for Edwin. She continued to gaze at Ethan, feeling compassion for this man who projected an image of conceited arrogance, and yet now looked so lost.

The room was almost pitch-black. A figure stood immobile in the centre of the room, eyes open but unseeing. Turning over in her cocoon of blankets, Kate returned to consciousness and cried out in fright as she saw Ethan staring at her. But she quickly realised he was sleepwalking again; untangling herself from her covers and net, Kate padded quietly to stand in front of him and looked into his blank eyes. Touching his cheek, she discovered his skin was icy cold.

'Kate?' His voice sounded strange, not quite his own.

The room was suddenly freezing; Kate shivered. 'I'm here,' she said softly. Through no will of her own, she began to stroke his cheek.

'Please forgive me, my love,' he whispered. 'Please…'

A lump rising in her throat, Kate fought to keep her voice quiet and steady. She felt love, *their* love, grow warm within her. She wanted, more than anything, to bring them all peace. Katherine, Edwin, Richard, David, Ethan and herself.

'I *do* forgive you,' she murmured. 'You must rest now, love. Everything's going to be fine.' Closing her eyes, she kissed his cheek. With a slight nod, he turned and walked stiffly out of the room.

CHAPTER 9

Sunday December 16, 2012

The rising sun cast a fiery glow over the desert, the light inching its way across the cliffs. The two horses cantered northeast, the tinkle of Mina's laughter drifting on the breeze towards the tower, taunting Kate as she watched.

Standing quietly at the top of the stairs, Ethan observed Kate's tense posture with reluctant pity. The idea that he might care how she felt was downright unnerving.

When working in the dig house, Mina often slept in a poky room next to the kitchen, while her uncle claimed more luxurious quarters as befitted his position. But Ethan knew that Kate was imagining the young Egyptian woman creeping along dark corridors in the dead of night, her destination David's bed, whether it was in the house or a tent.

He heard Kate sniff, her eyes fixed on the dust cloud kicked up by the horses' hooves, and he struggled to find something to say. Several attempts had him opening and closing his mouth again, a fish out of water. Finally, she turned away from the scene of her mental torture and looked startled to see him standing there.

'I'm sorry, Doctor Forbes,' she said quietly. 'I didn't hear you come up…'

'It's a nice spot to watch the sunrise,' he replied, stepping closer. 'And a good place to hide, sometimes…' He flicked a sidelong glance in her direction. She was looking towards the distant north cliffs, no doubt straining her eyes for a glimpse of the two horses.

'The horses are Ahmed's,' Ethan continued. 'His wife was a nightmare, so he traded her for two mares and a stallion…'

Ethan relished the raised eyebrow and pursed lips, precursors to one of Kate's quick-witted retorts. He experienced a fleeting memory of a fierce argument followed by a loving reconciliation. Or had he dreamt it? Last night's dreams had brought him another intimate encounter with a woman who looked like Kate. But then her countenance had changed to that of an Egyptian woman who looked a little like Mina, and tenderness had become primal lust.

The still-vivid sensation unsettled him, and for a moment he was rendered immobile. Swallowing hard, he returned to the present and noticed that Kate was moving towards the stairs.

'Friday, there's something you should be aware of,' he said swiftly. 'Mina's uncle has found her a husband. Suefy is a good man, and he loves his niece; I'm sure he's found a good match for her. He plans to marry her off as soon as he can.'

When Kate spoke, her dejection was obvious. 'Her feelings for David are plain for all to see...'

'Listen, David and I have known the family for years, and we helped with Mina's education – well, David did. There's no doubt that Anai wants her granddaughter to marry well and in the past, the old schemer probably had her eyes set on one of us. Obviously, Ali has put paid to that. But be assured that David has never shown any romantic interest in Mina. Although, he would do the honourable thing and marry her if he had to – if you see what I mean...'

He saw from Kate's crestfallen expression that his words had not helped to ease her distress. 'She's too young for him, at any rate. By Egyptian standards, he's almost old enough to be her father!'

At last, his words elicited a small, reluctant smile that quickly disappeared. 'I'm not certain. David's so...' Completely at a loss, Kate's voice trailed off.

'Kate,' Ethan sighed, suddenly weary of the nickname he had invented just to irritate her. 'David's mastered the art of appearing to be a closed book. But there's not much he can hide from *me*. I've known him for a very long time.'

'It seems I hardly know *anything* about him,' she confessed sadly, then turned away in another attempt to escape him.

'Then ask *me*,' he offered. Ethan was suddenly appalled by the realisation that he would say anything to convince her to stay on the roof with him. At that moment, he wanted just to be in her presence without either of them projecting a false façade. His voice softened. 'What would you like to know?'

Kate glanced at him uncertainly, feeling herself flush under his dark gaze. Ethan walked across to two folding chairs leaning against one of the chimneystacks. Setting them up, he gestured for her to sit. Reluctantly, she obeyed, her body language clearly exhibiting her desire to flee. Although she was eager to learn as much as she could about David, she wished she could learn from someone else. She wanted Ethan to be the inconsiderate, cold-hearted rake David had made him out to be. She didn't want him to remind her of Edwin.

'What was he like when you met him?' she asked hesitantly.

Ethan smiled gently. 'We met at university. He was a quiet, introspective lad just out of boarding school – a ramrod up his backside even then.' He laughed briefly at the memory. 'I was a loud, over-confident country boy. Somehow, we became good friends. He tried to keep me on the level, and I showed him how to enjoy himself.'

'You mean you introduced him to lots of loose women?'

Ethan grinned, finding her prudishness strangely endearing. 'It's no secret that I enjoyed being a student,' he replied diplomatically. 'But David was – and is – a very principled guy.'

'He wasn't all that principled at a certain Edinburgh nightclub last summer!'

Ethan's eyes burned into hers, and he frowned. 'Ah, you're referring to his one-night stand. Well, I take full responsibility for that one. I got him drunk, and I set him up with a tart. I'm sure he felt bad about it for weeks afterwards.' He stopped to gauge her expression. 'It wasn't typical behaviour for him, but he *was* completely lovelorn at the time...' Ethan immediately regretted the barb as Kate hung her head. He attempted to change the subject. 'He's never been a social animal – at university I literally had to drag him away from his desk to make him take a break.'

'Didn't he have girlfriends?'

Ethan snorted. 'Despite my best efforts, he never even indulged in a quick fling the whole time we were students.' He laughed again, Edwin's warm laughter. 'An all-boys boarding school had not prepared him for life with women – he was clueless. I do remember him having a huge crush, once. He was working on his thesis, and we both had jobs at summer school. It was the most distracted I'd ever seen him, but he never plucked up the courage to ask her out. She left the area; he bottled up whatever feelings he had and got back to work...' Something tugged at Ethan's memory, but he was unable to grasp it.

'So Diane was his first girlfriend?' Kate asked timidly.

Ethan watched her carefully. 'Well, there were two other short-term relationships before her. Nobody seemed to live up to his unrequited crush. He was with Diane for about a year.'

'What's she like?'

Ethan pursed his lips. 'Tall, dark hair, gorgeous of course. A complete ball-breaker. She's a lawyer, but she's done some modelling in her time. Quite wealthy, too – she owns a couple of properties in Edinburgh. David met her at some charity event -'

'She's a *lawyer*?' Kate sounded incredulous.

Ethan nodded, remembering that Kate's ex-husband shared Diane's profession. 'I never understood what he saw in her because she didn't seem to be his type at all. I never saw one shred of evidence that suggested they were even in love. But his parents loved her and thought she would be the ideal wife for our boy. As you're no doubt aware, David would make the perfect trophy husband. Diane started hinting about marriage and kids, but Dave would have none of it. He never even asked her to move in with him. In the end, she dumped him for someone more pliable. Thank God!'

Ethan fell silent, allowing Kate to absorb this new information, pleased that her natural curiosity had helped her relax in his presence. And something between them had changed, as though the atmosphere around them had lightened.

'There were lots of rumours about him at work…' Kate began. 'You know, about him being gay…' She coughed, embarrassed.

Ethan shook his head. 'I can explain that one easily. At the last Christmas party, he was pestered by one of the conservators but refused her rather obvious advances. You know how prickly he can get, and he eventually had to be quite blunt with the woman. She got her revenge by starting the rumours.' Ethan shrugged, admiring Kate's look of indignation. 'I think he thought that he would be left in peace if people weren't sure about his leanings…'

'It didn't work – he still gets pestered. Women are always flirting with him!' She blushed as Ethan smiled knowingly at her evident outrage.

'But I hear you keep the wolves at bay quite efficiently!'

Kate's eyes darted to his. 'He talks about me?'

Ethan gave her an incredulous stare. 'Well, our grumpy Englishman has been typically evasive – until last week, when we were staying at his parents' house in London. The night Steve phoned you for a blether, David spent the evening pouting like a stroppy teenager. I lightened his mood with a few glasses of his dad's excellent malt whisky, which also served to loosen his tongue. Then he wouldn't shut up about you.'

Kate's expression changed to one of trepidation, and she bit her lip.

'Don't worry,' Ethan smiled. 'He didn't reveal any secrets! He's always been annoyingly discreet.'

Sighing, he sat back in his chair and looked at the sky, as though trying to recount David's words. 'Let's see…you studied journalism, but for some reason changed your mind about that career. You have a kind heart; you looked after your aunt when she was ill, and she left you her cosy house in Ravelston. You married a sleazy lawyer who cheated on you, so you sensibly divorced him.' His eyes met hers. 'You're apparently the most beautiful woman in the universe, but you have a shocking temper when you're riled.

'You love horse riding, but you're very stubborn and independent. You have a fine work ethic, and the ability to drive him insane. Your brother's a paediatrician, and he has two cute kids who look like you but with an Italian twist thanks to their mother. Your nephew regularly emails David with questions about archaeology – and dinosaurs. You should know that Dave absolutely loves this.' Ethan smiled fondly.

'David told me that he enjoyed the barbecue at your home last May, but he wished your mother hadn't interrupted you in the kitchen…'

He gave Kate a questioning glance and watched her eyes grow misty. Ethan had discovered that there had been a brief encounter in Kate's kitchen; David had been about to kiss her when her mother had come into the room.

'In fact,' Ethan continued sharply. 'He listed every time you two have been "interrupted". Frankly, it just made me irritated with him for being so backward.' He stood up abruptly and began pacing. 'I've tried to teach him everything I know, and yet he -'

'He refuses to act like a man-whore!' Kate snapped.

Ethan stopped moving and stared down at her, surprised by her outburst. And yet, he knew she was correct in her estimation of him. At that moment, his bohemian lifestyle disgusted him.

'You know,' he began softly. 'Those weeks when you two were "estranged", he was unbearable to live with. I stayed with him for some of that time, and I've never seen him so close to losing the plot.'

Impulsively, he reached out towards Kate, and she shrunk away from his hand as he gently scooped the silver chain from under her sweatshirt. He held the locket in his palm, his fingers close to her chin. 'And all because of this?' As far as Ethan knew, the rift had been caused when Kate had rejected David's birthday gift. 'What was the problem? Is silver not good enough for you?'

Kate tucked the necklace back under her clothing. 'It's none of your business,' she responded, the tone of her voice making it clear the subject was not up for discussion.

'But you would have preferred gold,' Ethan murmured, distracted now by mental images which made no sense.

Kate's eyes scanned his face, seeing a puzzled expression on the dark, handsome features. Did he remember? Was he recapturing the memory of Edwin Ford presenting his wife with a gold locket? *But if he should remember, what then?*

'Wouldn't you have preferred gold?' he pressed.

Kate stood up slowly, her gaze searching his eyes for some sign of her soulmate. 'That wouldn't have been appropriate.' She fingered the engraved wings of her locket. 'And I like it just the way it is.'

'What do you keep in it?' His voice suggested some other challenge was about to come her way, that the bridge they had tried to build was about to collapse.

'Nothing,' Kate muttered wearily.

'An empty heart…' he mused.

'Are you referring to my locket,' Kate snapped icily. 'Or yourself? God, Ethan, I'm so sick of your incessant niggling!' She turned to leave.

'Kate,' Ethan called softly, and she halted. 'You have his heart – don't toy with it. If you don't want it, give it back and let him go.'

The look she gave him was filled with such torment that Ethan almost recoiled. He had received that look from her before, in some other place, when *he* had been the cause of her distress. Her expressive eyes sparkled with threatening tears, and he realised that, for some reason, Kate was suffering just as much as David.

'He no longer wants me,' she said softly, speaking now to the ground. 'I've become a burden. I shouldn't have come here…'

Suddenly desperate to escape this uncomfortable conversation, Ethan walked towards the stairs, suppressing an uncharacteristic desire to provide comfort. 'Well, it looks like we're making our own breakfast this morning. Fancy some scrambled eggs?'

David waited for Mina to enter the dining room before him, and then halted on the threshold. The feeling of calm he always enjoyed after riding evaporated as soon as he saw Ethan sitting with Kate at one corner of the table. They were tucking into scrambled eggs on toast, and David jealously wondered who had made breakfast. The knot in his stomach tightened further when he saw Kate laugh at something Ethan had said.

Her eyes downcast, Mina headed for the kitchen to begin preparing breakfast. The outing had been most unsatisfactory. She longed to tell David that she loved him, that she could be a good wife, and that she would live anywhere in the world with him. She had even performed a ritual under the light of the moon, in the hope that the goddess Hathor might intercede on her behalf. Before meeting David that morning, Mina had dressed carefully and anointed herself with a potion designed to draw him to her and inflame his desire. But he had been introspective during their morning ride; when he spoke, it was only to answer her questions about life in Edinburgh. Each reluctant reply had included an anecdote concerning Kate, the light of his life.

Steven entered the kitchen looking tired and dishevelled, and asked Mina if there was any coffee. With a harsh rebuke in Arabic, she pointed to the pot on the stove and told him to prepare it himself. Steven responded with a grimace, but he was too tired to argue. Like David, he had assumed some of Ethan's responsibilities to give the director time for his private quest. Each day Steven drove out to the main city to oversee the conservation work, and then compiled a progress report. Despite his lack of experience, the workers looked to him for occasional supervision. The demands of his job weighed heavily. Coupled with recent personal problems, Steven often felt as though he were drowning. Only the night before he had woken abruptly from a nightmare in which he had found himself slipping into the depths of the soil heap. A group of Egyptian workmen had laughed hysterically as sand flowed quickly over his head.

Ethan had chosen Kate's hometown as a neutral topic of conversation. She had been surprised to learn that he had escorted some artefacts to the museum last December and helped put them on display for the Fascinating Mummies Exhibition. This sparked a lively conversation about the enthralling exhibition that Kate had loved. As they enjoyed a hearty breakfast, they moved onto other places of interest in Edinburgh, namely Ethan's favourite nightspots. But all discourse ceased when they spied David glaring at them from the doorway.

'Well, that's a look I haven't had from him before…' Ethan whispered, seeing naked envy in his friend's eyes. He felt Kate tense as David approached the table.

'So, you've emerged from hibernation...' he muttered to Kate, voice rich with sarcasm.

'I have work to do,' she snapped back. 'We don't all have time to go cantering off for a dawn picnic!' She glared at him accusingly, hiding her pain behind a mask of righteous anger.

David's jaw tightened as he prepared for a verbal sparring match. In the early days of their tortuous relationship, he had enjoyed their spats and her sharp ripostes. But the playful, flirtatious mood had gone, leaving something darker in its wake. Her fiery glare smouldered, and David forced his eyes from her parted lips.

Ethan cleared his throat. 'Before you two start tearing a strip off one another, can we sit down and discuss the plans for the day?' He beckoned for Steven to join them and gestured for David to sit down. Kate rose from her seat and picked up her empty plate.

'Thanks for the scrambled eggs, Doctor Forbes,' she said politely, feeling David's eyes burning holes in her clothing. She started towards the kitchen, aware that Ahmed stood in the kitchen doorway, watching her every move as though she were a fascinating exhibit in a zoo.

'Wait,' Ethan called. 'As your boss keeps telling me, you're part of this team. Sit down, Kate.'

Kate complied, feeling awkward under the stares of the men in the room and perturbed by Ethan's changeable behaviour towards her. She dreaded the moment when he would resume his despicable nettling.

'Okay,' Ethan began. 'I take it that your group will be back in the field today?' He glanced at David.

David nodded in confirmation. 'This morning we'll be working on the other plots. We'll be doing some cleaning and cataloguing after lunch. I might take them out again when it's a bit cooler…'

Nodding, Ethan turned to his intern. 'Steve, are you still busy with that soil heap?'

'Yeah, we've lifted a fair bit of sand and found mostly fragments of pottery. Some of it is patterned or inscribed with glyphs. I'd like to keep going with it, although I have a lot of paperwork, too…' He looked dolefully at Ethan. 'I could use some extra hands…'

As if on cue, Jonathan, Amy and Celine entered looking exhausted. Camping in the desert was proving difficult to stomach. Toilet facilities were created by digging a ditch, but there were few secluded areas to be found which might offer a modicum of privacy. David had woken them before dawn to break camp, presumably so he could go riding before breakfast. The students were feeling resentful, but they were slightly mollified by Kate's sympathetic smile.

'Any volunteers for soil heap duty?' Steven asked the lacklustre trio.

The prospect of working with Doctor Brodie brought Amy to life. 'I'd love to help!' she gushed. Jonathan and Celine reluctantly offered their services, in the hope that compliance might earn them a proper bed that night. Steven nodded curtly, and then waved them away. The three slouched off for breakfast.

'I can help, too,' Kate offered timidly and saw Steven's expression harden.

'It may only be a soil heap, but I still need people who know what they're doing…' Steven asserted rudely.

'Doctor Brodie,' Kate said through gritted teeth. 'Almost everything I've learned about archaeology and excavating, I've learned from you. Are you saying that your tuition was somehow inadequate?'

'Touché, Doctor Brodie!' Ethan smirked, while David sat back in silent observation. 'Okay, that's settled -'

Clearly fuming, Steven drew himself up to argue.

Hurt by Steven's attitude, and dismayed by the strained atmosphere for which she felt responsible, Kate finally snapped. Her chair scraped loudly on the floor as she stood up quickly. 'On second thought, forget that I offered to help. I've got enough work to do here, where my ineptitude won't cause such offence.' She gathered up her plate and without thinking, picked up Ethan's as well.

'Yeah, you should stick to your strengths…' Steven muttered.

Leaning across the table towards him, Kate lowered her voice, but her soft tone held a distinctly menacing note. 'You mind that your "bolshie teenager" act doesn't earn you a skelp round the ear – *Doctor* Brodie.' With her chin in the air, she marched to the kitchen, aware that silence befell the three men at the table.

Worthless in the face of female emotions, Ethan cautiously stuck his head around the door of the computer room. Kate was efficiently organising her workspace for the day; evidently, she planned to finish digitising the records from the 1891 expedition. He saw her swipe at her eyes with one hand.

'Hey,' he began awkwardly, realising that he was making a habit of sneaking up on her. 'David said that Anai finally parted with her box of artefacts…'

Kate cowered beneath a cloak of aloof proficiency. 'It's only bits and pieces, I'm afraid. Notes and lists, pieces of old letters, some photographs. I doubt it has monetary value, but it does give us a glimpse of what camp life was like in that era …' She chewed her lip.

'Are you sure you want to be cooped up in here this morning?'

She hesitated as though caught off-guard by his concern and fidgeted with the pen she held, almost dropping it. 'I think it would be best. Besides, I want to finish this. And I have the reports to write for the museum.' Her expression became petulant. 'Of course, I won't send anything until you've checked it…'

Ethan sighed. 'Then let me know when you're done. I'll be in my office for part of the morning…' He loitered in the doorway, hands in pockets. 'Kate, I'm sorry about Steven. I'll have a word with him.'

'I don't need you to defend me!' she snapped, irritably throwing her pen on the desk. 'I just wish I knew what was wrong with him. We were fine until he came out here – now he can't stop telling me how inadequate I am.'

'I've given him a lot of extra work to do,' Ethan admitted ruefully. 'A lot of it is administrative, and he would naturally rather be gaining experience in the field. Perhaps he's just frustrated…' He shrugged, becoming slightly alarmed by the trembling of her lower lip as she lifted her hand to her brow. 'You're not inadequate,' he blurted. 'You're doing a – a very *adequate* job. Keep up the good work…'

Ethan fled to the sanctuary of his office, but he would not find peace in that room, either.

At the sound of a firm knock on the door, Ethan raised his head and invited the caller to enter. As Julian Noble stepped into the room, Ethan sat up in his chair and adopted an air of calm authority. Eyeing the fair-haired student, Ethan gestured to the seat on the other side of the desk. Unexpectedly, the overconfident young Englishman made himself comfortable and looked the director in the eye; evidently, Julian felt justified in disturbing him and was not intimidated by the older man's carefully honed dour expression.

'What can I do for you, Mister Noble?' Ethan asked tersely.

'I wish to lodge a formal complaint, Doctor Forbes.' He had the good grace to blush, but a moment later had regained his composure.

'Oh? Against whom?'

'Professor Young.'

For a moment, Ethan stared stupidly at Julian, not convinced he had heard him correctly. 'You wish to complain about *Professor Young*?' he repeated. 'I presume you have good reason?'

The words came out in a rush. 'Well, he wasn't here for the beginning of the expedition, for a start. He's not doing his job properly, and his behaviour's erratic.'

Ethan forced himself to appear objective and assumed an impassive mien. 'Please elucidate,' he prompted, one hand straying to the small rock he used as a paperweight. He picked it up and turned it over in his palm, fingertips stroking the rough surface as he prepared to listen and pass judgement.

Julian was forthright in his criticism of David's lackadaisical attitude towards the syllabus, his sadistic decision to take them camping when they had paid for proper accommodation, and his appalling behaviour at Meryre's tomb. In the student's opinion, Professor Young wasn't so much teaching as bullying and seemed more interested in socialising with the locals than spending time with the undergraduates. Julian was calm and concise throughout his denunciation, but Ethan detected an underlying malice.

'Have you discussed these complaints with Miss Grahame?' Ethan asked once the diatribe had ended. 'She is the student liaison and therefore your first line of contact.'

Julian looked briefly at the floor before fixing Ethan with a cold, meaningful stare. 'I believe Miss Grahame's objectivity has been compromised...'

Ethan suppressed a snort of incredulity but gave in to the desire to punish the student by making him squirm. 'In what way has she been "compromised"?'

'She and the professor are...involved.'

'So you are also questioning Miss Grahame's professionalism?'

The student was becoming flustered, and therefore irritated. 'I'm sure she's perfectly professional when she's doing her job in Edinburgh. That is to say, when she's working with kids.

'She's not qualified to work as Professor Young's assistant on an expedition. The day we uncovered the skeletons, she looked like she was going to faint; *that's* why Professor Young sent her away. Her role – or rather, the approved position of "intern" – should have been given to one of the fourth-year students...'

Julian's voice trailed off as Ethan smiled slowly in triumph. The boy had said too much, and revealed the underlying reason for his spite.

'And of course,' Ethan began. 'The job might have been yours had Professor Young not made you repeat your third year after you failed your exams.' He raised an eyebrow at Julian's look of shamefaced astonishment.

'Why so shocked, Mister Noble? I'm the field director; it's my job to know everything about the people working under my supervision. I've studied every student record and every appraisal. Now, why don't you admit that you're mad at Professor Young for pushing you back a year and this is your way of exacting revenge?'

'Whatever my personal feelings, Professor Young's conduct has been inexcusable! He should be made accountable for his actions -'

Ethan banged the rock back on the table, stopping Julian mid-tirade. His mind was already working to find a solution to this problem, but he needed to buy some time. 'If you wish to proceed with this complaint, you need corroborating evidence. So I'll talk to each of your fellow students. If they also complain about ill-treatment or poor value for money then I'll take the matter to the next level…' *Like hell, I will.*

Ethan knew that the other students would not support Julian; his pompous attitude had won him no friends among his peers. But Julian was also aware of this, and so he had chosen an extreme course of action.

'I've already emailed the university,' he told Ethan, sounding smug. 'And I just received an acknowledgement. They're taking my complaint very seriously.' He drew some sheets of paper from his jacket pocket and placed them on the desk. 'This is a copy of that correspondence.'

'I see.' Ethan's whole body tensed as he fought to maintain his self-control. 'So why come to me, if you've already contravened the chain of command and gone over my head?'

Leaning over the desk, he stared hard at the young man and enunciated his next words carefully. 'What do you want?'

'As I said, Professor Young should be penalised for his indefensible behaviour. I also believe that Miss Grahame should be sent home immediately, and replaced by someone more suited to the job.'

Feeling anger rising within him, Ethan knew he was on the verge of physical assault. Standing, he remained on his side of the desk. 'Your complaints are noted, Mister Noble. Please inform your fellow students that I will need to talk to them. Now, you should join your group; Professor Young will be leaving for the dig site any minute.'

He strode to the door and opened it with more force than was necessary. Perhaps Julian saw the murderous gleam in Ethan's eye, for he rose quickly from his seat and sped out of the room without another word.

Youthful resilience waning, the students spent the morning following orders barked at them by Steven and David. Perhaps in an effort to escape the hostile working environment, the youngsters took it in turn to return to the dig house with one malady or another, preferring Kate's quiet compassion to the truculence of their supervisors. Julian worked with his usual meticulousness, but for once did not try to belittle the other members of his team. Each time one of his colleagues was excused to seek first aid at the house, however, a small knot of fear tightened in his gut.

And so Kate spent much of her morning in the infirmary, dispensing painkillers, indigestion remedies, and first aid for minor scrapes and an assortment of aches and pains. Unfortunately, she lacked the authority to order them to their rooms to rest, and so reluctantly had to send them back into the line of fire.

Despite the interruptions, she finished adding the meagre contents of Anai's box to the records, disappointed that she could find nothing of relevance; she had hoped for more information on Richard. There was only one blurry photograph, a scene of the men at work on the plain, the back view of a lone horseman in the foreground. Kate knew, from the upright yet relaxed posture that this was Richard Yorke astride a huge, dark-coloured hunter.

Once she had added this last picture to the database, Kate went to the kitchen and made a sandwich that filled her empty stomach, but failed to excite her taste buds. Hearing women's laughter in the courtyard, she stepped outside and saw Mina, Samira and Anai sitting under the tree. Samira waved and invited Kate to join them. Kate wavered, wary of spending time with them alone, but the heat from the midday sun felt like a slap in the face, and so she strode quickly towards the shade provided by the leafy acacia.

Springing up from her seat, Mina fetched Kate a chair but avoided meeting her gaze. Thanking her with a grateful smile, Kate resolved to remain friendly but mindful, and to resist Anai's references to past lives or inferred duties.

Samira was shelling a huge bowl of peas. With a grin, she handed Kate a pod and gestured for her to help, showing her how to split the pod with a fingernail and push the plump green peas into a second bowl. Apparently, it was also acceptable to eat a few while one worked. Kate sat quietly, glad to be part of their amicable little group, content to listen to the quiet chatter in Arabic and English, unaware that Anai watched her shrewdly.

All too soon, the students and their masters returned for lunch. For once, Mina seemed reluctant to jump up and cater to David's every whim. She hid behind her aunt and grandmother, declaring that there was plenty to eat in the kitchen and her services should not be required. Kate smiled at what she assumed was a display of rebelliousness, blissfully ignorant of Mina's resentment.

The students did not appear in the courtyard, and Kate correctly guessed that they had sought the comfort of bedrooms they had hardly used. As David walked around the side of the house, her feeling of tranquillity dissipated, to be replaced with something a lot less comforting.

David felt as though he were walking towards a pride of lionesses, still and watchful, but lethal. Certainly, the woman he loved could cut him down with her words alone, or one flash of those eloquent eyes. She had weakened him, and now the only way he could control his growing desire was to nurture the discord between them.

He slowed as Ahmed marched towards the group from the opposite direction. As he made a beeline for Kate, Ali's son swiftly removed the straw Stetson he always wore, and ran a hand through his hair. The Egyptian dutifully kissed his mother and grandmother, and then moved to stand before Kate. With growing trepidation, David watched her look up at a smiling Ahmed.

'Are you enjoying your time with us, Miss Kate?' Ahmed asked courteously, in heavily accented English.

'Yes, thank you Mister Suefy,' Kate smiled. 'Your country is very beautiful – what I've seen of it, anyway.'

'I would like to show you more of Amarna,' he declared. 'If you are willing, perhaps you would accompany me tomorrow morning. I could show you the boundary stelae, the palaces, the tombs…'

She was stuttering, unsure how to reply, and David recognised the guarded look. Whether she liked it or not, he was going to interfere. Purposefully, he came to stand beside Ahmed, greeting him with a brief smile that did not reach his eyes.

'I'm afraid Miss Grahame can't be spared, Ahmed.' He ignored Kate's scowl of indignation.

'A pity,' Ahmed replied, giving David a pointed look. He turned back to Kate. 'Perhaps you will have some free time before you leave us, Miss Grahame.' With a few words of farewell to his family and a short bow for Kate, Ahmed continued on his way.

Feeling the Egyptian women eye him with a mixture of scorn and amusement, David focused his attention on his assistant. 'I need you to help with the cleaning and cataloguing of artefacts this afternoon,' he stated sharply.

'The students are all thumbs today and whining like babies!' David moaned. 'We've used up half a tank of petrol driving them back and forth for ruddy plasters and painkillers. They've emptied the first aid kit we took with us – probably buried everything in the sand so they could skive off!'

Standing, Kate drew herself up to her full height, which was still more than a head shorter than David. 'They're *tired*,' she replied through clenched teeth. 'Perhaps you could allow them to sleep in their own beds tonight. They've paid for room and board – not a tent in the desert and a trench for a toilet. They're not going to be at their best if they don't get a decent rest. Their days are long enough.'

'They shouldn't expect to be babied, either!'

Hearing Samira mutter something to Anai, David felt completely outnumbered and knew Kate's confidence would grow in the company of these spirited women.

Sure enough, Kate continued with her verbal attack. 'They might be more willing to work if you'd give them a bit of encouragement, instead of snapping and glowering at them!'

'I wish Kate to join us this evening,' Anai demanded imperiously. 'She will dance for me in her costume.'

Having stirred the pot, Anai relaxed in her chair and closed her eyes, a cunning smile on her wrinkled face. Mina and Samira exchanged a surreptitious glance.

Tilting her head, Kate assumed an expression of false obsequiousness. 'May I go to Anai's house tonight, Professor?'

Wishing he could pull her out of earshot of her co-conspirators, David crossed his arms. 'No, you can't.'

Kate pouted because she knew he found the gesture distracting. 'Why not?'

'I won't be here to ferry you there and back -'

Mina spoke up. 'I can do that.'

'No,' David said again, sounding less assured. Kate was frowning now, and tapping her foot on the mosaic tiles as she began to lose patience with his inflexibility.

Taking her arm, he led her a few steps away from the women, lowering his voice so as not to be overheard. 'I won't have you parading about the place in that costume when I'm not around...' He frowned; his words had come out wrong, and now she was smirking at him. 'I won't have guys like Taylor feasting their eyes on you.' Kate suddenly looked uncomfortable. 'Yes, I heard about you throwing coffee over him. But I also heard that he'd made improper advances.'

Her ability to unsettle him returned. 'Well, Taylor's not the only one guilty of *that*. And did you just imply that I'm a feast for the eyes when I'm wearing a belly dancing costume?' Kate smiled audaciously. She had issued a challenge, and David knew he would lose.

'I'm saying that you might convey the wrong impression if you flounce around half-naked.'

She could see he was getting flustered. 'I won't be half-naked. I'll be wearing a face veil, and a body veil -'

'Which is transparent.'

'It covers me up. Mostly. And I don't *flounce*!'

'*Hah!*' David started to retreat towards the kitchen door, where Ethan lounged, munching on an apple. Stopping abruptly, David turned back to Kate. 'And what's the point of using a face veil, when all of *this* -' He gestured at Kate's midriff. '- is on show?'

Kate was briefly lost for words as she watched him walk towards a chuckling Ethan. She strode after him, confused by the array of emotions tumbling about within her. Why couldn't they just stop fighting?

'I demand that you allow the students to stay here tonight!' she shouted, stamping her foot. Ethan choked on a piece of apple. David turned slowly and regarded his assistant with disbelief.

'You *demand*?' He raised an eyebrow.

'Yes!' Kate replied boldly.

'Come on, Dave,' Ethan coaxed. 'Show some Christmas spirit! Just because you'll be homeless this year, doesn't mean you have to act like a -'

'Ethan, shut up and mind your own business!' David barked. He pushed past his friend and disappeared into the kitchen.

Realising he had put his foot in it, Ethan glanced at Kate and groaned inwardly at the woman's crestfallen expression. Apparently, David had neglected to tell her that he wasn't planning to renew the lease on his Edinburgh flat. Their relationship seemed to disintegrate a little more each day, not unlike Akhenaten's tomb.

'Did you draft your reports?' he asked, in an attempt to stop her from descending into despair in front of him. She looked up at him with huge eyes; he almost flinched.

'Yes,' she muttered helplessly.

'Well, I'm going to get some more food, but then I can take a look at them. Why don't you go back and sit with the women and I'll give you a shout in a little while?' Reluctant to bear witness to her suffering any longer, he retreated into the kitchen in search of biscuits.

Samira clucked sympathetically as Kate returned to her seat under the tree, while Mina muttered darkly in Arabic about the pig-headedness of men.

Patting Kate's hand, Anai chuckled. 'The lion is angry, qitah. You have dislodged him from his seat, and he does not know where to stand.' She laughed outright and scrutinised Kate's face. Kate tried not to look away from the intense stare of the enigmatic octogenarian, who seemed to have the ability to peer into her soul. 'You feel powerful today, little one. You have stepped onto a different path, I think.'

Picking up a pea pod, Kate split it open and gazed sadly at the little green orbs snuggled together. 'I can't make sense of anything...' she murmured.

'Your eyes have been opened to the truth. You recall being here in another lifetime. You loved one man and felt great affection for another. But your marriage was not the wondrous unity of souls you imagined, because both you and he were flawed. It ended in tragedy and heartache.

'What you have witnessed through your dreams is a story that has happened many times through the ages. And, since it began in the time of the pharaohs, in this place you helped create and protect, your souls are drawn to Amarna. The three of you always end the story here: the golden lion, the jackal, and the little cat…' She began humming to herself, as though she had simply been discussing the weather.

Kate studied her carefully, searching for signs of dementia. The woman had spoken with complete authority, however, and Kate felt unable to dismiss Anai outright.

'Does the story always end the same way?' she inquired, forgetting her resolve to be vigilant.

Anai tilted her head. 'I feel that it will end differently this time,' she replied confidently. 'Because you can see the mistakes of the past. And because *you* are different.'

She fell silent, her piercing dark eyes holding Kate's gaze. Samira and Mina watched in silent anticipation, and Kate braced herself for another damaging exposé. Sure enough, Anai took a deep breath and slowly withdrew a drawstring bag from the folds of her robe. With trembling fingers, she pulled out a creased sepia photograph of a dark-haired couple wearing solemn expressions. The comely young woman held a baby wrapped in a shawl. Anai tapped the swaddled infant.

'That is me,' she explained, and Kate smiled. 'These are my father and mother. My father was born – how do you say it…' She turned to Mina, and there followed a short exchange in Arabic, during which Mina sounded as though she were begging her grandmother not to continue. Anai ignored the girl's pleas and returned her attention to Kate.

'There was no marriage between his parents,' Anai said sadly, shaking her head. She paused, assessing Kate's expression of curiosity. 'His mother was from a village near Luxor. His father was an English archaeologist. You understand, qitah?'

Kate nodded, understanding perfectly: a visiting archaeologist who took advantage of a naïve and love-struck young woman. Given Anai's approximate age, Kate estimated the scandal would have occurred in the Victorian era. Then a dreadful thought hit her like a bolt of lightning. 'When was your father born, Anai?'

Anai tilted her head as though mentally calculating, but Kate began to suspect that some new treachery was afoot.

At last, Anai declared, 'I think 1889.'

She handed Kate the tattered photograph. 'Look,' she commanded, but Kate drew back, unwilling. 'You *must* look.'

He was there, in the man's intelligent dark eyes. The same sensual mouth. An inscrutable expression she would never forget. This man's lineage was only half Egyptian; the rest was a unique blend of Italian and English.

Anai's father was Edwin's illegitimate son. Her soulmate's essence was in Anai, in Ali, in Ahmed, in Mina, and in Hassan. Edwin's marriage to

153

Katherine had been built on a lie. The chair toppled over as Kate stood up.

'No…' she moaned. 'He's not – he can't be…'

Pulling out another old photograph, Anai delivered her final, crushing blow of the day. 'Then look at *this*.'

There he was, her past life husband, standing in front of the house Anai lived in, his dark eyes gazing on the tiny baby in his arms – his son.

'I am sorry, little one,' Anai told her. 'Edwin Ford was my grandfather. He seduced my grandmother and promised to marry her. But he returned to your country instead.

'Nula came to Amarna when she discovered he was here searching for Akhenaten's tomb. Edwin met with her, told her of his new wife and family, and insulted her by offering her money for her silence. She gave birth to his son while he was here – as you see from the picture. But then he abandoned her once more.

'My grandmother was considered soiled and so no man wanted to marry her. Her heart was broken, but she used her gifts of sight and magic to help the women of her community, and these women helped her to raise her son.

'She taught me all she knew before she died, and now I continue her work. I have inherited her gifts; I can see the past, the future, lost souls and spirits. I can help others to do the same…

'But I will never forget the misery heaped upon Nula. Edwin Ford was a betrayer who brought a curse on this family. We have suffered terrible misfortune for four generations. His soul may reside in that jackal but it is forever damned! Ethan Forbes rots from within – he will never know peace!' Her vehemence brought on a fit of coughing, and Mina handed Anai a cup of water and helped her to drink.

Shaking her head in denial, Kate dropped the photographs and ran.

CHAPTER 10

As he approached the computer room in search of his assistant, David heard Kate's voice and Ethan's deeper tones in quiet conversation. Without making a conscious decision to do so, David stopped just outside the room and eavesdropped.

'I don't like this bit,' Ethan said.

'Which bit?' Kate sounded impatient and a little frosty.

'This bit here,'

There was the sound of a heavy sigh from Kate, followed by a few moments of silence. 'Is it technically correct?' she inquired. Yes, there was a definite hostility in her tone of voice.

'Yes, I suppose…'

'And you're happy that I'm not revealing secrets or writing anything that is detrimental to your worthy cause?'

'Hmm…'

'It's just my writing style which bothers you?'

'Only this bit. And maybe this bit…' There was laughter in his voice, as if he were attempting to provoke her for his entertainment, but it was clear that Kate was in no mood to be toyed with.

'Well, since this is *my* work, why don't you leave style and construction to me? I'm pretty sure I'm more eloquent than you are!'

Leaning against the wall, David smiled fondly, and then frowned as Ethan spoke again.

'Now see, I remember this attitude. Were we in the same class at some time? Remedial English, maybe?'

'I was never in remedial anything!'

'No, I bet you were a good little girl. Let me guess, you're Daddy's little princess, right?'

There was a short, heavy silence. 'My father died nearly two years ago,' Kate informed him quietly. 'I was never his "princess".'

Ethan's hesitation was longer than it should have been. 'Sorry…'

Kate made a noncommittal sound. 'Can I send this report?'

An exaggerated sigh issued from Ethan. 'Well, if you're happy with the style and construction…'

There was the faint sound of Kate's rapid typing. 'Ethan, can I ask you something?' So, they were on first-name terms now. Moreover, her tone had softened. Why was she so inconsistent?

'Oh God, do you have to? I'm not baring my soul again…'

Kate grunted derisively. 'I don't think you have one to worry about.' She paused, no doubt reflecting on the poignant remark. When she spoke again, her voice sounded strained. 'Is it possible to trace the family tree of one of the locals?'

'Who?'

'Anai.'

Ethan laughed. 'Anai? I sometimes think she was around when Akhenaten was a lad! In fact, she might have been the one who discovered the Amarna Tablets.'

'Never mind. I'll ask someone else.' Kate sounded annoyed.

'Stop scowling, Friday. I doubt there are proper records. Why are you interested?'

David finally made his entrance, in time to hear Kate mutter, 'It doesn't matter.' He tried to project an air of calm indifference and stifled the impulse to glower jealously at Ethan.

'Kate, would you join me?' he asked. 'I want to set up the room for cleaning the artefacts we found in the grave.' The room was already prepared; he just wanted to snatch a few minutes' peace with Kate.

Without argument, Kate stood and headed towards the door. One look at her face told David that something was very, very wrong.

'Actually, have you two got a few minutes?' Ethan queried. 'There are a couple of issues we need to address. Shut the door and sit down.' He waited until the door was closed, and Kate had returned to her seat. David, however, remained standing. 'First, I'd like to say that this is the worst expedition I've ever been on -'

'Well, *you're* the field director…' Kate grumbled.

Ignoring her insolent comment, Ethan continued. 'David, your boy Julian has made a formal complaint to the university -'

'About what?' David snapped. At the same time, Kate inhaled sharply.

'About your behaviour,' Ethan replied, shifting uncomfortably in his seat. 'And your unprofessional relationship with Kate…' He waited while David muttered a string of expletives and slumped in a chair. 'Look, he's miffed because you passed him over for the intern's position, and Kate's a sitting duck. The stupid laddie gave me a copy of his email…'

He passed the now wrinkled sheet of paper to David so that his friend could read the list of complaints. Slowly, David's face turned an unattractive shade of puce. Crushing the paper into a ball, David tossed it onto the desk.

Kate picked it up, smoothed it out, and read evidence of Julian's spite, an expression of mounting horror on her already wan features.

'He has all the eloquence of a donkey, right?' Ethan remarked, smiling gently at Kate. 'Julian could learn a thing or two about writing by reading *your* work.' The compliment was wasted on her; she read the missive a second time while chewing her lip. 'Don't fret – I've already sent my own message to the university -'

'You did *what*?' David groaned. 'Ethan, I can fight my own battles -'

'I know, mate. But you've pulled me out of more scrapes than I can count, so let me handle this one.' He squeezed David's tense shoulder. 'I told Julian I'd have to speak to the other students. I thought I'd call for them individually while you're doing the cataloguing this afternoon. If I make a big drama out of it, it might frighten him enough to think about the consequences of his actions...'

Rubbing his forehead, David grimaced. 'Christ, Ethan, haven't we got enough drama to deal with?'

'You're not going to like issue number two, then...' Ethan felt sorry for his friend, but he could not handle this problem alone, because he did not fully understand it. 'I've heard some gossip that might shed light on Anai's sneaky behaviour.' He glanced at Kate, who looked utterly desolate. David, meanwhile, remained resolutely in his seat, and Ethan felt a moment's irritation towards the other man. 'Ahmed's looking for a new wife.'

David's head lifted sharply, his face registering disbelief. Ethan continued with plaster-ripping bluntness. 'And although Kate's a bit long in the tooth for an Egyptian man's tastes, she's not past her childbearing years yet. More importantly, she has money.'

Kate seemed to shrink shamefaced in her seat and offered no counter-argument. With a heavy sigh, Ethan hastened to end this unpleasant discussion.

'I think we're all aware of Mina's feelings for you, Dave, and I think we can agree that you might be guilty of leading her on a bit – even if you didn't intend to. I've just discovered she wants to study medicine, preferably in Britain. Again, perfect trophy spouse with money and access to a British visa.'

Speechless, David stared at Ethan incredulously. Obviously, he had been unaware of Mina's dangerous infatuation. Ethan shook his head in frustration; David could be so oblivious to the feelings of those around him. He had always blamed David's lack of siblings for the Englishman's insensitivity.

'What about you?' Kate asked Ethan quietly. 'What are her plans for you?'

'A lifetime of torture?' Ethan suggested, trying to make light of a grim situation. 'We also have to deal with this witchcraft problem. I've noticed the appearance of talismans around the house, and Mina was wearing a love potion this morning, though I guess you were too preoccupied to notice.' He looked inquiringly at David, who shrugged in bewilderment. 'Anai probably believes she can manipulate us through hocus-pocus. She's using this suggestion of a shared past life to bamboozle you, Kate, because she feels you're gullible. I bet she's been using your ancestry against you, too, right?'

Kate's face turned white as she nodded and stared blankly at the desk. Ethan waited for elucidation, but she remained silent.

'Ahmed invited Kate out on a tour with him,' David revealed. 'And when she went to Anai's house with Marianne and Thea, Anai cut a lock of Kate's hair…'

'She might have used it to make a wax or clay poppet,' explained Ethan, catching Kate's look of fear. 'In Egyptian magic, they're used as a way to manipulate the will of others. But I'm sure she won't stick pins in it…'

The three of them sat for a moment, each of them feeling weakened and vulnerable.

'Kate,' David began, his hand stretching across the table towards her even though he was unable to reach her. 'I think it would be best if you didn't spend time with the Suefy family on your own. No more dancing at Anai's house.'

'I agree,' Ethan told her. 'I'll have to speak to Ali about the witchcraft thing -' He stopped midsentence as Kate snorted in apparent disgust. 'What?' he inquired.

'You!' she spat. Kate adopted a masculine tone, aping Ethan's voice. 'And "I'll have to speak to Ali"! As if everything will be fine if you clipe to the man of the house! You men think you can solve everything just because you're men!' She thumped her chest mockingly with her fists. 'Man talk – woman listen and obey! This isn't the dark ages – we have the right to ignore what you say and *do what we like*! Anai illustrates my point perfectly! And so does Mina – you can't believe that her uncle approves of the way she throws herself at David, but that doesn't seem to worry *her* at all!'

Glancing at David, Ethan realised he would receive no support from that quarter, for David's eyes were full of doting admiration.

'It's true that Anai is the matriarch of her family,' he replied tersely, forcing himself to remain calm in the face of her belligerence. 'But in this culture, women generally know their place -'

Kate's response was cuttingly swift. 'Two words, Ethan: "up" and "yours"!'

David tittered. Kate sat back and folded her arms, the very image of a sullen teenager.

Seeing she was unmoved by his warning look, Ethan took a deep breath and continued his attempt to solve their problems. 'I'm fairly sure Ali and Samira have had no part in Anai's machinations. Ali might be able to nip it in the bud. Just to be on the safe side, though, give me those talismans Anai handed out.' He held out his hand for the amulets.

'Why?' Kate asked, drawing the Bastet talisman from a pocket. 'I thought they were for our protection and good fortune?' She stroked the image of the cat goddess.

David pulled the image of Sekhmet from his trouser pocket and tossed it to Ethan. 'Not always.' He shook his head. 'They are sometimes used as a conduit for magic spells – allegedly…'

Standing abruptly, Ethan snatched the amulet from Kate's open palm and began to pace the room like a caged animal. 'Christ!' he spat. 'I can't believe we're even discussing such nonsense! I'm supposed to be an archaeologist, but I feel like I'm in a cheesy fantasy soap opera! What's next – vampires in El Till?'

David smiled sadly. 'Ethan, you have no idea…'

Sniffing, Kate kept her head down and wiped at the tear that had spilled onto her cheek. There was a short silence, as Ethan fought to compose himself; he needed to remain rational.

'Look,' Ethan began. 'Everything will be fine if we just keep our heads.' He gave David a lopsided grin. 'So please don't be tempted to give Julian a mud-encrusted rock to clean this afternoon. And Kate, if you want to go sightseeing, I'll be out and about tomorrow. You could come with me if you like…'

Ethan knew he was in danger of crossing the line, and sure enough, he saw the telltale tic in David's jaw. Kate looked up at David imploringly, but instead of offering his services as a tour guide, the professor looked away. Exasperated, Ethan shook his head and frowned at David.

'No, thank you,' Kate murmured to Ethan.

'Perhaps you could dance here,' David suggested. 'There's bound to be a room we can use, and appropriate music. I'm sure Marianne and some of the girls would love a lesson from you…' He fired Ethan a roguish grin, pleased with his ingenuity.

'That's a very good idea,' Ethan agreed, his eyes twinkling. 'But David and I get to watch.'

Realising that they were late for the artefact cleaning session, David rose to his feet, chuckling at Ethan's impudence.

'Choose a room with windows,' Kate responded, rising from her seat. 'And then you two can do your peeping-tom double act!'

Shamelessly, the men sniggered. David opened the door and gestured for Kate to precede him into the hallway. Ethan watched her as she passed him; she was strong, and she would rally.

'I've got it!' Ethan exclaimed, making Kate halt in her tracks. 'You were a stripper in a pub in Leith! *That's* how I know you. Naughty secretary, right?'

Rolling her eyes, Kate turned her head to scald him with an angry glare. 'You were a rotten tipper,' she retorted and walked out of the room.

As David followed her, admiring her spirit as well as her rear view, he heard Ethan call after her, 'I've never *had* to tip!'

Traipsing along the corridor, Kate seemed to deflate again before David's eyes. Falling into step beside her, he brushed her knuckles with his own, a small gesture of solidarity.

'Are you counting the days yet?' he asked carefully, tired of being at odds with her.

'I'm just trying to get through one day at a time,' she confessed. 'But yes, I have considered running home screaming to my mother.'

'Well, there are only five days left. And then you can go home…'

She made no reply, since every conversation led to an argument.

'Why are you interested in Anai's ancestry?'

'Don't ask, David; you don't want to know. And I appreciate your suggestion, but I really don't feel like dancing…'

They had reached the workroom, where the students were already sitting around the large table in the centre of the room.

'Look,' David said quickly, touching her arm. 'Ali's cooking on the barbecue tonight. Have dinner with me, and we can try to forget about the bad stuff for a while.'

She looked into his eyes, seeing gold flecks in the green irises. 'David, is there anything you would like to tell me?'

There was a moment's vacillation, before he replied, 'Not at the moment.'

Nodding resignedly, Kate walked into the room and took a seat between Jonathan and Dominic. All chattering ceased as David shut the door. Julian glared at Kate but avoided looking at his professor.

The discoveries from the grave of the two skeletons lay in three plastic containers that sat in the centre of the table, alongside a tray of cleaning tools and cataloguing materials. David cast a discerning eye over each artefact and began to distribute the pieces for cleaning. Pulling on latex gloves, Kate prodded the large nugget of caked mud that David placed on the work mat in front of her. Jonathan received some pieces of grimy broken tile while Dominic chose an object that resembled a sausage on a knobbly stick. Glancing furtively across the table at Julian, Kate eyed his work mat with concern; David had given the student an item that did in fact resemble a mud-caked rock. She caught David's eye and threw him a questioning glance, but he simply pointed to her mat and indicated that she should focus on her assignment.

After a few words of guidance from their teacher, the students and Kate began the exercise by taking preliminary notes and measurements. With infinite care, they then began to remove the layers of grime from their items with soft brushes and the cautious application of distilled water. They worked nervously, aware of David circling the table like a great hawk, watching them carefully and judging their technique.

He paused to crouch between Jonathan and Kate; she had tentatively rubbed at her relic with gentle fingers, loosening the mud until the piece was about the size of a walnut. Now Kate could see what looked like a smooth blue band, and was unsure how to proceed.

'It won't clean itself, Nefertari.'

Hearing an ancient queen's name used as an endearment, the students glanced up in surprise, and then awkwardly returned to their work. David allowed himself an artful smile; he had openly admitted his affection for Kate. Hopefully, Julian's implication that the professor was conducting an illicit affair would now carry less weight. Moreover, he had let Kate know that he hadn't given up on her yet.

Reaching across the table, David selected a toothbrush, a dish of water, and a pick that looked like a dentist's tool. He handed them to Kate, smiling at her discomfiture. As he got to his feet, his gaze met Julian's, and David raised an eyebrow at the student. Julian went back to scraping soil from the piece that now resembled a golf ball, and David resumed his role as invigilator.

'You know what Nefertari's name means, don't you?' Jonathan whispered out of the side of his mouth. Kate muttered in the negative, and the teenager gleefully explained, 'It means "most beautiful one of all"!'

Ethan stuck his head round the door and announced that he needed to talk to the students. Over the next two hours, he extracted each member of the group in turn. Julian looked increasingly uncomfortable, while David paced the room.

Meticulous cleaning revealed a small alabaster pot and several amulets. Some of Jonathan's tile fragments were pieced together to show part of a river scene. In Akhenaten's time the painting of blue water, green rushes and swimming birds would have been vibrant. Now its beauty would be held in high regard once more, even though the colours had faded, and the tile was incomplete.

The group was entranced by the baby's rattle that emerged from Dominic's oddly shaped clump of earth. The blue-green faience had been fashioned to resemble a hippo, the matching handle fragile but still intact. Dominic shook the hippo gently, and they heard a dry rattling sound from inside the hollow toy.

Julian's ancient Egyptian golf ball had a grill pattern etched into its surface, and some rudimentary hieroglyphics were faintly visible. The student recorded the glyphs in his notebook, but was unable to make sense of them. Although the ball was made of mud, fragments of pottery and bone had also be used in its composition.

161

Using a stainless steel scalpel, Julian made an incision in the ball and cut it in half. With David looking over his shoulder, the student used a pick to gently lever out the contents of the mud ball. A small parcel wrapped in discoloured linen was placed on the mat. It was tied with strands of dark hair and open at one end. After more brushing and close examination, Julian deduced that the mysterious item was in fact a metacarpal bone.

'Do any of you know what this is?' David asked the group. The students would only see their professor's usual po-faced demeanour, but Kate would see the sparkle in his eyes that betrayed David's excitement over this artefact.

'Is it a mud ball?' Russell asked hesitantly, afraid of sounding facetious. David nodded encouragingly. 'Aren't they pretty rare? And weren't they used in ancient Egyptian magic rituals?'

'Yes, yes and yes,' David replied with a smile. 'They've only been found in burials. We assume they were made for the protection of the deceased, but their true purpose is unknown. This discovery adds credence to our assertion that the woman practised witchcraft.' He looked at the other students. 'What else do we have which might back up our theory?'

'There are a lot of amulets,' Amy responded.

'What kind of amulets?' David probed. Amy was, as Kate had put it, a 'work in progress'. She always needed extra tuition, probably because she did not apply herself wholeheartedly to the work. Not his favourite type of pupil.

'Well, we've found a haematite headrest amulet, some jasper Eyes-of-Horus, a little heart-shaped stone, and some djed columns which are probably made of bone...' Amy floundered, and blushed as she became aware of everyone watching her in anticipation.

'Please tell us the significance of these particular pieces,' David ordered.

Amy took a deep breath. 'The headrest amulet was placed under the neck of the deceased and had a protective function. A string of Eyes-of-Horus might have been placed across the neck area. The heart amulet...well, it speaks for itself – it would have been placed on the chest.'

Someone sniggered, infusing Amy with confidence. She gave the professor an impish grin. 'Of course, sometimes a papyrus sceptre amulet was also placed on the chest, or a Knot of Isis. Scarabs were also important, as they were inscribed with a spell on the underside that implored the heart not to testify against the deceased during judgement, when the heart was weighed against the feather of truth.

'Faience amulets of the gods were also popular, made with loops in the back so they could be strung together. We've found one of Isis suckling Horus. Isis was a goddess of magic, as well as her other goddess-y skills...'

Celine laughed at Amy's humorous comment, but David remained unmoved.

'I see extra tuition with Doctor Brodie is paying off,' he remarked. 'When you're writing up your notes tonight, Amy, I want you to draw me a picture. Sketch the outline of a mummy, and mark the positions of the amulets. Write down the significance of each and the materials used to make them.' Noting Amy's crestfallen expression, he added, 'You can work on the grave tomorrow morning. Perhaps you'll find the "missing" amulets.'

Relieved to have pleased the professor, Amy grinned at her cohorts. David perched on the table and glanced around the group. 'So what conclusions, if any, can we draw from the items we've cleaned so far?'

'She was loved,' Celine spoke up with conviction. 'She and her child were buried with care and reverence. If she was indeed a witch, she was respected...'

'A little sentimental, but accurate,' David concurred. 'Anything else?'

'She didn't worship the Aten,' Julian put in, looking directly at the professor. 'All the artefacts indicate she followed the old, polytheistic religion.'

'Correct,' David said briskly, his face carefully neutral. 'Right. Those of you who've finished cleaning their objects, continue with *accurate* cataloguing, please. I want a sketch of each item, too. Jonathan, since you've completed the assignment already, you can take photographs of the pieces for the records.'

As they resumed their work, David walked around the table to stand beside Kate. She was brushing the last vestiges of dirt from a ring of blue faience. The oval bezel boasted an openwork design with two fan-shaped bouquets of flowers.

'It's so beautiful!' Kate whispered breathlessly, holding the ring in her cupped palm. She placed it back on the mat so that Jonathan could take a photograph, and then picked it up again to admire the workmanship.

Lowering himself to one knee, David took the ring from her. To an observer, it appeared as though he was offering the ring to Kate in a proposal of marriage. His eyes met hers.

'Very beautiful,' David agreed. 'She was indeed loved...'

All the lights went out.

'Remain in your seats,' David called calmly. 'It's probably a power cut.' Fishing his mobile from his pocket, he activated the inadequate flashlight; Russell and Jonathan followed suit. They pushed the artefacts on the mats to the centre of the table, out of harm's way. Within five minutes, the door opened and Ahmed and Ali entered, each carrying two hurricane lamps. Ahmed set a lantern on the table in front of Kate, smiling at her as he did so.

'Don't be afraid, Miss Grahame,' he soothed. 'We are used to power failures here, and so we are well prepared.'

'It'll take more than a power failure to frighten Miss Grahame, Ahmed,'

David informed the Egyptian. 'In fact, she's pretty frightening herself, which makes her an extremely difficult woman to live with.'

Ali asked David if they needed more light, but David decided they could manage. With a polite bow, the caretaker hurried from the room with his son following at a slower pace.

'Well,' David addressed his trainees. 'We can still work, so keep going. By the way, I'll be camping out again tonight. Those of you who wish to join me may do so, but I won't think any less of those who would rather sleep in their beds.'

He looked at Kate for a sign of approval and received a slight nod of acknowledgement before she commenced cataloguing the beautiful faience ring.

Steven brought in some torches as the session was ending, which were snatched up by the students when David finally dismissed them. Although the prospect of cold showers filled them with horror, the students agreed this was a small price to pay for the pleasure of sleeping in a proper bed with a roof over their heads. Dominic and Russell were keen to camp out, however, and Jonathan was undecided. He wanted to impress Celine, but the infatuated young man was unsure which course of action would prove more effective.

Once the six had departed, and peace descended on the room, David sat down next to Kate and sighed in relief.

'It went well, don't you think?' he asked her.

'You should tell *them* that,' Kate advised. 'They need to hear your praise, now and again.'

A teasing smile appeared on his lips. 'You're doing a good job.' David held her gaze. 'My Nefertari…'

Kate wearily pushed her hair back from her face. 'You mustn't call me that in front of people – we're in enough trouble. And stop coming over all caveman with Ahmed. I can deal with him myself. I do have a tongue in my head.'

His eyes darkened as he murmured, 'I'm aware…'

Kate threw him a warning glance and shook her head in disgust. 'Please, can we just finish up here? I'm very tired…' *And I'm angry and hurt, and confused.*

As she helped David pack the artefacts, file the paperwork, clean the equipment and tidy the room, Kate became increasingly withdrawn. Sensing her bleak mood, David remained silent. Once the room was pristine, they picked up the lanterns and used them to light their way to the dining room. Compared to the area they had just left, this part of the house was dazzlingly bright and a hive of activity.

Ali and Ahmed had fired up the barbecue and now carried plates of meat outside to the courtyard, which had been transformed into a magical grotto lit by flame torches and strategically-placed lanterns. The occupants of the house were already gathering in the courtyard, but the escalating noise quickly began to grate on Kate's nerves.

In the kitchen, Mina and Samira prepared vegetables, salads and other local delicacies. Appearing from the darkness behind them, Ethan entered carrying a case of beer, which he set down on the table. Deftly opening two bottles, he handed one to David and offered the other to Kate, who declined. Shrugging, Ethan took a long swig from the bottle.

'Julian is the only student who has a gripe,' he announced, after drinking half a bottle of beer in one draught. 'The rest of them fairly gushed about the pair of you. If I were a suspicious man, I'd wonder if someone had paid them…'

Before either David or Kate could thank Ethan, Mina rushed out of the kitchen brandishing a sample of spicy sauce on a wooden spoon, which she offered up to David's lips.

'Taste!' she commanded.

Complying, David made an appreciative sound and assured Mina that the sauce tasted delicious. As the girl returned exultantly to the kitchen, David was treated to a disapproving frown from Ethan and a look of sad resignation from Kate. Picking up a torch from the table, Kate braved the darkness and cautiously picked her way to her room. She was in no mood to join the party.

It was the dead of night and silent save for the distant bark of a lonely dog. Movement around him woke Ethan from a restless slumber. A powerful scent wafted up his nostrils, something akin to incense. As his eyes adjusted to the meagre light offered by a small window, he discovered he was lying on a camp bed in a rough mud hut. Dark shapes around him suggested a large trunk, a folding desk and chair, a washstand and miscellaneous boxes. But it was the slender shape gliding towards him that held his attention. When the silhouette folded itself gracefully to sit beside him, he realised the spectre was a woman.

With long, slim fingers, she traced the buttons of his linen shirt, and then stroked the exposed skin of his throat. Placing his hand firmly over hers, he halted her exploration.

'Stop,' he whispered hoarsely. A convenient shaft of moonlight shone through the window, bathing his visitor in a halo of soft light.

Long black hair fell around her shoulders and down her back. Her features were exquisite, as though carefully chiselled from flawless alabaster. Amber eyes stared at him in a manner that was almost feline. She tilted her head and gave him a mysterious smile. Leaning forward, she kissed him slowly, seductively. Ethan cursed his traitorous body. His anonymous guest, however, sat back and surveyed her handiwork, one hand straying to his thigh and moving upwards…

'I mean it,' Ethan rasped. He felt suddenly giddy. 'You have to leave. You can't be here…'

'You want me,' she stated confidently. 'And tonight I will claim you as mine.'

Standing, she unfastened the flimsy robe that covered her body and let it slide to the floor. Naked, she slipped under the rough blankets. 'You belong to Nula,' she whispered in his ear. 'You will be forever mine, Edwin Ford…'

Sitting bolt upright in bed, Ethan found himself bathed in sweat. Far from erotic, the dream had been too vivid, with an almost threatening undertone. Switching on the light by his bed, Ethan reached for the book he had left on the floor, his hands trembling. He tried to study the bewildering concept of astral projection until he felt brave enough to sleep.

CHAPTER 11

Monday December 17, 2012

Footsteps made Kate look up from pulling on her grimy boots and her eyes met David's briefly before her attention returned to her footwear. His unshaven face was inscrutable, and she wondered if this would be another day of discord.

Kate had nothing left to fight with; she had spent ten minutes standing under the pathetic spray of warm water in the shower, her mind blank. Already she felt the dust clogging up her pores and clinging to her hair. Her bootlaces were so dirty, they squeaked as she tied a double knot.

Ali had repaired the lock on her bedroom door just before the power cut, and Kate had gratefully accepted the gift of solitude while her colleagues had stayed up late carousing. When power had been restored just after nine o'clock, the tipsy housemates had cheered loudly and continued their merrymaking.

For Kate, another sleepless night had ensued but, thanks to her locked door, she received no visitors. Now she heartily wished she could banish David from her room and lock out the world for a little longer – or better still, until it was time to go home.

'You're up,' David observed pointlessly. 'Good. Come with me. Bring your gloves and wrap up. We're going out, and it's cold.' He strode out of the room.

Gathering up her gloves, scarf, and jacket, Kate hurried after him, unwilling to incur his wrath before the day had even begun. Anticipating her imminent questions, David put a finger to his lips to silence her, and led Kate outside into the muted dawn light.

A sombre-faced Ahmed waited on the other side of the house wall, holding the reins of two black Arab horses. The stallion was the huge, spirited beast that David had taken out with Mina. Today, the horse carried saddlebags. The mare was smaller and more docile. A striped rug protected her sleek back from the saddle.

The professor thanked Ahmed, who handed over the reins somewhat reluctantly then wandered into the house. David checked the horses and their tack, as was his habit, before turning to a dumbfounded Kate.

'I'm going to attach a lead rein,' he informed her, and Kate nodded meekly. David knew her acquiescence to be a sign of her flagging spirits. She looked tired and disconsolate, and not unlike the photograph of her ancestor. Without further comment, he attached a lead rein to both bridles, and then helped Kate into the saddle. Once he had helped her to adjust the stirrups, David mounted the prancing stallion and led the way down the slope and into the silent desert.

As the call to prayer sounded from the local mosque, David and Kate rode in the direction of the north cliffs, sand blowing lazily around the horses' hooves. Kate's body swayed in time with the horse's pace, her overloaded brain unable to focus on the business of commanding her mount. Tears lurked just behind her eyes, threatening to spill at the slightest provocation. In need of comfort, she stroked the horse's warm neck, and looked blankly at the barren landscape around her, which hid so many secrets.

Before long, her attention wandered to David's back. As ever, he was relaxed in the saddle, lost in thought. Kate lost track of time, but as they climbed upwards, she realised they were heading for the viewpoint Ethan had shown her. They kept going until the dirt track petered out at the barricaded entrance to a tomb. Here, David dismounted, and secured the reins on the rusting gate.

Dismounting slowly, Kate walked gingerly to the edge of the cliff and looked across the plain, automatically wrapping her arms around her body. A cold breeze ruffled her hair, and she shivered.

'I should've told you to bring your camera,' David chided himself as he came to stand beside her.

'It's okay,' Kate replied vaguely. 'I took pictures when -' She stopped midsentence.

David sighed. 'He already brought you here, didn't he? I should've known...'

Kate looked up, seeing disappointment on David's face. 'He brought me here and then interrogated me,' she explained, scared of antagonising him. 'The view didn't look as pretty as it does now, in the dawn light. And he brought me in a smelly truck, not on horseback.' She tried to smile, but found she was too weary.

There was a broad, flat-topped boulder a few feet away, which almost resembled a bench. Kate sat down heavily, but instead of admiring the view, she looked down at her filthy boots.

'I thought you might enjoy a morning ride...' David said, sounding disheartened by her lack of enthusiasm.

Kate's head rose sharply, her gaze reproachful. 'Was Mina busy?' she asked him, unable to hide her jealousy. She bowed her head once more.

David walked towards her and crouched down so that he could look into her face. She wanted to turn away so that he wouldn't see the dark circles under her dull eyes, but he touched her cheek to still the movement.

'I didn't bring you up here to fight with you.'

'Why did you bring me, then?' Kate knew she sounded petulant.

'So we could have some time alone -'

'I've been alone enough, thank you very much!'

David remained patient. 'So we could have some time alone *together*. To try to find our way...back. Things have been crazy, Kate. I hate the constant tension between us.' Briefly, he leaned his forehead against the clasped hands on her lap. 'I miss you...'

Kate eyed him warily, tempted to stroke his hair, but then David stood up and collected the saddlebags from his horse's back. Sitting down next to Kate, he opened the canvas bags and extracted a thermos flask and a bag of bread rolls. Her eyes widened in amazement as he then pulled out a small jar of chocolate spread and a knife. Spreading a linen cloth on his lap, he proceeded to cut open a roll and coat it with a thick layer of spread. Unable to contain a grin of triumph, he offered the bread roll to Kate.

Feeling like a complete fool, Kate fought to prevent her lip from trembling as she accepted his offering. 'You brought this for me?' she asked, her voice shaking with emotion even as she cringed inwardly at her overreaction to his thoughtfulness.

David smiled gently. 'How could I forget your fondness for all things chocolate?' he teased, and reached out to caress her cheek. 'Come on, eat your breakfast. You've missed dinner two nights in a row.'

As Kate obediently bit into the soft roll, David opened the thermos and poured some coffee into the lid. When he handed it to Kate, she shook her head apologetically.

'I think you might like *this* coffee,' David coaxed.

Not wishing to offend him, Kate sipped the hot liquid. 'It's my favourite instant coffee!' she exclaimed, her voice quivering as she felt the urge to weep outright. 'How did you -'

David smiled enigmatically. 'Enjoy it, you philistine!' he laughed. 'It can be our secret!'

He prepared a roll for himself, and they sat quietly for a while, savouring the tranquillity around them. At last, David broke the silence.

'So,' he began hesitantly. 'How are things?'

Kate shrugged. 'The students seem to be okay -'

'How are things with *you*?'

Lowering her head, Kate remained silent while she tried to formulate a reply. Finally, she looked up at him, her expression one of open honesty. 'I don't want to talk about it. I can't fight with you over this anymore. I – I don't know what to think or what to do for the best. I wish…' A sob caught in her throat, making her swallow hard. 'David, please stop camping out…'

Now it was David's turn to look away. 'I was trying to make everything…easier.'

'It's not making *anything* easier. Leaving me alone while you take the group camping is making me look bad, for one thing. Everybody thinks it's because I can't cope -'

David frowned. 'By your own admission, you hate camping. And I thought that if I stayed away, you and Ethan might -'

Kate's eyes widened. 'Did you really think I would meet Ethan and then automatically jump into bed with him?' She looked hurt. 'You don't know me at all…'

She had wounded him, and so he became defensive. 'In your heart, didn't you want it to be that way?'

'No!' she cried, tears running freely now.

'He seems to be remembering…'

'He thinks he knows me from *this* lifetime, David. He has no memory of that other life, and I'm not going to tell him. There is nothing between Ethan and me and there never will be. There's no chemistry. We haven't bonded. He's not even my type.' She rushed on without thinking. 'Edwin's marriage to Katherine was a mistake, a cruel joke. I've forgiven him as Anai suggested. But I don't think I should have -' Kate stopped abruptly, realising she had been about to reveal the latest, most shocking discovery about Edwin's life.

'How did you forgive him?' David asked suspiciously.

Despite her anger and sorrow, Kate still felt concern for a suffering human being. 'Ethan sleepwalks. He's been to my room, but it's like he…' She saw David's jaw tighten. 'I just…I just told him that I forgive him, and that it was time to rest...' She took a deep breath. 'Ethan's a lost soul, David. This arrogant, slutty persona of his is just a façade. He needs help to find the way forward. But that doesn't mean I'm going to tether myself to him in some misguided attempt to save him.'

Kate hoped that her eyes would impart her true feelings. 'Please, David, sleep indoors tonight. Or let me come out with you. I'll sleep better if I know you're not far away…'

'You're very trusting, given my recent behaviour.'

'As you say, things have been crazy…'

David gazed at her, tenderness warming his hypnotic green eyes. 'I'll give up my tent if you have dinner with me. Just you and me. No interruptions, no intrusions, and no fighting.'

'And am I expected to dress up for this dinner?' she asked archly, relieved to glimpse his playful side.

'Well, if you want me to behave like a gentleman, don't wear your belly dancing costume…'

She answered with an affectionate smile, and leaned her head against his arm as he poured more coffee into the single cup. Kate felt exhausted; she wished she could curl up beside him in a big, soft bed and sleep, free of nightmares. As he handed her the cup his other arm slid around her shoulders and she relaxed into his light embrace, inhaling her favourite scent: David Young.

'We'll have to go back soon…' she murmured regretfully.

'Not yet.' David lifted her chin to look at her face. A chocolate-coated crumb clung to the corner of her lips. Gently, he brushed it away with his thumb. 'Ethan's taking the students to the main city today, to help with the laying of new thresholds in parts of the temple. They'll also assist the American and Australian teams with a GPS survey. Your friend Taylor's planning to take aerial photographs with a camera attached to a balloon. It should be an interesting day. I can drive you over there and drop you off if you like.'

'Drop me off?' she repeated. 'What are you doing today?'

'Ethan and I have swapped jobs. I have to sort out the accounts for the last month, and he's going to try his hand at teaching.'

Kate's voice sounded bitter. 'Is that because there'll soon be a job vacancy at Edinburgh University?' She shifted away from him.

David sighed heavily. 'Another reason I wanted to bring you up here…'

'I heard about your job offer from Marianne. It would seem that everybody knows about your new job except me.'

'Kate, I only received the offer a week ago. I know I should've mentioned it before now, but – well, there's enough going on. I've only discussed it with Ethan and I haven't made any decisions yet. But I'll have to, soon…'

'And since you've given up your flat, I assume you've already packed your bags?'

A heavy silence followed, which seemed to last a very long time. Eventually, David spoke, his voice grave. 'Would you deny me the chance to make a fresh start, if I needed to?'

'Are you tired of living in Edinburgh?' *Or are you finally tired of me?*

'Kate, I have money and a good career. I'll be thirty-six on my next birthday; I want to put down roots somewhere. I want a family of my own.'

'In York…'

'York is a beautiful town – and an archaeologist's dream location. I've been offered a great position, with a good holiday allowance…'

'Which you'd no doubt use for travel and fieldwork.'

Realising she had no right to stand in the way of his happiness, Kate tried to sound supportive. 'It sounds like an amazing opportunity…'

'Edinburgh is only two-and-a-half hours away by train…'

As though Fate was demonstrating a twisted sense of humour, David spotted a camel train crossing the desert some distance away. Wishing to escape this difficult conversation, Kate stood up for a better look. Taking the hint, David packed the saddlebags and returned them to his horse's back.

'So, do you want a lift to the city?' he asked as she approached the horses. He raised an inquiring eyebrow when she shook her head. 'You haven't seen much of Amarna.' Kate shrugged. 'Are you still digitising your expedition?'

'I'm done with that expedition. Do you need help with the accounts?'

'Some of the receipts are in Arabic…'

'Then you can translate. I'm sure we'll get them done in no time.' She tried to sound more upbeat as she asked, 'So, are you cooking dinner tonight or are we having it delivered?'

David sidled closer, and Kate thought he might hug her. But instead, he patted the mare and checked the girth was tight enough. 'My cooking skills are ropey even with ingredients I recognise,' he commented ruefully. 'So it's probably best if we have it delivered. We can eat in my room…'

Kate eyed him suspiciously, but a small smile played on her lips.

'I promise not to behave like an arrogant thug.' He stepped closer and bent his head towards hers. 'You know, I'm not sorry I kissed you.' David paused and smiled, as if he enjoyed watching her blush. 'I'm just sorry I didn't make a better job of it…'

Pondering whether to offer him a second opportunity, Kate's gaze fell on his mouth. *No, I can't. I have to protect myself and prepare for a future without him.*

'Do I need a lead rein for the ride back?' she asked, pulling on her gloves and ignoring another look of disappointment from David.

'Yes,' he replied firmly. 'You're not wearing a hard hat and you're not familiar with the horse or the terrain.'

'You don't force Mina to use a lead rein,' Kate grumbled, but David pretended not to hear and busied himself with the stirrups.

'You're a beautiful horse,' Kate murmured lovingly, scratching the mare's nose. The stallion whinnied for a share of Kate's attention, stamping the ground petulantly.

'You say that about every horse you meet!' David chuckled, gesturing for Kate to mount up. She bounced up into the saddle, but when she looked down at him, David had a faraway look on his face. Fleetingly, Kate wondered if he had experienced more flashbacks of his past life. Perhaps he had helped Katherine Ford onto a horse once, before he had learned of her pregnancy. Had he loved her, as Richard Yorke? Did he remember?

She watched him return to the present, shake his head briefly, and walk over to his mount. 'We'll try some trotting on the way back,' he announced.

'Thank you – I'd like that. Does my horse have a name?'

'Hamar,' David told her, grinning.

Kate looked at him suspiciously. 'What does it mean?'

David bounced up onto the stallion's back. He started to laugh. 'Donkey.'

The chaos of the field director's office was testament to Ethan's disordered mental state. The large desk was laden with paperwork. Post-it notes had been stuck to the computer screen, almost covering it entirely. The wooden bookcase was so full, the sides bowed outwards. Some of the books and journals had been carelessly stuffed back into place and now sat askew in the rows of literature. A large filing cabinet occupied one corner; a thick pile of field reports lay on top. The water dispenser was almost empty; a dirty mug had been left on top of the water tank. A wicker wastepaper basket had not been emptied for days.

'He'd better clean this up before the field director comes back...' David muttered, puffing out an exasperated burst of air as he stood in the doorway.

'I thought he *was* the field director,' Kate said. Another snippet of information to add to her growing collection.

'The full-time field director's on sick leave,' David informed her. 'Ethan volunteered to stand in – which is very unlike him. The EES have made a fatal error in judgement because he's not up to the job. He should've taken more time to recuperate after the coma, eased his way back into work...'

So I'm not the only one lacking in the proper qualifications, Kate thought to herself. Nevertheless, she felt a twinge of sympathy at the thought of Ethan floundering his way through life, and resolved to help David clear up his friend's mess.

As David cleared a space on the desk, Kate's eyes fell on the opposite wall. A large noticeboard took up most of the plastered surface, and Ethan had filled it with photographs and sketches of a particular landscape. Several A5 snapshots were pinned next to one another, providing a panorama of the cliffs near the Royal Wadi. Ethan's detailed drawings were of the same area.

A feeling of familiarity pulled her to the noticeboard. 'I know this...' she murmured as David came to stand behind her.

'You probably saw it on the way to Akhenaten's tomb.'

Closing her eyes, she delved into the recesses of her mind, trying to recall where she had seen similar sketches. A voice whispered in her head, urging her to remember.

'No,' she replied, and at last she remembered. 'I saw it in Edwin's diary.'

With Edwin's loving presence at her shoulder, she had braved the dark and dusty attic of her home one grey afternoon in the spring. Hidden behind old pieces of furniture and other heirlooms, she had found a battered trunk.

To her amazement, the chest contained pictures of her Victorian family, and a family tree dating back to James Grahame's time. Kate had wept over the discovery of Katherine's engagement ring and wedding veil, and the engraved golden locket Edwin had given his wife on her twenty-first birthday.

She had also discovered Edwin's diary wrapped in a piece of old silk. As well as personal notes and observations, the book had included many sketches. Some of them had been almost identical to the ones she now stared at on the wall of Ethan's office.

'They're looking for a tomb in the same place...' she breathed, and then felt inexplicably cross. 'Idiots!'

'Did you bring the diary with you?' David asked tentatively.

'Of course not! Why would I do that? I gave everything to Ben just before I left Edinburgh.'

David looked perturbed. 'You gave him *everything*? Why?'

'Why? I didn't want it anymore, and he's keen to do some research for himself. His wife is always raving about her Italian heritage. Ben felt his children should know more about *our* family tree. These things are family heirlooms, so it's only right that Luca and Rebecca should inherit them.'

'But what about *your* children?'

Pain flitted across Kate's eyes, and she looked down at the floor.

'Did you give him all the photographs? Including the wedding photograph of Edwin and Katherine Ford?'

Kate nodded, her mind wandering back to Edinburgh.

'Ah,' David muttered. 'That explains why he's been in touch with me...'

He touched Kate's arm, bringing her attention back to him. 'I've had a frantic email from Jess, and two from Ben. They say they haven't heard from you, despite sending you numerous emails and texts. Why have you isolated yourself like this?'

'I learned it from you,' she retorted weakly.

Placing his hands on her shoulders, David made her look at him. 'I know this must be a nightmare for you, but surely you need people around who can keep you grounded, like -'

'*Grounded*? *Here*? How do you imagine I could be grounded in *this* place?'

'You've been keeping to your room, and refusing to mix with -'

'David, I don't *fit*. I have a reasonable working relationship with the students, but I can't mix socially with them. And I'm not "management". I have nothing to bring to that particular table.'

Frowning in consternation, he gazed down at her. 'That last statement is untrue. But if that's how you feel, then surely you would feel better if you spoke to your brother? He's really worried about you.'

'Ben is always able to tell when something's wrong with me, even from an email. I promised to Skype them, but I know that I would just end up blubbing like a wain...' She looked up in time to see him hide a smile. 'What's so funny?'

'You,' he chuckled. 'Your Scottish accent has become more pronounced since you arrived in Egypt. It's endearing.' David stroked her hair, and Kate felt somewhat pacified. 'Did you tell him everything about Edwin and Katherine?'

'No. He knew about my regression therapy, but I never gave him the details. Now that he's seen the photographs, he'll have put two and two together. Hence the frantic emails. No doubt he'll recommend psychiatric care upon my return...'

Pulling a chair to the desk, she flopped down and leaned her elbows on a pile of papers held in place by a small rock. Kate smiled sadly as she recalled that Edwin had also used a rock as a paperweight. 'The truth is, I haven't felt like talking to anybody. And as for Jess...'

'She's your best friend and you must forgive her, Kate. She cares about you, and she kept things from you to try to protect you. I was wrong to ask her to keep secrets. Be mad at *me*, not Jess.'

'I'm not mad at anyone anymore. Except myself...'

'Then it's time to forgive yourself and move on.'

Drawing up another chair, David sat next to her. 'If there's an internet connection, you could look at your emails now,' he suggested, switching on the computer.

'And what would you have me say to them?' Kate asked. 'That everything is perfectly wonderful?'

Once the field school ended, they both had a week's holiday. Secretly, Kate had hoped to spend it with David. Christmas loomed, and now she fretted over their plans for the festive season. Would they spend it together or in different parts of the world?

David pushed the grubby keyboard towards her. 'Sign on,' he ordered softly. 'And just read them.'

Concern and remorse oozed from Jess's long email, as she explained her reasons for concealing her knowledge about Ethan's resemblance to Edwin. She begged forgiveness and pleaded with Kate to reply to her correspondence. Two more emails followed as Jess became progressively anxious by Kate's stubborn silence.

Only a few hours ago, Jess's sister Erin had sent Kate a brief message. Erin had administered Kate's regression therapy and had become a good friend along the way. Intuitive as always, the therapist offered an impartial ear should Kate need someone to talk to.

The first email from Ben was chatty and informative, and passed on the news of their family, his work, and local gossip. The succeeding five missives were shorter and held an increasingly reproachful tone. Doctor

Benedict Grahame, clearly flexing his 'big brother' muscles, demanded she contact him. The latest email asked Kate to get in touch urgently as he had just opened the box of family heirlooms from her attic. The rebel lurking inside Kate blew a raspberry at her bossy older brother. Feeling cornered, she clicked on the video attached to the email.

Her beautiful niece and nephew appeared, talking over one another in their haste to tell their doting aunt about a trip to Edinburgh's Winter Wonderland. Full of excitement over Santa's impending visit, they showed her their Christmas tree and the decorations in the living room. The camera moved to the bay window and panned across the snow-covered garden while the children provided a running commentary. Tears filled Kate's eyes as she touched the screen, stroking their cherubic faces as they moved back in front of the camera.

'Oh, I miss them so much!' She wiped her eyes and sniffed, fumbling in her pocket for a tissue.

'They look so much like you…' David commented softly.

Ben's voice could be heard in the background, urging the children to conclude their bulletin. Four-year-old Rebecca held up a picture she had drawn. Squinting, Kate made out a castle with a tower similar to that of the dig house. In front of the blue door stood a stick woman with dark brown hair, holding the hand of a tall stick man. Grinning, David pointed out that the man's hair was a mixture of light brown and yellow.

'This is you, Auntie Katie,' the little girl piped. 'And your handsome prince. I hope you're still wearing your ring. I love you, Auntie! Please come home soon!' She blew several kisses and disappeared from the screen.

Glancing at the plastic mood ring on her finger, Kate realised that Rebecca's gift had maintained a muddy hue since she had come to Amarna.

Luca smiled shyly at the camera, brown eyes twinkling. 'I hope you're having a nice time, Auntie Katie, but I miss your chocolate cake.' The seven-year-old came closer, and his voice dropped to a loud whisper. 'Mum's cake isn't nearly as good as yours!' The camera trembled as Ben laughed abruptly. 'Please can you ask Professor Young if he's found any dinosaur bones? Or maybe you could bring him over for Christmas dinner, and I can ask him myself. Love you, Auntie Katie!'

The video ended, amputating Kate's lifeline. She stared at the screen, mulling over Luca's inadvertent invitation to David. Finally, she stretched her fingers over the keyboard and logged off.

'Accounts,' she said to David, in a brisk tone that implied there would be no invitations issued at present.

It took a long time to sort out Ethan's disorganised box of receipts. Sitting side-by-side, Kate and David separated the paperwork into receipts for equipment, food, maintenance, employees' wages, and 'miscellaneous expenses'. Many of the 'receipts' were hastily scribbled notes on napkins and scraps of paper, and many had an amount for 'baksheesh' added below the total paid out. A wage slip for two donkeys made Kate laugh outright.

Eventually, Kate was able to begin updating the accounts spreadsheet on the computer while David translated the bills written in Arabic and deciphered Ethan's scrawl. It was painstaking work, but the peaceful atmosphere around them was idyllic. Kate kicked off her boots and unconsciously rested one foot on top of David's. The familiar gesture warmed his heart, and he found himself once again weighing up the pros and cons of moving to York alone. The argument was not at all balanced.

By late morning, noises drifted along the corridor from the kitchen, announcing that preparations were beginning for the next meal. Sensual Arabic music floated through the open door of the office. It wasn't long before Kate started to shift slightly in time with the slow, hypnotic beat, completely unaware of the effect she was having on her companion. David was almost relieved when their task was finally complete.

'Thank goodness!' Kate breathed, packing away the receipts in an orderly fashion. 'I was starting to feel like a secretary…'

'Don't mention that to Ethan,' David muttered as he scanned the figures Kate had typed on the screen. Ethan was an experienced haggler, but the expedition budget would be insufficient to cover the season's expenses. If Ethan could not find ways to economise, there was a risk that the season would be brought to a premature end. 'He'll pass some remark about naughty secretaries again. And stockings…'

Her mouth curved in a mysterious smile, and Kate fixed David with an enigmatic stare that only served to stimulate his curiosity.

CHAPTER 12

Gazing critically at her reflection, Kate began to harbour doubts. If David was serious about moving to York, she should be distancing herself from him, not agreeing to a private dinner in his room. And what could they safely talk about, given that all conversational roads potentially led to disaster?

There was also the worrying possibility that he might expect to share something more than food. The insidious voice in her head whispered for her to claim illness and retreat to the safety of her bed. Another voice, full of longing, urged her to rush to David's side and enjoy every minute with him.

By the time she reached David's room, Kate's palms were sweating. Russell appeared from his room further up the corridor and headed towards her, looking a little flustered. Donning a winning smile, the dishevelled student stopped in front of Kate.

'You look nice,' he commented.

Immediately suspicious, Kate adopted a neutral expression. 'Thanks.'

'Erm…could I ask – that is, I wondered if -'

'Russell,' Kate interrupted. 'Take a deep breath. And then tell me what you need.'

The student took a deep breath. 'Condoms,' he blurted. 'Do you have any condoms on you?'

For a moment, Kate was struck dumb by embarrassment. Then, indignation took over. 'No!' she cried. 'And might I remind you that you're on a serious expedition. It's not a holiday camp!'

Russell blushed furiously. 'I'm sorry. I just thought that you might…you know…' He gestured vaguely towards David's bedroom door.

'Well, I don't!' Her eyes narrowed vindictively. 'Ask Doctor Brodie.'

His face scarlet, the student fled, and Kate saw that David had opened his door and was leaning against the doorframe, his eyes sparkling with amusement. It was Kate's turn to blush.

'So,' David drawled. 'You didn't bring any -'

'Not another word!' she warned him. 'Or you'll be eating dinner by yourself!'

He attempted to look contrite but remained in the doorway, forcing her to press against him as she moved into the room.

David had tried to create a pleasant atmosphere in the tidy room. The desk had been moved to the centre of the floor and was laid with a linen cloth, cutlery, glasses, and a flickering tealight. Music played softly from an iPod dock, reminding Kate that they shared the same musical tastes. Her eyes fell on the statue of Bastet, which sat on the top of the wardrobe looking down at them. It was very similar to the statuette Kate had inherited from her Aunt Margaret, except this cat goddess wore a red and green collar. A gold scarab hung around the cat's neck, and gold paint had been used to illustrate the eyes and ears.

'It's Ethan's,' David told her, following her gaze. 'He's had it for years. He claims it brings him luck.'

As they faced one another in the small space, David appraised her outfit. She was wearing jeans that fit her perfectly, along with a soft white shirt and a lace-edged camisole. Her locket glittered in the candlelight, on show for once and not hidden beneath her clothing. Her hair was still damp from the shower.

'You look lovely,' he remarked. She responded with a guileless shrug.

'Is the beard a permanent feature, then?' she teased, pointing to his unshaven face.

He scratched at the stubble on his jaw. 'I left my razor in Cairo. I'll buy another when I'm back in the city.'

So, he was returning to Cairo after the expedition. What was he going to do after that?

'What can we talk about that won't lead to trouble?' he asked.

Kate took a step towards him. 'I was thinking the same thing. In fact -'

There was a knock at the door, and David brusquely called for the gatecrasher to enter. Mina pushed a hostess trolley into the room, laden with little dishes of food. Smiling sheepishly at them both, she arranged the food on the table, all the while casting sideways glances at Kate. David thanked her in a voice edged with impatience. Before she made her exit, however, Mina laid a hand on Kate's arm.

'Kate, I am sorry about my grandmother,' she began urgently. 'She should not have told you. There was nothing to be gained by it -'

Gently, Kate extricated her arm from Mina's tightening grip. 'But she *did* tell me, Mina. And now I know the truth.' She firmly shook her head. 'No more. I appreciate all you've done – but no more.' Pointedly, Kate ushered Mina out of the room, leaning against the door once she had closed it firmly on the world.

Wisely, David asked no questions. Instead, he pulled back a chair and gestured for Kate to sit. With a comical flourish, he then produced a bottle of red wine from his wardrobe and poured them each a glass.

Dinner was the usual Egyptian fare, more enjoyable because they were alone. Kate asked David to tell her about his childhood, especially the time he had spent with his grandparents in Cambridgeshire. He had adored them, and so was happy to reminisce about wonderful holidays spent playing in the countryside. Kate encouraged him with questions, wishing only to listen to the sound of his voice. She had once jokingly called it a 'BBC voice', but she loved its rich, smooth tone.

Skirting difficult issues as though negotiating a minefield, they moved onto countries they had visited. David had spent time in China and Japan, and provided elaborate descriptions of landscapes, buildings and the extraordinary food he had sampled on his travels. From there, they lightly discussed books, films, and music. When Jack Savoretti began to sing softly in the background, their eyes met. The talented singer had provided the soundtrack for most of their relationship.

'D'you remember when we danced to this song?' David asked, as the words to 'Without' taunted them from the corner.

On the first Saturday of December, the museum had been the venue for a society wedding reception. Kate and David had danced together in the empty Egyptian gallery. And then he had taken her home and walked away, and she had let him go.

Kate smiled wistfully. 'Back when you had a razor…' Tentatively, she reached out to touch his bristly cheek, and wrinkled her freckled nose.

'It seems like a lifetime ago…' David sighed.

'It was only sixteen days ago.' The memory was bittersweet.

Capturing her hand, David kissed her palm. 'That night, I wish I'd…'

The wine had imbued her with false courage. 'I wish you had, too…' Lacing her fingers through his, she held his hand across the table.

There was a loud knock on the door, and Ethan entered without waiting for an invitation. A look of animosity crossed Kate's face as she turned to look at him, letting go of David's hand in the process.

'Oh,' Ethan muttered.

'What do you want?' David asked crossly. 'I told you I'd be having dinner with Kate this evening…'

Glaring at the intruder, Kate wondered if the interruption had been deliberate or just further evidence of Ethan's inconsiderate, apathetic nature.

'Sorry, Dave. I want to have a meeting to discuss tomorrow's trip.'

'Well, it can wait until after dessert.'

Ethan looked perturbed. He glanced at Kate, and then the bed, before returning his attention to David. 'How long do you need?'

Interpreting the question from Ethan's wavelength, David's expression became hostile. He picked up the plate of pastries Mina had left at the corner of the table. 'However long it takes to eat *these*.'

Ethan's answering leer made Kate want to hit him.

'It's fine, David,' Kate interrupted, reaching over to touch his fingers. 'We can do this another time -'

'No, no,' Ethan said quickly, still smirking. 'You go ahead and have your pudding. I'll see you *both* in half an hour in the lounge.' He winked at David as he left.

The bubble had burst; another headache prodded at the base of Kate's skull. Standing slowly, she gathered the empty dishes. As she moved around the table, David gently took both of her hands and pulled her towards him, tugging her down onto his lap. Discomfited and uncertain, she waited for his next move.

'Things never work out the way I plan them,' he grumbled. 'But at least I'm not to blame for *this* ruined date. How can I make it better?'

Helplessly, Kate shook her head and made no protest when he drew her against him. Resting her head against his solid, dependable shoulder, she sighed despairingly. 'It's just as well he's your best friend, otherwise I might thump him...'

David chuckled. 'You'd have to stand in line.' Testing his luck, he ran his fingers through her hair; she gave a little sigh of pleasure. 'You were right – he's lost his way. When we first met, he was ambitious, and he worked hard. But he changed in our graduate year and seemed to lose his motivation.

'Even so, he's done some excellent work over the years, especially in Amarna. Ethan has a love/hate relationship with this place, but he always ends up back here. I guess Anai would have an otherworldly explanation for that.'

Grunting derisively, Kate snuggled into his neck.

'When he woke from the coma, he was desperate to return to Amarna. But he seems unable to focus on the work, and he's becoming slapdash. I want to help him, but I don't know how...' David looked troubled as he confessed, 'He stands between us and part of me hates him for it.'

Kate sighed, pained by his words. 'Ethan has been your friend for a long time, David. You mustn't hate him, or blame him for our problems. He doesn't stand between us – we've put up our own barriers...'

'You are profoundly wise, Nefertari...' David murmured.

She gently poked him in the ribs, making him twitch. 'You're a good man, and I know you'll do the right thing and find a way to help. You always do...' One of her hands moved up around his neck, as she shifted to make herself more comfortable.

On the pretext of supporting her position on his lap, David placed a hand on her denim-clad hip and moulded his fingers over the curve. Aware that

David had developed a certain fondness for her hips, Kate giggled softly.

'Are you perhaps a little tipsy?' he asked, sounding amused and delighted all at once. She made a sound of affirmation. 'On one glass of wine?' He moved his hand to tickle her, eliciting a yelp and a burst of laughter. 'You'd better have some cake before we go to this stupid meeting. I had no idea you were such a lightweight!'

'I don't want cake!' she mumbled petulantly. 'I want ice cream – ooh, with Mars Bar sauce! And I don't want to go to this stupid meeting – I want to stay here!' She laughed at her childishness, and then surprised herself by seductively nuzzling his neck. 'You could ply me with more wine and then take advantage of me…'

With gentle hands, he manoeuvred her into a sitting position. 'You know I would never do that,' he told her solemnly. 'At least, not until we were married…' He gazed at Kate intently as her eyes widened and her cheeks flushed.

Kate was profoundly relieved to hear yet another knock on the door. 'Come in!' she hollered, getting off David's lap and moving quickly to the other side of the table.

'Would you like coffee?' Mina asked timidly. Her trolley now held two cups and a pot of coffee.

'Yes!' Kate replied swiftly, earning herself a quizzical stare from Mina as the girl handed her a cup of black coffee. Kate screwed up her face as she downed the bitter drink in one gulp.

Stopping just short of the doorway to the sitting room, David caught Kate by the wrist. His ill-judged comment had stilled further conversation and now hung awkwardly in the air between them.

'I overstepped,' he began quickly. 'I'm sorry.'

Did you mean it, David? Or were you just toying with me? 'Let's blame it on the wine, shall we?' she suggested, managing a weak smile. 'Maybe you're a lightweight, too.'

She walked into the lounge, surprised to find the room occupied by Ethan, Marianne, Steven and Yusuf. Obviously, Ethan's extra-curricular tomb hunting was not a closely guarded secret. Firing a bleak look at Ethan, Kate sat on one of the sofas. A small fire burned in the hearth; the room would have been cosy and welcoming were it not for the presence of the three condescending men.

'Did you enjoy dessert?' Ethan grinned, as David took his seat next to Kate. 'Friday, your cheeks look flushed…'

'Ethan, please get on with this!' Marianne sighed peevishly. 'I want to go to bed!'

Waiting until he had the full attention of his audience, Ethan pulled the rectangular coffee table closer to him and laid out the photographs from the notice board in his office.

'Tomorrow's trip will be about reconnaissance,' he informed them. 'Steven, Yusuf, David and myself will go and look over the site.' He glanced at David, his eyes revealing the respect he had for his friend. 'Fresh eyes might see something I've missed.'

'But, just to confirm, you haven't received official permission to do anything other than walk the site?' Marianne asked, perturbed.

'We will only look,' Yusuf confirmed. 'But, should we find anything, future work will be undertaken by *my* country.'

The implication was clear: if they found anything significant, Yusuf would take the credit. Kate wondered how David and Ethan felt about this exploitation of their skills. Yusuf wasn't even a qualified archaeologist. She saw the friends exchange a meaningful look, as though David were asking the same question. Ethan simply shrugged. Perhaps he felt he had spent too much time on this obsession, and that it was time to conclude the search and move on. Perhaps some small part of him realised he needed a change – both of his ways and his location.

'Now, Moumdah will be off-site in the morning but, should he return before us he will need to be distracted...' Ethan eyed his companions.

'I can help with that,' Marianne offered. 'I'll leave word for him to join us over in the city.'

'Good. We also have David's students to worry about.' He glanced at Kate and then dismissed her in favour of Marianne. 'Could you -'

'*I* can take care of our students,' Kate said firmly. 'I've already set their rotas for tomorrow. I'll supervise them in the field until David gets back.'

She glared boldly at Ethan and suddenly saw Edwin in his place. Anger rose from the depths of her soul, as she heard a voice whispering insidiously in her ear: *Your soulmate is a lying, philandering swine!*

'Very well,' Ethan conceded. 'We should be back by lunchtime, in any case. If we don't find anything, we can put this thing to bed. If we do, we'll plan our next move...'

'Very carefully,' Yusuf added, with a meaningful look at the temporary field director.

'Of course,' Ethan muttered.

'Where will we start the search?' Steven asked from his armchair.

Ethan launched into a detailed explanation of his investigations of the area, which suggested that an eroded path extended from ground level to two-thirds of the way up the cliff face. It ran horizontally for a short distance then disappeared, but there were several semi-eroded ledges at the same level. Unfortunately, they were hard to reach without proper climbing equipment. Ethan proposed they inspect the ledges from the top of the cliffs, where they might obtain a clearer view.

It all sounded very vague to Kate, and lacking in the level-headedness that David would have employed. As Ethan droned on, his voice was overshadowed by another voice in Kate's head. A calm voice, which gave instructions and urged her to speak.

Ethan stopped talking as Kate approached the coffee table and began to sift through the photographs of the north cliffs. Finding the picture she sought, Kate handed it to Ethan and pointed to an area of the cliff face.

In a halting voice, Kate said, 'Near the end of the range, before it turns into the ravine, there's a narrow, curved ledge. The limestone forms a kind of curtain across a recess in the cliff. You must look for...symbols. I think...' Her glassy stare was replaced by a slightly stunned look.

Ethan broke the puzzled silence. 'How do you know that?' He stared hard into her eyes. 'Are you hearing voices from the grave now?'

His disdain brought her resentment, and her defiance, to the surface. 'In a manner of speaking. The Victorian archaeologist who married my ancestor kept a journal, which I found in my attic at home. He, too, was obsessed with finding a tomb, although *he* was looking for Akhenaten's. In his journal, he made a sketch of the place I just mentioned. I'm guessing he shared your belief, as well as your ambiguity.' She walked back to the sofa and perched on the edge of her seat, fighting the desire to strangle her soulmate with her bare hands.

'Do you have this journal?' Ethan asked curiously, ignoring her sarcasm.

'No, I gave it to my brother. It's a *family* heirloom, not mine alone. I'm only related to Edwin Ford through marriage, not blood.' She swallowed as heartache welled up inside her. 'Although I realise now that I *should* have brought it, as it seems his line continues here...'

Kate's gaze locked with Ethan's, and the room and its occupants seemed to disappear. It was as though grief, guilt, bitterness and torment connected them for one brief moment, enclosing them in a suffocating bubble until David's voice retrieved them from the darkness.

'Ethan, when do you want us to leave in the morning?' he asked sharply.

Kate chewed her lip, vexed by her carelessness. She had partially revealed another secret, which she had concealed from David for his own benefit.

Tearing his gaze away from hers, Ethan gazed at the picture in his hand, his expression distant.

A nudge from Marianne brought him back to the present, although he looked somewhat unnerved. 'Just before dawn, I think...' he mumbled.

Yusuf began talking, but Kate blocked him out as she slumped back on the sofa. She was trembling as she slid next to David, moving as close to him as she could without drawing attention, ever mindful of propriety.

'I'm not ready to talk about it...' Kate murmured, pre-empting the question on David's lips. 'Please can I go to bed now?' His response was a resigned nod, and Kate stood up. She blushed as everyone stared at her as though fearing she might speak in tongues. After wishing them goodnight, Kate headed for the door. The whispering in her head had stopped, to be replaced with her own inner voice, screaming. At that moment, Kate feared insanity.

'Wait!' Ethan called sharply. '*Finally! I know who you are!*'

An unpleasant sensation washed over her, as though she were being held in suspension, awaiting a cruel fate. Fearfully, Kate turned to rest her eyes on the man who had become her tormentor. David, apparently no longer concerned about fuelling gossip, stood up with the clear intention of chaperoning Kate to her room.

'You lived a few doors along from us on Marchmont Road when we were students. You were Gemma Walker's room-mate!' His bark of laughter taunted her. 'Gemma and I had a very short summer romance, maybe ten years ago. Don't you remember, Friday?' Reminiscing, he shook his head, completely oblivious to Kate's horrified stare. 'Man, that girl was a handful! In *every* respect!'

As Marianne berated him for his vulgarity, and Steven and Yusuf sniggered like adolescents, Kate raced out of the room, her humiliation complete.

David considered the best course of action. His heart told him to follow Kate, but his head counselled caution. Frustration urged him to kick his best friend up the backside.

For most of his adult life, David had been sure of himself, and the path he wanted to take. Now he felt all that certitude slipping out of his grasp. It was unfair, an inexcusable blunder on the part of Fate. He waited until he and Ethan were finally alone, and then turned his angry gaze on his tactless friend.

'Can't you get through one single day without upsetting Kate?' he asked through clenched teeth, getting to his feet and blocking Ethan's path to the door.

'What did I say?' Ethan asked defensively. 'She *did* share a flat with Gemma, didn't she?'

The colourful assortment of expletives uttered in cultured English tones surprised even Ethan. 'You stupid moron!' David spat, once he had exhausted his arsenal of foul language. 'Gemma's the woman who slept with Kate's husband!'

Ethan shrugged carelessly. 'How was I to know?'

'You never bloody *think*, Ethan!' David cried in exasperation. 'You never think about anyone but yourself! Why can't you just grow up?' Unwilling to vent his rage further, David stormed off down the corridor in search of Kate.

She wasn't in her room, the courtyard, or the kitchen. Unfortunately for David, Mina was reading a magazine at the dining room table, and her eyes lit up when he stepped into the room.

'You enjoyed dinner?' she asked brightly.

'It was fine, thanks,' David replied, anxious to be on his way. His brain was flitting through all the rooms in the house, trying to ascertain where Kate could be hiding.

'But she has not stayed with you...'

Hearing a judgemental note in Mina's voice, David focused his attention on the girl. 'That's none of your business, Mina.'

'Perhaps she does not desire you...'

David's eyes widened in surprise at her offensive remark. 'Kate does not enter into such things lightly.'

'And yet you continue to let her tease you and break your heart.'

He hadn't foreseen this; Ethan had been right about Mina's desires. This misunderstanding was all his fault – and now ruthlessness seemed to be his only option. She stood in front of him, gazing into his face adoringly. And yet there was also calculation in those amber eyes, which suggested that Mina had been privy to Anai's plans from the outset.

'I love her,' David told Mina firmly, his eyes as cold as the deepest ocean.

'She is old,' Mina spat dismissively. 'She may not give you children. And her heart will always be with another.' Her voice took on an almost fanatical edge. 'She will never give all of herself to you. She will not love you as *I* love you. *I* can give you many children. *I* can make you happy, David!'

For a moment, David wanted to back out of the room; he was shocked, and almost fearful. If she, too, was a witch, what further misfortunes could she rain down on them? But then an inner voice began to speak with icy calm, and David knew what to say.

'I don't love you – I love Kate,' he declared, enunciating each word. 'There will never be another woman for me. Only *she* can be the mother of my children. You must stop this, Mina, for I have never thought of you as anything other than a friend or, at most, a little sister. But you and your grandmother have destroyed our friendship with your sordid little schemes.'

Her eyes wide and pleading, Mina stared at him, but David felt no pity. Taking her arm, he squeezed it and looked directly into her eyes. 'You and your grandmother will stop filling Kate's head with nonsense about the past. In fact, I *forbid* you to make anything other than polite conversation with her. You will not harm one hair on her head, do you understand? Make no mistake, Mina, I can make life very difficult for your family. And if you hurt Kate, I won't hesitate to destroy you.'

The still, heavy air felt charged with electricity, prickling the back of Kate's neck as she stood at one corner of the tower, staring with tear-filled eyes into the darkness. In the desert beyond, all was blackness. Somewhere in the distance, the wild dogs commenced their howling. A gunshot sounded, echoing around the cliffs; perhaps someone hoped it would frighten the animals, or perhaps one of the dogs had suffered a grisly demise.

'If anyone can hear me,' she whispered into the night. 'Please, please help me…' She felt sickened by the sound of Ethan's voice below, from a dark corner of the courtyard. Stepping back, Kate sank to the ground and hugged herself, longing for escape from…well, her whole life.

'I don't know what's up with him…' Ethan's voice was querulous.

'You've upset Kate.' It was Marianne, sounding vexed. 'You seem to be making a career out of it; of course David's going to be mad. What did you say this time?'

'The woman I had a fling with – Gemma – had an affair with Kate's husband. It's what caused their divorce. Although, if I had to live with *her*, I'd probably look elsewhere for some fun, too…'

Kate choked on a sob and hid her face against her raised knees.

'Ethan!' Marianne protested. 'That's an awful thing to say!'

'That's rich, coming from you!'

When she spoke again, Marianne sounded wounded. 'I don't understand what you have against her. She's a sweet girl. A little damaged, maybe – but which of us isn't?'

'She's so uptight she sets my teeth on edge! I don't know what Dave sees in her – *I* can't wait to see the back of her. Dave tried to tell me he was over her, but I don't believe it for a second! He's blind and stupid where she's concerned. She's brought him nothing but misery, ever since they met.'

'You're wrong about her, Ethan. I've seen how she and David look at one another, how they are with one another. They may be going through a rough patch, but they care about each other a lot. And she's brought him joy, too – I've seen it on his face. You've just been too busy looking for the bad stuff – maybe because you're jealous…'

He sounded as though he were replying through clenched teeth. 'I want her *gone*.'

Above him, Kate started to sob quietly.

After a short silence, Marianne sighed. 'Come to bed. You've behaved like a monk since David got here. Perhaps we can make you less of a grouch…'

It took a few moments for Marianne's words to sink in, but then Kate bit on her fist to stop herself from wailing in despair. Retching, she covered her mouth with both hands to keep the sound in, and fought to calm her heaving stomach.

'Bed? What's wrong with right here?' Ethan asked nastily. 'You never objected to a quick grope in a cupboard or a doorway last season, when you brought your idiot husband with you.'

'For God's sake, Ethan…' Marianne's voice revealed her distress. And even though the American was an adulterer, Kate felt sorry for her. 'What the hell's got into you?'

There was the sound of shuffling and a muffled protest from Marianne, but Kate couldn't listen anymore. Unsteadily, she made for the stairs and began to descend, her hands pressed against the walls to help her keep her balance. Tears blurred her vision, and her chest felt tight as she stumbled down the last few steps. She wanted to drop to the ground, curl into a ball and howl. Instead, she leaned against the wall for support as her head began to swim and bile started to rise from the pit of her stomach.

'Kate?'

She heard the note of concern in David's voice, but when she looked up she found her vision fading, the world darkening around her. Her knees started to buckle, and her ears filled with a deafening buzzing sound...

Moving quickly, David caught Kate as she fainted into his arms. Swiftly, he scooped her up and carried her to his room without being seen. Kicking the door closed with his foot, he laid her gently on the bed. As he stroked her deathly pale cheek, Kate regained consciousness and immediately tried to sit up, but David gently pushed her back against the pillow.

'Stay there,' he commanded and walked across the room to the desk. He returned to the bed with a small glass of whisky. Perching next to Kate's head, he slipped an arm under her back and helped her to sit up slowly. 'Sip it,' he told her, handing her the glass.

The whisky slopped dangerously as Kate took the glass between shaking hands and drank, wincing as the alcohol seared her throat. Clumsily, she scrambled to swing her legs to the floor and stood up unsteadily. David grasped her arm and pulled her back onto the bed. 'You're not going anywhere,' he told her firmly. 'Not until I'm sure you're okay.'

'I have to go,' she mumbled. 'I don't want to burden you with my problems anymore…' She gave way to weakening sobs, her fingers clutching the glass tightly. David took it from her and folded her in his protective embrace.

'You spend an inordinate amount of time weeping in my arms,' he murmured softly into her hair. 'Just once, I wish it were different.' He sighed wearily. 'Talk to me, Kate.'

What Ethan had thoughtlessly divulged to a room full of strangers had been shocking enough, but the discovery of his true feelings towards her threatened to destroy Kate's already battered self-esteem. Nevertheless, she would not tell David what she had overheard; she would not willingly damage the men's friendship. Instead, she haltingly revealed the equally distressing news of Edwin's illegitimate child.

'That – that *pig*!' Kate cried, pulling away from David. 'He said he loved Katherine, and all the time he -' She was losing the ability to form a coherent sentence or a rational thought. 'All those days he spent away from camp, when nobody really knew where he was – was he with another woman *and their child*? He would have met her during the expedition that brought him to Edinburgh. Richard was on the same expedition – did he know and keep it secret? How could he do such a thing?'

Gently cupping her chin, David lifted her face so she would look at him. Speaking slowly, carefully, he tried to alleviate her sorrow with logic. 'Angel, there can be no doubt that Edwin loved his wife. How could he not? Anai showed you proof that he had suffered one moment of weakness, but we know nothing of the circumstances surrounding it. We can't judge him. For all we know, this woman may have trapped him in the hope of escaping a life of poverty. I'm sure that when she confronted him in Amarna, he was utterly confounded. He probably thought that the best thing he could do was to give her money to provide for the child.

'You must try and remember that Katherine loved him, and most likely knew nothing of this. So she wouldn't have felt betrayed. Hold onto the knowledge that she died loving him…

'As for Richard, if he had suspected that Edwin was leading a double life with another woman and their illegitimate child, he would have intervened for Katherine's sake. I felt his love for her, Kate; he wouldn't have allowed Edwin to mistreat her.'

Tenderly pushing a lock of hair behind her ear, David took a deep breath. 'It's important that you identify the real reasons behind the pain you feel. I think you're still grieving over your marriage to Mark, which is understandable. You feel angry and hurt because of *his* betrayal -'

'It was my fault!' she wailed. 'I didn't try hard enough to please him!'

'Darling, you may have been dreaming about a past lover while you were married, but Mark was the one who had an affair.'

'Because I couldn't make him happy!'

'In what way did you fail to make him happy? You are the kindest, sweetest person I've ever met. If anything, your desire to please everyone is almost a flaw, because it sometimes has a negative impact on your own wellbeing.'

'He said I was…*oh*!' Her tears fell onto David's hand, as she recalled Mark's cruel remarks about her apparent coldness in the bedroom. 'I can't talk about it with you.'

Wiping her wet cheek with his fingers, David smiled gently. 'If you keep it bottled up, it will fester. And you'll pick at it until you make yourself ill. After everything we've been through, do you honestly think there's anything that could shock me?'

'You'll think badly of me…' Feeling her world crumbling to dust around her, Kate looked at him imploringly until he cuddled her against his chest. Hiding her face in his shirt, she confessed her greatest failing. 'I failed to make him happy in *that* way. He said -' She choked back a sob. 'He called me a frigid ice maiden.'

As David tightened his arms around her, Kate heard a muttered oath hiss from his lips. '*Swine!*' His disgust only served to open the floodgates.

David did what he had always done; he held her against him, stroked her hair and murmured soothingly, attempting to ease the heartache caused by another man. She sobbed into David's chest until she felt weak, her body trembling with exhaustion.

At last, her tears ran out, and Kate took a great, shuddering breath. 'David, did you know about Ethan and Gemma?'

'Ethan has had a lot of flings, Kate. I gave up trying to keep track of them a long time ago.'

Another thought entered Kate's head. 'She had lots of parties in our flat. If she was dating Ethan, then how did you and I never meet?'

There was a moment's silence while he considered his response. 'I wasn't very sociable. In fact, I'm still very fussy about the company I keep...'

'But you *do* know he's having an affair with Marianne?'

'Yes. It's been going on for several seasons now. He seems unable to help himself...'

There was a pause, and Kate knew he would be wondering if she were jealous of Marianne. Sure enough, she felt him take a deep breath.

'Does it upset you?' he asked warily.

Kate felt as though she were floundering in deep, black water. Choking down her tears, she tried to find the surface, air, the sun. 'Am I always to be thwarted by temptresses?'

It didn't answer the question, or put his mind at ease, but the remark made him smile. 'My beautiful Kate, you're more of a temptress than you realise. The charms you possess far outweigh those of any women I've ever met.'

'Don't, David. I know what I am, and it's not a temptress. Please don't mock me.'

Throughout their relationship, amid all the flirting and innuendo, David had always tried to maintain a playfulness and had never taken advantage of her vulnerability. It was as though he had guessed that she had not enjoyed a fulfilling intimate relationship with Mark, and had sensed the ambivalence she felt concerning this delicate subject.

'Sweetheart,' he began quietly, stroking her cheek. 'Mark's unsavoury comment only highlights his ineptitude...' He felt Kate's body become rigid, but continued to hold her gently, talking to the top of her head. 'It takes two to make love. Sure, there should be passion. But there also needs to be tenderness, trust, patience…' He smiled ruefully. 'And some creativity. He obviously didn't do his job properly. He should have worked harder to please you, especially if he was your first lover…' With his forefinger, he tilted her chin upwards. 'Although, I'm very glad he wasn't the first to kiss you…'

Now her gaze flew to his face. 'How do you know that?' she whispered, looking almost guilty as she recalled her first kiss. Her perplexed expression must have looked comical, for David began to laugh.

'Katie Grahame, we *have* met before. I can't keep this secret any longer.' Chuckling, he kissed her nose. 'Think back to the Christmas of 2001. There was a party at the Students' Union – the usual raucous affair. I had harboured a crush on you for several weeks, despite my best attempts to ignore it. You had a part-time job at our local café and thanks to you, I developed a serious coffee habit. You were always kind, always polite, but also a little sad and lost. To me, you were an angel sent to bring light and cake to my days.

'I was too cowardly to approach you, thinking myself beneath such a goddess. But on the night of the party, I finally decided to say something other than "black coffee and a piece of chocolate fudge cake, please" – although I admit to downing a vodka shot for Dutch courage. Standing on my own in a corner – Ethan had disappeared somewhere – I watched you laughing with a group of friends and then, to my delight, you were left standing alone. I waded through the crowd towards you – and the lights went out. I never knew whether it was a power cut or a prank or divine intervention, but I didn't waste the opportunity. I took your lovely face in my hands, and I kissed you. Then, like a scaredy-cat, I ran away.'

Leaning back, he surveyed her astonished but misty-eyed expression. She lifted her fingers to her mouth, remembering the light brush of warm lips. She had been stunned, and her heart had raced as she dared to respond to his kiss. The lights had come back on, and Kate had been disappointed to discover that her secret paramour had vanished.

'I remember…' she murmured softly, with a wistful smile. 'It was my very first kiss…'

'I'm glad,' he replied softly. 'Because for me it was a momentous event. You were naturally hesitant, and I knew then that I had taken advantage of an innocent girl. I thought you might slap me. But then, to my amazement, you kissed me back. It made me dizzy.' His smile was a little sad as he gazed at her lips. When he spoke again, his voice was hoarse. 'And for me, there's never been another kiss like it…'

'Why didn't you ever speak to me?'

'Unfortunately, I was a studious nerd in those days.' David kissed her forehead. 'I rarely socialised, and I was painfully shy – unlike Ethan, who was my polar opposite. All I did was work, because I was ambitious and eager to prove my worth.

'I was supposed to be working on my thesis, but there were times when I couldn't get you out of my head, and I cursed you as an unwanted distraction. I tried to forget about you. I tried staying away from the café, and took different routes to work to avoid bumping into you. I knew that I would be leaving the country and that romance was out of the question, but…' He gazed into the middle distance forlornly.

'You moved away, and I had no choice but to shut you out of my mind. I lost myself even deeper in my work. Within a few months, we were sent to Amarna.' David sighed wistfully. 'The rest, as they say, is history.'

'I left Marchmont because my Aunt Margaret had terminal cancer,' Kate explained. 'Dad wanted to put her in a hospice, but she wanted to stay in her house. I moved in with her to nurse her.' She paused as she experienced a sample of the grief from that time. 'But in the end, he got his way and she was moved to Saint Columba's Hospice.' She looked at him in wonder, her mind still trying to comprehend his confession. 'When we started working together at the museum, you never said that you knew me…'

'It didn't seem appropriate. Too much time had passed, and we were both involved with other people. I accepted that we'd taken different paths and resigned myself to the constraints of a working relationship. For a while, at least…' He took a deep breath. 'But now, that's no longer enough.'

David did not readily bare his soul; he was watching her carefully, hoping she would not trample on it. Kate knew he was waiting for some words of encouragement or consolation, but she could find nothing to say. They had wasted so many opportunities and made so many mistakes. There were still many obstacles to overcome – perhaps too many…

Her lip quivered, but no tears followed. Instead, she reached up tentatively to push a lock of hair from his eyes, and then kissed him lightly on the cheek.

'I'm sorry…' Kate whispered. 'I'm sorry everything's so tangled up. We're like flies caught in a spider's web.' She leaned back into his embrace and sighed heavily, but the voice in her head nagged her to escape.

'I should go,' she decided, trying once again to rise. 'We have to be up early, and I need to -'

'Stay here tonight,' David finished. Kate stared at him, startled by the suggestion. Correctly interpreting her expression, David rephrased. 'I don't mean what you think I mean. I'll find a bed elsewhere, or take out a tent. You should stay here and get some peace. I know you don't like sleeping at the other end of the house by yourself – at least here there are rooms on either side.' He stood and took her empty glass to the tiny sink, creating distance between them, giving her space to contemplate his offer.

Kate watched him, her thoughts in turmoil. He was gathering items to take with him to another room, his attention carefully focused on what he was doing. 'Don't leave,' she blurted, ignoring the voice of good sense. 'Please stay with me.' He stopped fiddling with the contents of a drawer and stared at her, eyes questioning. 'Just for company…' she clarified.

'I'll go and get a sleeping bag…'

Kate looked at him bravely. 'Can't you just…hold me?' Her voice dropped to a murmur. 'You'll be rid of me soon enough…'

Avoiding her gaze, David asked if she needed anything from her room, but Kate shook her head. Did she want to borrow something of his? Awkwardly, she declined. Somewhat shyly, he presented her with his spare toothbrush, still packaged, and gestured towards his tiny shower room.

Keeping their eyes averted from each other, they removed boots, belts, watches and shirts. With butterflies in their stomachs, they slid under the covers, automatically arranging themselves like spoons in a cutlery drawer, each slightly awed by how perfectly they fit together. Almost immediately, Kate felt blissfully peaceful. He was stroking her arm, lulling her to sleep. Through a warm, soporific haze, Kate heard his velvety voice close to her ear.

'I'm sorry I brought you here, sweetheart. I wish I could have protected you from this.'

'Stay with me,' she murmured sleepily. 'Don't leave…'

'How could I ever leave you, when I…'

Kate drifted off to sleep.

The sound of weeping floated down a dark, narrow street in El Hagg Qandil; a young woman's grief pervaded the walls of the simple dwellings. Women who understood her pain shook their heads in sympathy and cursed the man who had caused it.

Inside Anai's house, Mina lay prostrate on the rug before the fire, sobbing as though her heart might break. Over by the sideboard, Anai finished crushing herbs with an old pestle and mortar. Draining the resultant oils into a shallow dish, she began to mutter an incantation in an angry voice. Dipping her fingers into the dish, she anointed the female wax poppet with the malodorous unguent, saturating the lock of dark brown hair stuck to its head.

'She will dream,' Anai assured Mina, who had curled into a foetal position on the floor. 'She will dream of those she loves, and she will be tortured by their betrayal. Her soul will not be reunited with either of them in this life. We will have our revenge, Tasmina.'

Mina's body shook as her sobs grew increasingly anguished. Anai's face became a mask of hatred as she picked up one of the male effigies, which now sported a few strands of dark blond hair. Shuffling over to the fire as she uttered another invocation, Anai placed the little man upright on the high mantelpiece, next to the statue of Isis. Raising her voice as she came to the end of the spell, Anai swept her hand across the mantelpiece, knocking the figure off its perch. As it fell to the tiled floor, the wax effigy broke in two.

David woke with a start, disorientated in the dark room. He had moulded his body against Kate's back, his arm resting protectively across her body. She was murmuring anxiously in her sleep.

'Father?' he heard her call softly. 'Father, is that you?'

Kate peered around James Grahame's dimly lit study. A fire roared in the hearth, the familiar smell of wood, whisky and cigars swirled in her nostrils. From a dark corner, James stepped into view, and Kate gazed lovingly into the kind face of her cherished Victorian father.

'Lassie,' he said in his deep, soothing voice. He took Kate's hands in his, and Kate felt hot tears roll down her cheeks. 'My poor lassie…'

'Oh, Father!' Kate cried. 'Everything has gone wrong! Edwin told me he would be waiting in Amarna, but where is he? Is he in Ethan?' A sob escaped from her lips. 'Why is Ethan so cruel? And why did Edwin betray me?'

James emanated an almost angelic tranquillity, soothing Kate's distress with his calm demeanour. 'Always so many questions...'

'Where is Edwin?'

'He is where he should be, lass…'

'He said he would be *here*…'

Her father's expression was grave, and she felt him squeeze her hands. 'He did not. Edwin told you that you would find what you were looking for in Egypt. You *have*, my darling. And it is *not* Edwin.'

'Father, please stop talking in riddles! Please speak plainly and *tell me what to do*!'

James pursed his lips and stared at her sternly. 'What have you learned, Katie? What has this experience taught you about yourself? All of this has not been about finding romance – it has been a journey to find out about *yourself*.'

Kate hesitated, unconsciously wringing her hands as she struggled to order her thoughts. She was becoming confused about her identity, aware of Katherine Ford's spirit mingling with her own. James, however, seemed unconcerned that the woman before him was not his daughter, but a much weaker relation.

'I was once told that during each lifetime we have a lesson to learn and another to teach,' Kate began. 'If we do not complete these tasks we return to try again until we succeed.' James nodded encouragingly, so she continued, hearing her voice grow stronger. 'I have allowed myself to be tied down and bullied, by people and society's "rules", even when it made me unhappy.'

Her eyes widened as realisation dawned. 'It was the easiest solution, the dutiful option. Demanding my freedom seemed like a selfish choice – and too much of a struggle. And yet, I've made myself a martyr in the process and so caused suffering in the people around me…' Ashamed, she hid her face in her hands.

James nodded sagely. 'At last!' he smiled. 'Now you must have faith, and listen to the voice of your *heart*. Do not be dictated to by your excessive sense of duty. Stop allowing people to run roughshod over you and stand true to yourself, for you need no longer feel restricted. You will make the right choices…' He lifted a hand to stroke her face. 'And you will not have to repeat the lesson. As for the teaching part, you are making progress and in this you will also succeed.'

'Is Edwin in Ethan? Am I now bound to him?' The thought disturbed her, and she almost dreaded James's response.

'You need be bound to no one, Katie. And be assured that Edwin did not betray you. The laddie loved you and was a faithful husband.'

Another pressing question formed in Kate's head. 'Father, what happened to Richard? I think I -' Kate stopped as she became aware of the light in the room becoming brighter. She turned towards the half-open door, sensing another presence just beyond the threshold.

'Mother?' she called, desperate to see Eleanor Grahame once more. She heard the rustle of skirts and caught the scent of violets.

'My beautiful Katie,' James drew her attention away from the doorway. 'Listen to me. There are those who wish you harm, those who tell you one thing whilst hiding another. You must be mindful. There are also those who love you, but who are growing weary of this struggle. But know this: your trials are almost at an end.' He looked past her and sighed heavily. 'It's time to go, Katie. But never forget how much you are loved, my darling girl…'

The edges of the room began to blur and fade. 'No!' she cried. 'Don't go yet! I want to see Mother…'

David realised he was eavesdropping on a meeting with James Grahame. Misery had induced Kate to find a place of safety in her dreams. Her voice was muffled, the words a little indistinct, but David was spellbound by the change in her accent, the soft lilt in her tone and altered pronunciation. But whether she was dreaming as Kate Grahame or Katherine Ford, her torment was obvious.

'Hush, angel,' he soothed softly, kissing her head and gently holding her writing body. 'It's alright…'

'Please don't leave me…' Kate moaned, still dreaming. She turned towards David, her body shifting until it nestled against him, her arm sliding around his neck. 'I love him, Father, but he will want to leave me too…'

'Who, Kate?' David whispered. 'Who do you love?'

'David…' she murmured, and finally relaxed into a peaceful slumber.

CHAPTER 13

Tuesday December 18, 2012

Quietly, Kate closed the door of David's room and crept along the corridor, carrying her boots. It was nearly dawn, and the house would soon come to life. She didn't want to be in David's bed when he woke; it would be awkward, to say the least. Or it might lead to something else which would make their situation even more complicated. On the other hand, Kate thought as she climbed to the roof, waking up in his arms had been...wonderful. Gazing upon his handsome face, serene in sleep, had been wonderful. Kissing him gently before she left his bed had been wonderful.

Her blissful reverie fizzled into the ether when she stepped onto the roof and spotted Mina standing at one corner. Anai's granddaughter faced the impending sunrise, arms outstretched, and her long scarf fluttering in the breeze. From Kate's position, it looked as though Mina held the rising sun between her hands. The girl was whispering, as if in prayer.

Before Kate could creep back downstairs, Mina turned towards her. Kate was startled by the girl's gaunt complexion, and the dark circles under her eyes. Her normally exquisite bone structure looked strangely harsh in the dawn light. Smiling only with her lips, Mina beckoned Kate to join her, and the pair stood together near the edge of the roof. Silence reigned while they watched another glorious sunrise, the blood-red light seeping over the desert.

'You have slept in your clothes,' Mina observed at last, her exotic eyes on the horizon. 'But not in your bed, I fear.' She flicked a reproachful glance over Kate's crumpled clothing.

Kate offered no defence; like her grandmother, Mina's intuition was almost preternatural. The Egyptian women seemed to know everything, including a person's innermost thoughts. Why, then, should she explain her actions?

The Egyptian girl's demeanour altered, and she regarded Kate with a cryptic smile. 'Tea?' she offered.

The closing of the door woke David from a dreamless sleep. In the darkness, he rolled over to the space still warm from Kate's body and pushed his face into the pillow still filled with her scent. Lying there, he attempted to order his thoughts and harness his emotions, wondering what this day would bring.

It brought a loud knock at the door, followed by a draught as the door opened, and blinding illumination as Ethan switched on the overhead light. David groaned in protest.

'Why aren't you ready?' Ethan barked. 'Move yourself, you lazy beggar! I want to get out of here before everybody else gets up.'

Amy did not appear for the morning briefing in the dining room. Once the others had dispersed to gather their equipment, Kate made her way to Amy's bedroom. She was surprised and a little peeved to find the girl still in bed, the covers pulled up to her chin. When Kate leaned over the student, she saw that the younger woman had been weeping. Amy turned her face into her pillow like a petulant child.

'What's the matter, Amy?' Kate asked, sitting on the edge of the bunk. She held back an irritable sigh; she would like nothing more than a day in bed herself. Well, perhaps not by herself...

'Are you ill?'

Instead of offering a coherent explanation, Amy set about howling like a grief-stricken child. Kate's shoulders slumped, but she patted the lumpy covers in the general area of Amy's back. 'I can't help you if you won't tell me what's wrong.'

'I've done a really stupid thing!' Amy wailed, her voice muffled by the pillow.

'Well, I'm sure it's not as bad as you think...' Kate tried to sound consoling.

'I slept with Doctor Brodie!' she cried, sobbing loudly.

Dumbfounded by the revelation, Kate chewed her lip. Steven had a girlfriend in Edinburgh, and Kate had thought him smitten with the bubbly Megan. But since coming to Egypt, the once affable archaeologist seemed to want to imitate Ethan in every way.

Kate had been aware of Amy turning her attentions from David to Steven, but had felt sure that the young man would sensibly rebuff the misguided girl.

Suddenly, Kate's strait-laced nature took over; she was tired of the drama and the evident promiscuity enjoyed by her colleagues. As Ethan had said, the expedition was becoming like a soap opera! Conveniently, she failed to consider her own part in the show.

'Presumably he didn't take you by force,' Kate reasoned, trying hard to keep the coldness from her voice. Amy sniffed wetly, and Kate reached for the box of tissues on the floor beside her. 'And you *have* been flirting with him a lot...'

'I know...' Amy blew her nose loudly.

'Then why are you crying?' Kate asked, and allowed her sense of humour to enter the scene. 'Was Steven rubbish?' She hoped Amy would not regale her with details.

'No, but he made it clear it was just a one-off. He made me leave his room immediately afterwards.' Another bout of dramatic sobbing ensued. 'I feel so used!'

Her wailing was so fierce she sat up abruptly and dashed to the sink, where she vomited ferociously. Wearily, Kate straightened the bed linen and fetched the half-empty bottle of water from the desk. When Amy had cleaned herself up, Kate tucked her back into bed.

'I'll take your place on the dig today,' she told the shivering girl. 'Stay here and rest. I'll check on you later. Do you need anything? Toast, maybe?'

Amy shook her head, looking more like a little girl than the femme fatale she tried to emulate. 'I don't feel like eating...'

Kate nodded briskly. 'I'm going to borrow your hat. Try to get some sleep – and forget about Steven Brodie. Instead of chasing unsuitable guys, focus on your work and your future. You don't need the validation of men to get on in life...'

Amy looked up at Kate gratefully, a little intimidated by the older woman's firm tone and determined expression. 'Thanks, Kate.' She huddled under the covers and squeezed her eyes shut against a cruel world.

Accompanied by Hassan, Ahmed drove the Edinburgh group down to the cemetery and helped unload their equipment. Determined to embrace her temporary role as supervisor, Kate organised the students with swift efficiency. Hassan wanted to stay and watch; Kate agreed as long as kept out of their way. To Ahmed she was polite but indifferent, and offered no encouragement to the Egyptian who apparently wished to win her favour. She was relieved when, having emptied the pickup truck of their gear, Ahmed drove back to the dig house.

After checking and repositioning the poles and strings of their area of excavation, Julian, Jonathan and Celine began to sieve the gravelly sand. Only one workman had been assigned to them that day, and Kate felt a little disappointed that the man had brought a wheelbarrow instead of a sad-eyed donkey.

Russell took up his position at the head of the grave of the alleged sorceress and quietly began to work. Kate resisted the mischievous impulse to embarrass him by asking about his evening, as the shamefaced young Scot had done his best to avoid her gaze all morning. She had eavesdropped on a whispered exchange between Dominic and Jonathan, which revealed that Russell had enjoyed a night-time rendezvous with one of the American students. Naturally, the young men were full of envy and grudging admiration for their colleague.

Kate knelt beside the centre section of the grave and set out her tool kit. Humming an Irish air under his breath, Dominic set up a canvas screen to give them shade and then took his position at the foot of the burial plot. Working methodically, the three began to sift a final ten centimetres of ground.

For a while, no one spoke, but not because they were miserable. In fact, Kate felt an atmosphere of camaraderie around her. The temperature was comfortably warm, and there was only a slight breeze, which thankfully did not blow sand in their faces. A few wispy clouds drifted lazily across the sky. Occasionally, she spotted a swift movement in the sand or between the rocks, but Kate did not look too closely for its source. She had not encountered any snakes or scorpions yet, and had no desire to do so.

Around mid-morning, Kate announced a break for 'second breakfast' and opened up the large cooler packed with snacks for the group. Hassan, who had amused himself by helping the Egyptian man, immediately ran off with a couple of filled rolls and a bunch of grapes. Once they had refuelled, everyone returned to work. Energised by a tasty sandwich, the Egyptian workman began to croon snatches of old pop songs and soon the students had joined his hilarious rendition of 'I'm Too Sexy', singing loudly while they toiled.

It had been the general opinion of the group that they would find nothing more in the open grave, so Russell called out in surprise when his trowel gently knocked against a piece of metal. Selecting a small, flat-edged trowel, he sought the edges of the piece and used his fingers to push the earth away from an object about fifteen centimetres long. It resembled an ankh without the crosspiece.

The next task was to photograph the piece in situ, and take measurements, and then Kate watched in fascination as Russell carefully extracted it from its resting place. He brushed the dirt from its surface to reveal an engraved pattern on the circular end. Two holes had been punched near the bottom edge. Russell placed it gently in the plastic tray behind them, and they went back to sifting with renewed fervour.

A short while later, Julian called Kate's attention to another discovery. He had designated himself as the unofficial overseer of his section, pompously directing Jonathan and Celine to work on particular parts of the plot. But while Julian had spent hours sifting worthless pebbles, Celine had uncovered a human hand and radius, and Jonathan had found a skull.

'We can assume this grave has been looted,' Julian told Kate coldly. 'The bones have probably been scattered over the ground...' His gaze became calculating. 'We should just cover it up and move on, instead of wasting our time.'

Kate realised he was testing her authority. 'Professor Young gave us explicit instructions to dig out another ten centimetres,' she said decisively. 'So keep excavating the plot. And of course, record and photograph the finds as you go.' She smiled at Celine and Jonathan. 'Good work, you two!' With a brisk nod in Julian's direction, Kate returned to her own little patch of earth.

Time slipped by without Kate noticing as she became immersed in her work. Even the sounds around her faded into the distance. Her perseverance was rewarded in the early afternoon, when the sun and glare were becoming uncomfortable. Digging out what she assumed to be a small stone, Kate was surprised and elated to find a small bead, about half a centimetre in diameter. Further probing unearthed a fragment of a collared necklace; four strands of beads joined together with brittle cord.

'Look!' she cried to her companions. 'I've found part of a necklace!'

The boys leaned over and examined the piece, both of them offering words of praise.

'The piece I found must be the counterpoise,' Russell beamed. 'The prof will be well pleased!'

Kate brushed the sand from her treasure, gently stroking the arrangement of discoloured blue and yellow beads. Reverently, she placed it in the container and turned back to the ground, where she soon began to find individual beads of varying sizes, some of them a faded shade of red and shaped like almonds. There were so many, she decided to place them in a separate reed basket. When she heard the engine of the pickup truck drawing closer, Kate felt downright irked at the interruption.

'Kate,' Russell tapped her on the shoulder, as he and Dominic stood and began to pack their equipment. 'It's time to go in.'

Wiping dust from her face with her sleeve, Kate looked up. The other group had tidied their site and now walked towards the truck. A different driver disembarked and cheerfully greeted the workman, who was also preparing to leave for the day.

'I think I'll stay here,' Kate decided. 'You two go on. Take this morning's discoveries back to the house with you. I'll see you when you come back this afternoon.'

'Are you sure?' Dominic asked, frowning in concern. 'It's pretty hot now, and you'll be on your own. I'm not sure Professor Young would want us to leave you…'

Hassan dropped to his knees beside Kate and peered into the basket of beads. Kate smiled up at the two young men who were reluctant to incur David's wrath.

'It looks like I won't be alone after all,' she chuckled.

The boys fetched Kate an extra bottle of water from the cool box and thoughtfully adjusted the screen for her before joining the others on the back of the truck. Kate watched the vehicle bump its way back towards the dig house, and then ruffled Hassan's hair.

'Well, Edwin's great-great-great grandson, it looks like it's just you and me.'

The little boy grinned at her, uncomprehending. Kate used hand signals to convey the message, 'Don't touch anything!' then she continued her search for the witch's beads, determined to reunite the Egyptian woman with her jewellery.

As Hassan played and sang to himself, Kate toiled for another hour, oblivious to the sun that now shone mercilessly on her head. She felt at peace, connected to the earth and the past. Her mind wandered calmly to the vivid dream she had experienced while sleeping in David's bed. The vision had provided reassurance; like a portly guardian angel, James Grahame had given her hope, strength and clarity.

Dark thoughts were forced out of her head as she enjoyed the present. They were replaced with memories of being cuddled by David all night, feeling his warm breath against the back of her neck and his arm clasped around her waist. Kate's face glowed with a secretive smile as she continued to daydream…

Kate yelped in surprise when a hand squeezed her shoulder. Turning her head, she looked into Ethan's face as he crouched down beside her. Gently, he reached out and lifted the brim of her hat. Kate stiffened as his fingers brushed her cheek; equanimity vanished on the breeze, to be replaced by confusion.

'You're directly in the sun,' he observed. 'How long have you been out here?'

She shrugged, perplexed by this apparent concern for her wellbeing. And yet a part of her still craved his goodwill. She silently berated herself.

'I – I guess I lost track of time,' she stammered. 'But look, I found a piece of a necklace. And now I keep finding all these beads…' She gestured to the basket, now almost half-full.

Ethan dipped a long forefinger into the collection of beads and swirled it round thoughtfully.

'They might be part of a menyet,' Ethan mused. 'A necklace which was held in the hand, rather than worn around the neck. Menyets were owned by ladies and priestesses who were devotees of Hathor. It supposedly guaranteed the protection of the goddess....' He paused, and Kate knew he was watching her as she sifted a measure of sand. Another small yellow bead was added to the basket.

'You're going to stay out here until you find every last one, aren't you?' he asked with a wry smile, as if he knew her character. How could he be so two-faced?

As usual, he made her feel stupid. 'I wanted her to have her necklace...' She fiddled with the handle of her trowel. 'Can it be reconstructed?'

Ethan considered the contents of the basket then looked up at Kate, his expression deadpan. 'Come back to the house, and I'll get you some string...' Kate stared at him uncertainly, then pursed her lips as she realised he was teasing her.

'I thought Amy was supposed to be in this group today,' Ethan continued. 'Where is she?'

'Not feeling well,' Kate mumbled, not looking at him. 'I told her to stay in bed.' She leaned over her work area and resumed digging with her small trowel.

'And you're wearing her hat in the hope that you might fool David into thinking you're her...' Kate refused to answer. 'You don't think he'll recognise your backside from, say...' He looked over her head as the Land Rover trundled across the sand. Parking a safe distance from the excavation site, David jumped out of the vehicle. '...twenty metres? He spends enough time ogling it.'

Kate looked over her shoulder then quickly lowered her head. David was striding purposefully towards them, and even from a distance, Kate could read his stern expression. '*Nuts!*' she muttered under her breath.

'Your language is becoming appalling, Miss Grahame!' Ethan teased. 'By the way, our boy's in a good mood this morning, although he looks exhausted. I take it you had a good night?'

Fumbling for words, Kate couldn't decide on an appropriate response. But it didn't matter, because Ethan was grinning at his friend as David drew closer. 'Hey, Dave! Got some interesting stuff here!'

Kate kept her head down and waited for a severe reprimand. To be honest, a part of her relished the thought of bickering with him because now she was ready to solve all their disputes by exercising her feminine wiles.

'Well done, *Kate*,' David growled. Kate looked sideways at the sandy boots that had lain discarded next to hers the night before, and grinned.

'Where's Amy?' demanded David.

Standing, Ethan gallantly took Kate by the elbow and helped her rise clumsily to her feet. She stepped quickly away from Ethan's grip as David watched them with unconcealed jealousy.

Pushing her hat to the back of her head, Kate stretched and rubbed at the small of her back, stiff from kneeling in the same position for too long. As she had hoped, David's eyes followed her movements as though hypnotised.

'She's ill,' Kate informed the professor. 'I thought it best to let her stay in bed, although she was reluctant to do so and sorry to miss today's dig.'

'I'll bet!' David muttered sarcastically.

'Kate made the right decision,' Ethan piped up. 'Can't have the students vomiting all over the dig site.' He began to tidy the site. Hassan, who had been sitting a short distance away, ran over and folded up the sunshade. 'Dave, do you want a lift back or would you rather walk?'

'Walk,' David and Kate said together.

'Thought so...' Ethan murmured, picking up the basket. 'It's a long way to walk in the hot sun, mind...'

'We'll manage,' David said, his attention centred on Kate. 'So what exactly is wrong with Miss Reardon?'

Kate raised her chin defiantly, and prepared for a delightful battle of wills. 'Women's problems,' she stated flatly.

Ethan grimaced. 'I'll leave you to it, then,' he said and loped back to the car with Hassan at his heels.

Kate and David regarded each other, eyes challenging. Kate waited to see if David was intimidated by mention of the mysterious workings of the female anatomy, as Ethan seemed to be.

'And that requires a day in bed?' he asked, refusing to give in.

Kate saw the twinkle in his eyes that told her he was suppressing a smile. 'Lots of things require a day in bed...' she observed, grinning when she saw him look flustered. 'By the way, thanks for putting me up last night.' She lifted her hand and rested it on his forearm. The sound of the car's engine receded in the distance. 'I'm sorry if I disturbed you...'

'I'm used to it,' he commented drily, his gaze fixed on her lips. 'But I think *you* might have been disturbed – you were talking in your sleep. Did you have a nightmare?'

Kate's eyes grew wistful. 'Not a nightmare, no. More like a helpful, comforting dream. A shove in the right direction, if you like.' She looked down at his sleeve, and rubbed at a stain on the cuff. As she tilted her head, she exposed a fading red mark that extended from her jaw down the side of her neck. David reached out to stroke the irritated skin.

'What happened here?' he asked.

Kate blushed and smiled shyly at her feet. 'Stubble burn,' she murmured, remembering her gleeful grin when she had noticed the mark that morning. She had donned a wide cotton scarf to hide it from view, but had loosened it when the students had gone for lunch. 'Your beard is very rough...'

'Oh,' David muttered bashfully, but Kate heard a note of pleasure in his voice. 'You left very early.'

'I didn't want to outstay my welcome.'

'It's probably just as well. If you'd stayed five more minutes, you would have run straight into Ethan…'

Kate raised her eyes to his and shrugged dismissively. 'I wouldn't have cared…'

David's eyes widened in surprise at her declaration, and he seemed momentarily lost for words. Kate pretended to look at the scenery while her hand still played with his sleeve.

'Did you have a productive morning?' she asked, sounding nonchalant.

'Yes,' he spluttered, caught off-guard by the question. 'We found a curtain of rock shielding what looks like a blocked passageway, just like you said. And through binoculars, we could see symbols carved into the limestone curtain. We're going back in the morning with climbing equipment. Kate -'

She looked up at him intently. 'Yes?'

He touched her sun-flushed cheek with the palm of his hand. 'You're hot.'

Kate smiled coquettishly. 'Why, thank you, Professor Young! You're not so bad yourself…' She giggled as he blushed.

'Are you trying to distract me from Amy's skiving?'

Kate's eyes flashed impishly. 'Is it working?'

David attempted to reassert his control. 'Her performance out here is important, Kate.'

Brazenly, Kate raised both hands to pluck non-existent fluff from the front of his shirt. She looked up at him with wide eyes. 'I know, David, but she's in pain today. You asked me to deal with their issues, so let me deal with them.'

'I don't want them taking advantage of you. I know you've been helping some of them with their field notes – I recognised your writing style -'

'I didn't *write* their field notes,' Kate grumbled. 'I only read them and made suggestions – kind of…'

'Uh-huh.' David didn't look convinced. 'I have to write a performance review for each of them. So please make sure Amy's ready to work this afternoon.'

His hands moved to cup her elbows as he gazed into her eyes, and Amy was forgotten. 'I don't suppose you would consider swooning at my feet again tonight, would you?'

Kate's palms rested flat against his chest as he drew her a fraction closer. 'I've never swooned at *anyone's* feet!' she protested, her voice silky. 'And precisely *what* are you suggesting?'

He raised an eyebrow suggestively, and Kate pretended to look shocked. 'What is it about this place that makes everyone abandon all pretence of propriety? There's so much bed-hopping going on, it's like Ibiza without bikinis!' His hands felt hot as they slid up her upper arms.

David gave her a seductive smile and asked, 'Have you ever been to

Ibiza?'

Kate pouted. 'Yes.'

'And?'

She frowned. 'I didn't like it. Nobody ever wanted to go sightseeing. They spent every night clubbing and every day in bed...' She blushed as she replayed the words in her head.

David chuckled and leaned his forehead on hers. 'I wasn't suggesting we behave like rutting beasts, Miss Grahame.' He rubbed the tip of his nose against hers, and Kate relished the intimate gesture. 'We could just stay up and...talk.'

Kate gave him a disbelieving look, and he had the good grace to grin ruefully. She wanted to slide her hands around his neck and run her fingers through his hair. Instead, she moved back a little and smiled up at him.

'I don't want to behave like the others,' she told him. 'It would feel... indecent. Not special at all.'

'I agree,' he replied, rubbing at a smudge on her cheek. 'And even out here, I feel as though we're being watched. But I don't think we can keep pretending to be "just colleagues" any longer. For one thing, it's exhausting.'

'And also, I don't think anyone believes us anyway. But we should be discreet. We can still try to set a good example for the remainder of the expedition – if that's even possible, anymore...'

'And then?'

She gazed at him, thinking his half-smile irresistible. Instinctively, she raised herself up on her toes to be closer to those tantalising lips, pushing all her concerns out of her head. 'Well, then the students go home. And we're on holiday...' She held her breath as he lowered his head to hers....and then let out a squeal of surprise as a hot, wet tongue licked the length of her cheek.

'Oh, for God's sake!' David whined, and abruptly released Kate.

A long black face butted its way between them, velvety ears tickling Kate's nose as the Arab stallion nuzzled her pockets in search of mints. Giggling, Kate brought a packet of Polo mints from the thigh pocket of her trousers and fed one to the horse. By way of thanks, the horse nuzzled her neck and cheek. Patting the strong, velvety neck, she murmured to the animal in a loving tone and inspected his burnished black coat. She was relieved to see that the welts were healing. The horse was wearing a harness today instead of a bridle, and its abused mouth also seemed to be recovering. Given the owner's reticence, Kate wondered if David had supervised the horse's care in his spare time. The stallion certainly seemed familiar with David, as he nudged the professor's shoulder.

'You're a blooming pest!' David muttered to the horse. 'You're timing is rotten, as usual. So don't bother giving me that look – you're going home!' He gathered up the dragging reins and turned the animal towards the main road.

Dusting off her satchel, Kate settled it across her shoulder. After a final inspection of the dig site, she returned to David's side. 'What look?' she asked, amused.

David frowned testily. 'The same look you give me when you want your own way, and the pouting and foot-stamping hasn't worked.'

'Hey!' Kate protested. It wasn't fair that he knew her so well! She looked longingly at the horse's bare back. 'Can I ride him?' As David turned towards her, she imitated the horse's doe-eyed stare. 'Please? It's such a long way back to the house...'

'No, you can't,' he said firmly, and gave her a half-hearted scowl. 'Not ten minutes ago, you said you wanted to walk!' He started walking across the sand, refusing to be drawn into a wrangling session with her. The horse whinnied, blowing the hair on the top of David's head. 'Shut up!' he growled at the animal. 'You've ruined a perfectly good opportunity, fleabag!'

Kate laughed quietly as she trailed behind, enjoying the sight of a beautiful man arguing with a beautiful horse. Joyfully, she ran up to David's side and slipped her hand in his. 'Don't be so grumpy, Forest Face!' she scolded.

David laced his fingers through hers. 'He ruined the dream.'

'What dream?' He didn't answer, so she squeezed his fingers. 'Tell me.'

'I had a dream, months ago. We were here, in the desert, with two horses.' He gently poked the horse's muzzle. 'But neither of them pushed in between us!'

'Oh? What were we doing?' Kate's voice became coy.

David kept his gaze on the horizon. 'Never mind.' He waved at the Egyptian boy who approached them from the road, the same youth they had met on their first day in Amarna.

'Spoilsport!' Kate grumbled. By mutual consent, their hands dropped to their sides.

The boy was out of breath but refrained from scolding the horse in front of Kate. Instead, he spoke quietly to David, his manner deferential. Kate listened to David responding in Arabic, his voice almost musical as he caressed the syllables, and very different from Ethan's harsh tones.

'Miss Grahame,' David addressed her formally, his eyes dancing mischievously. 'Are you satisfied that this horse's condition is much improved?'

Aware that the boy was looking at her expectantly, Kate made a show of examining the horse, running her hand along the sleek flank as she moved from nose to tail on both sides. At last, she nodded.

'I'm satisfied for now. But I'll be watching...'

David translated Kate's warning. The boy raised an incredulous eyebrow but nodded humbly. Listening intently to David's conversation with the youth, Kate managed to understand a few words that confirmed her suspicions.

'You've been taking care of the horse, haven't you?' she asked David.

Raising an eyebrow, David gave her a look that was mildly reproachful. 'When I took Mina riding, I visited your precious stallion. Mina and I were *not* picnicking – or anything else.' Patting the horse's neck, David bid farewell to the prancing horse and its owner.

Once the boy had led the horse away, David slipped his arm around Kate's shoulders and they headed back to their responsibilities. They followed the main road, which ran from the southern tombs, past the dig house, then joined up with the Royal Road. It was a long walk, as Ethan had warned them, and there was no shade from the sun, but they walked without complaint. One of the expedition drivers passed and offered them a lift, but they declined, keen to eke out this trip for as long as possible.

She should have been enjoying their time together, but Kate's thoughts shifted to the house and its occupants quicker than her feet, and she started to grow uneasy. Sliding her arm around David's waist, she leaned against him.

David, too, became introspective, as if he wished to broach a subject that might prove problematic. Eventually, he inhaled deeply then told her, 'I found out what happened to Richard Yorke…'

'I thought you didn't want to know -'

'But *you do*. So I did a little research, with the help of a historian at the university in Edinburgh and the EES archives.' He hesitated, which meant the news wasn't good. 'He died, Kate. His regiment served in South Africa at the end of the Boer War, and he was killed in action in May 1902. Two days before peace was declared.' David squeezed her shoulders, offering solace.

'He would've died with honour,' Kate declared with certainty. 'But it's a shame. It's almost as if the three of them were cursed – perhaps they really were. Perhaps Nula *was* a witch, and she blamed the three of them for -'

'Or perhaps they were just destined to die prematurely,' David cut off her rambling. 'And perhaps they've found each other again and are finally at peace.'

He was right; she should hold onto that notion instead of torturing herself with the thought of three lost souls trapped between realms. They continued meandering along the road as the sun blazed down on them. Inevitably, Kate found herself fretting about the future.

'I heard some potentially good news today,' David began, as though he could read her mind and knew she needed to hear that at least one of their problems had been solved. 'I received an email from the university regarding Julian's letter of complaint. Apparently, the other students sent their own emails to the head of my department, singing our praises. Although there will be a formal debriefing, I don't think there will be serious repercussions.' He kissed the top of her head. 'I don't want you to worry about it anymore.'

'That's great, David.' Kate breathed a sigh of relief. 'They're such a good bunch of kids…'

'I'm kind of shell-shocked that they would do that, given what a sod I can be…' He chuckled, sweetly bemused.

Kate turned to kiss his hand as it rested on her shoulder. 'Well, I'm not surprised at all. Although I agree, you can be a right sod.'

His laugh was infectious, and it felt good to be light-hearted for these precious stolen moments. The dig house loomed ahead, and Kate could see people milling around outside the building. Voices carried on the breeze towards them, and Kate steeled herself in preparation. Only a few more metres…

Her feet stopped moving. The butterflies thrashing about in her stomach seemed to have razor-tipped wings.

'You've come too far to go back, angel,' David told her, turning her to face him. 'Only two more days to go.'

'I feel like I'm standing at the edge of a cliff, overlooking a stormy sea,' Kate murmured. 'I'm scared I'm going to fall – and sink.'

David smiled indulgently at her. 'That's very poetic – you should consider writing something more than just reports and blogs.' He toyed with the errant tendril of hair across her cheek. 'But you would fly, not sink.'

Impulsively, Kate hugged him, touched by his faith in her. Stretching up on her toes, she tilted her face upwards in invitation. But he didn't move, just gave her that mysterious, sexy smile.

'Are you going to make me beg?' she asked huffily.

'No,' he chuckled hoarsely. 'But I'm going to make you wait – agonising though that might be.' Stroking her cheek, he looked into her eyes. 'I want to give you my full attention, and I want us to be completely alone. Right now, we're not.' His eyes flicked towards the house.

As Kate followed his gaze, she saw Mina standing on the roof, watching them. Waves of enraged disapproval surged towards them from her amber eyes, and then the girl turned and disappeared from view. Kate's shoulders visibly slumped as she trudged the final few steps to bedlam.

When they reached the front of the house, David turned to Kate, his lips pursed in speculation. She could see that he shared her wish for seclusion, and perhaps the opportunity to share an intimate meal in some quiet place. But there was nowhere to hide, and responsibilities weighed heavily on those broad shoulders.

They had no choice but to join the other residents, and Kate couldn't face the hubbub.

'I'll go and make sure Amy's ready to work, and then I'll check up on the rest of the students,' she said decisively. 'I'd like to write my report for the museum while this morning's still fresh in my mind.' She looked down at her dusty clothes. 'I think I might do some washing, too…'

His expression told her that he knew she was avoiding their colleagues, but he offered no reproof. 'Make sure you eat. I have some dull stuff to read, so I'll join you in the computer room in a little while.' He paused, as though mulling over an idea. 'Maybe you could take me for a night-time drive later…'

Wearing a tight smile, Kate groaned inwardly. 'David, I hate driving – always have. Why must you always push me further than I'm willing to go? Am I not good enough as I am?'

Disregarding all she had said about setting an example, David seized her hand. 'It's not about being good enough, Kate. It's about reaching your potential and being able to enjoy your freedom. I want to help you do those things in any way I can. Driving along a straight, empty road is a very tiny step forward. Think about it, okay?'

With a doubtful nod, Kate disappeared into the cool shade of the dig house. Perhaps she could wash away some of her troubles under a warm shower.

Smooth, toned legs stretched out under the table, beaded flip-flops dangling from toes whose nails had been painted a shimmering gold. David's eyes travelled from those wriggling toes up the shapely legs to the hem of Kate's pastel green shorts. He guessed that all her trousers were tumbling around in the washing machine and the shorts and vest were the last of her clean clothing. Certainly, she would never wear such an outfit around the men in their company, and probably assumed she would remain unnoticed by leering eyes if she stayed behind a desk in the office. She had been very, very wrong in her assumption.

David wondered if Kate was aware of the effect she was having on him as she slowly shifted her legs under the table, paying little attention to him as he sat in the corner allegedly reading. He had refrained from telling her that he had been sent information from York regarding accommodation and terms of employment.

Marianne sat at the table opposite Kate, busy with her own paperwork. The two women conversed quietly, and David suspected they had lowered their voices just to annoy him. The conversation seemed to take a more intimate turn, for Kate giggled in embarrassment, a rosy flush creeping into her cheeks. Involuntarily, she glanced quickly at David then looked away. Marianne began to chuckle. The women reminded him of teenage girls, and he suddenly felt like a gawky adolescent. Clearing his throat, he pretended to focus on his work, while straining his ears to eavesdrop on the women's intriguing conversation.

Kate was glad to hear Marianne's laughter. The archaeologist had been working in the room when Kate had arrived. Marianne had looked downcast, but she had offered Kate a welcoming smile, as though glad of her company.

Kate found she held no animosity towards the older woman; Marianne had shown her nothing but kindness. For the first time, the two were able to connect as women of the world, and Kate found that they actually had a lot in common. It wasn't long, however, before the Texan began to talk candidly about subjects Kate would normally deem too private to discuss. Kate suspected that Marianne had steered the conversation in this direction purely because David was present. Even so, the brash American's outrageous frankness made Kate laugh, and reminded her of happy times spent with Jess, a bottle of wine and a pizza.

At last, Kate's report was finished and she decided it didn't need Ethan's approval. With a contented sigh, she pressed the send button, hoping that Deputy Director Gray would be satisfied with her narratives of the expedition. Her fingers hovered over the keyboard as she contemplated answering the emails from Jess and Ben, but her hands dropped stubbornly to her lap. They would know from her blog that she was safe.

Shutting down the computer, Kate pushed back her chair and stood, emitting an involuntary groan at the pain in her lower back.

'Are you alright, honey?' Marianne asked.

Kate grimaced as she rubbed her aching back, but gave Marianne a small smile. 'Sore back,' she explained, stifling a yawn. 'I can't wait to have a long bath…'

'You and me both,' Marianne agreed. 'There's a bottle of herbal muscle rub in the infirmary. Why don't you go and take a break?'

'Good idea. Thanks, Marianne.' Kate sauntered towards the door, her eyes wandering to where David sat with his feet on the desk and his tablet perched on his lap. Their eyes met, and Kate hoped her look expressed an invitation. She wandered down the hall towards the infirmary.

David chewed his lip, his unseeing eyes fixed on the screen full of words that made no sense. He had finished reading a while ago, but had stayed in the room in the hope that Marianne would leave. Now he wanted to follow Kate, but his departure would surely give them away.

'And the perfect English gentleman remains in his seat…' Marianne observed, giving David a pointed look. She smiled knowingly as the professor lurched to his feet.

'I-I've left something…in my room…' he muttered. Annoyed at himself for sounding flustered, he strode out of the room, ignoring Marianne's burst of laughter.

He found Kate in the sick bay, her cotton vest hiked up above her waist, trying to apply oil to her back. Pushing the door closed behind him, he took the brown glass bottle from her hand. 'Let me do that,' he offered. 'Lie down.'

Kate looked uncertainly at the door, and then her gaze shifted to his face. 'We shouldn't,' she murmured half-heartedly. 'It's inappropriate…'

David rolled his eyes. 'Kate, I've seen you in a swimsuit. I've seen you belly dancing. I helped you out of a stubborn corset last Halloween…' His voice tailed off, as he recalled that particular event. She had taken part in a ghost tour around the museum, dressing up as a jilted Victorian girl who had allegedly committed suicide in the building. When Kate had gone to change she had been unable to untie the corset laces and he had been the only one available to help. The act of unlacing a corset had been undeniably erotic…

'Hoi!' Kate poked him in the stomach. 'Get your mind out of the gutter!'

Returning to the present, and another potentially sensual encounter, he grinned at her. 'Given how much of you I've already seen, you can't possibly become all prudish over me rubbing some oil on your back. Now be accommodating for once, and get on the bed.'

She complained about his bossiness, but he saw her smile as she lay down on her front on the squeaky hospital bed. Making herself comfortable, she sighed into the pillow. 'I ache all over…' she mumbled.

David admired the view before him. 'Stop wriggling your backside at me,' he commanded. 'I'm only a man, after all!'

Kate became completely still, hiding her blushes by resting her face on her folded arms. David felt her body jump in reaction to his hands sliding slowly up her sides, moving the vest up out of the way.

'I don't suppose you would consider taking this off?'

'Nope.'

'Oil stains are hard to shift – I might ruin it.'

Sighing with what he suspected was feigned irritation, Kate tugged the vest up so that it bunched up around the back of her neck but still covered her breasts. David admired the satin bra straps edged with pink lace; briefly, he fantasised about what the view from the front might be. He heard her gasp as he deftly unhooked the bra.

'*David!*' she hissed, and her whole body tensed.

'It's in the way,' he explained, trying not to sound gleeful. 'Now settle down and let me work.'

David warmed some oil in his hands before applying it to Kate's smooth back with long, firm strokes. The scent of lavender, black pepper and rosemary filled his nostrils

'Oh God, that feels so good!' she blurted.

Unfortunately, David had not closed the door properly. Ethan's head appeared around the door, eyebrows raised at the scene before him. David gave him Ethan a look that clearly indicated he was to leave silently. Ethan grinned, and then retreated, gently pulling the door closed behind him.

Now assured of some privacy, David continued his efforts. He began working on Kate's lower back, his fingers straying just under the waistband of her shorts. The incursion met with no resistance so he invaded further, his hands stroking around the top of her hips and returning to her spine in one fluid movement. He repeated the stroke several times before moving further up, kneading each muscle group in turn, and paying particular attention to the knots he found around her shoulder blades.

In David's opinion, her hourglass figure was perfect and her skin was flawless. A toned back tapered to a slim waist, which led to those deliciously rounded hips. He wanted to see more. He wanted to touch more. He took a deep breath, letting out the air in a trembling exhalation. His imagination started to wander…

Kate was aware only of his skilled hands, confident in their movements and suddenly scorching. He was testing her limits, his magical fingers straying beneath the boundaries of her clothing. Instead of restricting his contact to her back, his hands now strayed towards the front of her torso. She felt his fingertips marginally breach her displaced bra before sliding back towards her shoulder blades. She wanted to raise her body off the bed to allow him better access, but modesty prevailed. As he kneaded and stroked his way to her shoulders, finding and eradicating every nodule of tension on the way, Kate wondered exactly how he had acquired his impressive massage skills.

'Where did you learn to do this?' she asked, a note of suspicion in her voice. Perhaps he had dated a massage therapist. Unwelcome images burst into her head, and she pushed them away, unwilling to spoil this decadent experience.

'Sometimes the horses get tense…' came his reply, and Kate heard the laughter in his voice. She opened her mouth to offer a retort, but only a groan came out as David kneaded her tight shoulders.

'You need to move this,' he told her, tugging at the bunched-up vest which prevented access to her neck. Obediently, she reached back and pulled it over her head, pushing it down so that the whole garment demurely concealed her bosom.

All too soon he had finished, and Kate felt unaccountably indignant as he expertly refastened her bra and briskly told her to sit up. Slipping her vest back over her head, Kate manoeuvred into a sitting position on the bed, fixing David with an accusing stare.

'What?' he asked innocently, his eyes twinkling with mischief.

She refused to voice the observation that he was obviously well acquainted with women's lingerie. Instead, she pouted sulkily.

'We all have a past,' he pointed out, moving to stand in front of her and using his hips to shift apart her knees so he could get closer.

His proximity was suddenly unnerving. Egypt had worked a kind of magic on David, making him less controlled and much more unpredictable. A tiny shiver ran up her spine as he leaned towards her ear and whispered, 'I promise that, from now on, you'll be the sole beneficiary of my talents…'

Kate giggled helplessly; he was incorrigible. Turning her head slightly, she kissed his rough cheek. The stubble grazed her own cheek as he turned to seek her lips, and Kate closed her eyes in utter bliss. Her lips parted under his, her hands slid around his shoulders to pull him closer. It was a gentle, soulful, loving kiss full of promise.

David held her tenderly at first, but as he felt her body press seductively against him, his arms tightened around her back. Almost overcome with the desire to consummate their relationship, he gently ended the kiss and looked into her eyes, immensely pleased with her glassy-eyed stare.

'I wish we were somewhere else,' he murmured.

'Where?' she asked, sounding almost breathless.

He clasped his hands behind her back, reluctant to release her from his embrace. 'Somewhere nice, and definitely secluded. With some champagne maybe, and chocolate. A huge bath…' Her cheeks flushed pink. David kissed her nose. 'And a nice, big bed.'

His lips moved lightly from her temple to her ear, dropping feather-like kisses on her warm skin. He breathed deeply, the scent of her addling his brain. 'Come to my room…' he whispered, his hands moving stealthily under her vest and over her ribs. 'I can't wait any longer.'

Reluctantly, Kate pushed his hands away. 'No. You can't have your wicked way with me yet, however much I want you to…' Realising she had crossed her ankles behind his thighs, she tried to adopt a more demure position.

'You have to get back to work…' She whimpered as he kissed the soft skin of her neck, instinctively finding the sensitive spot below her ear. Kate fought the desire to lie back and surrender. They had to stop before the fire he had ignited took hold.

Tenderly, Kate pushed him away but clasped a handful of his shirt because she didn't want to let go of this moment. She received a look of utter devotion.

'Oh, Kate, is it too soon to say I -'

Kate placed her fingertips over his lips. 'Don't, David,' she whispered. 'Don't say it. Not yet.' She cupped his cheek as his loving smile faded. He was silent, his eyes showing confusion.

'You're *still* holding back…' His words, delivered softly, were rich with accusation.

'No.' Kate shook her head, her other hand still holding onto his shirt to keep him close. 'I don't want to hold back, but it's true that I'm still not sure...' She tried to read his expression. 'You have decisions to make about your future. Are you even coming back to Edinburgh?'

His expression became guarded, as he evaded her searching gaze. 'I have to pick up some things from my flat.'

'I thought you had already surrendered the lease?' Kate began to grow suspicious.

'My landlord offered to store my stuff.'

'That was kind of him...' She got the feeling that another bombshell was about to be dropped on her head.

'*Her.*' He glanced at her briefly. 'She offered to store my things because...well...' He bit his lip. 'Kate, Diane is my landlady. It's a convoluted and very boring story. But once we broke up, she became *only* my landlady. I didn't tell you because it's not important. *She's* not important.' He took her hands in his. '*This* is important. And what I want to say to you is important...'

The intensity in his voice broke through her defences. She could see his uncertainty, along with a hint of resentment because she had made him feel vulnerable.

'I want to wait until we're on neutral ground,' she decided. *Another secret he's kept from me. How many more?*

David stepped back from her, breaking the physical connection as she was picking away at their emotional link. 'And where is neutral ground?' he demanded, his voice strained. 'We take our pasts with us wherever we go. Only you have *two* to carry around -'

'I told you, I want to leave it behind -'

'Do you? Do you *really*?' His stared at her coldly.

'Yes! You're the one who can't seem to let it go!'

'That's because – thanks to you – my head is filled with images of you and *him*!' Anger welled up inside David, and he was unable to keep from raising his voice. Kate had hopped off the bed and was heading towards the door, preparing to escape from his wrath. 'Every time I look at my best friend, all I can see is him with his arms wrapped around you!'

On the other side of the door, Amy, Russell and Jonathan huddled together as they eavesdropped. Far from delighting in the battle between their supervisors, the students felt concerned. They had never heard their professor raise his voice; chastisement was usually delivered in icy, level tones. Kate had been their supportive friend, a positive influence, a trusted confidante. The anguish they heard through the door filled them with compassion. The words they heard brought confusion, for they could make no sense of them.

Fearful of David's barely-harnessed rage, Kate flattened herself against the wall next to the door. 'I never forced you to undergo regression! I've never asked you for anything but time -'

'Yes, time alone with your memories of Edwin Ford! You've clung to them for so long, it's a wonder you can face reality -'

Tears sprung into her eyes. 'David, that's not fair!' she whimpered. In a heartbeat, he was in front of her, gripping her arms fiercely. She found a morsel of bravado. 'Don't you dare kiss me in anger!'

He pushed away from her. 'Why kiss you at all? I can't compete with a ghost!'

'That's all in your head! I've never compared you to anyone else -'

On their way to one of the workrooms, Ethan and Steven came upon the snooping students. Kate's painful weeping could be heard from within the infirmary.

'What are you doing standing here?' Ethan barked. 'What's going on?'

'The Professor and Kate are fighting,' Amy told him quietly.

'Shouldn't we do something?' Jonathan asked.

'You can get back to work and stop listening in,' Steven said. 'Come on.' He led them away.

Ethan remained in the hallway, one hand on the door.

Kate slid down the wall and sat on the floor, her knees pulled up defensively. How had they come to this? Tears streamed freely down her cheeks.

'I know you have memories of being intimate with him, Kate!' David accused as he wiped a hand over his face. 'There have been many times when I looked at you and I just *knew* you were thinking about Ford. I could see it on your face...'

There was no point in denying the truth. There had been too many secrets, too many half-truths and concealments. 'Yes, I held onto memories of that life for a while. How could I not, when my life was falling apart? Mark left me feeling like a failure – remembering my past life brought me comfort -'

He rounded on her once more. 'You had *me*, damn it! I was ready to give you comfort, and anything else you desired!'

'And at the first sign of trouble, you ran off and slept with a stranger!' she shouted back. 'How was I supposed to trust you, when you did exactly what my husband had done?' She lowered her head to her knees, her body shaking. 'Oh, I want to go home!'

David had been pacing the small room, but now he returned to stand before her. 'To ground bloody zero?' he roared. 'Where there's no neutral ground *anywhere*? He's everywhere we go – even in your house! There's no escape! *There never will be!*' His voice started to shake as though he were fighting tears; he turned his back and faced the cabinets.

'Then you should go to York! Make your fresh start and – and leave me alone!' Staggering to her feet, she reached for the door handle. 'I'll go home tomorrow. I'll ask Marianne if I can travel with her to Cairo.'

He remained unmoved. Kate covered her mouth to stifle a fresh round of weeping and rushed out of the door. She stumbled into Ethan, who steadied her with his hands at her elbows. Briefly, their eyes met and Kate saw a flicker of compassion as she stared at him in dismay. Wrenching herself free from his grasp, she bolted to her room.

Rooted to the spot, Ethan regarded David through the open door. But before he could speak, David strode past him, his face suffused with anger and grief.

'I can't even bloody look at you!' David bellowed as he escaped to the solitude of his room.

Ethan watched him go, feeling utterly helpless. The jigsaw of scattered memories was slowly rebuilding itself, but the missing pieces eluded him. Of one thing he was certain: his friendship with David was in jeopardy, and Kate was to blame.

CHAPTER 14

Time seemed to stop in Kate's tiny room as she lay face down on her bed and wept. Everything had fallen apart, hope had evaporated, and there seemed to be no way to repair the damage. At last, she ran out of tears and curled up facing the wall, exhausted and struggling to draw an even breath.

Her befuddled brain fought to construct an alternative course of action. She desperately wanted to return to Edinburgh and the protection of her family. Running away would prove that she was weak, but she didn't care. She couldn't stay in Amarna any longer, and she couldn't live a life that included both Ethan and David. The last few days had proven that, should they remain together, the three of them would tear each other apart.

Finally, Kate sat up and moved unsteadily to the hand sink to wash her face. The distorted visage reflected in the small, cracked mirror was pale and gaunt. The eyes staring back at her were ringed with dark circles and red-rimmed from weeping. Frowning at her reflection, she willed herself to salvage some inner strength so that she could proceed to the next hurdle in this tortuous path.

'This isn't *all* your fault,' she told herself, her voice ragged. 'But it's time to go home.'

Checking her watch, Kate realised that the house would soon be full of hungry, noisy people. Although she had no appetite, Kate felt thirsty, and so she furtively made her way to the kitchen for a bottle of water. As she walked through the quiet house, she tried to fill her head with images of home, and the people she loved. But David's face was ever present in her mind.

Fate had not finished with Kate that day for, on the return trip to her room, she met Steven heading in the opposite direction. He was dusty and dishevelled, but his self-righteous contempt was evident from metres away.

'Are you happy now?' he sneered, stopping in front of her. 'Did you get a big kick out of giving David hope and then shredding him?'

Kate had suffered enough of his intolerable behaviour. 'Do you get a kick out of sleeping with students behind your girlfriend's back?'

'I no longer have a girlfriend,' he replied, his derision weakening. 'She dumped me as soon as I left Edinburgh. Found somebody "more reliable".' His anger returned. 'You're all the bloody same!'

They had been friends, and so Kate immediately felt sorry for Steven, but she quelled her sympathy in order to vent her fury. 'That doesn't excuse you from sleeping with a student! You have a position of authority here -'

'She was begging for it!' Steven's snapped maliciously; his next words would damage their friendship irreparably. 'Not everybody's as frigid as you!'

Kate's response was to slap him hard across the face, causing Steven to stagger. Fresh tears stung Kate's eyes as she absorbed the insult as the truth.

'Hey!' Ethan shouted from behind them. 'What the hell's going on?'

Looking from one to the other, he waited for an explanation. None came. 'Right then – Brodie, on your way. Grahame – my room. *Now.*' Taking Kate by the arm, he pulled her to his room, thrust her inside, and closed the door.

Standing in the middle of the floor, Kate faced him uncertainly. She wanted to back into a corner, or flee this untidy space that smelled of him. His dark eyes burned into hers in a way that made her feel naked.

'You've caused nothing but trouble on this trip,' he said fiercely. 'I wish you'd never come here!'

'You needn't worry,' Kate snapped. 'I'm leaving tomorrow.'

Ethan took a step towards her. 'Good! You certainly won't be missed, for you've done nothing that Steven or even Mina couldn't have handled with their eyes shut. Even Amy has been more useful than you!'

Kate knew her reply would sound like a feeble excuse for her presence because she now believed it to be so. 'David wanted me to help with the students, and I've -'

'Rubbish! He's managed without a "student liaison" for his entire teaching career – an intern's always been good enough for him. Someone with *appropriate qualifications.*' Ethan snorted scornfully. 'He's gone to great lengths – and great expense – to get you into bed. You've been a waste of time and money – the most overpriced, underwhelming lay I've ever seen.'

He took another step towards her; she backed away and hit the wall. Kate felt a rising panic. She didn't know what to do, or what would happen next.

'Was Steven right?' Ethan asked quietly, his eyes fixed on hers. 'Did his insult strike a nerve? Did he reveal a shortcoming? Is that why you're keeping David at arm's length – because you're scared he'll find out and quite rightly ditch you?'

His cruelty stabbed at her heart, and she no longer had the strength to defend herself.

'I hate you!' she cried and moved to push past him and make her escape.

She almost cried out when he pushed her back, his hands resting on the wall either side of her shoulders.

'Do you?' His voice was suddenly weak and rasping. 'Deep down in your soul, do you *really* hate me?'

As they stared at one another, Kate saw turmoil as well as anger in Ethan's eyes, as if he were locked in some internal struggle. She could have enlightened him, she could have eased his uncertainty, but she cruelly refused to come to her soulmate's aid. She could *never* be tied to this man. Their connection was lost.

'Let me go,' Kate said evenly, and his hands dropped from the wall.

Kate willed her legs to stop shaking as she opened the door and gained the fresher air in the hallway, where she came face to face with David. His stricken expression revealed that he had made an assumption that would drive the wedge even deeper.

'It didn't take you long,' he said icily, and kept walking.

Marianne knocked on Kate's door for the third time. 'Come on, honey, open up.'

The door opened slowly to reveal a distressed and shivering young woman. Closing the door behind her, Marianne put a comforting arm around Kate's shoulders and led her to sit on the bed. Maternal instincts taking over, the archaeologist hugged Kate, rocking her gently. The sound of revelling students drifted in from the courtyard, which seemed very far away from this isolated little room. Night had fallen some time ago, but Kate hadn't bothered to switch on a light.

'You're freezing,' Marianne observed and rose to find a sweater in the wardrobe. As Kate pulled on the oversized jumper, Marianne switched on the lamp, closed the half-open window, and then returned to sit on the bed. With a great deal of trepidation, she handed Kate a paper bag. Kate looked vacantly at the contents: her passport and return tickets to Edinburgh.

'I asked David for these,' Marianne told Kate gently. 'You're coming to Cairo with me tomorrow, and we'll get you on a flight home. You need to get away from here, honey. Away from *them*. I can't stand by and watch them trample on you anymore.'

'Did he say anything?' Kate asked weakly.

'He said that you're relieved of all duties.' Impulsively, she wrapped her arms around Kate, feeling the younger woman slump limply against her. 'And honey, if I were you, I'd run for the hills. You're nobody's chew toy.'

'I don't know *who* I am anymore,' Kate said hoarsely. 'I feel like I'm losing myself.'

'That's because you spend all your time trying to change who you are in order to please other people.'

Outside, voices started singing. In Kate's room, the two women sat in silence, both in need of comfort. A short while later, there was a tentative knock at the door.

'Kate,' Jonathan called hesitantly. 'It's only us – we just wanted to make sure you're okay…'

'Well,' Marianne smiled, pushing Kate's tousled hair away from her face. 'I guess we know where *their* allegiance lies. Are you up for visitors?'

Nodding, Kate sniffed and sat up, rubbing ineffectually at her tear-ravaged face. 'I'm fine, Jonathan. Please come in…'

He wasn't alone; Amy, Celine, Russell and Dominic followed Jonathan into the room in an anxious huddle. Kate watched them eye her cramped quarters. No doubt they had expected her to have been allocated a better room than theirs, with a double bed and perhaps some little extravagances appropriate to her alleged position as the professor's concubine.

'I'm sorry,' she said, trying to keep her voice level. 'I only have one chair.'

'That's alright,' Dominic said awkwardly. 'We won't stay long.'

The cheerful singing continued outside, American voices with one or two Egyptian tenors in the mix. An awkward silence threatened to settle heavily in the room.

'Did you need me for something?' Kate asked, sorry that she had allowed her personal problems to encroach on her professional duties. Regretfully, she suspected that her row with David had spread to every member of the household.

The students murmured in the negative. Quiet, kind Jonathan had apparently been appointed spokesperson for the group. 'We wondered if *we* could do anything for *you*,' he explained tactfully with a sympathetic smile. 'We didn't see you at dinner, so we've asked Mina to fix a plate for you. She'll be along shortly.' He glanced at his fellow students, clearly wishing that one of them would say *something*. 'Is there anything you need?'

I need to be teleported out of here and taken back in time about ten years, Kate thought ruefully. Instead, she smiled at the students. 'No, thank you. You've been very thoughtful. Listen,' Kate's gaze moved to each student in turn. 'I'm leaving tomorrow. But I want you to know that I've enjoyed working with all of you, and I wish you all the best in your studies, and in whatever path you choose to take.'

Standing, she delivered an opportunity for the group to make a graceful departure, and was surprised to receive a self-conscious hug from each of them, along with their thanks for her companionship. In a sombre mood, the five trainee archaeologists filed out of the room.

As they departed, Mina entered, carrying a tray of food, tea, and water. Marianne took the tray from Mina's hands and set it on the desk, implying that the girl should leave them in peace. Although Marianne was unaware of the details of Kate's relationship with the Suefy family, she had overheard enough to know that Kate did not need Mina's disruptive presence at this moment. But Mina had other ideas.

'Kate, I would like to talk with you -' the young woman stammered, wringing her hands.

'Mina,' Marianne began firmly. 'This isn't a good time.'

Dropping to her knees in front of Kate, Mina looked up at her in supplication. 'Please,' she begged.

Dragging her hands through her hair, Kate shook her head. 'Mina, I can't listen to any more. You and Anai must leave me alone. There's nothing I can do about the past. Or the present, for that matter.'

'There is much you can do about the present,' Mina retorted vehemently. 'And about your future. But that is not what I wish to discuss. I respect your wishes.' She bit her lip, and visibly drooped. 'Today my uncle told me that I am to be married.'

'Congratulations…?' Marianne commented, bringing Kate a cup of tea and reoccupying her seat on the sagging bed.

'No,' Mina shook her head. 'I do not wish it. Once I am married, I will have no freedom to choose. I will not be permitted to work here. I will not be allowed to see…' She looked at the floor. '…all of you.'

You mean David, Kate surmised. *You won't be allowed anywhere near David.*

Mina's fearful eyes darted from Kate to Marianne. 'What is marriage like?'

The two women on the bed sighed in unison. 'We're not the best people to ask,' Marianne said forlornly. She caught Kate's eye. 'But marriage is different for everybody. Many, many people have a happy life with a loving spouse. I'm sure your husband will care for you...'

'Will he beat me?' Panic crept into her voice. The other women shook their heads unconvincingly. 'Will he try to change me?'

Kate snorted bitterly. 'Do men know any other way?' Suddenly, she was sick of being compassionate. 'Mina, most men want to change us into a more "suitable" shape, be it physically, emotionally or spiritually. It doesn't matter what culture or religion you belong to – all women suffer the same maltreatment at some stage in their lives. We are expected to perform our wifely duties – and they are too numerous to count – or be subjected to our husband's disappointment and sometimes, his contempt.'

Horrified, Mina looked at Marianne, who shrugged weakly. 'We can't promise that you'll live happily ever after, Mina, because that hasn't been our experience.' She paused meaningfully. 'All we can tell you is to hope for the best. You'll both have to work hard to find a way of life which suits you.'

Had Mina been a Western woman, Kate mused, she would have been urged to maintain her personality, carve a life for herself alongside her role as a wife, and demand equality and respect. But Mina was from a different culture, where such behaviour would undoubtedly be considered rebellious and unseemly.

'Then you are not happy, Doctor Deveraux?' Mina persisted.

Kate saw sadness and remorse cross Marianne's beautiful face. 'I was, once. But I've found it difficult to maintain my marriage *and* build a career for myself. Archaeologists work away from home for weeks at a time, and absence doesn't always make the heart grow fonder. In my case, my husband and kids made a life for themselves without me. Now I'm a visitor in my own home, but I guess I'm mostly to blame...'

'Do you love Doctor Forbes then?'

Kate gasped in horror. '*Mina!*'

Marianne touched Kate's arm. 'It's alright, Kate.' She looked earnestly at Mina. 'Mina, infidelity is wrong, no matter what the circumstances. My relationship with Ethan grew from a need for comfort and a need to feel wanted and beautiful. We have ended it, because that's the right thing to do. But it still hurts – at least, for me it does. I don't believe Ethan is capable of love...' Marianne looked miserably at the threadbare rug under her feet.

'Mina, you should talk to your Aunt Samira about marriage,' Kate said softly. 'She and your uncle seem to be very happy. She would guide you well, I think.'

Mina left the room looking worried. The vivacious, carefree girl had vanished.

'I was too blunt,' Kate muttered remorsefully.

Marianne shrugged. 'You were honest. Listen, Kate, those pig-headed men are going back to the cliffs in the morning. I said I'd keep our students busy, so if you don't feel like working you don't have to. A bus will be coming for my team early afternoon. It's not the best time to travel, but we should make Cairo in time for dinner. Does that sound okay?' Kate nodded wearily, and Marianne stood up. 'Have something to eat, and get some sleep. Pack your case in the morning. If you need me, holler.'

She leaned down to hug Kate goodnight. 'D'you know who *I* think you are, honey? You're the woman who belly dances with unreserved joy. Don't ever stop.'

With a sad smile, Marianne left, closing the door firmly behind her.

A sudden flash of lightning lit up the room, closely followed by a rumble of thunder that seemed to shake the walls. Within seconds, torrential rain battered the windowpane, chasing the housemates indoors. Still dressed, Kate curled up under the mosquito net and blankets, and listened to the storm raging over her head until she finally fell asleep.

Irrational fear clutched at Ethan's heart as he waited for Anai to open the door. Behind him, a bolt of lightning cracked the darkness from sky to desert, closely followed by an angry rumble of thunder that echoed around the cliffs. The rain soaked through his jacket and shirt, and seeped through his worn boots.

At last, the door opened a fraction, and Anai's wizened face appeared. She appraised him with her beady black eyes, her gaze both mocking and disdainful. 'So,' she sighed. 'Finally, you have come…'

'I need to talk to you, Anai,' he told her. 'I need to talk to you about Kate, and David, and me. I've been having dreams I don't understand, and I think it's because of the potion you gave me…'

Opening the door wider, Anai ushered him inside but her manner was not welcoming. She left him to stand dripping in front of the fire, offering neither a seat nor refreshment. The flames in the hearth were the only source of light in the stuffy room. Mina stood in the doorway to the bedroom, long hair cascading down her back, body covered from neck to ankle in a voluminous nightgown. Like her grandmother, the girl's expression was hostile.

'The potion awakened that part of your memory which you had sealed…' Anai declared in Arabic.

The use of her native tongue was another ploy to unsettle him, Ethan realised. He would be unable to express himself as fluently in this difficult language; she was set on maintaining the upper hand. Nevertheless, he needed her help. 'And so?' he prompted.

'And now that you have been reunited with your twin flame, the memories of your past life have been brought forth.'

'My what?' Ethan tried to appear scornful. 'This all sounds utterly ridiculous! What the hell is a "twin flame"? And who is mine?'

'Twin flames are two souls who are connected for eternity, but they are seldom able to find peace and happiness together in their mortal forms. These souls burn so brightly they bring only harm to each other. You and Kate are twin flames. She has known this for many months.'

'I don't believe you.' But deep inside, Ethan feared it was the truth.

'Then tell me of your dreams,' Anai suggested.

'I've been dreaming of a woman,' he stuttered. 'The dreams are – are intimate, but I'm certain I've never met her…'

'And do you feel guilty, having despoiled this woman?' Anai snapped, eyes flashing.

'I – I don't know…' Ethan looked at the floor, ashamed of his next confession. 'I've been dreaming about Kate, too.'

The old woman turned towards the sideboard, muttering. Ethan thought he heard the word 'whore', but couldn't be sure.

'Look, Anai, I know you gave David and Kate a potion so that they might see a past life -'

'They *did* see their past lives.'

Ethan gaped at her, and Anai smirked triumphantly. 'Did they not tell you? You were all here together, more than a century ago – two men who loved the same woman. She married one of the men, but had no right to him. He was already bound to another who had borne his child in this very house.'

'What do you mean? Kate was married to David?'

'No, fool – she was married to *you!*' Her expression became almost murderous. 'But you had already made a child with my grandmother and then abandoned her for your Western trollop.

'While you were here in 1891, Nula gave birth to your son but you shunned both her and your child. Meanwhile, your sainted wife and your friend became lovers behind your back. My grandmother cursed you. Your wife's early death was her punishment for stealing you, and *your* punishment for abandoning the one who truly loved you.'

'I was Edwin Ford...' Ethan gasped. Kate had been his wife. 'That explains so many things...'

'You were – and are – a soulless jackal!'

'I want to see for myself,' Ethan demanded. 'Anai, I need you to perform whatever ritual you used on Kate and David.'

'Why should I do this for you? You carry the soul of the man who ruined my family!'

'Then perhaps I can atone.' Ethan's eyes narrowed slyly. 'If I'm able to understand what happened, perhaps I can find a way to redress the balance.'

Anai pointed to Mina. 'You need to make it up to *her*,' she hissed. 'For she carries the soul of the one you abandoned.'

Ethan swallowed; this was too far-fetched, and impossible to accept. And yet, he felt he should play along. 'You're saying Mina's the reincarnation of the woman I allegedly married before I met Kate – the woman who gave birth to your father?'

Anai nodded slowly, but Mina looked panicked. Perhaps the girl was not a willing co-conspirator, after all. 'And what is it that you want me to do in order to make amends?'

'Take care of her, as you should have done before -'

'I will not go with him!' Mina cried. 'I want nothing to do with *him!*'

'You're not getting David,' Ethan countered, fixing her with his black gaze. 'You will leave him alone.'

'She wants to be a doctor,' Anai continued, ignoring her granddaughter. 'She wants to live in your country. You can make this happen. If she marries the boy Ali has chosen, her life will be like mine. I do not want that for her.'

Mina begged her grandmother to desist, but Ethan pursed his lips as he mentally composed terms for a treaty with the local witch.

'Let me see into the past,' he told Anai. 'And then we can talk about Mina's future.'

'*No!*' Mina screamed. 'I will not be at his mercy! I will not be his slave!'

Anai clutched the girl's arm. 'Enough from you! Leave us!' She pushed Mina out of the room.

He had taken the foul brew, but instead of lying on the floor, Ethan was made to sit in Anai's armchair. A small table had been placed before him and on it sat a large mirror with a gilt frame. The ornate looking glass seemed incongruous in these surroundings. Ethan stared at his shadowy reflection as Anai chanted her spell in a grating tone, waving the athame around his head in what he hoped was not a threatening gesture. A mist seemed to invade his mind, and the corners of the room, as he began to feel groggy.

The reflection in the glass shimmered, and Ethan struggled to focus on the image of his own brooding face. It was changing, ever so slightly. His short dark hair seemed to grow longer, the tired features became more youthful, and the brown eyes appeared less cynical. His black sweater became a white, collarless shirt. Ethan found himself becoming calmly acquiescent as he floated down a dark tunnel – and found himself in the Royal Scottish Museum in Edinburgh, in the year 1890…

'Return to the present moment, Ethan Forbes!' Anai called loudly, and Ethan's eyes snapped open.

She handed him a drink, which he swallowed obediently as he endeavoured to hold onto the visions he had experienced while in a trance. He clung to the smiling image of a lovely girl of eighteen, his employer's headstrong daughter. She was the love of his life, and his soulmate…

Through the scenes that had played out in his head, he had seen the highlights of their life together. A short, passionate courtship had preceded a difficult but nonetheless loving marriage. The problematic expedition to Amarna had resulted in their child's conception, and also its demise.

From this point, the images that followed had rushed through his mind. Katherine's premature death had flashed by in seconds. The cold and lonely journey back to Scotland with her body had lasted only an instant. He had faced her bereft family, and had stood at her graveside on a wet winter's day as they lowered her wooden coffin into the cold earth. He could still hear her mother weeping.

Ethan knew that several long, empty years had followed before he had reluctantly joined another expedition to Egypt. It had been his last; after a mysterious illness, Death had brought him blessed relief.

But somehow he had returned, briefly. He had gone back to the museum, and to a house in Edinburgh. He had spent time with the Kate who now slept in the dig house. He had been her guide, a consolation of sorts in her time of need...

And then he had resumed his existence in *this* hell.

'I was with her when I was in a coma...' Ethan spoke to the mirror, seeing his own face reflected in the polished glass. His expression was distorted with grief; he could still feel Edwin's heartache as if it were his own. He looked up at Anai. 'How is that possible?'

Shrugging as if such phenomena were commonplace in her world, Anai replied, 'Your body was in paralysis, but your shadow was not. Freed from the burdens of your everyday concerns, your soul was alerted to her need for your help. You were able to walk in her world as spirit, for a time. But it was not your time to die. All the parts of you had to reunite so that you could come here – and *do your duty*.'

'My duty...' Ethan breathed. He should have been a better husband, and then his Kate would not have died. They could have been a happy family. Perhaps that was why he shied away from commitment in this lifetime. Perhaps his soul had never recovered from the tragedy.

'Did you relive the betrayal?' Anai asked harshly.

The betrayal had been his, all his. He had been faithful to his wife, but he had neglected her in his pursuit of an illustrious career and with his obsession over Akhenaten's tomb.

Throughout his regression, Ethan had been hit with wave after wave of emotion. Yes, there had been love and sorrow. But he had also felt a restlessness in his soulmate, a yearning in those beautiful eyes.

In one of the flickering tableaux, he had seen Katherine dancing with David in a ballroom, but his friend had been wearing a military uniform. Ethan had sensed a certain energy between the pair, had seen a look of adoration in David's eyes. Even so, Ethan had no doubt that Katherine Ford had been loyal to her husband. She had loved him despite his faults. He would never find such love again.

'Did you see Nula?' Anai pressed.

Unsteadily, Ethan got to his feet. 'I did not,' he stated. 'I saw my life with Kate – a life filled with love. Kate didn't betray me with another man.' He staggered towards the front door. 'All these tales you've been telling us about our role as guardians of Amarna – it's all rubbish, isn't it? You couldn't care less about protecting a heritage site – you want our money for your family and others like you.' He shook his head in disgust.

'We may have a little money, but we're not rich and we can't give you handouts. We're not a charity.' Ethan started to feel sick, but he kept going; he had to put a stop to this.

'You've used this past life stuff to try and manipulate us. But what it all boils down to is jealousy and your twisted desire for revenge. You feel we're somehow responsible for your humble situation here, but we're not. We employ your family and pay them well for their service. That's where our benevolence ends.'

As he pulled open the door, a blast of wind showered him with cold rain. His expression was desolate as he turned to deliver one last callous strike. 'I learnt something from my dreams, Anai. You rant about Edwin's merciless seduction of your grandmother – but it's another lie. It was entrapment, and *Nula* was the perpetrator. She seduced him like a common whore in the hope she would earn herself a comfortable life.'

With narrowed, pitiless eyes, he regarded her ashen face. 'You will get nothing out of this.'

'You have promised to take care of Mina!' Anai shrieked.

'I made no promise, Anai. Now leave us alone.'

A string of ancient curses issued from Anai's dry lips as she pointed at him. Her last words were in English: 'The three of you are damned!'

'Damned?' Ethan snorted, his face contorting with the anguish he felt. 'That's a way of life for me.'

Once he had parked the Land Rover, Ethan's feet took him to the bedroom door of his lost soulmate, but he did not attempt to gain access. His mind reeled; his suspicions had been solidified into a strange reality, but he should not have been surprised to learn of the bond he shared with Kate.

Gently, he leaned his forehead on the door. *I'll keep you safe this time, I promise. I'll make sure you and Dave are happy and I won't interfere.*

Tears slipped down Katherine's fevered cheeks as the scissors sliced through her long tresses. Amelia Hamilton held her own emotions tightly in check as she worked, her heart full of pity for the young woman. Katherine Ford had suffered unbearably, and death would be her only reward.

'I'm so sorry, Katherine,' Amelia said gently. 'I do this only as a last resort to bring your temperature down.'

The usually cheerful bedroom was dark and airless, the scent of despair hanging heavily over the large bed which supported Katherine's small and weakened body. The wooden shutters had been closed, muffling the noise from the street below, and banishing the bright sunlight. Gently flickering candles added to the heat of the room. Amelia was at a loss as to how to make her patient more comfortable, but she had done what she could. Against Katherine's wishes, she had sent a message to Edwin and demanded his immediate return.

'Please, Amelia,' Katherine rasped. 'Open the shutters a little…'

Sniffling, her eyes filled with tears, Amelia gestured to her maid to gather up the fallen tresses, and then walked to one of the tall windows to open the shutters just enough to let in a little sunlight. Silently, the maid placed the lengths of hair in a basket, no doubt calculating how much money she might earn from selling them on the back streets of the city.

A soft knock sounded on the door, and another servant appeared. She whispered to her mistress and then left. Composing herself, Amelia moved back to the bed and sat on the edge. She picked up Katherine's limp hand.

'Dearest, the minister has come.' She smoothed soft auburn curls away from her young friend's face. 'Would you like to see him?'

Katherine sighed, her breathing laboured. *Not long now.* 'Yes, please. He has been kind to me, and I should prepare…'

Reverend Donaldson had been hovering in the doorway; on silent feet, he entered the room and stood at the foot of the bed.

'I apologise for my appearance, Reverend,' Katherine whispered. She attempted a weak smile. Beside her, Amelia stifled a sob in her lace handkerchief.

'I place no importance on outward appearances, child,' the minister replied with a benevolent smile. 'And neither does the Lord.'

'Will the Lord accept me into Heaven, do you think?'

'Why would he not?'

'I have sinned…'

'You have not, Katherine!' Amelia cried. 'Oh, you have not!'

'I tricked my husband,' she said hoarsely. 'He did not wish to be burdened with a child, but I disobeyed his wishes. And then I lost Edwin's baby. I have not been a good wife to him – I am to blame for everything…'

'The Lord has His own plan for us, child,' Donaldson advised, adopting a suitably ecclesiastical tone. 'Although it is not always clear what His motives are…' Mercifully, he refrained from using the stock phrase about the Lord working in mysterious ways.

'There is another sin for which I should be punished…' Katherine whispered. A gasping sob escaped from her dry lips and tears flowed down her cheeks, staining the bed cover that had been tucked around her. She began to slip once more into unconsciousness. 'I love them both. May God forgive me – I love them both…'

Her own tortured cries woke Kate, and she stared into the darkness, listening to the sound of anguished whispering around her. She no longer felt afraid, and she finally understood the lesson. 'You're forgiven, Katherine,' she whispered. 'Now please rest in peace.'

The whispering stopped.

CHAPTER 15

Yusuf and Ahmed were the only ones talking as the pickup truck bumped along the uneven ground. The Egyptians sat in the cabin, engaged in a loud conversation about local politics.

On the benches in the back of the truck, Ethan, David and Steven sat lost in sombre contemplation. To their left, the spectacular vista of Amarna and the Nile spread as far as the eye could see. To the right, there was only hostile desert, and the sun rising above the horizon. Heavy rain had persisted through the night, leaving a freshness in the early morning air. The men ignored the scenery; they felt cold, both inside and out.

Steven was overcome with guilt over his mistreatment of Kate. Having finally confessed the reason behind his unacceptable conduct, he now craved the opportunity to tell her all about his break-up with Megan. With the selfishness of youth, he needed Kate to provide comfort, clemency and hope.

David's mind was not on the dangerous task ahead; he didn't care about lost tombs or even lost careers. He had lost Kate, and already she had betrayed him with Ethan. He fought to distance himself from his emotional state and to function instead as an automaton. If he could make it to the end of the expedition, he would allow himself to vanish from his world for a time so that he could nurse his broken heart.

The subject of betrayal occupied Ethan's thoughts. Not the treachery from his past life, but David's recent duplicity. He tried to catch David's eye, but his friend stared blankly at empty space. How were they to discuss the matter that weighed so heavily on them?

David had always been the most honest, sane and logical person in Ethan's life. How long had he been keeping his knowledge of their past lives a secret? The fact that David could so readily accept the idea of their reincarnation was extremely troubling.

Kate obviously knew even more about this than David, given her family connection. But how could he discuss this with her?

Most disturbing of all was David's decision to bring Kate to Amarna, knowing that she would be reunited with a soulmate. He claimed to love this woman, and yet David had metaphorically thrown her into the lion's den.

It was a messy, destructive triangle. And yet, it seemed they were bound together for eternity.

They had reached their destination. Ahmed stopped the truck and yanked on the handbrake, but Ethan remained hunched over on the bench. *All the bickering, all the strife between Kate and David – it's all because of me.*

Standing over him, David shoved at Ethan's shoulder to rouse him from his miserable deliberations.

The abseiling equipment was ancient, and any experienced climber would have discarded it as unsafe. But, given that it was the only gear available, they would make do. Once Ethan had selected the area they would use for their descent, Ahmed and Steven secured the anchors into the rock. Yusuf busied himself taking photographs while Ethan and David checked the ropes.

Climbing into a grubby yellow body harness, David was too distracted to notice that the waist strap was frayed at the side. He allowed Steven to help fasten the harness snugly around his shoulders and thighs, and then David locked on a rusty carabiner and prepared the line for his descent.

The plateau where they stood was perhaps a hundred metres from ground level. From this position, the eroded path could be seen winding its way up the side of the cliff. It petered out at a narrow ledge, which led to that tantalizing curtain of rock marked with what could feasibly be a cartouche.

In unison, Ethan and David began their controlled descent, while Steven, Ahmed and Yusuf watched anxiously from above. Ten metres passed without incident, then twenty. The men landed softly on the ledge.

Feeling something poking into his abdomen through his sweater, David unfastened the harness buckle around his waist. The rain had pooled on the shelf in the night, softening the earth. He took a tiny step backwards, the limestone crumbled under his boot, and suddenly David was falling, swinging against the cliff and slamming his head and right shoulder against the rock.

The safety knot in the rope came into play; he was jerked roughly and dangled, flailing. The fraying strap gave way, and he began to fall.

Without thinking, Ethan threw himself flat on the ledge and seized David's right arm. Reaching out, he managed to grab hold of David's other arm, but was unable to haul him to safety. David's weight strained the anchor, and it began to loosen from the rock. On the plateau, Steven grabbed

David's rope while Ahmed fought to secure the anchor, sending a shower of loose stone over David and Ethan.

Ethan's shoulder muscles screamed in protest as he hung onto David's arm, sharp pieces of rock tearing into the front of his torso as he struggled to maintain his prone position. The harness straps tugged uncomfortably, hampering his range of movement. He could see that David's unclipped harness would not hold him much longer. When it finally slipped, David would plummet to the ground.

'Find a foothold,' Ethan gasped, but David's feet slid uselessly on the wet cliff face, unable to find purchase. The rope slackened slightly as Steven slipped under the weight of David's suspended body. 'Pull that line, damn it!' Ethan screamed. The rope tightened again as Steven was aided by Yusuf and the anchor was finally repositioned.

David's eyes focused on Ethan's strained face. He felt dizzy and nauseous, and his arms felt like they would soon rip from their sockets. And yet, he found he was unafraid, strangely detached from the fear in the air around him.

'If I fall,' he muttered to Ethan. 'Take care of Kate. Make sure she gets home safely.'

Ethan tightened his grip on David as much as he was able, but he was losing his strength. He needed David to help him soon, or all would be lost.

'Oh, I'll take care of her alright,' he sneered with a lascivious grin. 'I'll be a good guardian to our feisty lass. I bet she's a real firecracker in the sack!' Ethan saw David's eyes widen. 'Of course, you know I get bored easily. But I'll put her on a plane home when I'm done. And I promise not to tell her that you loved her – can't have the poor girl carrying *that* burden.'

David was completely unaware of the harness ripping apart at the seams. *She hasn't slept with him. He hasn't touched her. There might still be hope...*

Suddenly he was filled with rage. 'I'm going to kick your backside!' he snarled at Ethan.

'Then *find a foothold*!'

David kicked a hole in the soft soil of the cliff face and stuck the toe of his boot into it. Ethan felt David's weight shift and with renewed strength pulled him up enough to grab onto the belt of his trousers. Within moments, David was sprawled on the ledge, Ethan lying exhausted beside him. Groggily, David got to his knees and futilely attempted to refit his broken harness. Leaning against the cliff face, he struggled to his feet.

'We're up!' Ethan shouted to the others, as he stood up and reached out to steady David. He swore as David's fist connected with his jaw, throwing him backwards against the wall of the ledge. David sank to his knees, and then passed out.

Almost falling out of bed, Kate realised that she had overslept. Rising too quickly, a sudden wave of dizziness forced her to sit down again; stress, tiredness and lack of food were beginning to take their toll. Slowly, she made her way to the desk and the unopened bottle of water. The tray of food had gone, implying that Mina had returned to the room after Kate had fallen asleep. Gulping down the tepid water, Kate glanced towards the closed door and noticed that someone had pushed a piece of paper under it. Hope swelled as she hurried to pick it up, but disappointment reigned as she read a note from Marianne.

'Bad weather has made the ground unsuitable for digging,' Kate read. 'I'm giving your students a short lecture on bones, and then I'll let them have some free time. Once you've packed your gear, take some time to relax, if you can. And eat something! Marianne.'

Feeling a hollowness inside her, Kate made the bed, tidied the room and packed her case. She then made her way to David's room and knocked on the door. Relieved that there was no reply, she entered, and laid the silver locket gently on his desk. Then, pushing back tears, she made her way to the kitchen and prepared a hasty breakfast of fruit, bread and honey. The American team moved about the house industriously, packing their belongings and equipment, glad to be going home for Christmas. Taylor joined her in the kitchen briefly, helped himself to coffee, nodded to her in acknowledgement, and then went about his business.

Feeling as though a door was closing on another chapter of her life, Kate walked outside and sat on a bench against the wall. The warmth of the sun was comforting; Kate had felt cold and shivery since her fight with David. As she closed her eyes, Kate tried to restore balance within her, but she felt drained, almost desiccated.

'You must not leave!' Anai commanded, as she hobbled towards Kate.

Sighing, Kate gathered what little strength remained. 'I have no reason to stay. I'm going home.'

'You have a duty -'

Kate's eyes flashed angrily. 'My *duty* is to myself! I have no place here, and no desire to find one. My home is in Edinburgh, with my family and friends. I must look to my future – not the distant past.'

'You must make reparation for Edwin Ford's sin,' Anai snapped bitterly. 'You are of his line...'

With a sad, tired sigh, Kate pushed her hair away from her eyes. 'I am *not* of his line, Anai. Your grandfather was his only heir.'

Anai looked perplexed. 'That is not so,' she disagreed, her voice betraying her uncertainty. 'Nula said that Edwin spoke of another child, left behind in your country -'

The words provided Kate with a means of escape, and she allowed herself a brief, grim smile of victory. 'Then this tale has not been handed down intact. The child you refer to must be the offspring of Katherine's brother, John. *I* am descended from *John's* line. *My* family has no connection here, and so we're not duty-bound to give you anything. Not our time, our devotion – or our money.' The last remark was cruel, but Kate had reached the end of her tether. She would no longer be swayed by Anai's insinuations, which were based on misinformation. She wanted to sever all her ties to this inhospitable place.

'I want you to let Edwin rest,' Kate demanded. 'I want you to stop referring to his great "sin". It took two people to make the child who was your grandfather, Anai. If the child was conceived out of love, there is no sin in that. Stop holding this grudge, for it will eat you up and destroy you. And allow Ethan to find his own peace – he can't be held accountable for something which happened long before he was born.'

Anai tried a different tactic. 'You are needed here, qitah. I wish to pass on all that Nula taught me, so that someone can carry on my work once I have passed on to the next life.'

'You have Mina -'

'Mina will be married soon. Besides, she does not have the gift, nor any desire to learn about the old ways.' Anai pointed a shaking finger at Kate. 'You have the ability, qitah. With the proper guidance, you could replace me and help the women of our community. You would lead a fulfilling life…'

Kate shook her head, grudgingly impressed by the woman's tenacity. 'No, Anai. I don't want that life.'

Crestfallen, Anai made one final attempt to retain her hold on Kate. Her eyes narrowed shrewdly. 'I can show you how to help Edwin and Ethan find peace. Your love can ease their tortured soul -'

She almost wavered, but then Kate remembered James Grahame's warning. 'Edwin *will* rest in peace, and his love will always be with me. I need to go home, to be with the ones I love. Please understand…'

Recognising defeat, Anai's imperious demeanour finally left her. She struggled to lower herself onto the bench beside Kate, taking the younger woman's proffered hand to descend into a comfortable sitting position.

'You will return one day?' she asked, hopefully.

Sadly, Kate shook her head. 'I don't think so.'

Still holding Kate's hand, Anai squeezed it, and then clasped it between her own. 'We will miss you, qitah. But we will never forget you…'

They sat together in the sun, a devoted lifelong custodian, and the understudy who had irrevocably rejected the role.

Fragile peace was shattered by the screeching of brakes, the banging of doors and loud male voices shouting in English and Arabic. Running around the building to the source of the commotion, Kate was horrified to see Ethan and Ahmed gently drawing a stretcher from the back of the pickup truck. She saw Yusuf climbing out of the passenger seat and Steven standing up on the back of the truck. Kate cried out in alarm when she realised that the inert body on the stretcher was David, and then she bolted towards the group.

'What happened?' she demanded, elbowing Ethan out of the way so she could see David's face. He was unconscious, his face ashen. Blood ran down one side of his face from a wound at his temple. His right shoulder was also bloody, his sweater torn.

'He slipped off the ledge and his harness ripped,' Ethan replied, taking up the other end of the stretcher and moving quickly towards the house. 'The doctor's on his way.' He glanced over his shoulder and spoke to Ahmed. 'We'll take him to his room – it's closer than the infirmary.'

Turning back to Kate, he issued more orders. 'Get a medical kit from the infirmary and bring it to David's room.' He saw Kate reach out to touch David's lifeless hand, her face crumpling. 'Go, Kate! Now!'

The sharpness of his voice spurred her into action and she rushed to comply. By the time she got to David's room, the men had placed him on the bed. Ethan asked for the medical kit, intending to clean David's wounds while they waited for the doctor.

'I'll do it,' Kate said firmly.

'I don't have time for petty squabbles,' Ethan snapped. 'Give me the kit!'

'You get away from him!' Kate snarled. '*I'll* clean his wounds!'

Her ferocity made all three men back away slightly, allowing her to set the first aid kit on the chair next to the bed. With shaking hands, she extracted the equipment she would need to clean and dress David's visible injuries. The cut on his temple was deep, but Kate managed to staunch the bleeding. As she began to clean the wound, David began mumbling incoherently.

'It's alright,' Kate soothed. 'Everything's going to be alright.'

'Did you find him?' David whispered in a ragged voice.

'Who?' Kate leaned close to his face and spoke softly.

His eyelids fluttered, and David grimaced. 'Our son!' he croaked. 'He was digging a hole in the sand. Did you find him?'

Kate gasped. David was hallucinating about their son, a cherished phantom from her own dreams. A beautiful little boy with dark blond hair and warm brown eyes. Ethan and Steven looked uncomfortably at their feet while Yusuf and Ahmed exchanged quiet words in their own language.

'He's safe, darling,' Kate murmured. 'There's no need to worry.' She stroked his cheek, forcing back a sob, and resumed her work.

Voices outside the room heralded the arrival of the doctor, and Ahmed opened the door to admit a burly, balding man in his fifties wearing a light brown suit. Astonished to see Kate tending the patient's wounds, he waved an arm to evict her from the room. Kate stood her ground, and demanded that she be allowed to stay. Ethan gently took her elbow and led her from the room.

'I want to stay!' Kate cried as Ethan shut the door behind them.

'I know you do, but arguing with the doctor is delaying his treatment. David's hurt his head – he needs to be examined *now*.'

Kate's chest tightened. 'This is all your fault!'

Ethan felt the full impact of Kate's words. 'I know. But right now, we have to focus on David. I'll come and get you once the doctor's gone…'

'I'm not moving from this spot!'

With a resigned nod, Ethan went back into the room. Kate looked helplessly at the door as though it were an impenetrable barricade.

'He'll be alright, honey,' Marianne said from behind her; she had brought the sexist surgeon to the room. 'David's tough as old boots.'

'I can't leave…' Kate murmured. 'Not until I know he's okay.'

The older woman nodded in understanding. 'Then I guess this is goodbye…' Impulsively, she pulled Kate into a fierce hug. 'I'm so sorry this trip has been such a nightmare for you, Kate. But listen to me – you have to do what makes *you* happy, not what you think will please other folk. Promise me you'll remember that?'

Sniffing, Kate nodded against Marianne's shoulder.

'And promise me you'll keep in touch?'

'I will. Good luck, Marianne. And thanks…'

'When I finally make it to Edinburgh, we're going to have some wild nights on the town, okay?'

Having elicited a fleeting smile from Kate, Marianne kissed her cheek then departed, hiding her own tears behind a curtain of copper-coloured hair. Sliding down the wall, Kate sat on the floor and allowed herself to cry unchecked.

The men emerged from David's room looking cautiously relieved, and quietly discussed the allocation of duties. Steven offered to supervise the students; Yusuf volunteered to take over Ethan's responsibilities; Ahmed vowed to have sharp words with the reprobate who had supplied the climbing equipment. The three men dispersed.

Ethan crouched down beside Kate, who sat with her knees pulled up, arms wrapped round them and face hidden from view. Tentatively, he touched her shoulder, making her look up at him with reddened eyes.

'It's a mild concussion,' he told her gently. 'He has to rest and the doctor will leave some Amitriptyline. He'll need to be checked out a hospital, just to be on the safe side. None of his wounds need stitches, but someone will have to stay with him for the next twenty-four hours. We can take it in shifts...'

'Can I see him?' Kate asked. 'I want to stay with him.'

Ethan looked pained, as though it were an effort to keep his voice level and non-confrontational. 'I think it would be best if I take the first shift. He has to stay calm...' Pausing, he studied her features. 'Why don't you check in on the students, keep yourself busy for a little while, and then come back later?'

'Has he regained consciousness?'

Shrugging, Ethan's gaze slipped sideways. 'Kind of...'

'He doesn't want to see me, does he?' Kate bit her trembling lip and slowly got to her feet. 'He saw me leaving your room yesterday and he thinks -'

'I know what he thinks!' Ethan interrupted. Suddenly, he took Kate's hands and stared earnestly into her eyes. 'Kate, I *will* fix this. I won't mess it up again.'

Kate's eyes widened in disbelief. He *knew*. His sad gaze conveyed his acceptance of a life shared and lost.

'Please don't cry,' he said hoarsely and stepped back to lean against the opposite wall as if he didn't want her to touch him. 'Just do what I've asked. I promise I'll make this right...'

He slipped back into David's room and shut the door on her.

At the other end of the house, it was business as usual for the Suefy family and their temporary staff from the village. As soon as the American team had been waved off in their minibus, the Egyptians commenced cleaning the vacated rooms, chattering cheerfully as they worked. Kate curbed the instinct to tell them to be quiet and show respect for the man lying injured nearby. Instead, she sought out the students who were her responsibility.

Steven had gathered them in the dining room for lunch and relayed the news of their professor's injury. As Kate entered the room, Steven was being plagued by questions. How had Professor Young hurt himself? How bad was the injury? What would happen now? Were they going home? All Steven could do was shrug and promise to keep them informed. He looked relieved to see Kate, but she avoided his gaze as she proceeded to the kitchen and poured herself a cup of the coffee she hated.

On automatic pilot, she sat with the students and tried to reassure them that all would be well. Her numb brain refused to comprehend the task Steven set for his charges, but she was aware that they left looking uncertain and anxious. Steven, however, remained standing at the table.

Dumbly, Kate stared into the cup of black liquid, imagining she was staring into a representation of her own future.

'Kate,' Steven began cautiously. 'It's my fault he fell.'

Looking up slowly, Kate's stared at him uncomprehendingly. 'How is it your fault?'

'I helped Ahmed secure the anchors, but I didn't give them a final check. I fastened David's harness, and I should have noticed the straps were damaged. But we were all so distracted…'

To Kate's ears, he was implying that she was the cause of their inattentiveness. Pushing back her chair, she stood up, glaring at him with fiery eyes; his crestfallen expression had no effect on her.

'Katie, I'm sorry,' Steven said in a rush. 'I've behaved badly. I was mad at Megan and I've been taking out on you. I -'

'You don't deserve my forgiveness,' Kate hissed, stumbling towards the kitchen. '*Doctor* Brodie.'

The day wore on. Steven left to oversee the work at the Great Aten Temple, the students remained in the dig house, struggling to concentrate on the written task Steven had set purely to keep them busy and in one place. A box of medical supplies arrived and Kate was putting them away in the sick bay when Yusuf disturbed her. The inspector asked if she would type up one of Ethan's rambling, haphazardly-written reports and help him make sense of the muddled pile of papers on the field director's desk. By the time she had performed these secretarial duties it was early evening, and Kate felt like screaming.

A hot wind had picked up, and the sunset appeared almost subdued in the brooding evening sky. Clouds were rolling in from the south. Steven, Kate and the students sat around the dining room table for a quiet dinner of lentil soup followed by a selection of stuffed vegetables. Nobody spoke; morale was non-existent.

Near the end of the meal, Ethan entered with Ahmed close behind him. The Egyptian disappeared into the kitchen in search of food, but the field director looked worried as he cast his eyes over the group.

'There's a sandstorm coming from the south,' he announced. 'I'm making arrangements for us to leave. I want you all to pack your things then see what you can do to help Ali and the others batten down the hatches here. No wandering past the boundary wall.'

'How bad is it?' Amy asked, looking fearfully at Ethan.

'Isn't it too early for sandstorm season?' Julian asked. 'Don't they usually happen in the spring?'

'Well, perhaps the gods are angry,' Ethan said evasively, catching Kate's eye. 'Once you've finished here, get moving. I'll keep you updated…'

'Doctor Forbes,' Jonathan began. 'How's Professor Young?'

'He's resting,' Ethan replied, then glanced at Steven and Kate. 'Doctor

Brodie, Miss Grahame – a word, if you please.'

Kate and Steven followed him down the corridor out of earshot.

'It's a severe storm,' Ethan told them. 'It's caused havoc in the south. I have to find a way to get us out of here as soon as possible. At least we were due to leave tomorrow, so there should be no cries for compensation. Steve, I need you to pack up all our equipment and make sure we've downloaded all the relevant data. All the work we've done here needs to be properly finalised as though it's the end of the expedition. Every artefact must be locked in the magazine. I'll come and help as soon as I can. Obviously, it's important we remain calm.'

Steven nodded in compliance and rushed off. Ethan glanced down at Kate. 'I need you to stay with David. He's been talking gibberish, which the doctor says will wear off. Keep him calm and hydrated – and don't engage in any inflammatory conversation. He was knackered before he fell off the ledge, so hopefully he'll just sleep. I'll check in on you later.'

She, too, nodded submissively, before running to David's room.

Moving quietly about the room, Kate packed David's possessions into his large rucksack by the light of a single lamp. Her locket still lay on the desk; she stowed it carefully into one of the inner pockets of the backpack along with David's watch.

Hearing him murmuring in his sleep, Kate moved to the side of the bed and put her hand on his forehead. He felt clammy, but there was no sign of a fever. Rinsing out a flannel in the sink, she gently dabbed at his forehead, avoiding the dressing at his temple. With a light touch, she tried to wipe away the dried blood that clung to strands of his hair. Somehow, they had managed to change his clothing; the torn sweater had been balled up and tossed in a corner.

David's eyelids flickered, and his eyes settled on Kate's face. 'Katherine...' he whispered.

Kate's voice stuck in her throat, but she calmly continued her ministrations. He lay propped on several pillows; supporting his shoulders with her arm, she helped him drink some water through a straw then settled him comfortably on the bed. The room was beginning to feel cold, so Kate pulled a blanket over David, absently smoothing the creases with her palm. Outside, the wind began to howl and rattle the window panes.

'Thank you,' David murmured sleepily.

'Are you in any pain?' Kate asked softly.

'Not sure...' He drifted back to his dreams.

When Ethan slipped into the room an hour later, he found Kate lying on the bed, tucked into David's left side with one hand resting protectively on his chest and her face pressed against his shoulder. As he covered the sleeping pair with another blanket, Ethan dropped a kiss on the top of Kate's head and left them in peace. The house was silent save for the whispering voices, warning him of imminent disaster.

Ethan hammered on Anai's door until it rattled on its hinges. At last it swung open, and Mina stared at him with huge, fearful eyes.

'What have you done?' he snarled and shoved his way into the house.

Anai sat calmly in her chair by the fire, the black cat curled in her lap. Leaning over her, Ethan was revolted by her look of nonchalance. 'What did you do?' he shouted. 'David nearly died today!'

From her position in a corner, he heard Mina gasp in horror. 'Is he badly hurt?'

'He has a concussion and some cuts and bruises,' Ethan snapped. He returned his attention to Anai, gritting his teeth in an attempt to control his rage. 'Did you have something to do with this? Is this one of your so-called curses, or did Ahmed deliberately give us rotten equipment and then fail to secure the anchors properly?'

The look she gave him was almost insolent. 'I told you that the three of you would be cursed. The gods have done what I asked of them.' With one gnarled hand, she stroked the cat.

Ethan could scarcely believe what he was about to ask; he would have preferred to think human error was to blame, or that Ahmed had acted out of jealousy. 'What will it take for you to stop this and leave us alone?'

'I will never leave you alone,' she replied, her voice like ice. 'I will torture your soul until it leaves your rotting corpse.'

He gaped at her, feeling her senseless hatred swirling around him like a black mist. His defeat seemed inevitable, but he would plead for the freedom of those he loved.

'I'll do whatever you ask, if you will let David and Kate go in peace. I'll do anything…'

Her thin smile made Ethan shudder. Anai emanated spiteful calculation. 'You will marry Mina,' she proclaimed, and her granddaughter gave a small scream and cowered in the corner in a tight ball. 'You will be a loyal and generous husband. You will work hard for us. Your money will be our money. We will be your family – your *only* family. Your dedication to us will be your redemption, Ethan Forbes.'

His throat constricted, his heart pounded in protest, but Ethan remained outwardly calm. 'And Kate and David will be safe? You'll stop using your dark magic on them?'

'I give you my word.'

'Then I agree. Once Kate and David have safely left Egypt, I'll do what you want.'

Rummaging in his jacket pocket, he extracted the three amulets and tossed them into Anai's lap. The cat snarled at Ethan and jumped to the floor. 'Don't give them any more of your little souvenirs.'

With a passing glance at his sobbing future wife, Ethan left Anai's hovel and drove back to the dig house. Halfway along the road, he stopped the car and leapt out. Stumbling into the desert, he startled a pair of wild dogs when he let out a despairing howl into the darkness. Then, hunching over, he vomited into the sand.

Satisfied that she had at last ensured financial security to her household, Anai retired to bed. Shock had kept Mina rooted to the floor as she finally realised that her grandmother only wished to use her to further her own ambitions.

Over the years, Anai had tried to regress Mina on several occasions, but the girl had never managed to see scenes from any past life, and had no recollection of being Nula. Nevertheless, Anai had stubbornly maintained that her granddaughter was the reincarnation of poor, sullied Nula, perhaps due to the resemblance between the two. Mina, however, did not share Anai's belief and had staunchly refused to let it shape her life.

Crawling across the floor to the sideboard, Mina decided to take matters into her own hands. Carefully, making as little sound as possible, she removed the remaining male wax figure, the requisite herbs and the pestle and mortar. Sitting cross-legged on the floor, she repeated the spell her grandmother had used two nights before, anointing the pliable little body with the liquid from the crushed herbs. As she whispered the words of the incantation, Mina smoothed the unguent over the lock of black hair fixed to the effigy's head. Purring, the cat fixed its golden eyes on the figure, its nose twitching at the scent emanating from the little wax man.

Holding her breath, Mina placed the poppet on the floor and held her scented fingers out to the cat. Holding the animal's attention, Mina tapped the figure in a playful motion, moving it a few centimetres.

With narrowed eyes, the cat crouched as though stalking prey. Then it pounced, grazing the wax figure with needle-sharp teeth. Drawing back, it stretched out one elegant paw and swiped at the effigy, tossing it across the floor. It hit the wooden leg of the table and broke in half.

Mina picked up the cat and, nuzzling its soft fur with her cheek, thanked the animal for its service.

241

CHAPTER 16

Thursday December 20, 2012

Angry gusts of wind whistled around the house, and the clatter of something falling over outside woke Kate. Her body ached from having slept fitfully in the same position all night; David hadn't moved, either. As she shifted her weight, she disturbed him.

'Katherine…' he murmured. 'You must return to Edwin. You'll be missed…'

Leaning up on one elbow, Kate searched his shadowed face, trying to discern whether he was dreaming or delirious. 'I don't want to leave you,' she whispered, speaking for herself and the woman she had once been. She didn't hear the door opening softly. 'I love you.' Tenderly, she kissed his dry lips. 'I should've told you a long time ago…'

'Kate,' Ethan called gently from the corner. Startled, Kate flinched, then quietly came to stand before him. Behind her, David began to stir.

'What time is it?' she whispered drowsily.

'It's just after four. How is he?' Ethan kept his expression carefully composed.

'He just slept…' she reported.

'Good,' Ethan replied. 'Because we're leaving in an hour. The bus is on its way to take us to Cairo. Hopefully we can outrun the sandstorm.'

'Do you think David's well enough to travel?'

'He doesn't have a choice. The doctor's coming in to take a look at him. Thankfully, he's managed to get David an appointment with a neurologist in Cairo.

'I need you to get the students organised – without raising a panic. Samira is preparing breakfast.'

Ethan's gaze moved past Kate to where David was attempting to sit up. Turning, Kate took a step towards the bed but was held immobile by the look of utter contempt on David's face.

'Go on, Kate,' Ethan muttered. 'I'll see to him.'

Tearfully, Kate hurried from the room.

'Stop shuffling those stupid papers and *listen* to me!'

Ethan slapped his hand on the desk, making David wince as the sound reverberated through his throbbing head. He was aimlessly organising his paperwork, trying to prepare for departure. Feeling suddenly dizzy, David flopped down on the chair. Ethan had related the details of Kate's argument with Steven the night before, succinctly emphasising that Kate had received a reprimand from the field director and nothing more. But David remained skeptical.

'Dave, when we brought you in yesterday she wouldn't let any of us tend to your injuries. She was like a bloody tigress! The doctor practically had to throw her out, and she would have sat on the floor outside your room for hours if I hadn't given her some work to do. She spent the whole night with you...'

Angrily, Ethan banged on the desk again with a clenched fist. 'For God's sake, Dave – concussion is no excuse for pig-headed stupidity! Didn't you hear what she said to you this morning – when you woke up in her arms?'

David rubbed his forehead but said nothing. He only knew that he wanted to be back in her arms, whatever the cost.

Bastet stared haughtily from the top of the wardrobe; Ethan retrieved the dusty cat and shook it at David. 'She told you that she loved you,' he said, his voice edged with bitterness. 'You great stupid half-wit!'

Ethan hurled the cat against the wall beside his friend's head. The cat goddess shattered.

Thanks to Ali's strong sense of propriety, four generations of the Suefy family gathered at the front door to give the British group a courteous sendoff. Despite dust-filled gusts of wind, the Egyptians shook the hands of the students and wished them well. The youngsters said goodbye in Arabic then hurried to the waiting minibus.

Yusuf was treated to a less formal adieu as he would be back within the month to oversee another expedition. Anxious to return to his hometown, the inspector hastened to the Land Rover and made himself comfortable in the back seat.

Steven and Ethan emerged from the house, with David between them. Despite a crippling headache, the professor had been deemed fit to travel and was clearly growing impatient of his friends' solicitude. Steven bid the Suefy family a perfunctory farewell and boarded the minibus.

David's demeanour was guarded and distant. When Mina threw her arms around his neck, he quickly disengaged himself and offered a brittle smile.

Anai merely nodded sombrely, and David walked unsteadily towards the Land Rover.

Having issued several orders to Ali and Ahmed, Ethan ruffled Hassan's hair and lightly kissed Samira's cheek. Mina's eyes told him of her hatred and the misery to come. Anai's calculating stare warned him of the consequences should he break his promise. With a heavy heart, Ethan followed David to the Land Rover and wordlessly climbed into the driver's seat.

Kate was last to emerge. Having discovered that her mood ring had slipped off her finger, she had made a frantic search of the house but had failed to recover Rebecca's gift. Hopefully, the little plastic ring had somehow entangled itself among her possessions and was somewhere in her suitcase.

She shook Hassan's hand, smiling at the boy as he executed a low bow. Ahmed gave her a curt nod and firmly shook her hand. Ali embraced her like an uncle and wished her good fortune. Kate drew ever closer to tears as she passed along the line of men who had continued Edwin's bloodline, and shared some of his once-treasured features.

Samira's embrace was crushing and came with a small parcel of pastries for the journey. Mina's face was cold and expressionless as she shook Kate's hand. The Egyptian girl kept her eyes lowered, hiding the guilt which lurked in their amber depths.

Holding both of Kate's hands in hers, Anai solemnly touched her forehead to Kate's and whispered words of protection.

'Ila al'likaa, Anai,' Kate said in a trembling voice. 'Goodbye.' The softly-spoken word was lost on the wind.

Anai kissed both of Kate's cheeks and looked into her eyes for the last time. 'You are free,' Anai proclaimed gravely. 'Be well, little one.' She hobbled away, and Mina followed.

The Land Rover had already started down the road by the time Kate made her way to the bus. She stood for a moment and looked back towards the silent ruins of Amarna, as the wind swirled the sand around the remnants of the city. She felt as desolate as the dead metropolis. Silently, she bid farewell to Akhenaten's masterpiece and boarded the bus, taking a seat at the rear.

Kate's face was an impassive mask behind her dark sunglasses, her body language making it clear to the students sitting in the front section that she did not wish to be disturbed. Tossing her bag onto the seat next to her, she curled up and looked forlornly out of the window. The driver started the bus and accelerated away from Amarna, and the sandstorm that would soon be in pursuit. Kate no longer cared if they evaded the storm or not. What did it matter? Her whole life felt like one big sandstorm. The students talked quietly, subdued by recent events. Kate closed her eyes, tears trickling beneath her lashes. By the time they crossed the Nile, she had sobbed herself into an exhausted slumber.

Back at the dig house, Mina crept into an empty bedroom. Locking the door, she turned to survey the room her beloved David had slept in. The room he had slept in with Kate. Inhaling deeply, she fancied his scent still lingered in the air, and imagined him moving about the cramped space. In her mind, she heard his laughter, his soft voice as it spoke to her in French or Arabic. She saw his beautiful smile, his mesmerising green eyes.

Stepping to the unmade bed, Mina sat down heavily and took the wax effigy of Kate from her pocket. With a slightly vindictive look in her eyes, she placed the figure on the pillow Kate would have used; indeed, she found a strand of reddish-brown hair caught in the pillowcase.

With blatant disregard for the tenets of her culture and the wishes of her family, Mina had decided her own fate. Carefully pulling a phial from another pocket, she opened the cap and swallowed the liquid within. Then, settling herself on David's bed, her head resting on his pillow, Mina waited for Anubis to claim her.

An hour or so from Cairo, they stopped at what passed for a service station. The weather had cleared on the journey, and the December sun shone brightly from a cloudless blue sky. The group stretched their legs and made use of the meagre facilities. Kate handed out Samira's pastries to the ever-ravenous students, hoping the sweetmeats had not been laced with any questionable substances. Although the bus and the Land Rover had parked at opposite ends of the large car park, Kate waited expectantly for David to find her. Surely he had heard her declaration of love? Surely he would want to say…something?

Instead, it was Ethan who approached her as she stood alone near the bus, in the skimpy shade of a scrawny palm tree. As he came to stand beside her, he told his heart to brace itself for loss, but found himself defenceless.

'I just heard that the storm has hit Amarna,' he said unhappily, pushing his hands into his trouser pockets. 'It doesn't seem to be moving any further. I expect there will be some damage…'

'I'm sorry,' Kate replied softly. 'Will you be going back?'

Ethan stared at the southern horizon. 'I have no choice.'

'How's David?'

'He's grumpy as hell and feeling car sick. I've given him some of his pills and a plastic bag.'

There was a short, awkward silence, before Ethan sighed and spoke again. 'They've managed to do a digital facial construction of the female skeleton already. It's obviously not precise, but I have a picture – would you like to see it?'

Kate shook her head. 'We removed her from her place of rest – I don't need to look her in the eye as well.'

'I think you should take a look…' He handed her his phone, and Kate's eyes widened at the digital face of the female skeleton – an eerie likeness of Mina.

'Perhaps Anai meant it when she said the skeleton was family,' Ethan mused, but Kate would not add her own speculation. Feeling as though he were trying to break down an impenetrable barrier, Ethan kept trying. 'The students will be staying in a very basic hotel in Cairo. We should be able to keep them entertained until they fly home tomorrow.'

'I'm not staying in Cairo, Ethan,' Kate said firmly. 'I'm going straight to the airport. David clearly doesn't want me here. And neither do you.'

Ethan had never experienced such overwhelming regret. Solemnly, he considered his reply.

'We have to leave the past behind, Kate.' Their eyes met. 'I know you love David, and he's been crazy about you for…well, forever. He hasn't stopped loving you just because of the things that have happened here, but he's proud and stubborn…'

He surrendered to the urge to push the wayward lock of hair from her face; they were behind the bus, safe from accusing green eyes. 'I've booked him a room at the Hilton. I'm going to ask the bus driver to drop you off there while I take David to the hospital. Then I'll bring him to the Hilton and you two can talk this out…'

Mournfully, Kate shook her head. 'No, Ethan. It's too late.'

'Kate, I'm trying to make this better, but you have to meet me halfway!' He placed his hands on her shoulders. 'Please give it one more chance. If you can't make it work, I'll take you to the airport myself and you won't hear from either of us again.' He watched a familiar expression cross her face, one that showed she was considering his proposal.

'Has David agreed to this?'

'I haven't run it by him yet. Yusuf won't let me get a word in edgeways and I can't discuss this in front of him, anyway. I was going to do it now, before we all get back in the car.'

'He might not want to see me…'

'Sweetheart, I spoke to him before we left Amarna and I'm pretty sure I convinced him that there's nothing going on between us.' Ethan swallowed. 'I'm confident he'll jump at the chance to make up with you.' He grinned, trying to make light of this hellish situation. 'And then make out with you…'

She studied his face for a long moment, as though waiting for divine inspiration. At last, she sighed. 'Alright. But if it doesn't work, I'm going home. And we're done.'

Impulsively, and because he knew there would never be another opportunity, Ethan kissed Kate's cheek. 'I understand. Good luck...' He made to leave, but stopped. When he turned to face her once more, he saw a tired, anguished expression on her sweet face.

'Kate, Anai told me things the other night...' He fumbled for words. 'She hypnotised me – or something – and I saw another life with you and David. Anai said that you've seen it too. Is it true? Have you experienced...us...in the past?' With his eyes, he begged her for a truthful answer.

Kate stared at him, a lonely tear sliding down her cheek. 'Ethan...I *can't*. I want us all to be free of this.'

'Were we...happy, in that other life?'

Her eyes looked sad, but she gave him a weak smile. 'Edwin and Katherine loved each other, Ethan. Yes, they were very happy.'

'How long have you known?'

Her expression was one of utter disenchantment as she murmured, 'A few months...'

He could see that she awaited his scorn, expecting to be ridiculed as a lunatic. But he could not mock her, for he knew Anai had not lied to him about *this*.

'Why did you come out here?' he asked gently. *Was it to be with David, or to find me?*

'It was a mistake to come here.' Her reply evaded the question, and now she looked to be fighting tears.

So Ethan took a deep breath and tried to hang onto one last, connective strand, even though he knew it was absolutely the wrong thing to do. 'Perhaps, when you're ready, you could write to me? I'd like to know more...'

'Knowing has only brought me misery, Ethan. And David, too.' Kate looked at the ground as she confessed, 'I don't want that for you...'

Lifting her chin, Ethan gave her a weak smile. 'Love, I'm already miserable.' He pressed a tattered business card into her hand. 'Please, Kate, if you can bring yourself to do it one day – write to me.'

Reaching into his trouser pocket, he pulled out a small stone scarab and gave it to her.

'No more talismans,' she said quickly, shaking her head.

'Take it,' he told her gently. 'It's a symbol of rebirth.'

'Another one of Anai's lucky charms?'

Ethan squeezed her hand. 'No, this one's mine. Maybe it'll work better for you.' Turning, he started to walk back to the service station to collect his passengers. He could feel her eyes burning into his back.

As she watched him go, Kate had the dreadful feeling she might never see him again.

'Ethan!' she cried out.

Her soulmate turned and, as she saw his tortured countenance, Kate's heart lurched. Still concealed by the empty bus, they stumbled into each other's arms and held on tightly. Both of them knew this was farewell, the severing of their soul connection.

The knowing smile on the male receptionist's face made Kate cringe; she felt like an escort waiting to greet her next appointment. However, once Steven mentioned Professor David Young, the immaculately dressed hotel employee became deferential and business-like. After a few minutes, he left his post to bring Kate the room key card personally.

'If you would please wait a few moments, Miss Grahame, I will call a porter to take your bags to your room.' He executed a sharp bow, gesturing to someone behind Kate. A second later, a glass of cold orange juice had been placed in her hand and she was invited to sit down.

'Looks like you're all set,' Steven observed.

Although she could see the remorse on his face, Kate was not yet prepared to forgive him. She could feel a chasm yawning between her and all those she had trusted and loved. She stood on the edge of the abyss, teetering towards a suffocating darkness.

'Thanks, Steven.'

'Kate,' he began awkwardly. 'I spoke to my mum yesterday, and she'd like to invite you for dinner sometime over Christmas…'

As she gazed at him, Kate felt the strengthening of her defences. 'You'd better get back to the students, Doctor Brodie.'

Turning away to take the proffered seat, she dismissed him. Glancing back, she watched the young archaeologist striding towards the exit. Miserably, Kate sipped at her drink and contemplated her current situation. *What the hell am I doing here?*

'Katie Grahame, is that you?' a woman's voice asked. 'It *is* you!'

In the next moment, she was pulled to her feet and tightly embraced by a young woman in the uniform of a holiday rep. When she finally got a proper look at the woman's face, Kate recognised her as a classmate from school.

'Paula!' Kate exclaimed.

For the next five minutes, Paula supplied Kate with an abridged version of her life since their carefree school days. In short, she was single and enjoying her career as a representative for an exclusive tour company.

Avoiding the trials she had faced in her own life, Kate talked briefly about her job at the museum and the recent expedition. When asked about her marital status, Kate replied without shame that she was divorced and single. At the last word, she heard herself sound resolute.

'Katie, it's been so good to see you,' Paula said sincerely. 'And I'd love to hear more about your Egyptian journey of discovery. But I'm taking a group to the airport and I have to get them on the bus…'

Paula looked at her old classmate carefully. 'D'you need a lift?'

CHAPTER 17

David's eyes swept the room, finding no sign of Kate or her belongings. He sat slowly on the bed, all hope dissolving. She had gone. He had lost her. Again.

The bathroom door opened, causing David to jerk his head up from his hands and wince in pain. Kate emerged from the steam-filled room, dressed in one of the large complimentary bathrobes. He was rendered speechless, uncertain of how to act or what to say. Kate's mobile phone broke the heavy silence, ringing from somewhere in the bathroom.

The call was short, Kate's replies to her caller giving nothing away. When she returned to the bedroom David observed the familiar guarded look that indicated she had raised her defences. She eyed the bed nervously, apparently reluctant to come any closer. Pulling the robe tightly around her body, she stood with her back to the wall next to the bathroom door.

'Who was on the phone?' David asked, quietly because the sound of his own voice hurt his head.

'There's a seat on tomorrow's flight…' Kate murmured

David got up slowly and crossed to where she stood, taking her hand in his and kissing the knuckles. 'I don't want you to go.'

'I need to go home, David.' Kate's voice trembled, a warning that tears were not far off.

'So the words you whispered in my ear – you didn't mean them?'

Her eyes widened. 'I thought you hadn't heard me,' she whispered. 'Or that you didn't care.'

David wiped the tear that slid from the corner of her eye. 'I thought I had imagined it. I've dreamed of you so often it seemed the most likely explanation. But Ethan spoke to me this morning and set me straight on a few things.'

He cupped her face gently in his hands, looking deep into her eyes. 'I love you, Kate. I have *always* loved you.'

Kate grasped his wrist, her expression angst-ridden. 'Until you're angry with me, and then you ignore me for weeks or treat me like something you found under your shoe!' She shook her head. 'I can't take any more, David! I want to start over -'

'Then let's do it *together*! I'm sorry about the past, Kate, but I don't want it to haunt us anymore -'

Kate pulled his hands away from her face. 'You don't trust me, David. Deep down, you'll always believe that I have feelings for Edwin – or Ethan. But the truth is, I gave up my ridiculous dreams of finding Edwin long before we left Edinburgh.' A sob escaped her throat, and she thumped David's chest. 'I wanted to be with *you* – you stupid, stupid idiot!'

'Then marry me.'

Kate stared at him, incredulous. 'You're joking!' she blurted.

David looked unperturbed. 'Hardly.'

'Then you're being stupid -'

'Again with the stupid…' David sighed, his eyes never leaving her face.

'David, you've hurt your head -'

'Yes, and I'm fine. Thanks for asking.'

'I'm sorry – are you *sure* you're fine?'

'Almost as good as new. Or I will be, as soon as you agree to be my wife.'

'No.'

David hid his dismay. 'Why not?'

'We hardly know each other…'

David snorted. 'Rubbish! You know me better than anyone else – almost.'

'Well, you don't know *me*…'

'Stop deluding yourself, Kate. You know that's not true.' He watched her fumbling for excuses.

'We haven't dated properly, or for a reasonable amount of time.'

'Now you sound positively Victorian! Don't you think we're past the dating stage?'

David placed his hands against the wall on either side of her shoulders, effectively trapping her.

'We haven't discussed any long-term goals,' she stammered.

'Such as?'

'What about your job in York?'

'Forget about York. I'm coming home with you – to Edinburgh.'

'Where would we live?'

David didn't hesitate. 'In your house, of course.'

'You wouldn't have…issues about living there?'

'I've told you already – the past is old news. Your house has felt like home since the first time I ate in your kitchen. My home is wherever you are, Kate. But I will insist on two things: a new bed and a new nameplate for the door. Assuming, of course, that you wish to take my name…'

'I bought a new mattress just a few months ago…' she informed him, her voice sounding strangled. She reminded David of a rabbit, squirming under the stare of a ravenous predator.

'Then that's a fair compromise,' he replied genially, his gaze on her lips. 'I can help you break it in…'

'W-what about your expectations?'

David stepped back slightly, his brow furrowed in puzzlement. 'My what?'

'What do you expect from me?'

'What do I expect?' David was taken aback by the question. He paused to consider which answer would most likely win her approval. 'I expect us to be two consenting adults committed to building a relationship based on equality, democracy and respect.'

Kate rolled her eyes and sighed. 'You make it sound so romantic!'

David raised his hands in despair. 'What am I supposed to say? I want you barefoot and pregnant in the kitchen, surrounded by a brood of my offspring?'

The thought of procreating with Kate made him lean closer. This time he clasped her waist and lowered his head to kiss the sensitive spot beneath her left ear, causing her to inhale sharply. David commenced kissing her ear, lightly nipping the lobe with his teeth.

'S-so you really want children?' she squeaked, shivering as his lips traced a path down her neck.

'Yes,' he murmured, nuzzling her neck. 'Two, ideally. No more than three, though one's okay, too. Must look like their mother.' David kissed the hollow above her collarbone. 'Horse riding skills essential. But I would like us to wait a year or two, so we can build a solid foundation before submitting to the challenges of child-rearing.' He tightened his hold on her as he felt her slip down the wall a fraction, and David wondered if he had at long last caused her to feel weak at the knees.

'You've really thought this through…'

David lifted his head and looked into her eyes. 'Angel, I've thought of little else for the last six months. I want to be with you. I want you in my life.' His lips moved towards hers. 'For the rest of my life.'

'But what about -'

David's voice dropped to a whisper. 'Stop. Talking.'

He ceased her questions with a kiss, feeling her hands clutch the fabric of his shirt. Moving to kiss the other side of her neck, he murmured, 'I love you. And you said you loved me. Marry me, Kate…'

'I can't…'

David continued his seductive ministrations, sensing the weakening of her resolve. 'Why not?'

Kate shoved him gently, forcing him to stop and look at her. Her gaze was earnest. 'I'm scared, David. I don't want to disappoint you like I -'

'Stop right there!' he said sharply. 'Stop reliving the past and stop picking over your alleged imperfections! I can't believe we're going over all this again! Your marriage to Mark didn't work because you weren't right for each other. He wanted an obedient trophy wife and you're...well, you're definitely not obedient.' He smiled gently. 'I will not curtail your freedom. I want you to be content. I want you to be *you*.'

David took her hands in his. 'Kate, I will do *anything* to make you happy. I lost you ten years ago – I'm not losing you again.'

'If only I hadn't left Marchmont Road,' Kate sighed wistfully. 'We might have had a chance, and we might never have learned about...' She faltered. 'We could have lived in blissful ignorance.'

'You wanted to be with your aunt, so don't regret the precious time you spent with her. And you shouldn't regret finding out about your ancestors, either.' Running his fingers through her damp hair, David smiled. 'Besides, I'm pretty sure that, had we dated back then, you would have given me up as a cold-hearted bore.'

She opened her mouth to fire an insolent retort, but he stopped her with another toe-curling kiss.

'There has never been another for me,' he murmured. 'Nor will there ever be. Only you.'

Kate scrutinised his face and then, to David's immense relief, slipped her arms around his neck and hugged him. They held each other tightly for a long time, their breathing the only sound in the room.

'I feel like I'm holding a Polar bear!' David complained after a while, a sly look in his eyes. His hands toyed with the tie belt of the thick bathrobe. 'Aren't you hot in this thing?'

Without waiting for her response, he untied the belt and slipped his hands inside the robe, fingers itching to touch bare flesh. He was dismayed to find that she was not naked beneath the androgynous dressing gown. 'Damn it, Kate!' he whined, and then discovered that what she *was* wearing was not altogether unappealing.

The white boy shorts that she wore were sweetly decorated with pink polka dots and adorned with a small pink bow at the front. Her torso was modestly covered with a white silk camisole, flimsy enough to reveal the bra that matched the shorts. David eyed her outfit with open appreciation, although he would have preferred to appraise Kate's shapely figure without the distraction of lingerie.

Kate suddenly tensed, and wrapped the robe around her once more. Seeing her anxiety, David decided to lighten the mood, to banish the tension that had crept into the room.

'I need to lie down,' he declared. 'I have a concussion, you know.'

Despite the chagrin of only a moment ago, Kate snorted. 'That's not even remotely subtle!' she scolded, but David caught the ghost of a smile on her lips.

'Well, let's *sit* down, then!' he sighed, and led her to the foot of the bed, despite there being a sofa in the room. He sat down heavily, pulling her down beside him. 'See – we're sitting!'

Catching a glimpse of her bare thigh before she modestly covered it with the bathrobe, he took a deep breath. 'Alright, Miss Grahame. I've answered your questions and addressed most of your concerns. Any *other* concerns you may have will be addressed...' David's eyes wandered up and down her body lasciviously. '...in due course. Now, let's break this down into the simplest of terms. Do you love me?'

'Yes,' Kate muttered reluctantly.

'That's inspiring, Kate,' David remarked drily. 'Do you like being with me?'

The look she gave him was haughty. 'Sometimes.' She squealed as he lunged at her and pushed her back on the bed, the robe falling open and allowing him to slide a hand up her side.

He leaned over her, supported on one elbow. 'Do you miss me when we're apart?'

'Maybe.' She pouted, and he raised an eyebrow in warning. 'Yes...'

His hand slipped beneath the camisole, his fingers lightly tracing the edges of the bra, making their way to the clasp at her back. He dipped his head, his lips kissing the length of her collarbone.

'Do you want me?' he asked, his voice low and seductive. The hand which had been about to unfasten her bra now snaked its way over her hip, his fingertips moving lightly along the waistband of her panties. Kate gasped, her hips jerking involuntarily at his touch. His hand caressed the length of her thigh. He couldn't make up his mind where to touch her first.

'Yes,' she whimpered, as his teasing fingers moved over the front of her polka-dot shorts.

He watched her, assessing every reaction to his touch, admiring her flushed cheeks, hearing her breathing become more rapid. She raised her hips towards him in invitation. David smirked as he contemplated Mark Forrester's ineptitude as a lover. He moved down to kiss the polka dots, relishing the delights that awaited him, his headache and injuries forgotten.

'Will you marry me, Kate?' he breathed.

'Yes!' she cried feebly. 'You're a rotten pig! I'll never be able to tell anyone how you proposed to me!'

He lifted his tousled head, a broad grin on his unshaven face. 'Thank you,' he said politely, and kissed her tenderly on the lips.

Kate's fingers worked to unbutton David's creased shirt, her hands sliding at last over his tanned chest. Whatever inhibitions she harboured were forgotten as she pressed her body against his, her hands tentatively exploring his torso as their kisses became more passionate. Finally, her fingers reached boldly for his belt. His hand gripped her wrist, stopping her abruptly.

'No,' he told her firmly.

She looked at him incredulously. 'No?'

He shook his head. 'No. Not until we're married.'

Kate looked horrified. 'You're joking!' she whined. For a moment, she looked as though she were mentally calculating how long it would take to organise even the simplest wedding in Edinburgh. 'Aren't you?'

He gave her a rueful smile. 'I only plan to have one wedding night. I want it to be…spectacular.'

The fire left her eyes. 'No pressure, then,' she mumbled, and then attempted to wheedle. 'Don't you think it would be better to have a trial run?' With one finger, she traced the line of coarse hair that bisected his lower torso, eliciting a shudder. 'Supposing it's rubbish?' she asked innocently, as he shifted and stood up.

David snorted as he buttoned and tucked in his shirt, one eyebrow raised in disbelief. Discarding the robe on the bed, Kate clambered to a kneeling position and pouted.

'I hate your self-control!' she grumbled petulantly, folding her arms across her chest, deliberately creating tantalising cleavage.

David's willpower wavered as his eyes swivelled to the swell of creamy flesh. He knelt on the bed in front of her. 'Stop pouting, you feisty wench! I've told you about this before – when you pout like that, you're just asking to be kissed. Hard.' Pulling her to him, he proved his assertion, smiling against her lips until her irritation subsided and she wrapped her arms around him.

'Sometimes, I could thump you!' Kate grumbled.

David gave her a lopsided grin. 'And sometimes I want to smack your pert backside. But that will definitely have to wait until after we're married.' He chuckled as she sat back on her heels, flabbergasted by his remark.

'You wouldn't -' she squeaked.

David pretended to look thoughtful. 'Hmm. You'll have to wait and see…' He moved backwards off the bed but Kate scrambled to hold him.

'I don't want to wait,' she murmured, nuzzling his cheek. 'I don't mean I want you to smack my backside. I mean I don't want to wait until we can organise a wedding -'

David's hand caressed her back. 'You once told me that the extravagance and ostentation of a big wedding wasn't important to you. So marry me now. Today. Or tomorrow. Or as soon as we can arrange it. I don't want to wait, either. You're far too tempting.'

Kate leaned her head on his shoulder, holding him tight. 'Alright,' she whispered against his neck.

David smiled tenderly against her hair, suddenly overcome with emotion. 'I love you, Kate,' he said softly.

Her response was to undulate against him provocatively, as though she were dancing to some seductive melody in her head. David placed his hands on her hips, feeling her subtle movement against his palms. Laughing as he pushed her away from him, he scrambled off the bed. 'Stop it, or I won't be able to think straight!' He backed towards the door, knowing that if he stayed much longer his resolve would collapse altogether.

'You're leaving?' Kate asked, scowling.

'Time is clearly of the essence!' He grinned.

'You realise we have to share a bed tonight?'

'I do,' he answered, his voice husky. 'If necessary, I'll sleep with my clothes on.'

'I don't wear anything in bed,' she commented archly.

David opened the bedroom door, eager to make his escape from his very seductive fiancée. 'Oh, well. By the time you've finished in the bathroom, I'll probably be sound asleep.' He closed the door as she threw a cushion in his direction.

'I do. I definitely do....'

'Dave! Come on, wake up...'

Ethan shook his friend's shoulder until David opened his eyes. He looked disorientated as he stared around the sterile white treatment room. 'What's going on?' he murmured, groggily.

'You dozed off,' Ethan explained. 'You were talking in your sleep.'

It had all been a dream? A figment of his imagination? 'I was getting married...'

'So I gathered. You've got the all-clear.' Ethan held up a paper bag. 'According to the scan, your noggin is intact. The doctor prescribed rest and painkillers. I've paid the bill, so we can go.'

'What's the hurry?' David mumbled. 'Just let me sleep. At least let me get past my wedding night...' He groaned as Ethan yanked him into a sitting position. 'Knock it off, Ethan! My head's still throbbing...'

'You have an appointment, remember?'

'Do I?' David searched his foggy memory.

'There's a certain lady waiting for you at the Hilton...'

'Damn!' David cursed. 'How long have we been here? Why didn't you wake me sooner?' Jumping to his feet caused a moment's giddiness, and Ethan reached out to steady David as he swiftly gathered up his belongings.

'I was enjoying listening in on your dirty dreams. Now take it easy – we don't want you to suffer from performance issues!'

Laughing, David led his friend from the room and began searching for the exit. 'There's absolutely no chance of that, Ethan. I need to make a phone call.'

'To whom?' Ethan asked, puzzled. 'To Kate? That's not very romantic, Dave. Far better to make a big entrance…' He sniggered at his own double entendre and jogged after his friend.

Once outside the impressive Dar El Fouad hospital, Ethan commandeered a recently vacated taxi and they sped along the 26th July Corridor. David spent the twenty-minute journey cursing the lack of phone reception and the taxi driver's appalling road sense.

Finally, they crossed the Nile by way of the 6 October Bridge and the taxi dropped them off at the first safe stopping place, a few hundred metres from the Hilton. As always, the streets were chaotic; David found a suitable place to stand without being jostled, and took out his phone.

'Who the hell are you calling?' Ethan asked impatiently, dodging out of the path of two men carrying a large wicker laundry basket. 'I can hardly hear myself think!'

'Ssh!' David admonished, sticking a finger in one ear while he held the phone to the other. His eyes glazed over as he listened to the ringing tone. At last, the line crackled and a deep male voice said, 'Doctor Benedict Grahame…'

David grinned, feeling excited and nervous at the same time. 'Ben? It's David Young. I'd like your permission to marry Kate.'

As he ended his phone call, a slow grin spread over David's face that eradicated his haggard appearance.

'Well,' Ethan urged. 'What did he say?'

'He said it was about time.'

'Then you'd better move your backside to the Hilton…'

David looked up and down the busy, dusty street until he found what he was looking for. 'I'm not going unprepared – she's had time to think up a whole tome of excuses. I need something to distract her, to stop her in her tracks until I've managed to persuade her. I'm buying a ring.'

Ethan's eyes widened, but he did not smile. 'You're buying a – what?' He watched as David removed his rucksack and searched the numerous pockets for his wallet. 'David, wait -'

'No. I've waited long enough. I've been patient, and I've let her have her way. There will be no more excuses, and no more procrastinating. Her brother has given me his blessing. I'm buying a ring at the jewellery shop across the street and then I'm going to propose to Katherine Grahame.'

'You might get the wrong size…'

Fumbling in the pocket of his trousers, David pulled out Kate's plastic mood ring. 'I found this in my room. It's like some kind of omen…' Shoving his rucksack at Ethan, David used a gap in the traffic to dart across the road. He disappeared into the shop, leaving Ethan speechless.

As he stared after his friend, Ethan was overcome with a feeling of loss so excruciating that he sank into a rickety chair that had been left on someone's doorstep. Closing his eyes, he allowed an unwelcome memory to resurface. He returned to 2002, and could almost smell the fresh Edinburgh air…

He was walking along Marchmont Road, on his way home from his temporary job at the university. Having recently obtained his degree in archaeology, he was helping with summer school while he waited to hear about a job application to the Egypt Exploration Society. He and David were still sharing a flat, but his antisocial friend was always either working or studying. David was also helping with summer school, and was a far better teacher than Ethan.

It was a beautiful summer's evening, and as he wandered along the street, Ethan noticed a girl crouching down some way along the pavement. She was stroking a black cat who curled itself around her legs. Something about the girl caught his attention and held it fast. Her dark auburn hair was long and curled around slim shoulders. Some of the silken strands glinted red in the sunlight.

As he approached, she glanced up at him with sparkling eyes, a smile playing on her lips. When their eyes met, she looked shyly away, returning her attention to the cat. But that one look had been enough. Something about her had tugged at his soul. From that day onwards, he couldn't get her out of his head.

By some strange and happy coincidence, they lived on the same road, a few doors apart. Every time they passed each other in the street, or happened to visit the corner shop at the same time, Ethan's heart leapt. She wasn't like the usual type of woman he bedded – and there had been many. There was something pure, almost angelic about her. Her lovely eyes always held a faraway look, as if she resided on some other plane of existence.

He found himself looking for her everywhere, ecstatic whenever he caught a glimpse of her luxuriant tresses. Sadly, she seemed not to notice him, seemed always to be lost in reflection. His longing and frustration drove him mad, but he did not confide in David, for fear his friend would ridicule or scold him. Ethan had fostered a reputation as a lothario, which had earned him many derisory comments from his flatmate. Besides, David had been even more introspective than usual recently; he would be unlikely to offer any kind of support.

After some snooping, which made him feel rather like a stalker, Ethan discovered that the object of his affection lived with a girl who shared his own dubious reputation. This young woman brazenly approached him in a local bar one night and shamelessly began to flirt with him. She was beautiful, arrogant, and superficial, and used to catching whatever man took her fancy. Her name was Gemma.

Ethan responded to her overtures, claiming to have noticed her many times on the street. He slyly asked if she lived alone, to which Gemma informed him that she had only that day lost her flatmate, her good friend Katie Grahame. Katie had moved in with her terminally ill aunt, to nurse the lady in her final days.

On hearing news of Kate's departure, Ethan felt as though he had been stabbed. His angel had flown; he had lost her because he hadn't voiced his admiration in time. Young, foolish and in pain, Ethan got drunk that night – and then went home with Gemma.

A short affair followed, which allowed Ethan to glean snippets of information about Kate. He knew that he was treating Gemma badly, even though their relationship did not extend beyond the bedroom. The affair ended abruptly when Gemma grew tired of his questions about Kate and verbally abused him before kicking him out of her bed.

Years passed; Ethan worked hard in Egypt, answering the call from Amarna and basing himself in that area. He met up with David regularly, even though their careers had taken different paths. Relationships with women were always casual and short-lived. No other woman touched Ethan's soul the way Katie Grahame had.

Near the end of 2011, he took a temporary job at the National Museum of Scotland to help with the exhibition on ancient Egypt. He was thrilled to be working with David again, amused and delighted that his friend had earned the deserved title of 'professor'.

His contract ended in January, and Ethan decided to spend some time with his parents before setting off on a climbing expedition in the Scottish Highlands. The day before he was due to leave for Carlisle, he arranged to meet David for lunch. As Ethan waited on a bench in the museum's entrance hall, he saw a figure he knew well; her face had been etched indelibly on his heart. Katie Grahame walked across the gallery floor, accompanied by an older woman. Kate looked a little overwhelmed, but she was just as lovely as Ethan remembered.

Without thinking of the consequences, he stood up and walked towards her, willing her to look at him with those soulful eyes and remember him. When she was no more than two metres away, she raised her left hand to tuck a stray wisp of hair behind her ear.

Ethan slowed as her wedding band shimmered in the light. Their eyes met for a single moment, and Ethan felt sure he saw a spark of recognition. A smile forming on his lips, he opened his mouth to speak to her, although he had no idea what to say. And then David was standing in front of him, talking about something insignificant. And Kate vanished out of sight.

Life continued, as difficult and unrewarding as ever, and gave him no time to mourn the loss of the elusive Katie Grahame.

He became aware of David's new love interest in late spring, but did not discover her identity until the professor announced he was bringing her to Egypt. With endearing pride, David showed off a photograph of his reluctant beloved and confessed to worshipping her from afar when they had all lived on Marchmont Road.

His worst fears realised, Ethan's misery gradually turned into indignation, which in turn exploded into a burning, groundless rage. A rage he directed at Kate from the minute he shook her hand outside the Hilton.

She did not know him as Ethan Forbes – her memories of him came from another lifetime, another incarnation. His bittersweet memories of unrequited love were now meaningless, for Kate had made it clear that she did not care to nurture the flame that united them.

They had condemned Anai and Mina as witches, but surely *Kate* was also guilty of sorcery. Like a siren luring hapless sailors to their death, she had drawn him to her and rendered him powerless. David, too, had fallen under her spell. In at least two lifetimes, she had enslaved them but refused to give all of herself in return. She withheld her favour while radiating discontent. And then, cruel woman, she abandoned them…

Ethan shook his head to dispel the memories, and sighed heavily.

She'll leave soon. She always leaves. Or perhaps this time, she'll go with David, and I'll have to smile and be happy for them, and hope she doesn't destroy him.

He knew that he would have to stay away from Kate, for both their sakes. But perhaps in their next incarnation, she would once again sing the siren's song…

From the stuffed rucksack, David's phone rang. Drawing in a shuddering breath, Ethan pulled it out of a side pocket and answered the call.

With profuse apologies, the receptionist from the Hilton explained that Professor Young's guest had taken a bus to the airport. A letter from Miss Grahame awaited the professor at reception.

Ethan listened with a heavy heart, thanked the man, and hung up. While he considered how best to relate the terrible news to his friend, Ethan absently scrolled through the photographs on David's phone. He found a picture he vaguely remembered, but had never expected to see. A sepia picture of a Victorian couple on their wedding day, the bride's auburn hair piled high on her head under a lace veil. Love in her eyes as she gazed at her husband – the tall, dark-haired archaeologist named Edwin Ford. His eyes on the photograph, Ethan prepared to cross the street.

Boarding pass in hand, Kate joined the long queue at the departure gate. Part of her wanted to run back to him, or crumple up in a heap on the floor and wail about the unfairness of life. But, contemplating the trials she had faced in her past life – and her own life – had helped her to find a new strength.

As a Victorian woman, she had battled convention but had not emerged victorious. Marrying the man she loved had not brought fulfilment, nor granted her the freedom she coveted.

Born again as a daughter of the twentieth century, she had once more suffered constraints. Her parents, though loving, had expected her to behave in a particular way. She had always tried to be a 'good girl' but had continually sensed her father's disappointment in his unexceptional daughter.

She had married a man who had also expected conformity, but had eventually sought his pleasure elsewhere.

Her conclusion? She was not designed for matrimony, for she brought only misery to men who sought to mould her into the perfect mate.

She loved David, but enjoying his love would come at the price of her autonomy. Even if she moved with him to York, she would have to resign herself to a lifetime of proving that she loved only him. Her existence would revolve around convincing him that she no longer craved Edwin Ford, and harboured no feelings whatsoever for Ethan Forbes. History would forever taint their future, and they would never know peace.

And so her only choice was to sever her connection to both David and Ethan, in the hope that they could each find happiness. It was time to shape her own life, and accept a necessary solitude.

In their case, love would not conquer all.

As the queue of travellers shuffled forward, Kate thought about her Aunt Margaret. That strong, passionate woman had remained resolutely single all of her life. No doubt she had experienced love, but she had refused to surrender her independence through wedlock. She had travelled, she had studied whatever sparked her interest, and she had imparted her vast knowledge of the world to her niece and nephew. She had always told Kate to follow her heart.

Kate was asked for her boarding pass by a grinning attendant, and then she followed the other passengers out of the building and across the tarmac to the plane. Halfway up the aircraft steps, a sudden pain in her chest made Kate gasp. She rubbed at the spot, thinking it either heartburn or heartache.

For the last time, Kate looked out at the shimmering Egyptian vista. She would not return to this wild and mysterious place, for it would forever trigger painful memories. Beautiful, grey Edinburgh was her home.

The portable steps shook slightly and Kate gripped the handrail. Her gaze fell on her right hand, no longer adorned with Rebecca's mood ring. She would buy another to give to her niece, and advise her that a woman did not need a man at her side in order to lead a rewarding life. She could be her own knight in shining armour. She could nurture her own soul...

Bennu turned up the radio and sang along to Billy Joel's 'Uptown Girl', grinding the gears as he manhandled the clutch of the decrepit delivery truck. He was behind schedule, and so had not stopped for lunch. Instead, he had bought some food at Macdonald's and now attempted to eat while he drove through the busy Cairo streets. One-handed, he turned off the main road onto a quieter street, taking a mouthful of his drink before returning the cup to the drinks holder on the dashboard. Haplessly, he missed the cup holder and the drink fell to the floor, splashing his sandaled feet with icy Coke.

Cursing, Bennu glanced down at his feet and tried to kick the rolling cup away from the pedals. He didn't see the black-clad man step out into the road as, quite by accident, his foot pressed on the accelerator. Too late, he heard someone shouting for him to stop. Too late, he hit the brakes and screeched to a halt. Too late…

A mobile phone lay on the asphalt, its screen cracked but still glowing faintly. The sepia image flickered as fingers stretched out to stroke the Victorian bride's face in a weak caress. A rivulet of blood flowed slowly past the handset. As the screen went blank, the fingers trembled and were still…